the Lost Story *of* Sofia Castello

BOOKS BY SIOBHAN CURHAM

An American in Paris
Beyond This Broken Sky
The Paris Network
The Secret Keeper
The Storyteller of Auschwitz
The Secret Photograph
The Stars Are Our Witness
The Resistance Bakery

The Scene Stealers
Frankie Says Relapse
Sweet FA

NON-FICTION
Something More: A Spiritual Misfit's Search for Meaning
Dare to Write a Novel
Dare to Dream
Antenatal & Postnatal Depression

SIOBHAN CURHAM

the
Lost
Story
of
Sofia
Castello

bookouture

Published by Bookouture in 2025

An imprint of Storyfire Ltd.
Carmelite House
50 Victoria Embankment
London EC4Y 0DZ

www.bookouture.com

The authorised representative in the EEA is Hachette Ireland
8 Castlecourt Centre
Dublin 15 D15 XTP3
Ireland
(email: info@hbgi.ie)

Copyright © Siobhan Curham, 2025

Siobhan Curham has asserted her right to be identified as the author of this work.

All rights reserved. No part of this publication may be reproduced, stored in any retrieval system, or transmitted, in any form or by any means, electronic, mechanical, photocopying, recording or otherwise, without the prior written permission of the publishers.

ISBN: 978-1-83525-632-9
eBook ISBN: 978-1-83525-631-2

This book is a work of fiction. Names, characters, businesses, organizations, places and events other than those clearly in the public domain, are either the product of the author's imagination or are used fictitiously. Any resemblance to actual persons, living or dead, events or locales is entirely coincidental.

For Judith Chilcote, Erzsi Deak and Jane Willis – formidable literary agents and wonderful women. I feel so fortunate to have had you by my side during my writing career.

We delight in the beauty of the butterfly, but rarely admit the changes it has gone through to achieve that beauty.

— MAYA ANGELOU

PROLOGUE
LISBON, 1941

I stare at the television screen, gripped, as the memorial procession slowly makes its way along Avenida da Liberdade. The tree-lined pavements on either side are filled with mourners. The men all clamping their hats to their chests, eyes lowered, the women's faces obscured by black veils. The camera zooms in on a group of *varinas*, and even though the footage is in grainy black and white, I can tell that the fisherwomen have swapped their usual bright costumes for black dresses. Several of them are crying, which catches me off guard, and a lump begins forming in the back of my throat.

The footage cuts to a shot from the front of the procession as it reaches Rossio Square.

'And now, those closest to Castello will make their way into the Queen Maria II Theatre,' the broadcaster announces, 'where some of the biggest names in the entertainment industry will be performing in a tribute concert to her.'

The camera zooms in on an unshaven man, his eyes puffy and ringed with shadows. It takes me a moment to realise that it's Emilio, and my heart aches at his obvious sorrow.

'One can only imagine how devastated Emilio Almeida

must be to have lost his musical partner,' the show's host continues in voiceover.

'Yes,' the voice of his female co-host chimes in. 'Almeida and Castello were such a formidable duo. And they'd only just begun.'

'Absolutely,' the man agrees. 'Who knows what they might have gone on to achieve – but one thing's for certain, she really did leave an incredible legacy from her three-year career.'

I feel a sharp stab of pain, followed swiftly by a flush of anger. It's all so unfair. So frustrating. But then another, deeper, more protective instinct kicks in, and I turn away from the television and finish packing my case. There's no turning back now. For my plan to work, I need to let my anger fuel me, not frustrate me. It's not just my life that's at stake after all. I shove the lid of the case down and click the silver catches shut.

When I look back at the screen, they're showing a heart-shaped wreath of lilies, beneath a photograph of the deceased. A photograph of me.

I turn off the television and the picture shrinks to a tiny dot, then disappears completely. And just like that, I cease to be.

1

LONDON, FEBRUARY 2000

A couple of years ago, I ghostwrote the autobiography for a breakfast TV presenter renowned for her vibrant power suits and equally cheery disposition. The book was titled *Rise and Shine!* – the exclamation mark was obligatory as everything she said was an exclamation of some kind, even 'please could you pass the salt!' – and the pages were crammed with positive platitudes such as 'happiness doesn't cost a thing!' and 'the sun is always shining, even behind the clouds!' I think of this last quote now as I stand, crammed into a rush-hour Tube, trying not to be asphyxiated by the aftershave of the man squashed beside me. There's no denying that my life has been 'cloudy' for quite some time. Ten months to be precise, after Robin, my partner of sixteen years, left me for another woman.

 I scan the crowded carriage, trying to find a glimmer of anything that feels like sunshine. My gaze falls upon a gum-chewing man sitting to my left. His legs are spread so wide, the poor woman beside him has had to suck herself in to the width of a pencil, but his curly black hair and chiselled jaw put him in the category of textbook attractive. I continue to stare at him, willing my body to feel something – anything – vaguely resembling desire, but there's nothing.

The man glances up and his eyes meet mine with such cold indifference, it's like I can feel a film of frost forming on my heart. I fight the urge to lean down and push his stupid legs shut. But then I have a flashback to the last time I saw Robin, the day he moved out, and the same dead look in his eyes as he told me goodbye, and a lump begins forming in the back of my throat.

I quickly glance at the adverts lining the curved wall above the windows. *Beat the winter blues*, one of them reads, above a picture of a tropical beach. Maybe I should go away, I muse as the train veers to the right and the man reeking of aftershave topples into me. Perhaps if I went somewhere where the sun isn't perpetually stuck behind a thick bank of cloud, I'd finally rediscover my mojo. I mentally photoshop myself onto the powdery sand in the picture, and the tension in my shoulders begins to loosen a little.

The train finally judders to a halt at Covent Garden and belches a wave of relieved passengers onto the platform. I take the lift up to the ground level and emerge into the dank grey day. There was a time when a meeting with my literary agent, Jane, would have filled me with excitement, especially when the meeting is to talk about a new ghostwriting client. But the last couple of jobs I've done – the autobiography for a monosyllabic boyband member and a novel about forbidden love in a Dubai stable for a glamour model who doesn't even read books, let alone write them – have left me feeling distinctly underwhelmed. Even though I don't know who the job is for yet, I wonder if I should turn it down and tell Jane I need to take a break.

A double-decker bus goes sailing past, a streak of red cutting through the grey, spraying my legs with dirty puddle water. My urge to escape to the sun grows ever stronger. The green crossing sign lights up, and I step into the road, only to almost get mown down by a courier on a bike.

'Watch where you're going, stupid!' he yells over his shoulder, and all the reasons why this complete stranger on a bike is right and I am stupid start scrolling like a ticker tape of headlines across my mind. *You can't get your own books published... You couldn't keep your partner... You can't even have children... You're thirty-five years old and you're all alone...*

By the time I reach the other side of the road, I feel so small I half expect to not be able to see my reflection in the shop window in front of me. But there I am, just about, grim-faced and thin in my customary outfit of black jeans, leather jacket and high-tops, my red fringe poking out from beneath my hood. And then, in a flash, a small child appears beside me in the glass. Her hair is the same shade of auburn as mine, and she's hugging the bottom of my leg. 'No!' I mutter, and I close my eyes tight. When I open them again, she's gone. Now I'm in no doubt – I need to go away.

I march along James Street mentally rehearsing how I should break the news to Jane that her most reliable and efficient ghostwriter wants to do a runner. Perhaps I should capitalise on the 'new millennium, new me' craze doing the rounds now that we've realised the computers aren't going to crash and send planes falling from the sky. But I don't want her to think that the new millennium me is work-shy.

I was wondering if I could take a holiday, I recite in my head as I arrive at the agency and take a seat on one of the plush leather sofas in the reception. *An extended holiday,* I add as I wait for Jane to appear. I used to be proud of the fact that I could ghostwrite books at breakneck speed, and I loved the challenge of writing in someone else's voice, but since Robin left, it's as if all the tears I've cried have caused my brain to rust. Now, the thought of having to churn out 80,000 words in a couple of months fills me with dread, especially if this new client is anything as difficult and uninspiring as the last two.

Finally, the lift doors ping open, and Jane walks out to greet me. Her white bobbed hair is immaculate as always, and she's wearing a wraparound dress in a vibrant paisley print, making me instantly feel drab and underdressed.

'Lily!' she cries, holding out her hands, causing the gold bangles on her wrists to jangle. 'It's so great to see you.'

'You too,' I reply, and as she hugs me and I inhale her signature floral scent, I'm filled with a rush of warmth. Over the thirteen years we've worked together, she's become so much more than an agent to me. When I was dropped by my first publisher for disappointing sales, Jane plucked me from my despair and suggested I reinvent myself as a ghostwriter, enabling me to forge a successful and lucrative writing career, albeit anonymously. And when Robin left, she took me out for lunch and, unlike my other well-meaning friends, told me to resist the urge to instantly get over it and change my life for the better.

'You need to embrace the butterfly soup,' she said, before explaining that when a caterpillar builds its cocoon, it doesn't just sprout a pair of wings and burst out, magically transformed. Instead, it completely dissolves in its own digestive juices and marinates for a while. Even though it was kind of gross, hearing this did make me feel better by easing the pressure a little. The trouble is, I've been marinating in a soup of apathy and indecision for almost a year. I need to do something to haul myself out of it.

'Come,' she says, ushering me inside the lift.

I catch a glimpse of myself in the mirrored wall and can't help grimacing at how pale I look.

'How are you doing?' Jane asks, her smile fading into a look of concern.

'OK. I didn't sleep very well last night,' I say, trying to explain my wan appearance.

'Are you eating properly?' She looks me up and down.

'Yes. Kind of.' The truth is, I stopped bothering to cook anything other than ready meals and various things on toast after Robin left. It seems pointless going to all the effort of cooking from scratch for just one person.

'Well, I've got us some coffee and pastries,' she says in her clipped upper-class accent, so customary in the UK literary world.

As she gives my arm a squeeze, I feel dangerously close to tears. Growing up in foster care left me with a bone-deep longing for proper parents – and when I say proper parents, I mean the kind you see in Hallmark movies, the kind who give each other affectionate nicknames and hug and squeeze their kids.

I need to take a break, I mentally rehearse again. *I need to see the sun to prove to myself that it does still exist.*

The lift arrives at the top floor, and the doors slide open. We make our way along the book-lined corridor to Jane's corner office at the far end. The walls are made entirely of glass, and the views across London are stunning. As I gaze out at the skyline, I have a flashback to my first meeting here, thirteen years ago when Jane had just got me a deal for my first – and last – novel in my own name. It was a warm June day and the sky had been bright blue, instead of the gunmetal grey of today. I'd felt on top of the world – literally and metaphorically. Not only had I landed my dream career as an author, but I'd also just moved into an apartment in London with my university sweetheart. Despite my decidedly shaky start in life, I'd managed to turn things round. I was a success!

Now, as I perch on one of the leather armchairs in front of Jane's desk, I have to push away my feelings of failure yet again. My novel only ended up selling a couple of thousand copies, and my university sweetheart eventually ended up leaving me for someone brighter and shinier and no doubt more fertile. I catch a glimpse of the little red-haired girl peeping out at me from behind one of the giant potted plants. I clear my throat and try to compose myself. *I was wondering if I could take a holiday...*

'Coffee?' Jane asks, picking up the jug on her desk.

I raise my eyebrows. 'Do you really need to ask?'

She laughs. 'What was I thinking! I'm so sorry.'

'That's OK; just don't let it happen again,' I joke, taking off my jacket and sitting back in the chair.

'Are you sure you're OK?' she says, bringing a steaming mug over to me.

I wrap my cold fingers around the mug and inhale the rich aroma. Perhaps it would help to tell her the truth. A problem shared is a problem halved and all that, and if she knows the full story, she might be more understanding when I turn down this new job. I take a sip of coffee to embolden me. 'Do you remember the day you took me out for lunch and told me about what happens to a caterpillar when they're inside the cocoon?'

She nods. 'The butterfly soup?'

'Yes. Exactly how long does a caterpillar marinate in its own juices?'

'Hmm, about two weeks, I think.' She sits down in the chair across from mine and crosses her slim legs.

'OK, well I've been in the soup for ten months now, and I can't seem to find the energy or enthusiasm to pull myself out. When does the caterpillar know it's time to change?'

'When it feels the calling of the butterfly from deep within its cells,' she replies dreamily.

I let out a sigh. 'That's very poetic, but I'm not feeling anything calling to me from within, so I was wondering if—'

'Well then, this is perfect timing,' Jane interrupts. She picks up the basket of pastries on the coffee table and offers them to me.

'It is?' I take a plump golden croissant and put it on a plate.

'Yes. I think this new ghostwriting job might be exactly what you need.'

My heart sinks. 'Are you sure? The last couple of clients weren't exactly inspiring.' I glance at the wall by the door which is lined with the framed covers of bestselling books by some of Jane's authors. At least five of them were written by me, including the autobiographies of the six-time Olympic gold athlete Joyce Daniel, and one of Britain's most successful and beloved actors, Sir Lawrence Bourne – both of whom were a joy to work with.

'Oh, trust me, this job will be nothing like those last two.' She smiles mysteriously. 'In fact, it will be nothing like any job you've ever done before, which was why I wasn't able to tell you about it over email.'

'What do you mean?' Despite my overwhelming desire to do nothing but lie on a sunny beach for a month, possibly even two, I feel a prickle of interest.

'It's top secret,' she replies, lowering her voice. 'So top secret in fact that only I know about it.'

My interest grows. 'Who's it for?'

'I can't tell you until you sign the NDA. I have it on my desk ready.'

'But...'

'Trust me, Lily, this is like no other job I've ever handled before.' Her eyes sparkle with excitement. 'And I think it's exactly what you need to get out of the soup.'

Now she really has my attention. 'Can't you give me any clues before I sign my life away?'

'If you were to take the job, you'd have to go abroad – to meet the client initially, and then, if all goes well, to write the book. So it would mean being away for a couple of months, maybe more, and a complete change of scenery.' She glances through the window at the grey sky. 'And somewhere a lot warmer and sunnier too.'

I feel a burst of excitement. This has never happened before. Everyone I've written for previously has been based in the UK. And how bizarre that it should happen right when I realise that I need to escape. 'Where exactly?'

'Portugal.' Jane leans closer. 'Trust me, Lily, this could be the most incredible experience of your career. And the client has asked for you specifically.'

I nod, unsure why she thinks this is such a big deal. I've ghostwritten so many books, I'm well respected within the publishing industry, even if no one outside of the industry knows me.

'If you knew who she was, you'd realise what a magical opportunity this is,' Jane continues, placing her hand on mine. Her huge diamond ring glints up at me as if to emphasise the magic of this opportunity.

One of the things I like most about Jane is her no-nonsense, unflappable attitude. I've never seen her so excited by a job before, so I know I should take it seriously. But more than anything, the opportunity to leave the relentless gloom of the UK in February is hugely appealing.

I grin. 'All right. I'll do it."

'Wonderful!' She leaps up and goes to her desk to fetch the NDA.

'Go on then, put me out of my misery – who's the client?' I ask as I sign it, praying I won't be disappointed.

'Sofia Castello,' she replies enigmatically.

I frown. 'The singer?'

'Yes!' She smiles.

'The singer who sang "Ocean Longing"?' I ask, certain I must be mistaken.

'The very one.'

'But it can't be.' A shiver runs up my spine. 'She's been dead for years!'

2

LONDON, 2000

Everyone knows Sofia Castello is dead. Just like Marilyn Monroe and Janis Joplin, her tragic untimely death became an intrinsic part of her identity, elevating her to that almost angelic status of one taken too young. The terrible, violent nature of Castello's death made it even more heartbreaking, dying in a plane crash during World War Two. But her songs lived on, and to this day her wistful ballad 'Ocean Longing', about pining for an absent love, continues to get airplay, an evergreen hit on a par with 'La Vie en rose' by Edith Piaf. There's a resonance to the lyrics and the plaintive, soulful tone of her voice that reaches deep inside the listener, transmuting their pain into something almost beautiful. I played it on a loop after the doctor told me I wasn't able to have children.

'I don't understand,' I say. 'Everyone knows she's dead.'

'Everyone *thinks* she's dead,' Jane replies with an excited smile. 'But it turns out that she's not, and now she wants to tell the story of what really happened.' Her smile grows. 'And best of all, she wants you to help her tell it!'

My skin prickles with goosebumps. If this is true, then Jane is right – this is a ghostwriting job like no other, the job of a lifetime. But how can it be true? If Castello didn't die in the plane crash, why didn't she tell anyone? Even if the crash had caused her to lose her memory, wouldn't other people have recognised her?

'Are you sure this isn't some kind of prank?'

Jane shakes her head. 'No, her old manager was the one who reached out to me. I represented him way back in the day, when I first started out as an agent. I got him the deal for his autobiography back in the 1960s and we've remained friends ever since. I trust him implicitly.'

'But how could she have survived the plane crash without anyone knowing? It doesn't make sense.'

She shrugs. 'I don't know, but that's what makes this job so intriguing.'

'Wow!' I lean back in my chair, feeling slightly dazed at this unexpected turn of events.

'So, how soon would you be able to go to Portugal?' Jane asks, snapping back into business mode. 'She's very eager to get things started and has requested a meeting in Lisbon next week if possible.'

'Oh – uh – yeah, that wouldn't be a problem.' I don't need to check my diary. Over the winter, I've retreated further and further into my post-break-up cocoon. I didn't even go out on New Year's Eve to celebrate the arrival of the year 2000.

'Excellent.' Jane goes back over to her desk and takes a file from a drawer. 'Apparently she lives in a coastal village in the north of Portugal. But she wants to meet you in Lisbon first, just to make sure it's a good fit. You know the score.'

I nod. Every ghostwriting job begins with a preliminary 'get to know you' meeting. I used to love the challenge of only having an hour or so to bond with a potential client and win their trust, especially if it was someone I really respected. My favourite had to be my meeting with Sir Lawrence Bourne. He might have been in his eighties, but he still had all the youthful exuberance of a boy, and he shattered my preconceptions of aristocrats being pompous and aloof – after our first meeting he took me to lunch in his favourite greasy spoon café in Camden for pie and mash. More recently, of course, that challenge has faded, but for this job... I shiver at the prospect – this could be the most thrilling and nerve-wracking preliminary meeting I've ever had.

Jane hands me the file. 'All of the details about when and where to meet are in here.'

'OK.' I clutch the file, my heart thudding. 'Are you sure this is for real?'

Jane nods firmly. 'How long have we known each other, Lily? There's no way I'd send you on a wild goose chase. And look at it this way. Even if the meeting doesn't go well and you don't end up writing the book, you're still getting an all-expenses paid trip to Lisbon.'

I feel a strange sensation in the pit of my stomach, and it takes a moment to recognise what it is. For the first time in what feels like forever, I'm genuinely excited. I'm not one of those people who believes in a benevolent universe – discovering that your long-term partner is cheating on you and your womb is working against you tends to make one a tad cynical – but even I have to admit that there's something magical about this morning's events. Could it be that, just like the butterfly, I'm being helped to feel the call to transform?

And so, two days later, I find myself on a plane bound for Lisbon. As we speed down the runway and into the air, my spirits soar in tandem. I'm nervous about what lies ahead, but it's a good kind of fear, the kind that is laced with excitement rather than dread. This is the first solo trip I've ever taken, but it feels exhilarating to be pushed out of my comfort zone, to be jolted wide awake.

I spend the two-hour flight studying the notes I've made about Sofia Castello after some hasty research. She was born in 1920 in a town called Ovar in northern Portugal, then, at sixteen, she headed to Lisbon to work in the harbour selling fish to escape a childhood full of pain and abuse. Two years later, she was spotted singing one night in a bar and, in a classic rags to riches tale, she was whisked out of her life of fish and into the glamourous world of musical stardom. Initially, she was only famous in Portugal, but then her iconic song, 'Ocean Longing', catapulted her to worldwide fame in 1941. Later that year, her life ended when the Germans shot down the passenger plane she was travelling on, killing everyone on board – or so everyone was led to believe – and there was a global outpouring of grief. There have been several books written about her, and a couple of documentaries and a film, all claiming to tell the true story of her life, and all, it turns out, completely wrong – about her death at least.

The flight passes by in a flash, and as we begin our descent, I press my face to the window and drink in the scene below. Hills lined with rows of buildings in beautiful pastel shades of yellow and pink, all with terracotta roofs. The reality that I'll soon be wandering those streets, in a country I've never been to before, and where I don't speak a word of the language, suddenly hits me, and I quickly turn to the back of my notebook where I've scribbled down some essential phrases. *Bom dia, um café, obrigada, por favor*, I chant in my head. *Good day, a coffee, thank you, please.* All of the essentials, along with *desculpa, sou inglês*, meaning, *I'm sorry, I'm English*, which will hopefully cover a multitude of sins.

In the whirlwind of preparing for my unexpected trip, I'd thought these words would suffice, but as the plane gets lower and the streets of Lisbon draw closer, I feel increasingly nervous. What if the locals hate people who can't speak Portuguese? What if Sofia Castello can't speak any English?

She must be able to though – why would she have asked for an English ghostwriter if she didn't? It wouldn't make any sense.

None of this makes any sense, I remind myself and fight the nervous urge to laugh. There's still a part of me expecting this to be a giant prank. But it's a measure of how bad things have become that I really don't care. At least I'm feeling something – even if it is increasingly anxious, it still beats the numbness of the past ten months.

As soon as I step out of the plane and down the steps onto the tarmac, I'm hit by a wall of heat. After a relentlessly cold and gloomy British winter, it feels so alien to breathe in warm air, but so, so good, although I'm instantly regretting my decision to wear a roll-neck sweater, jeans and boots.

Passport control is surprisingly quick and easy to navigate, but then the nerve-wracking part begins. After narrowly avoiding getting on the wrong train, and sweltering in the muggy air, I make it to the city centre. I've been booked into the Hotel Avenida Palace where I'm due to meet Sofia Castello tomorrow, close to Praça do Rossio, which my Lonely Planet Guide to Portugal informs me is one of the main squares in Lisbon.

I have yet another pinch-myself moment as I turn the corner. With its ornate water feature and black-and-white mosaic floor, Praça do Rossio is absolutely breathtaking. I stop walking and drink it all in, my feeling of disbelief growing. Just a few days ago, I was crammed on a Tube train in London, just about losing the will to live, and now here I am, in a country I've never been to before to meet a legendary singer who's come back from the dead. And, best of all, she wants me to help her tell her story, and what an incredible story it must be.

I carry on walking, my nervous excitement growing with every step. In all my years as a writer, I have never wanted a job more.

3

LISBON, 2000

It's impossible to miss the Hotel Avenida Palace. An imposing five-storey building with an ornate façade and huge stone pillars either side of the entrance, it sits on the corner of another beautiful, cobblestoned square. I check my notebook to make sure I have the correct address. It looks incredibly grand and super expensive. But then I guess Sofia won't be poor, given the longevity of her success. 'Ocean Longing' featured on the soundtrack of a smash hit film just a couple of years ago which sent it catapulting back up the charts. But how would she be able to claim the royalties from her music if she's supposed to be dead? This is just one of the hundreds of questions I've been plagued with since my meeting with Jane. Still, I guess I won't have long to wait to get some answers.

As I approach the hotel, a porter in a pristine uniform springs to attention and gives me a dazzling smile. I glance down at my jeans and scuffed boots and hope they let me in.

'*Bom dia!*' he says warmly.

'*Bom dia!*' I reply. '*Desculpa, sou inglês.*'

'No need to apologise; the English are our friends!' He laughs warmly. 'And I speak some English, so it's all OK.'

'Oh that's great. I would have learned more Portuguese, but this is a very unexpected trip. I have a reservation,' I gabble nervously.

'Very good, please...' He opens the door and ushers me inside.

'Thank you. I mean, *obrigada*.'

I step into a beautiful foyer. A huge chandelier instantly draws my attention, glittering from the centre of the ceiling. Thankfully, the air is much cooler inside and is perfumed with the sweet scent of lilies in large gilt vases dotted around the place. The mahogany reception desk gleams in the soft light, and two leather sofas have been arranged in an L-shape in front of it. A man is sitting on one of them reading a newspaper, which obscures his face, but I'm relieved to see that he too is wearing jeans and a pair of scruffy trainers.

As I make my way over to the desk, the woman behind it smiles warmly.

'*Bom dia!*' she cries.

'*Bom dia!*' I reply. 'I have a reservation for this evening.'

'Wonderful, welcome to the Avenida. What is your name please?'

'It's Lily. Lily Christie.'

As she consults the leather-bound register on her desk, I feel a brief moment of panic as I once again wonder if this might all be a huge prank. Maybe there are cameras hidden behind the huge potted ferns and vases of flowers filming my reaction for one of those candid-camera TV shows. I glance around and see that the man on the sofa is now looking at me over the top of his paper. He has wavy chestnut brown hair, piercing green eyes that glimmer emerald-bright against his tanned skin. As soon as our eyes meet, he ducks back behind his paper as if embarrassed to be caught looking at me.

I turn back to the desk, aware that my cheeks are starting to flush. It's been so long since I've been noticed by a man. It's been so long since I've wanted to be noticed. The double whammy of learning that I can't have children and the revelation of Robin's affair caused that part of me to shut down to protect myself from further hurt. For the past ten months, I've drifted around London wearing nothing but black and grey, trying to blend into the background.

'Ah, yes, here you are,' the receptionist says. 'You're in Room 412, on the fourth floor. It has a stunning view,' she adds.

'Oh that's great.' So, it isn't a prank then. I feel a rush of excitement. My life really is about to begin again, and in the most extraordinary way.

She hands me my room key. 'The elevators are over there.' She points over to the left, her glossy red nail polish shining in the light. 'And the restaurant and bar are through there.'

As I turn to look right, I see that the man has left the sofa and is striding across the lobby towards the bar.

I make my way over to the lifts, marvelling at the excitement and anticipation I'm experiencing. Moments later, I emerge onto the fourth floor to discover a wine-coloured carpet so plush and thick it feels like walking on a cloud, and when I open the door to my room, I can't help gasping – it's almost as big as my London apartment. The elegant wooden furniture gleams in the soft lighting, and the burgundy-and-gold velvet drapes perfectly match the bedding.

I head over to the window and look outside. The receptionist wasn't lying; the view is stunning. I take off my jacket and throw it on the bed and start to laugh. This all feels like an incredible dream.

After a quick shower to freshen up, I put on my jeans and the one T-shirt I brought. It's still only 5 p.m., so there's plenty of time to explore.

I head back downstairs and out onto the square. It looks even more magical in the twilight as the lights begin to come on, sparkling like stars against the deepening blue sky. I head towards Avenida da Liberdade, which Lonely Planet informs me is Lisbon's equivalent to Paris's Champs-Élysées. As soon as I reach the top of the avenue, I can see why. Both sides of the wide boulevard are lined with two rows of trees forming inviting canopies of green to stroll beneath. The pavement is covered in a mosaic of tiny tiles creating ornate patterns in black and white. My side of the street is filled with market stalls selling everything from leather bags and purses to brightly coloured scarves and clothes. With every step I take, I feel more emboldened. I'm no longer the unseen woman who drifts around London like a ghost. I'm a woman who travels the world solo. I'm an intrepid explorer who can navigate the Lisbon Metro. I'm a writer on an intriguing international assignment. I'm—

My thoughts come screeching to a halt as I reach a stall selling clothes. Hanging on a rail in front of me are an array of beautiful silk dresses in radiant swirling prints. I'm instantly drawn to one in teal and gold. I had planned to wear a pair of smart black trousers and a grey blouse to my meeting tomorrow, but just a couple of hours in Portugal has convinced me that this dress would be far more appropriate. Before I have time to overthink, I take the dress from the railing.

The stallholder, a beautiful woman with olive skin and long grey hair, treats me to a smile and says something in Portuguese.

'*Desculpa, sou inglês,*' I reply, which is starting to roll off my tongue effortlessly.

'That is OK. I speak some English,' she replies. 'This dress, it would suit you very well. The greeny-blue, it matches your eyes and will make that lovely red hair light up like fire.'

'*Obrigada!*'

'And it is silk, so it packs up very small. Perfect for travelling,' she adds, and I feel a burst of joy as I realise how she sees me – a traveller with hair like fire. I'm so grateful, I have to fight the urge to hug her.

'I'll take it,' I say without even checking the price. Thankfully, it's very affordable, and feeling buoyed, I continue on my way.

As I walk past a restaurant, I catch a delicious waft of grilled meat, and I'm ambushed by a sudden and acute hunger. I was so nervous about finding my way to Lisbon, I didn't eat a thing on the plane and hardly anything for breakfast. I remember seeing a beautiful old taverna on the square near the hotel and do an abrupt about-turn.

As I look back down the avenue, I notice a man a few yards away also come to a sudden halt and quickly turn to look at a stall full of bric-a-brac. There's something familiar about him, which confuses me as I've only been here a couple of hours. But then I realise where I know him from. It's the man from the hotel lobby, the one I caught looking at me over his paper. Is it a coincidence, or did he see me leave the hotel and decide to follow me? But why would he be following me? A terrible thought occurs to me. What if he knows why I'm here and who I'm here to meet? What if he's a journalist who's got wind that Sofia Castelo is still alive? But how could he? Jane was adamant that nobody else knows.

I stare at him, bent over the stall, engrossed in something, or pretending to be. What if he's some kind of stalker or a thief? What if he spied me arriving at the hotel on my own and thought I'd be an easy target?

My new-found joy drains from my body, replaced by a feeling of growing unease. Is my dream assignment about to turn into a nightmare?

4

LISBON, 2000

I stand frozen to the spot, wondering what to do. Then I remember the rape alarm my best friend Nikki insisted I buy before leaving the UK. 'Just to be on the safe side,' she'd said. I'd nodded along to humour her, never thinking that I'd actually need it.

I open my bag and feel inside just to check it's there and take a breath. *It's OK, there are loads of people about – even if the man is following you, what's he going to do?* I try reassuring myself. I think back to the council estate I grew up on and the gangs that used to roam the tower blocks in packs. My life might have been a middle-class dream since meeting Robin and leaving university, but that scrappy, street-smart kid is still there inside me.

I glower at the man's back, daring him to turn round and face me, but he appears to be transfixed by an old carriage clock. I march past him in the direction of the hotel.

When I've got about halfway down the avenue, I suddenly stop and turn, hoping to catch him out again, but there's no sign of him. I breathe a sigh of relief and tell myself off for being paranoid, but I still feel a little shaken, so I decide to forgo a visit to the restaurant and return to the hotel and order room service instead.

As soon as the food has arrived, I double lock the door, as I realise that the man probably overheard the receptionist telling me my room number. I know I'm probably overreacting, but this is the first time I've travelled to a brand-new country on my own and I can't help feeling a little vulnerable. Besides, there are just hours to go before what could be the biggest, most intriguing job of my career and I don't want anything, or anyone, to ruin it.

After I've eaten, I turn out the light and go and perch on the wide windowsill. The lights of Lisbon twinkle below and a balmy breeze drifts in, bringing with it the laughter and chatter of diners sitting outside the taverna. I kick myself for being a coward and ordering room service, but then I remind myself that, whatever happens tomorrow, I'll be staying in Portugal for at least a week. If I don't get the job, I'm going to take a holiday here instead. The beauty and vibrancy of Lisbon has already worked its way inside of me, and I crave more of this feeling. I sit for ages watching the crescent moon slowly arcing its way across the sky, full to the brim with gratitude for the magic that seems to be at work in my life right now.

It turned out that I had no need to bring my travel alarm clock with me, as I wake every hour throughout the night, full of nervous excitement. I decide against going to the hotel restaurant for breakfast, just in case I see the creepy guy again and it unsettles me before my meeting, and I venture out onto the square instead. I find a beautiful little café just around the corner, which the sign informs me has been in business since 1880, and I order a coffee and a pastel de nata – the traditional pastry of Portugal. The coffee arrives in a tiny espresso cup, along with a delicious-looking custard tart, the top burnished gold and sprinkled with cinnamon. I take a bite and can't help gasping in pleasure. The pastry is flaky and buttery and the vanilla custard rich and creamy. It's so different to my normal breakfast of Marmite on toast and once again I feel jolted awake by the freshness of the new.

The coffee might have been small, but it really packed a punch, and I return to the hotel buzzing from a cocktail of nerves, sugar and caffeine. There's now only an hour to go until the meeting. Only an hour to go until I meet a music industry legend back from the dead. It's impossible to wrap my head around the enormity of it, and to stop myself from spinning out entirely, I take a bath with the complimentary magnolia-scented bath oil, then put on my new dress.

I'd been fully expecting to feel ridiculous in it, but to my surprise, when I look at my reflection in the wardrobe mirror, I'm actually happy with what I see. The woman who sold it to me was right: the teal really does bring out the colour of my hair and eyes, and it seems to have brightened my complexion too. I smooth down the silk and take a deep breath. This meeting is going to be bizarre to say the least, but I can handle it. I've ghostwritten for some very big stars before – admittedly none of them had come back from the dead, but still...

'*Bom dia*, Sofia! I'm Lily Christie,' I say to my reflection, extending my hand. 'It's a pleasure to meet you.' My voice wavers slightly, so I try again, and again, until I'm saying it with just the right tone of calm confidence.

Realising I ought to check my emails just in case there's been any last-minute change of plan, I plug my laptop cable into the socket in the wall and wait as the air fills with the ping-ping-whir of the dial-up tone. 'You've got mail!' my AOL account cheerily informs me, and I see a message from Jane wishing me good luck. My stomach flips. The meeting is on and only five minutes away.

I put my laptop in its case, along with a notebook and pen, and grab my bag. I take the lift up to the top floor and make my way along the corridor to the suite Sofia has hired for our meeting, my nerves growing with every step.

But just as I reach the door, I hear a sound from the end of the corridor. My stomach lurches as a man steps through the door from the stairwell and into the corridor. It's the same man from yesterday – the man from the lobby and the market. My mind races as he starts striding towards me. Was he watching my room? Did he see me take the lift and quickly race up the stairs to catch me?

I slip my hand in my bag and wrap my fingers around the rape alarm. As he draws closer, the corridor appears to grow narrower, making his broad, muscular frame all the more menacing. I take the alarm from the bag and press the top hard. A piercing shriek fills the air, causing the man to jump in shock, and he mutters something in Portuguese. I'm hoping he'll turn on his heel and flee, but to my horror he keeps marching towards me. *What the hell?*

Feeling I have no other choice, I hammer on Sofia's door. This is the worst possible way to meet a potential client and especially one of such stature, but what else can I do? The alarm in my hand is so loud now, I hope someone from another room might appear.

The man gets closer and closer, and I see a look of confusion on his face as he says something again in Portuguese, which I can barely hear over the piercing shriek. Then the door flies open.

A tiny woman in a black silk dress printed with pink roses stands staring up at me. Her short hair is dyed jet black and her eyes are accented with kohl in a dramatic cat eye. Her olive skin might be lined, but there's no sign of sagging, and she still has the most incredible, prominent cheekbones. Even in the chaos of the moment, I instinctively know that I'm face to face with Sofia Castello. She stares at the alarm shrieking in my hand, then at me and then at the man, and she shouts something to him in Portuguese.

'*Desculpa*, I'm Lily Christie,' I say, but she can't hear me over the alarm.

'What?'

'I'm Lily Christie,' I yell, 'and this man has been following me.' I point the screaming alarm at him accusingly.

She looks at me blankly for a moment, and my heart sinks. I've blown it before I've even set foot in the room, and all because of some crazed stalker.

I glare at him. 'Why the hell are you following me, you creep?'

He takes a step back, holding his hands up in some kind of half-hearted surrender.

I hear something above the sound of the alarm and turn and see Sofia leaning against the door frame hooting with laughter. She attempts to say something but is clearly too amused and bends over double, clutching her waist.

I stare at her, shocked. Why on earth would she find this funny?

5

LISBON, 2000

'Oh my dear, I'm so sorry,' Sofia eventually says, reaching out and touching me lightly on the arm. 'There's no need to worry. I asked him to keep an eye on you.' She looks at the man and shakes her head. 'Why did you have to do such a lousy job?'

'I am happy I did a bad job,' he replies in faltering English. 'Who wants to be good at following a woman?'

I stare at them both, incredulous.

'Is there any way you could turn that off?' Sofia says, looking back at me. 'I can hardly hear myself think.'

'Oh, uh, I don't know.' I start pressing at the alarm, but it continues to shriek. I'd been so certain I'd never need to use it that I didn't bother reading the instructions.

'Gabriel?' She looks at the man hopefully.

'Please?' he asks me, holding out a hand. His tanned skin is scuffed at the knuckles.

I pass him the alarm, trying to process these latest developments. Sofia had asked the man to follow me, so I don't need to be scared. But why would she do that?

The man, Gabriel, tries pushing and pulling at the alarm, but it continues to shriek.

'*Meu deus!*' Sofia exclaims. 'Someone is going to call the police if we don't stop it. Come, come,' she says, ushering us both inside a large suite of rooms.

Gabriel disappears into a side room, and there's a loud bang and then silence. He reappears holding the smashed alarm and holds it out to me, with a laboured sigh, as if I'm entirely to blame for the fiasco.

'I beg your pardon,' he mutters, which sounds so weird and formal, it makes me want to laugh.

'It's OK.' I take a breath, my ears still ringing. 'I thought you were going to attack me.'

Sofia lets out another snort of laughter, and I'm reminded of my first meeting with Sir Lawrence Bourne when I'd snorted with laughter at something he said. Being frightfully posh, I'd assumed he'd be horrified at my lack of decorum. But when I apologised, he smiled and shook his head. 'I love people who snort with laughter, darling,' he'd said in his plummy voice. 'It shows they're uninhibited in their joy. It demonstrates a freeness of spirit.'

Gabriel's face flushes. 'I beg your pardon,' he mumbles again, but looking more annoyed than sorry.

'Well, that's certainly got things off to an interesting start,' Sofia remarks, still chuckling to herself. 'And I'm very sorry too,' she says to me with a warm smile that reaches her dark brown eyes, making them sparkle. 'I really didn't want to scare you; I just needed to be sure that you were here alone. That you hadn't notified the press or anything. Given my slightly unusual circumstances, I'm sure you can appreciate that I can't be too careful.'

'Of course.' I start to relax a little. Maybe I haven't blown it after all.

'And I'm glad to see that you have a feisty spirit,' she adds.

I'm about to say, *I do?* but manage to bite my lip. 'Oh, well, yes,' I stammer instead.

'A woman after my own heart,' she continues and gives Gabriel a pointed stare. 'Who won't take any bullshit from a man.' She starts laughing again.

'OK, OK,' he says, rolling his eyes.

'Why don't you make us both a drink?' Sofia says, winking at me. 'To help poor Lily recover from her ordeal.'

He nods.

'I brought some red and white wine from my local vineyard,' she says to me.

Normally, I never accept an offer of alcohol at a first meeting with a client as I like to have my wits about me, but this is no normal meeting and my pulse is still racing from the whole alarm fiasco, so I nod. 'Red would be great, thank you.'

Gabriel disappears into another of the rooms, and Sofia ushers me to sit beside her on the elegant royal-blue sofa, which feels oddly intimate given that it's our first meeting. We're so close I can smell her rich, musky perfume, laced with the faintest trace of cigarettes. I glance around the room at the gleaming mahogany desk and matching shelves and the huge floor-to-ceiling windows.

'So,' Sofia says, folding her hands in her lap. She's only wearing one piece of jewellery, a beautiful silver ring in the shape of a crescent moon, with a jewel glimmering at the bottom, like a star.

I smile at her. 'It's lovely to meet you.'

She instantly frowns and shakes her head. 'One thing you need to know about me right from the start is that I can't abide phoney pleasantries.' She claps her hand on my leg, causing me to jump. 'I always say exactly what is on my mind, and I want you to be the same in return. And given the circumstances, I suspect you might be feeling something other than *lovely* about meeting me.' She looks at me expectantly, and the old ghostwriter instinct kicks in. This is it – an opportunity to win her respect and trust.

'Fair enough,' I say calmly. 'In that case, it's bloody insane to meet you!'

There's a moment's silence and I hope I haven't overdone it, but then she leans back and lets out one of her guffaws. 'Bloody insane!' she hoots. 'Oh, how I love the way you Brits speak. I have a feeling you and I are going to get along famously.'

'I bloody well hope so,' I say with a grin, and she laughs again.

Gabriel reappears with two glasses of red wine and a dish of olives on a tray.

'Your Royal Highness,' he says to Sofia teasingly as he places them on the coffee table in front of her.

'Thank you,' she replies.

'I'll be in my room if you need me,' he says to her before giving me a pointed and slightly warning stare. I wonder how they know each other. I guess he could be some kind of minder she's hired, but there's a warmth between them that suggests that it might go deeper than that.

'I'm sorry you and Gabriel got off to such a bad start,' she says as he goes into an adjoining room. 'He's a good boy.' She sighs and shakes her head. 'How can you tell when a person is eighty? They call a thirty-four-year-old man a boy!' She picks up her wine and takes a sip.

'Does he work for you?' I ask casually.

'Oh no. He's actually a fisherman – which explains his complete lack of talent at tailing you. If you'd been a mackerel, he might have had more success.'

Now it's my turn to laugh.

'He's from the village where I live,' she continues. 'I was very close to his mother, so I've known him all his life. And since his mother died, he does odd jobs for me, fixes things around the house, drives me places, that kind of thing.'

'I see.'

She settles back on the sofa and takes a sip of her wine. 'I imagine you must have a lot of questions for me.'

'I feel like that's something of an understatement!'

She grins. 'I love your accent so much. Please can you do me a favour?'

'Of course.' I put my glass down, assuming she's going to ask me to fetch her something.

'Can you say, "How do you do? I'm so frightfully pleased to meet you," as if you're the Queen of England.'

'Oh.' I start to laugh. 'OK.' I clear my throat and hold out my hand. 'How do you do? I'm so frightfully pleased to meet you.'

Sofia hoots with laughter as she shakes my hand. 'You're bringing back a lot of memories. I knew some Brits during the war.' Her smile fades. 'Anyway, due to the nature of this situation – and by that I mean the fact that everyone thinks I'm six feet under and pushing up the daisies – I'm afraid I won't be able to answer what I'm sure is the most burning question you must have. And by that I mean – how the hell am I still alive?'

I nod, feeling disappointed but unsurprised – we have only just met after all.

She leans forward and takes an engraved silver box from the coffee table. I watch as she opens it. Her fingers are surprisingly long for one so short, and her nails are painted as black as her hair. 'What you will come to realise if today goes well and we both want to proceed with his project,' she continues, taking a cigarette from the box, 'is that my supposed death is not in fact the most shocking thing about my tale. Far from it.'

I stare at her as she takes a lighter from the box. What could possibly be more shocking than the fact that she isn't dead?

She puts the box back on the table and lights her cigarette, leaning back on the sofa and exhaling a thin plume of smoke. 'So, what I propose is that I start telling you my story from the beginning, with the first instalment today. And if we both want to continue, we'll begin the project in earnest, but I need to stress that this isn't going to be an easy job – for either of us.'

'Why not?' I ask.

'Well, the fact that I've kept silent for almost fifty-nine years ought to tell you something,' she says, slightly shortly. I remain quiet as she takes another drag on her cigarette, acutely aware that I'm now engaged in the delicate dance of winning her trust. 'When – *if* – my story becomes public, it's going to ruffle more than a few feathers.'

'I understand,' I say softly.

'No,' she replies sharply. 'You really don't.'

I feel a burst of dismay that I might be losing her.

'How could you?' she continues, and to my relief her tone is gentler. 'You have no idea what happened to me. But I have it on very good authority that you're one of the best ghostwriters in the business.'

'Oh, I don't know about—'

She puts up her hand to stop me. 'Please, no false modesty. You wouldn't be here if you weren't. So, shall we see how we get along? Take it a step at a time, a chapter at a time, and when we get to the trickier parts, I'll have a better idea of whether I want to go there – or whether I want to abandon ship.' She gives a nervous laugh.

'That sounds like an excellent plan,' I say calmly, although inside I'm buzzing. This isn't just going to be the most exciting job of my career; it looks like it's going to be the most challenging too – but in a way that fires me up rather than depresses me. There's no way I want Sofia to abandon this project. I need to do everything I can to win her trust and make her open up to me.

'OK then.' Sofia clears her throat. 'Shall we begin?'

6

LISBON, 1936

One of the most frustrating things about the whole world thinking you're dead is having to read the utter horse shit some people say and write about you. In a way, it's as if I really have been a ghost these past fifty-nine years – able to see and hear what's going on but unable to respond, until now of course. So, the first thing I need to do is tell the story of how I came to Lisbon. The true story.

Legend has it that I came from a terrible background – everything from an alcoholic and violent father to a neglectful mother – but nothing could be further from the truth. The truth was, I never knew my father and I never knew anything about him – my mother remained tight-lipped on the subject until her dying day, when she passed from cancer when I was just sixteen. So it wasn't abuse or neglect that drove me to Lisbon; it was the spirit of adventure.

I've always been able to take care of myself – something else the biographers and journalists always get wrong, calling me the songbird with the broken wing and other such tosh. I was taking care of my sick mother from the age of twelve, so of course I could take care of myself. And once she'd passed, I was faced with a choice: to stay in my hometown of Ovar, haunted by loss and grief, or to change my surroundings and start again. And what better place to start again than Lisbon, our wonderful capital city. Lisbon also offered a unique opportunity for a Portuguese woman at the time – the chance to earn your own money working in the port selling fish.

Many women and girls from Ovar had been tempted to make this journey – so many in fact that the Lisbon fisherwomen came to be known as Ovarinas, which was then shortened to *varinas*. But this is another part of my story that's been misrepresented. So many times I've had to read that those were the unhappiest days of my life. That being a humble *varina* and selling fish was somehow akin to being a leper, when the truth was, I loved it.

From the moment I got off the train at Rossio and made my way to the bustling harbour, I felt alive again. Caring for my sick mother, especially in the final year, made it feel as if my world had shrunk right down to the inside of her bedroom – and I wouldn't have had it any other way, I hasten to add. It felt like such an honour to take care of her and help her in her final days. We shared such a close bond. But arriving in Lisbon was the perfect antidote to all the sorrow. The busyness and the physical aspect of the job felt so cathartic. With every box of fish I'd carry down the gangplanks from the fishing boats, I felt myself working the grief out of my body. And then taking the fish into the city to sell, and walking up and down the steep Lisbon hills, released more grief from my limbs. And as the pain left my body, there was space for something new to come in – excitement.

I loved the challenge of trying to win customers. There were a lot of us *varinas* walking the streets, and we were quite a sight to behold in our colourful costumes, with baskets of fish balanced on our heads. At first, I found the competition intimidating, and my mind would freeze every time I tried to think of a witty slogan to capture people's attention. But then one day, I made up a song about the shrimp I was selling, and as soon as I started to sing it, people started buying from me. I soon became known as '*o canto varina*' – the singing *varina* – and the job became even more enjoyable. I'd always loved to sing, so much so that I often thought in song too, and when my mother became bedridden, I spent hours making up fun little ditties to entertain her with. So, I was just doing what came naturally.

Then one day, after I'd been in Lisbon for about six months, I was selling a basket of mackerel outside a taberna in the Madragoa neighbourhood where I had lodgings. I'd got a little carried away, to be honest, composing a mournful ballad about two mackerel who'd fallen in love but then one of them was dragged off in a fisherman's net, never to be seen again, and I'd become quite overwhelmed with the emotion of it all. I was singing the immortal line, 'Oh how I miss your slippery kiss,' when a ruddy-faced middle-aged man came marching out of the taberna.

'And the pout of your mouth,' I sang, my voice tapering off as I waited for the inevitable scolding but, 'Oh,' was all he said.

'Oh to you too,' I replied.

'Was that you singing?' he asked, even though he'd just seen me with his very own eyes.

'Er, yes,' I replied, wondering if he had perhaps indulged in a little too much wine.

'How old are you?' he asked, and I instantly bristled.

'Old enough to be able to kill a man with my bare hands and fillet him like a fish,' I snapped with a scowl.

He burst out laughing and raised his hands. 'It's OK; I'm not going to hurt you.'

'I know,' I said defiantly, mentally preparing my next move, which mainly consisted of throwing the basket of fish in his face and running like the blazes.

'My name's Joao Paulo and I own this place,' he said,

pointing to the shabby taberna. It was named after Santo Antonio, the patron saint of couples and marriage, amongst many other things, although as I took in the grimy windows and shabby paintwork, I couldn't think of anywhere less conducive to romance. 'And I'm always looking for fado singers.'

'Fado?' I'd never really considered myself a singer of the melancholic Portuguese folk music, although, on reflection, my ballad about the lovesick mackerel could have been categorised as such.

'Yes, and yours is one of the most powerful voices I've heard,' he continued. 'It's quite incredible, coming from one so small.'

'Size isn't everything, you know,' I said, straightening myself into my full five feet, one inch. 'A germ is tiny, but it surely can cause a lot of mayhem.' This was one of many lines my mother had given me to say whenever bigger kids picked on me. And it worked. By the time I was ten, I was able to pack quite a punch, mentally at least – and when I unleashed a verbal volley upon a boy in my class for calling me a sprat, no one ever bothered me again.

'Hmm, I'd never thought of it like that, but you're right,' he said with a grin. 'So, anyway, if you're looking for a way of earning some extra money, you'd be welcome to come and sing here.'

Now he had my full attention. 'How much are you talking?' I said in my most businesslike manner. Bearing in mind I was still only sixteen at this point, not to mention knee high to a grasshopper, I'm not sure how he kept a straight face.

'It depends on the tips you get from the customers,' he replied, creating a spark of excitement deep within me. This was exactly the kind of challenge I loved.

'I'm in,' I said. 'When do I start?'

He laughed. 'Well, how about I give you a trial slot on

Saturday night, around ten? Come and sing a couple of songs and we'll see how it goes.'

'OK.' I held my hand out to shake his, as it seemed like the fitting way to end our business transaction. Again, he gave me an amused smile, but he shook my hand, and just like his smile, his grip felt friendly and warm.

It was only when I was heading down the hill back to Ribeira Market that the enormity of what I'd just agreed to hit me. I had a gig as a fado singer and only two days to prepare some songs.

7

LISBON, 1936

For the next two days, I rehearsed my songs as I walked the streets selling fish. I'd somehow landed myself an unexpected opportunity and I was going to grab it with both hands. When it came to a subject matter for my first song, there was no competition. Fado is the musical expression of the word *saudade*, a word unique to the Portuguese, meaning a profound longing for a beloved person or place; that almost indescribable bittersweet feeling. So I wrote my first proper song about my mother, and in composing something about the love I'd lost, I discovered, a new love – for music and songwriting. My previous ditties had either been designed to sell fish, or to make my mother laugh and take her mind off her pain; writing a piece of music that was a channel for my own pain opened my eyes to a whole new way of singing and creating.

The night of my debut performance, I gave myself a transformational makeover involving a set of hair curlers, a black kohl eyeliner and a ruby-red lipstick, and as I gazed into the mirror, I learned something really important, something that would prove to literally be life-saving in the future and something I can see forms a key theme of my story – we don't have to remain stuck in our lives or identities; we have the power to completely change any time we like or need. That night I changed from a scrappy, street-smart *varina* into a glamorous songstress and singer – or I began the transformation at least.

I set off for the taberna feeling excited and confident, but once I'd climbed the steep hill to get there and was covered in sweat, I felt a little less so. In a place as hilly and hot as Lisbon, one has to accept that it's not always possible to be elegant, and you have to make peace with frequently frizzy hair and a flushed face. So I arrived feeling more than a little flustered, especially when I could hear the raucous laughter from inside the taberna from the end of the street.

I suddenly felt very young and inexperienced. It was a feeling I hated, so I forced myself onwards, and I imagined the spirit of my mother cheering me on. I'm not sure if she'd have been all that keen on me going to sing in a bar at such a tender age, but that's the good thing about loved ones who are deceased – you can conveniently imagine them supporting you in all kinds of endeavours without any objection. Over the years, I'd have to say that my poor mother has become my Patron Saint of Anything Goes!

What happened next was something of an anticlimax as no one appeared to notice me enter the taberna at all. The men at the bar were all engaged in boisterous conversation, and those sitting at the small round tables were watching a pot-bellied man playing the guitar. A blue-tinged cloud of cigarette smoke hung in the air, mingling with the sickly-sweet aroma of alcohol sweating out through the patrons' pores. Of course, I'd been inside tabernas before and knew what to expect, but when I'd been dreaming of my singing debut, I'd dared to hope for something slightly less raucous.

I made my way over to the bar in search of Joao Paulo. At

first, all I could see was a buxom older woman in a gypsy-style dress and hoop earrings, and again I was hit by a wave of panic, but then he appeared through a door at the back.

'*Boa noite,*' I greeted him as confidently as I could muster.

He stared at me blankly, and I realised that either he'd forgotten me entirely or my transformational makeover had been a little too good.

'I-I'm the girl who sings love songs about mackerel,' I stammered, which, to this day, remains the most mortifying way I've ever introduced myself to another human being. But it worked and his eyes instantly lit up.

'Wow!' He looked me up and down. 'You look so different without a basket of fish on your head.'

'Yes, well I thought I ought to make the effort if I'm going to sing in your fine establishment.' Perfectly on cue, the man sitting next to me at the bar let out a loud belch. Meanwhile, over by the guitar player, another man began to jeer.

'Play something good for God's sake,' he heckled before almost falling off his chair.

'Looks like you're just in time,' Joao Paulo said, grabbing my elbow and steering me over to the tiny stage.

'You want me to sing straight away?' I squeaked. I'd been hoping to have the chance to freshen up in the bathroom first, although the air in the taberna was twice as sticky as it was outside.

'I think it's probably best,' Joao Paulo yelled at me over the growing din. 'The natives are getting restless.'

The good thing about a baptism of fire is that pretty much anything that comes after it will seem relatively easy. That first night at the taberna proved to be quite a reassurance to me over the following years, when I faced challenges like flying across the Channel in the middle of the war, liaising with spies and encountering some of the most duplicitous characters I've ever had the misfortune to meet. At least you're not about to get on stage at the Santo Antonio taberna, I'd tell myself and instantly feel soothed. Of course, it couldn't prepare me for everything I would encounter – but then nothing can prepare a person for the ultimate betrayal.

Joao Paulo strode up onto the tiny platform and took a mic from its stand, gesturing at the guitarist to stop playing. 'And now, ladies and gentlemen, I have a real treat for you.'

'You're going to take the guitarist outside and have him shot?' the heckler yelled, to a chorus of braying laughter.

'Er, no, but I do have a very special guest for you.' He looked at me and smiled, and I could sense a blind panic in his eyes. My heart sank as I realised he was counting on me to keep his patrons from starting a riot. 'Here to sing some traditional fado songs, we have—' He broke off and looked at me. In his rush to get me on stage, he'd forgotten to ask me my name.

'Sofia Castello,' I called. Another trait that I credit from my years taking care of my sick mother is that whenever the chips are down, and it feels as if things are going south fast, some kind of survival instinct kicks in, overriding my anxiety or fear. I felt it that night in that hot, sweaty bar, and I've felt it again many times since. I had to take control of the situation before all hell broke loose.

'Sofia Castello!' Joao Paulo announced, gratefully handing me the mic as I stepped onto the stage.

I put the mic back on its stand, not wanting the crowd to see my hands trembling and took a breath. *I'm with you, my darling*, I imagined my mother whispering in my ear.

'Is it all right if I sing one of my own compositions?' I asked the guitarist.

He nodded eagerly, clearly grateful to have someone save him from the spotlight. 'That's fine; I'll pick it up as you go,' he replied.

I contemplated telling the audience that I was going to sing a song about my dearly departed mother, but none of them were paying any attention, so I just cleared my throat and began.

Almost immediately, I felt a potent cocktail of all the emotions I had experienced at the time of her death swirling inside of me. The loss, the pain, the longing, the love. As I reached the end of the first verse, I gripped the microphone tightly and closed my eyes, and I heard the guitarist join in. Somehow, he knew exactly which notes to play and hearing him strengthened me, and I sang louder and with more conviction as tears began streaming down my face. I still had my eyes shut tight when I reached the end of the song, and it was only then that I realised the taberna had become deadly silent. Had I horrified them speechless? I cautiously opened my eyes a crack and saw everyone looking at me, even the heckler, whose mouth was gaping open.

'Thank you,' I squeaked, preparing to flee, but then the place burst into rapturous applause.

I turned and looked at the guitarist incredulously. He raised his eyebrows and shook his head like he couldn't believe it either.

'More! More! More!' the heckler yelled, banging his wine bottle on the table. Others began joining the cries. I looked at Joao Paulo behind the bar and he nodded eagerly.

So I sang my ballad about mackerel, which thankfully everyone loved – I guess it appealed to their drunken sense of humour – and I left the stage with their hearty laughter and applause ringing in my ears.

Joao Paulo was delighted with my performance, mainly I think because I averted a riot. But he invited me to perform a regular weekly slot, and over the next year, I honed my craft, writing and singing songs for a drunk and unforgiving crowd, which, with hindsight, really was the best training. After all, you don't learn anything from having smoke blown up your arse. By the time I got my big break, at the ripe old age of eighteen, I felt like a seasoned professional.

Of course, what I couldn't have anticipated back then was that something far more threatening than a bar full of drunken hecklers was building on Europe's horizon. Something that would alter the course of my life in the most dramatic of ways.

8

LISBON, 2000

Sofia sits back on the sofa and shoots me a sideways glance. All the time she's been talking, she's been staring straight ahead, as if watching her memories play out on a screen in front of her.

'I take it that the sinister thing building was the war,' I say, pressing stop on my voice recorder.

'Yes, it's hard to imagine now, but some terrible things happened here during World War Two. Terrible things.' She closes her eyes, as if trying to block them out.

'Here in Lisbon?' I ask, surprised and intrigued. I can't remember my school history lessons ever mentioning Portugal during the war.

'Yes, and here in this very hotel.' She opens her eyes. It's hard to be certain, but I think she looks frightened.

'This hotel—' I break off, not wanting to appear stupid.

'It was a favourite haunt of the Gestapo.'

'But I thought Portugal was neutral during the war.'

She gives a tight little laugh. 'Supposedly, but that brought its own set of difficulties. Spies from all sides came here, to try to win the support of Portuguese dictator Salazar. And refugees fled here from all over Europe, trying to escape to America and other relatively safe places. It was a lethal mixture.'

I think back to what she said a moment ago about singing in the tavern preparing her for what was to come. 'Were the duplicitous characters you met members of the Gestapo?' I ask cautiously.

'What duplicitous characters?' She stares at me, her eyes narrowing.

'You said a couple of minutes ago that singing in the tavern prepared you for liaising with spies and some of the most duplicitous characters you ever met.'

'Hmm. I can see that you aren't going to miss a trick.' She places her empty glass on the coffee table and stands up. 'Why don't we have a quick bathroom break? Please do help yourself to more wine.'

I nod but don't take her up on the invitation. One thing's for certain – I'll need to have my wits about me for this job. Getting Sofia to open up to me is going to take all of my skill in tact and diplomacy, not to mention human psychology.

I go over to one of the huge windows and gaze outside. Sofia's room, like mine, looks out onto the square, and as I watch the people bustling about down below, it's almost impossible to imagine this vibrant city flooded with refugees and crawling with spies. I remember feeling the same way about London on a visit to the Tate art gallery when Robin told me that the pockmarks on the walls were shrapnel damage from the Blitz. Thinking about the ghostly imprint of those dark days had made me shiver and, as if realising, Robin had wrapped his arms around me.

I gulp down a sudden wave of sadness at the memory and think of the Portuguese word Sofia mentioned about longing for a person or a place. *Saudade*. It perfectly sums up how I've been feeling these past ten months. But now is definitely not the time or the place to be thinking about Robin or our time together.

I glance down at a small side table next to the window and see a folder with my name printed on the front. I fight the urge to look inside. Knowing my luck, the minute I'd open it, Gabriel would pop through the door, but still...

I hear the toilet flushing and quickly lift the bottom corner of the folder just an inch. I see a handwritten note in what I assume must be Portuguese and the bottom of some newspaper cuttings, which puzzles me initially, until I realise that they're probably reviews or features about some of the books I've ghost-written. Before I can take a better look, I hear the bathroom door open, and I quickly move back to the window.

'Quite a view, isn't it?' Sofia says, and I turn and nod.

'It's stunning. I'll just pop to the loo before we carry on.'

'Pop to the loo!' she shrieks with delight. 'You Brits have such wonderful turns of phrase.'

I grin, relieved to see her happy and relaxed again, and I make a mental note that the next time she seems stressed all I need to do is say 'by jingo' or 'golly gosh' and hopefully she'll be smiling again.

The bathroom is as plush as the rest of the suite and about as big as our living room back home. My heart sinks as I realise that I still think of the flat as *ours*. A couple of months after the break-up, when Robin had moved in with his new partner, Nikki came over and helped me redecorate the living room. We painted it a vibrant shade of orange with a stencilled green vine border – something Robin would never have agreed to, having always preferring a muted palette, both in his clothes and home decor. The room makeover made little difference. The jaunty stencilling was about as effective as a sticking plaster over a gaping wound, and it did nothing to mask the memories imprinted into the walls from our thirteen years living there.

The saying 'wherever you go, there you are' pops into my mind. I'm not sure where I heard it; Oprah, probably, but it's annoyingly accurate and slightly depressing to realise that even meeting a world-famous singer risen from the dead isn't enough to wipe Robin from my mind.

I'm torn from my thoughts by the sound of a door opening and Sofia speaking in Portuguese. Obviously, I can't understand what she's saying, but I'm sure I hear my name being mentioned, and there's an urgency, almost anger, to her tone. I hear the low deep cadence of Gabriel replying, and it sounds as if he's trying to placate her.

I flush the toilet and all goes silent in the room next door. As I wash my hands, I wonder if they were arguing about me, and I really hope it isn't anything that might jeopardise me getting the job. If I'm to have any hope of moving on from Robin, I need to write this book. I need to fill my brain with the mystery of Sofia's story, so there's no more room for memories of him and us. No more room for *saudade*.

I come out of the bathroom to find Sofia sitting on the sofa lighting a cigarette and Gabriel standing by the door, putting on his coat, his expression grim.

'Is everything OK?' I ask cautiously.

'Yes, Gabriel is just going to get us some lunch,' Sofia says with a smile, but there's a definite tightness to her tone.

Gabriel gives a laboured sigh. Ignoring him, Sofia pats the sofa beside her for me to join her.

'Now I'm going to tell you about the night I lost my virginity and how it dramatically changed my life path,' she says loudly, and Gabriel beats a hasty retreat. As the door to the suite slams shut, she laughs. 'I knew that would get rid of him.'

I grin and get my recorder ready. But just as I'm about to press play, I glance at the table by the window and I see that the folder with my name on it has mysteriously disappeared.

9

LISBON, 1939

In the event of my untimely demise, various men scuttled like lice from the woodwork, eager to share tales of their encounters with me. Another fascinating aspect of being alive when everyone else thinks you're dead is that you get to see what other people thought of you. What fascinated me the most – and when I say fascinated, I really mean infuriated and astounded – is how people I'd seen as mere extras in my story, people who wouldn't have even warranted a line in my autobiography, suddenly claimed to have been a central character. Perhaps that's more to do with my fame and their wanting to cash in, but still, it annoyed the hell out of me, not being able to tell the world that that's not how it happened at all, and how little they meant to me.

Bing Jefferson is a perfect example. Bing was an American pilot for the Pan Am clipper line that began flying from New York to Lisbon in the summer of 1939. I can't stress what a big deal those flying boats were back then, and I have to admit that I was absolutely fascinated by them. I'd seen photographs of them in the papers, but I hadn't realised quite how huge they were until I saw one on the Tagus River – like a giant metal whale with wings! Given the technical challenges of having to land on water, and often in harbours dense with fog, the crew had to be the best of the best, so being a clipper pilot around town in Lisbon made one akin to a Hollywood star. And Bing Jefferson had the chiselled jaw and dazzling smile of a Hollywood star to boot, so his fame was assured.

By the late summer of 1939 when I first met him, I'd graduated from selling fish and singing in the Santo Antonio tavern and had secured a regular slot in the bar of the Hotel Tivoli on Lisbon's swankiest boulevard, Avenida da Liberdade. The manager of the hotel had spotted me singing in the taberna and offered me the slot, and although the clientele in the swish bar with its chandeliers and cocktails were a lot easier to please, and the increase in income meant I could now afford to rent an apartment by Commercial Square, I missed the raucousness of the tavern and the banter with the audience.

Most of the Tivoli clientele were businessmen and their glamourous lady friends. So when Bing strode in, clad in his pilot's uniform complete with the telltale gold lapel pin, all the female eyes in the room, and I dare say a couple of the male, swung his way. I was midway through singing a particularly emotional fado ballad, so I was less aware of his presence. It was only when the song came to an end and I was graciously receiving the audience's applause that I noticed he'd sat down at a table close by the stage and was gazing up at me. I'd been hit on enough times by married men by then that my eyes were always instantly drawn to his ring finger. Seeing no ring and no companion, I returned his smile and gave him a swift nod before exiting the stage.

About ten minutes later, I was relaxing on the chaise in my dressing room, having a cigarette and practising blowing smoke rings, when there was a knock on my dressing-room door.

'Come in,' I called.

In walked the concierge, Francisco, holding a folded sheet

of the hotel's creamy thick writing paper. 'You have some fan mail,' he said with a grin.

'Oh, not more,' I quipped, putting the back of my hand to my brow in mock despair. Francisco was also from a small town in the north of the country, and I felt a natural affinity with him – far more so than with the uppity hotel guests.

I took the paper from him and began to read.

Your singing is divine, it said in Portuguese. *Please will you join me for a drink. You are a wonderful carrot.*

I frowned at the note. 'Who is this from?'

'A pilot in the bar.'

'He called me a carrot!' I showed Francisco the note, and he burst out laughing.

'*Senhora, cenoura* – it's an easy mistake.'

'Yes, if you're a dummy,' I replied. 'But it is a wonderful opportunity for me to have some fun at his expense.'

Francisco grinned and raised his eyes heavenward. 'Heavenly Father, please protect that poor soul from what's about to hit him.'

I stood up and spritzed myself with scent.

Returning to the bar, I found the pilot still at his table but now with a bottle of wine and two glasses. My first thought was that he'd found another woman to call a wonderful carrot. But as soon as he saw me, he raised one of the glasses in my direction with a beaming grin.

'You came!' he said in English with a slow American drawl.

'I did, but only out of pity and a touch of morbid curiosity,' I replied, also in English, as I sat down.

'Say what?' He stared at me, eyes wide with shock.

'I had to see what kind of man doesn't know a woman from a root vegetable.'

'What do you mean?'

I showed him his note. 'A *cenoura* is a carrot.'

He burst out laughing. 'Gee, I'm sorry. But, in my defence, I did just fly all the way across the Atlantic and I'm seriously deprived of sleep.'

'Hmm, I'm not sure I'll be taking a clipper flight any time soon,' I quipped. 'Who knows where we might end up.'

There was a moment's silence, and I watched his face keenly, wondering if he'd pass my test. I cannot bear a man who can't take a little gentle banter at his expense. I love it when they give it back too. It's so much more fun than gushing platitudes. To my relief, he gave a hearty laugh.

'OK, you got me.' He threw his hands up in mock surrender. 'It could have been worse though.'

'Really? How?' I widened my eyes in surprise.

'I could have accidentally called you a potato. I feel like a carrot is a far more attractive vegetable.'

'If I were you, I'd quit while you're not even ahead and pour me a drink,' I said.

'Of course!'

While he poured us both a drink, I lit a cigarette and gazed around the bar. I was trying to look cool as a cucumber, but inside my pulse was quickening. With his square jaw, sandy hair and blue eyes, Bing was undeniably handsome, and he could take a joke *and* he knew how to fly a clipper! How could I not be excited?

We spent the next few hours talking effortlessly, although the conversation mainly revolved around Bing and his opinions and achievements; he only asked me a couple of cursory questions about myself. At the time, I wasn't all that bothered. I was still so young and trying so hard to fit into a grown-up world. I didn't yet have the life experience to fully flesh out the feisty, wise-cracking persona I was busy creating for myself. Hell, I was still a virgin – although not for long.

After I'd quizzed Bing endlessly about the clipper, he asked if I'd like to come and see it down in the harbour. Now that was an offer I really couldn't refuse, so off we set, arm in arm, along the avenue. I guess it must have been about three in the morning and the city was finally quietening down. The trams had stopped running, so the streets felt deathly quiet without their constant rattle and bell ringing. Every so often, we'd hear a burst of music and laughter from the last of the night's revellers, and I felt so happy as we strolled along. I'd seen enough of life's dark underbelly by then to know that fairy tales were works of fiction – but still, on that balmy summer's night, walking arm in arm with a clipper pilot after singing at the Tivoli, I allowed myself to imagine that maybe, just maybe, my fortunes really had changed, and that this was the start of my happily ever after. Oh, the irony, knowing what I do now about what was to come.

As soon as we reached the banks of the Tagus, the temperature dropped a little and the tiny hairs on my arms pricked up in the cool sea breeze. Bing quickly whisked off his jacket and placed it around my shoulders. It was such a simple gesture, yet it triggered a yearning in me that made me realise how long it had been since I'd felt taken care of. I'd become so accustomed to being the carer, for my mother and then myself. I have to admit that part of me began to melt.

We made our way through Commercial Square and past a man sitting on the ground playing the guitar. I thought for a moment of the guitarist at the Santo Antonio taberna, and I marvelled again at how much my life had changed. Finally, the bulky outline of the clipper on the water came into view. A gangplank had been lowered onto the dock, and a man in uniform stood guard at the end.

'Good evening, Pedro,' Bing said, causing Pedro to instantly tip his cap.

'Good evening, Captain.'

Now, with hindsight and the wisdom of age, I can see that Pedro's lack of surprise at Bing suddenly appearing with a woman on his arm in the middle of the night should have set alarm bells ringing, but I was so excited at the prospect of going on board, I couldn't think straight. To my mind, this was going to be the closest I ever got to flying on a clipper.

We followed Pedro up the gangplank, and he opened the door in the side of the craft, then stepped aside.

'Thank you.' Bing took some money from his pocket and handed it to him, then ushered me inside. As he turned on a lamp, I let out a gasp. It was like stepping inside a luxury salon, complete with leather armchairs and gleaming wooden coffee tables.

'This is amazing!'

'You're amazing.' He stepped towards me and took hold of my hands.

'Can I see the cockpit?' I asked, too enraptured by the plane to pay attention to his advances.

'Of course.'

He took me along a narrow passageway and up some stairs and there I was, inside a clipper cockpit. I gazed out of the window. The moonlight was forming a silvery path on the water like a magical runway. As a nineteen-year-old who'd never left her home country, the notion of flying across entire oceans and continents was entrancing to me.

'It must be such an incredible experience, flying one of these.'

He nodded. 'Take a seat.'

I sat down, and he showed me some of the controls. At one point, his hand brushed mine, and my skin prickled with goosebumps. I felt as if I was a character in a movie.

'Shall we go get a drink?' he asked softly after he'd given me the full inventory of the cockpit. I nodded and followed him back downstairs and into a bar.

'This is more like a hotel than a plane!' I exclaimed.

'Sure is. There's even a bed in one of the rooms. We call it the honeymoon suite.' He gave me a look that was so charged, I felt as if my legs had turned to liquid. And then, just like that, we were kissing.

A couple of hours later, we emerged from the clipper into the pale dawn sunlight.

'Thanks, Pedro,' Bing said as we reached the bottom of the gangplank.

'You're welcome, Captain.' Pedro winked at Bing but looked right through me like I didn't exist.

Not that I cared. I'd lost my virginity to a clipper pilot and this was the start of a beautiful relationship, surely. As I gazed up at the wisps of cloud glowing like spun gold in the rays of the rising sun, it felt like the perfect backdrop for such a momentous occasion.

When we reached the street, a tram rumbled past, and one of the newsboys that rode them, yelling the day's headlines, hopped off right in front of us, wiry as a monkey.

'Germany has invaded Poland!' he shouted before scampering off and hopping onto another tram travelling in the opposite direction.

Bing stared at me.

'What does this mean?' I asked, a chill passing right through me.

'It means that Europe will soon be at war,' he replied, ashen-faced, and just like that, the seeds of my fate were sown.

10

LISBON, 1939

After the newsboy's declaration, Bing and I retreated to a tiny café on a cobbled back street to try to digest what had happened over a cup of coffee.

'Surely the rest of Europe won't get dragged into what's happening in Poland,' I said, and Bing's attitude towards me instantly changed. His eyes no longer full of rapture – or perhaps lust would be the more accurate term – he stared at me as if I was the most ignorant creature ever to have walked God's green earth.

'Of course they will!' he exclaimed. 'Do you really think France and Britain will sit back and wait to be invaded by the Germans? Everyone knows that Hitler's plans don't stop at Poland.'

I sat back in my chair, feeling embarrassed and stupid. It was not a feeling I was accustomed to, and I didn't like it one bit. The truth was, I'd been so concerned with keeping my mother alive and then taking care of myself, I hadn't paid much heed to world affairs.

'Yes well, you'll be all right, you're an American,' I muttered.

'I'm a pilot,' he snapped, his look of disdain growing.

'But America isn't going to get dragged into any European war.'

He leaned forward, propping his elbows on the table, resting his square jaw on his hands. 'Have you not heard of the Great War?' he said condescendingly. A shaft of sunlight slanted in through a gap in the shutters, falling on his face like a spotlight. He suddenly looked a whole lot older, not to mention meaner, than he had the night before.

'Of course I have,' I replied. He had me on the back foot, but I wasn't out for the count just yet. 'I guess being a fighter pilot must be a terrifying prospect when you're only used to flying passenger planes.' I leaned back and took a bite of my pastel de nata and an imaginary boxing commentator in my head started going crazy. *What a comeback from the dumb kid!*

'I'm not afraid,' he blustered, his face flushing. 'I'd be happy to serve my country.'

'Of course you would.' Now it was my turn for the condescending tone, and he didn't like it one bit.

'Perhaps you should stick to singing, sweetheart, and leave the politics to the men.'

'Yes, because the men have done such a good job of things so far, haven't they,' I retorted before taking another sip of my coffee. Now I had some caffeine in my veins, I could feel my mental agility sparking back to life.

'Oh no, you're not one of those women, are you?' He rolled his eyes.

'What women?' I asked coolly, although my blood was beginning to boil.

'Those women who think they're just the same as men.' He took a bite of his tart, and to my immense satisfaction a dollop of the custard filling plopped onto the front of his pilot's blazer.

I downed the rest of my coffee and stood up. 'Oh, I don't think I'm the same as men,' I replied drolly. 'I'm not in the habit of putting myself down.' And with that I turned and marched outside.

It was only when I reached the top of the hill that my bravado faded, replaced with a growing feeling of disappointment in myself, made all the worse by the dull ache between my legs. I'd always dreamed of losing my virginity to someone loving and kind, but I'd lost it to an absolute asshole. After that, Pan Am clippers really lost their shine to me, and imagine my horror when, a year after my supposed demise, Bing was interviewed for a memorial TV show about me, claiming to have been my first love. I mean, really!

I slunk back to my lodgings and took a long, hot soak in a lavender bath. I was too embarrassed to try communing with the spirit of my dead mother about what had happened, so I decided to pray to Santo Antonio instead.

'Please, Santo Antonio, I beg of you, help me make better decisions when it comes to men and romance. And help me to atone for my sins,' I added, for extra effect. I was so disillusioned in men that I decided to focus on far more meaningful pursuits. 'From this moment forth, I shall dedicate my life to helping others less fortunate than myself,' I promised from the bathtub, inspired by how Santo Antonio had dedicated his own life to helping the poor. 'And I shall read at least two newspapers every day so that no arrogant asshole will be able to patronise me about world affairs ever again,' I swore, blissfully unaware of how powerful these vows would prove to be.

The very next morning, I marched down to a café on Rossio Square and read the *New York Times* and the London *Daily Mail* from cover to cover. It made for grim reading. Britain and France declared war on Germany three days later, and it wasn't long before refugees began arriving in Lisbon.

As soon as I saw them emerging from Rossio station bundled up in their woollen overcoats, blinking in the dazzling sunlight like startled rabbits, I also saw an opportunity to atone for my stupidity. I would help these poor people in the best way I knew how – I would feed them. I'd stopped working as a *varina* about eighteen months previously, but I was still in touch with my friends in the fishing industry. In just a couple of weeks, I'd persuaded a handful of fishermen to donate some of their haul to my charitable cause, and I also managed to convince Joao Paulo to open his taberna to the refugees every lunchtime, where I joined the chef in the kitchen to help cook the fish. Every time I arrived at the taberna, I'd look up at the faded sign of Santo Antonio and say a quick prayer of gratitude for this opportunity to repent.

Of course, someone needed to let the refugees know where they could get their free lunch, so I had some flyers made, and every morning, after my coffee and newspapers, I'd stand outside Rossio station and greet the new arrivals. My experience as a *varina* meant that I had no qualms about loudly proclaiming things in the street, and I soon had my welcome patter down. The fact that we were able to give these people a relatively safe haven when so many other countries in Europe were closing their borders made me proud to be Portuguese. And the response I got from the refugees was a balm to my soul; every relieved smile and grateful handshake or hug I received helping to heal the hangover of shame and regret I'd been feeling since Bing. It made me realise that I wasn't a stupid person; I'd simply done a stupid thing, and I was capable of clever and kind things too.

Then, one fateful morning, in early 1940, I learned that I was capable of incredibly brave things too. I'd just welcomed a new train load of German refugees to the city and had headed across the square to have a much-needed coffee.

As I sat down outside the café, I noticed a teenaged girl emerge from the station in a tatty overcoat. Her long dark hair hung down her back in a thick braid, and she was anxiously looking this way and that. Realising that she must have been a straggler from the refugee train, I downed my espresso and got to my feet.

A man in a suit who'd been sitting at the table alongside mine stood at the same time and started heading in the same direction. I thought nothing of it at first. Many people stopped for a coffee on the square before boarding a train. But as we drew closer to the station, I saw that the man was also looking at the girl, who was now moving off towards a side street, walking with quite a pronounced limp, as if she was in pain. To my surprise, the man turned and started heading towards the same side street. Was it a coincidence, or was he following her? Perhaps he was here to welcome refugees too, I thought as I followed them. But, in his smart black suit and fedora hat, he looked more like a businessman, and his blond hair told me that he wasn't Portuguese.

The girl disappeared down the side street, and, sure enough, the man followed. My pulse began to quicken. Why would a grown man be following a young girl like this? If he knew her, he would have surely called out to her.

The man took something from his pocket, and I saw a glint of silver as the sunlight hit it. My mouth went dry as I realised it was the blade of a knife. What the hell? My fear morphed into anger. I had to protect the girl from this monster. As she limped around the corner at the end of the street and disappeared from view, the man broke into a sprint.

'Oh no you don't,' I muttered, starting to run too.

I rounded the corner to see the man gaining on the girl, who was oblivious to the looming danger.

'Please, Santo Antonio, help me!' I silently implored, and as if in direct response to my prayer, a *varina* appeared from a side street, stepping in between the man and the girl.

'Stop that man!' I yelled at the top of my voice in Portuguese. 'Please stop him!' I yelled again to the *varina*.

What happened next seemed to take place in slow motion.

The *varina* stepped out in front of the man, blocking his way, and he crashed into her, sending the basket of fish toppling from her head and all over his suit.

The man started yelling at her in words I didn't recognise, and as I drew closer, my blood ran cold. I couldn't tell what he was saying, but I was certain it was in German.

The *varina* began yelling back at him in Portuguese, and then, to my relief, just as I drew level with them, the man darted across the street – away from us and away from the girl, who was now nowhere to be seen.

I quickly explained to the *varina* what had happened and ran on, trying to find the girl, but it was as if she'd vanished into thin air. I returned to the *varina* to help clear up the fish and gave her some money to help cover the loss. But for the rest of the day I couldn't shake an unsettled feeling. For so long, I'd read about the Nazis and what they'd been doing in Germany and Austria. Had I now experienced it first-hand, on the streets of Lisbon? It was a thought that filled me with dread.

11

LISBON, 2000

'More wine?' Sofia asks, leaning forward for the bottle on the coffee table.

'Oh, yes please,' I reply. I'd been so engrossed in her story it was as if I'd been transported back in time to Lisbon during the war, and it takes a moment to get my bearings. 'That sounded so scary.'

'Huh.' She gives a sarcastic-sounding laugh. 'That was nothing – compared to what was to come.'

I think back to the biography of Sofia that I'd speed-read in preparation for our meeting. In the chapter on her death, the writer hinted that the Germans had been targeting her when they shot down the plane she was travelling on due to her support for the Allies – apparently she'd travelled to London to perform in a show during the Blitz. I wonder if I ought to ask her about this now, then think better of it as she's already warned me not to skip ahead.

'Have you ever really regretted meeting someone?' she asks, handing me my drink.

I instantly think of Robin. In the months since our break-up, I've definitely had moments when I've wished that our paths hadn't crossed in the Student Union on Freshers' Week. If only I hadn't joined the film society, I might never have met him and been spared the anguish of him leaving me sixteen years later.

'Yes,' I reply softly.

'Would you care to elaborate?' She raises one of her perfectly drawn eyebrows.

'My ex-boyfriend,' I mutter.

'Oh dear!' She shifts sideways on the sofa so she can properly look at me. 'And dare I ask why that might be?'

I sigh. I know that me opening up to her will help us to bond and benefit our working relationship, but by the same token, I don't want her to think of me as pitiful. 'He ended up causing me a lot of pain,' I reply, studiously avoiding eye contact.

'Did he cheat?' she asks matter-of-factly.

'I'm guessing so. He left me for another woman.'

She nods. 'How long ago was this?'

'Ten months.'

'Ah, so you're still in the weeds of the break-up.'

'Yes.' I look at her and give a weak smile. 'But I'm trying really hard to get out of them. That's why—' I break off, embarrassed.

'Why?' she echoes.

'Why I jumped at the chance of this job.'

'Do you mean to tell me that it wasn't because you'd found out that a world-famous singer had come back from the dead?' she exclaims with a look of mock outrage so dramatic I burst out laughing.

'Well, obviously that was a big hook too,' I reply. 'But, on a more personal note, I was so, so grateful for the chance to get away from London and my apartment, and all the memories.'

She nods enthusiastically, like she really understands. Then she leans towards me and clasps my hand. Her grip is warm and surprisingly strong. 'Do you know what's interesting about me preparing to tell my story?'

'Er, everything?' I joke.

She grins. 'To you maybe, but what's really interesting to me is realising how some of the things that felt so catastrophic at the time were actually blessings in disguise.'

'Such as?'

She lets go of my hand. 'Such as Bing the asshole Jefferson.'

I wasn't expecting this and can't hide my surprise. 'How do you mean?'

'Well, I've realised that if I hadn't been so easily impressed by that stupid Pan Am clipper and made the mistake of getting intimate with him, I wouldn't have ended up in that bathtub, begging Santo Antonio for forgiveness and vowing to atone for my stupidity. And then I wouldn't have ended up helping the refugees.'

I nod in agreement. 'Helping them must have felt so rewarding.' The biography I'd read hadn't mentioned Sofia's work with refugees, and I'm intrigued to know more.

'Yes, it was, and because of them, something even better happened. Or, rather, some*one*.'

'Another man?'

'You'll have to wait and see,' she says enigmatically. 'But, in the meantime, I want you to hold on to that thought whenever you feel angry or sad about your rat of an ex. You never know – one day you might be able to see that his leaving you paved the way for something – or someone – so much better.'

'That's definitely a comforting thought.' I take a sip of my wine.

'Good!' She gives me a warm smile. 'So, shall we continue, and I'll let you see just how rewarding my brief encounter with that rat Bing proved to be?'

'Yes, please!' I raise my glass with a grin.

12

LISBON 1940

Another interesting thing about reflecting upon one's life as if it were a story is that you get to see how some of the seemingly innocuous choices you make end up becoming crucial plot twists, like the day I chose to say yes to Alexandre Fernandes.

Like me, Alexandre was born in rural Portugal and came to the city to seek his fortune as a teen. He began by working in the clubs as a cloakroom attendant, but he always knew he was destined for far greater things. His big dream was to become a music manager. He had no experience in this field, other than watching artists perform in the clubs where he worked, but, thanks to his whip-smart brain and a huge dose of chutzpah, he didn't let a little thing like inexperience stop him. And by the time I met him in January 1940, he was one of the most respected figures in the Portuguese music business – at the grand old age of thirty.

I'd heard about him from other singers on the circuit, who would speak of him in the reverential tones one might reserve for the Pope. But I guess he did pretty much offer the promised land to singers back then. If Alexandre represented you, it pretty much guaranteed billing on the best stages in the city.

Given my natural disposition towards cynicism, not to mention my bruising experience with Bing, I couldn't help feeling slightly suspicious of this much-revered man. So, when he appeared in a club off Avenida da Liberdade that I sang in every Friday night, I felt a strange inner conflict. On the one hand, I didn't want to be like all the other fawning singers so desperate to grab his attention, but on the other, I wanted to prove my worth as a singer and stand out from the crowd. So, I pretended I hadn't noticed him sitting at a table right under my nose, and I decided to sing my latest comedy composition – a fado-style ballad about a sardine who wished his scales were shinier.

As I started singing about the sardine imploring the moon to shine some of her silvery light into his skin, I noticed Alexandre gazing up at me, mouth agape, cigarette hand frozen in mid-air. Realising that I'd captured his full attention, I poured every ounce of emotion I could into the song. When I reached the end, where the moon grants the sardine's wish and he swims off all shiny and pleased with himself – only to be spotted by a lurking fisherman – I heard Alexandre cry out, 'No!'

As I placed the microphone back on its stand, everyone burst into rapturous applause – apart from Alexandre, who stared up at me, shaking his head.

'How could you have killed him off when his dream had finally come true?' he called as I stepped down from the stage.

'Because I'm a realist,' I replied. 'And besides, it's fado; it's supposed to be sad – hadn't you heard?' I added this last bit deliberately, to try to make out I didn't have a clue who he was.

My tactic worked.

'Please, won't you join me for a drink?' Alexandre said, pulling out the chair beside him. He was slender, with a boyish face and a mop of brown hair that gleamed like a chestnut in the soft lamplight of the club. Even an old cynic like me couldn't fail to be excited at this development, but I tried damn hard not to show it.

'OK, I have about ten minutes,' I said, sitting down.

'Before your next set?' he asked, and I couldn't help noting that he looked hopeful at the prospect of me singing some more.

I shook my head. 'Before I go to bed.'

'Oh.' He seemed momentarily stunned. 'Well, I'd better speak quickly then if we're on the clock. I assume you must be the infamous singer of fish fado I keep hearing about.'

I took a breath to compose myself. 'The very one.'

He gazed at me intently, but not in the lascivious way in which Bing did. This was more the inquisitive look someone might give an abstract painting in a gallery when trying to make head or tail of it. 'I have to say, you have a very interesting take on music.'

'I don't see why it's causing such a commotion,' I retorted. 'I was a *varina* before I became a singer. I used to make up songs to sell my fish. Now I sing about fish to sell my career as a singer.' I laughed. 'To me, it's simply a natural progression.'

'Well, yes, when you put it like that.' He smiled, revealing a perfect set of white teeth framed by a pair of dimples that wouldn't have looked out of place on an advertisement for tooth powder.

He retrieved a pack of cigarettes from his pocket and offered them to me. I took one and leaned closer so he could light it. His cologne was fresh and smelled of pine trees.

'It's a very interesting backstory,' he said, nodding thoughtfully. 'And very Portuguese.'

'I suppose it is.' I took a long slow inhale on my cigarette to try to calm my nerves. The man I was smoking with had the power to send my career into the stratosphere if he so wished.

'Have you heard about the Portuguese World Exhibition starting this summer?' he asked, lighting his own cigarette.

'Who hasn't?' I replied. The whole city was abuzz in anticipation for the double celebration of the founding of Portugal 800 years previously, plus 300 years of independence from the Spanish. Half of the city was under construction in preparation too, with a marina and monuments and pavilions being built specially. While the rest of Europe prepared for war and built bunkers and defences, our neutrality enabled us to focus on more positive things. For the time being at least.

'The government is looking for artistic contributions to the celebrations,' Alexandre said, and my nervous anticipation grew.

'Really?'

'Yes, including pieces of music that celebrate what it is to be Portuguese – but I'm talking about a Portuguese person rather than a fish,' he added with a grin. 'I don't suppose you ever write about the human condition, do you?'

'I have been known to.'

'Excellent.' He took a sip of his drink. 'I'm sorry, I should introduce myself. I'm Alexandre Fernandes. You might have heard of me?' He didn't ask this in an arrogant way; if anything, he sounded slightly bashful. It was a pleasant and refreshing surprise.

I shook my head. 'I'm sorry, no. Oh wait, the name sounds kind of familiar…'

He looked at me hopefully.

'Did you used to be a fisherman?'

He laughed. 'No, I can categorically say that I've never been involved with fish in any way other than eating them.'

'Ah, what a shame.' I grinned, and he laughed again. My plan to be refreshingly irreverent appeared to be working.

'So, what name do you go by then, other than the creator of fish fado?'

'Sofia. Sofia Castello.'

He reached his hand across the table for me to shake. His grip was just the right mix of firm yet friendly. 'Nice to meet you, Miss Castello. Now, how would you like to change your life forever?'

13

LISBON, 1940

Well, it was an offer I couldn't refuse. Yes, I was relatively happy with the life I'd created for myself in Lisbon, but I was still only twenty, don't forget, and I burned with the hunger for adventure only the young possess.

Over the years, I've often thought back to that night and how different things would have been if I'd just said no to Alexandre and gone to bed. But after those dark times in my teens where my world shrank down to my mother's room, with the spectre of death hovering in the corner, I craved experiences that made my world feel expansive and me feel alive, which is hugely ironic, given that it would all end in me having to die – to the rest of the world, at least. So, I said yes to his offer, and he gave me more details over a bottle of fruity Alentejo.

Essentially, I was given a week to compose a song that was emblematic of the Portuguese experience, then we would meet in his office by the Marques de Pombal and I'd find out if I'd made the grade. If I did, Alexandre would introduce me to one of his musical producers who would put together a backing band so we would go into a studio to rehearse and make a 45 record. And if that wasn't intimidating enough, I would be invited to sing the song at the opening ceremony of the exhibition, in front of the Head of the Portuguese State no less. Alexandre made it clear that I wasn't the only singer in the picture and, without naming names, I'd be up against some stiff competition. That didn't intimidate me though; it inspired me, firing up the spirit of the underdog that has always strained on the leash inside of me.

For the next few days, I decided to forgo my normal morning newspapers at the café, choosing to stay home where there would be fewer distractions so I could focus on writing my song. But there was something about being told to write on demand that caused my imagination to refuse to play. It was infuriating. I tried everything – drinking coffee, dancing around my apartment, praying to Santo Antonio – *begging* Santo Antonio – but to no avail. I was only able to come up with the most insipid of ideas, and then my fears would start chiming in like an out-of-tune chorus. *Maybe all you're good for is writing about fish. This is what happens when you get ideas above your station. Perhaps you should give up singing altogether and go back to being a* varina.

The day before my meeting with Alexandre, in a fit of despair, I left my apartment to try to drown out my fears with the sounds of the city. I made my way down the cobbled street to the bottom of the hill, relishing the rattle of the trams and the ding of their bells and the clip-clop of horses' hooves pulling their carts of fruit and vegetables to the market. As always, somewhere in the distance there was the melody of a guitar being played. It really was the most glorious cacophony, and unique to Portugal, I was certain, and the beginnings of a song idea began taking root.

I hurried to Praça dos Restauradores where I bought a copy of the London *Daily Mail*, but to write on rather than read, and dived into the nearest café and sat down at a table. Now I just had to find something to write with.

I glanced around at the other tables. They were filled with men hunched over their tiny coffee cups, talking and smoking, but in the corner, I spied a girl, face creased in concentration as she scribbled away in a notebook. I could tell instantly that she was a refugee. The thick stockings and the knee-length tweed skirt gave it away. Most Portuguese women still wore dresses and skirts that hung well below the knee. I wondered if she had a spare pencil. From the feverish way in which she was writing, I very much doubted that she'd want to share the one she was holding. But I needed to capture my idea on the page before it fluttered away, so I picked up my purse and paper and made my way over to her table.

'*Bom dia!*' I greeted her cheerily.

She peered at me over her glasses, clearly confused. Her shoulder-length brown hair was jagged at the edges, as if she might have cut it herself.

'Do you speak Portuguese?'

She looked at me blankly and shrugged.

'Do you speak English?' I asked in English, and she nodded with a relieved smile. 'Excellent!' I exclaimed. I pulled the other chair out. 'Do you mind if I join you?'

'Oh – uh – all right,' she replied in what sounded like a German accent.

'I have a confession to make,' I said as I sat down. 'I do have an ulterior motive for joining you.'

She instantly looked alarmed.

'It's not that you don't look like a very interesting person – you do. In fact, in normal circumstances I would be intrigued to discover what you're writing about so furiously in your notebook, but these aren't normal circumstances – these are very urgent circumstances.'

Her look of alarm grew. 'Why? What has happened?'

'Oh, don't worry, it's nothing to concern you, it's just that I've been trying all week to get my imagination to work, but to no avail. Then, the second I leave my apartment, and all of my writing implements, my inspiration comes flooding back.'

She continued staring at me blankly.

'What I'm trying to say is, please could I borrow a pencil or pen?'

'Oh!' Her face broke into a relieved grin. 'Yes, of course.' She rooted around in her bag and produced a pencil and handed it to me.

'Thank you!' I put my newspaper on the table and began scribbling ideas in the margins.

'Would you like a piece of paper too?' the girl asked, gesturing at her notebook.

'Oh, yes please, if it's not too much trouble?'

'Of course.' She tore me out a couple of sheets, and we both resumed writing.

I jotted down a list of the sounds of Lisbon, then a list of the sights, and the tastes, then I tried conjuring up the story of someone pining for their senses to be stimulated in such a uniquely Portuguese way again. But once more my imagination refused to play, and I couldn't think of a compelling enough idea. I stopped writing and took a sip of my coffee. The girl also stopped writing and took off her glasses, which changed her appearance entirely, making her look a lot less schoolmarmish. With her heart-shaped face and freckle-speckled nose, she reminded me of an illustration from a children's book.

'My name's Judith,' she said, extending her hand.

'Sofia,' I replied, shaking her hand vigorously. 'I'm so sorry, I should have introduced myself before; I was just so desperate to capture my ideas before they disappeared.'

She laughed. 'Don't worry, I know that feeling.'

'Are you a writer?' I nodded at her notebook.

'No, I am a botanist. Or, at least, that's what I dream of

being. Plants are my passion.' She looked down at the table glumly.

'Are you from Germany?'

She nodded.

'Jewish?'

She nodded again.

I glanced around for any sign of someone who might be with her. 'Are you here alone?'

'Yes. Why do you want to know?' She stared at me suspiciously.

'Oh, I'm sorry, I didn't mean to pry; it's just that you look so young.'

'I'm seventeen,' she said defensively. 'Well, I will be in two weeks. And I'm perfectly able to take care of myself.'

I liked her spirit. I *recognised* her spirit. 'Of course you are. I also came to Lisbon on my own at sixteen.'

Her expression softened. 'Where from?'

'A town called Ovar, on the north coast.'

She nodded. 'I'm sorry, I didn't mean to be rude; it's just that—' She broke off, casting furtive glances around the café as if she were some kind of fugitive, which of course, thanks to the Nazis, she was. I thought of the girl I'd seen being followed by the German man and my heart ached that this should be happening.

'No, I'm sorry. I shouldn't have been so inquisitive.' I wracked my brains, trying to think of something plant related that might cheer her up. The jacaranda trees that line the streets of Lisbon immediately sprang to mind. Their bright lilac blossom with its intoxicating perfume always added a magical air to the city during the months of May and June. I quickly scribbled jacaranda on my piece of paper as another idea for my song. The jacaranda was perhaps the most beautiful of all the symbols of Portugal – surely it would make a fitting subject for my song. 'Have you heard of Lisbon's jacaranda trees?' I asked.

Her face lit up. 'Oh yes. I only wish I was here to see them in bloom.'

'They really are something.' I smiled. 'Well, in that case, I have a proposition, and a way of thanking you for the pencil and paper.'

'Oh, there's no need for you to do anything. I was happy to help.'

'Yes, there is,' I said firmly. 'Because you haven't just lent me a pencil and paper; you have given me a brilliant idea – or the beginnings of one, at least.'

She gave a smile of surprise. 'Oh! Well, I'm very happy to hear that, although I really don't understand how I did!'

'I'll explain later, but first I would like to take you to the Ajuda Botanical Garden, here in Lisbon, where you will be able to see the very first jacaranda trees that were planted in the city.'

'The ones that were brought here by Félix de Avelar Brotero?' she asked, her brown eyes wide as saucers.

'If he's the guy who brought the seeds here from Brazil, then yes,' I said.

'How wonderful!' Her eyes shone with such joy, it stopped me in my tracks. It felt so heart-warming to have such a positive effect on her, especially given the circumstances. 'When would you like to go?' she asked hopefully.

Part of me felt that I ought to stay there writing and strike while the pencil was hot, so to speak, but another part, realising how much this meant to her, decided that my songwriting would just have to wait.

'How about now?' I asked, and for a moment I thought she might burst into tears, she looked so overcome with emotion.

'This is so kind of you,' she said, and again, it caused a bloom of warmth in my heart.

'Enough talk,' I said briskly, putting my notes into my bag and handing her back her pen. 'Let's go.'

We gathered our things and got up to leave, and as I followed her through the café towards the door, I noticed something that stopped me in my tracks. Just like the girl I'd seen being followed by the sinister German man, Judith was walking with a limp.

14

LISBON, 1940

The botanical gardens were about a thirty-minute train ride away, along the river. As we settled onto our bench seats opposite each other, I studied Judith closely. Her long tatty overcoat was similar to the one the girl had been wearing the other day, and she was the same height and build. The only thing missing was the long braid, but she could have cut it off since I last saw her. The uneven edges of her bob certainly gave the impression of a haircut done in haste or by a non-professional – or both.

'So, when exactly did you arrive in Lisbon?' I asked casually.

'A few days ago,' she replied, and my curiosity grew, along with my confusion over what to do. If she was the same girl, how could I tell her that I'd saved her from a knife-wielding monster? I didn't want to unnerve her. She seemed jumpy enough as her gaze darted this way and that around the carriage. Almost every seat was taken, and the warm air was filled with chatter and laughter.

Judith shook her head and sighed. 'You have no idea how wonderful this is,' she said, leaning closer so I could hear her above the din.

'The noise?' I asked, raising my eyebrows.

'Yes! It's so joyful. I honestly thought—' She broke off and looked out of the grimy window. Despite the warmth, she kept her long coat wrapped around her.

'What?' I asked softly.

'I thought I'd never hear such laughter again. Or, at least, I'd never be able to be a part of it. You are so lucky to live here. To be from here.'

I'd heard and read all about the horrors the Nazis had inflicted upon the Jewish people in Germany and Austria, but this was the first time I'd met someone who'd actually experienced it. Someone who brought to life the hurt and fear in a way that no amount of newsprint was able to. My inner conflict grew. If she was the girl I'd seen the other day, shouldn't I warn her that I'd seen her being followed?

'How did you come to leave Germany?' I asked, hoping that if I learned more about her, it would help me decide what to do.

'Have you heard of Kristallnacht?' she asked.

I nodded. 'The night of the broken glass.'

'Yes. My father was captured during the attacks and sent to a prison camp, along with thousands of other Jewish men.'

I shook my head in horror.

'He'd anticipated something like that happening,' she continued. 'The Nazi regime had been in power for five years by then, and they'd already taken away our right to work and study, so he felt certain it wouldn't be long before they took away our liberty. He drummed it into me that if anything happened to him, I should try to escape.'

'What about your mother, or any brothers and sisters?' I asked.

'I don't have any siblings, and my mother died when I was a child.' As soon as she said this, I felt a tug of connection between us, making her story feel even more poignant. 'I have an aunt in France, and my father had already mapped out the safest possible route for me to take to get to her.' Judith gave a sad smile. 'I finally made it there, but after a few months, my aunt urged me to come here as she's convinced that the Germans are going to invade France too. Now I have to try to get my passage to New York. I have a distant cousin in Brooklyn. It's literally my last chance.' She gave a tight little laugh. 'The end of the line.'

'Wow!' I exhaled sharply and gave her a sympathetic smile. I'd thought I'd had it tough, but Judith had made her way across an entire continent. And, even worse, she'd been fleeing something terrifying rather than seeking her fortune. I couldn't begin to imagine how that must feel, and I knew that I had to do everything in my power to help her. 'I'm so sorry you've been through all of this, but you're not alone now, OK? You have a friend here in Lisbon. I'm talking about me,' I added, just to avoid any confusion.

'Thank you so much,' she said, her voice cracking slightly.

'Can I ask you a slightly strange question?' I asked, leaning closer.

'That sounds intriguing.' She smiled. 'Please do.'

'Did you have long hair when you first arrived here? In a braid down your back?'

Her mouth fell open in shock, and I knew that my hunch had been correct. She was the girl from the other day.

'It's OK,' I said, placing my hand on her arm to try to reassure her. 'I think I saw you arriving at the station. When I saw you today, I thought that you looked familiar; I just wasn't sure why.'

'Oh, I see.' She looked relieved. 'Yes, I cut my braid off. It was too much trouble having to take care of so much hair. I thought it would be simpler, easier.'

'That makes sense,' I replied, but I couldn't help wondering if the real reason was that she'd been trying to change her appearance. Had she realised she was being followed?

'That's so funny that you saw me arrive and then we bumped into each other in the café.' She smiled. 'Maybe it is *bashert* that we should meet.'

'What is *bashert*?'

'It's Yiddish for destiny, or for people we're destined to meet. A lot of Jewish people use it to talk about meeting their soulmate, but it can be used for friends too.'

I nodded thoughtfully. It certainly was a weird coincidence that I should have run into Judith twice in such a short space of time. 'Maybe we were destined to meet so that I can look out for you,' I said.

She looked at me curiously. 'What do you mean?'

I didn't have the heart to frighten her – not yet anyway. 'I can help you get settled in Lisbon, until you receive your passage to America.'

Her smile grew. 'That would be wonderful, thank you.'

I smiled back at her before looking out of the window. I would tell her about the man on our way back, so she could enjoy the gardens first.

When we got to the botanical gardens, I took Judith straight to the two jacaranda trees.

'Isn't it incredible to think that the seeds that grew these trees came all the way from Brazil,' I said, gazing up into the leafy branches.

'Absolutely.' Judith smiled. 'Brotero was doing the job of the birds.'

'What do you mean?' I asked, intrigued.

'Well, normally birds are the ones who spread the seeds of plants from place to place. I love how Brotero did that for Portugal. What a gift.'

'It really was. I hope one day you get to see them – and smell them – in bloom,' I replied.

We stood in silence for a moment, and I felt the seed of a new song planting itself in my mind. I didn't need to scribble it down though. There was no way I was going to forget this moment.

'In a way, you are like a jacaranda seed,' I said, still gazing up at the trees.

'How do you mean?'

'It's as if you've been carried across Europe on the breeze.' I turned to look at her. 'You say you are lucky to have ended up here, but we are lucky to have you too.'

To my surprise, her eyes filled with tears.

'I'm so sorry.' I touched her arm. 'I didn't mean to upset you. I know you would rather be in your home country with your loved ones. I just wanted you to know that I'm really glad to have met you.'

'You haven't upset me.' She took off her glasses and wiped her eyes. 'It's just that that's the first kind thing anyone's said to me in a very long time. Thank you.'

Acting on impulse, I flung my arms around her and hugged her tight. Her body seemed to collapse against me, flimsy as a rag doll, and I felt her sobbing into my shoulder.

'I'm so sorry,' she cried. 'It's just been so hard. I've had to be so strong.'

My own eyes filled with tears as I thought of how it had been for me at her age, trying to keep it all together for my mother during her illness and then coming to Lisbon to start a new life for myself. I coughed to try to clear the lump forming in my throat.

'It's all right. You're not alone anymore, you hear?' I held her arms and looked her right in the eyes. 'You've got me now, and I'm going to help you...' I paused and took a breath. 'Just like I helped you the other day.'

She stared at me, her eyes glassy with tears. 'What do you mean, the other day?'

'When I saw you leaving the station, I was going to give you a flyer about a place I know that gives free lunches to refugees.'

'That sounds lovely.' She frowned. 'But why didn't you?'

'Because I saw someone following you – a man – a German man.'

All the colour drained from her face. 'How do you know he was German?' she whispered.

'I heard him say something.'

'What?' she cried, panic-stricken.

'I don't know; it was in German, but he wasn't happy. I got someone to try to stop him from following you, and he ended up with fish all over his suit.'

Judith's look of confusion grew. 'Did he have blond hair and a thin moustache?'

'Yes.'

'This can't be happening,' she gasped. 'He can't be here.' She looked around the garden as if the man might be hiding in the trees.

'It's OK – he ran away, and you disappeared before I could tell you what had happened.'

Judith leaned against a tree, looking utterly defeated.

It was as if her fear was contagious, and it caused my stomach to churn. 'Do you know him?'

She nodded. 'Unfortunately. His name is Kurt Fischer and he's in the Gestapo.'

'Gestapo?' My fear grew. I'd read all about the Nazi secret police.

Judith gave a grim nod. 'I thought I'd managed to give him the slip. He's been chasing me since I left Germany.'

15

LISBON, 2000

Sofia sits back on the sofa and clears her throat, clearly emotional. And she's not the only one. Gabriel had returned midway through this latest instalment of her story, and we'd both been sitting there, totally rapt.

'Oh boy,' she says before taking a sip of wine. 'It still gets to me, even all these years later.'

'I'm not surprised,' I reply. 'It sounds terrifying.'

'Yes.' Sofia stares down into her drink. She looks tired suddenly, and older, the lines on her forehead more pronounced.

'Did you manage to protect Judith and help her get to America?' I ask.

Sofia shifts uncomfortably, and I hope that I haven't overstepped the mark again by allowing my curiosity to get the better of me.

'I think that's enough reminiscing for one day,' she says brusquely. 'I'm getting bored of the sound of my own voice.'

'Why don't we have some lunch?' Gabriel gestures at the brown paper bags he'd brought back with him. They smell delicious and are shiny with oil. 'I got pork sandwiches.'

'Excellent.' Sofia turns to me. 'So, what do you say?'

'Pork sandwiches sound great.'

'No, I mean about the job. Do you want to help me write this book, or at least attempt to write it?'

'Maybe you should take a little more time before deciding,' Gabriel says, instantly making me bristle. Why is he sticking his nose in?

'I'm eighty years old,' Sofia responds. 'Time is not something I can afford to be frivolous with. Plus, if I have to wait too long, I might get cold feet and ditch the entire idea.' She places her glass on the coffee table and stares at me intently. 'So, are you up for the challenge?'

'Abso-bloody-lutely!' I reply, shooting Gabriel a defiant look.

'I'll go and get some plates,' he mutters, heading off into an adjoining room.

'That's bloody brilliant!' Sofia replies with a smile in a mock British accent. 'You can come and stay with me in my place up north. How soon do you think you'd be able to join me?'

'Straight away if you like,' I reply as Gabriel returns with some plates.

'Really?' Sofia raises her thin black eyebrows. 'You don't have any other commitments back in the UK?'

I shake my head, aware that this might make me seem pitiful, but I honestly don't care. There's no way I want to go back to my empty flat with all the pain of the past year soaked into its walls. This isn't just an incredible work opportunity; I'm starting to see how much I could gain from it personally too. Sofia might be a little tricky to handle, but she's fascinating and inspiring – the kind of woman I feel I could learn a lot from. Jane was right: this could be just the thing to get me out of the butterfly soup.

. . .

And so I find myself a few hours later in the back of Gabriel's car, speeding along a bumpy road somewhere in the middle of Portugal. In the passenger seat in front of me, Sofia has wound her window down to smoke a cigarette, and the warm breeze ruffles my hair. I gaze out at the darkening sky and the remnants of the sunset glowing red on the horizon, and I feel as if I'm made of air. Maybe this is how the butterfly feels when it finally flies free from the cocoon, I think as I look down at my backpack on the seat beside me. And it dawns on me that this is the first time in my life that I've really thrown caution to the wind.

My childhood was so chaotic and unstable, it left me craving normality. When I met Robin at university, I loved how he seemed to personify normalcy, with his happily married parents and their three well-rounded children, two bounding Labradors and magazine-perfect home. It was the blueprint for the kind of life I desperately needed – or at least, I thought I did. But in all the years Robin and I were together, even before the strain of trying to get pregnant, I never felt this excited and free.

I close my eyes and a scene from my last holiday with Robin comes back to me. It was about a year before we broke up, and we were driving to his parents' holiday home in Provence – another feature from their perfect life – and we had made most of the six-hour journey in silence. But not the warm, companionable silence that comes with time. This silence was heavy and awkward and punctuated only by a petty squabble over whether or not we should have taken a right turn about an hour out of Paris. As I sat there staring blankly through the windshield at the French countryside rolling by, I realised that I could think of absolutely nothing to say. Or, more specifically, nothing to say to him. It was as if we had exhausted all topics of conversation. Plus I'd grown tired of bringing something up, only for Robin to make a sarcastic retort or not understand what I was trying to say.

I open my eyes and gaze out at the fluffy clouds glowing pink and gold in the setting sun. I feel so relieved that I'll never have to endure a torturous car journey like that again – although I can't help feeling that Gabriel would prefer it if I wasn't here. I glance up and catch him looking at me in the rear-view mirror. He quickly looks back at the road.

By the time we arrive in Sofia's village, it's completely dark, and as we bump our way along a dirt track, all I can see from the car window are the countless stars dusting the sky. It's not a sight I ever get to see in London due to the light pollution, and it's breathtaking. As Gabriel brings the car to a halt, a beautiful old cottage with terracotta walls and pale blue shutters appears in the beam of the headlights.

'Home sweet home!' Sofia exclaims.

I want to ask how long she's lived here, but I bite my lip, remembering how she doesn't like to be pressed when it comes to telling her story.

Gabriel gets out of the car and hurries round to open Sofia's door. I step out and breathe in the cool fresh air. It smells of honeysuckle and the sea, and sure enough I hear the soft lap of waves coming from somewhere nearby.

'Do you live right by the beach?' I ask Sofia.

'I do indeed,' she replies. 'Just wait till you wake up tomorrow and see the view from your room. You're in for a real treat!'

'Sounds amazing!' I take my backpack from the back seat, experiencing another pinch-myself moment that this is actually happening.

Gabriel opens the boot and takes out Sofia's case, and the three of us form a slow procession up the path to the front door, with Sofia leading the way. She takes an old iron key from her bag and unlocks the door and steps inside, and a moment later we're bathed in golden light. I follow Gabriel into a spacious hallway. The walls are painted forget-me-not blue, and the floor is covered with large rust-coloured tiles. A rug has been placed in the middle, woven in brightly coloured stripes. Gabriel puts the case down and says something to Sofia in Portuguese.

'Yes, of course, and thank you so much,' she replies before turning to me. 'Gabriel is going to leave now as he has to be out on his boat at four.'

'Ah, OK,' I reply, trying to hide my relief. Maybe it's the unfortunate way in which we first met but I still can't quite get a handle on him.

He says something to Sofia while shooting me a sideways glance, and I get the distinct impression that he's talking about me. I catch a couple of the words – '*a verdade*' – and I make a mental note to look them up in my Portuguese dictionary later.

'*Não, não, não,*' she says, frowning and ushering him out of the door.

'It was lovely to meet you,' I call after him, hoping he'll detect the sarcasm in my tone.

Sofia shuts the door behind him and takes me by the arm, leading me into a cosy living room off the hall. The walls are painted fern green, perfectly complementing the wooden furniture. My eyes are drawn to a beautiful lamp made from driftwood by the fireplace. Then I notice a framed photograph on the mantelpiece. It's a black-and-white portrait of a young woman with an uneven haircut and round, wire-framed glasses.

'Is that Judith?' I ask, pointing to the picture.

'What? Oh...' Sofia instantly looks a little flustered. 'Yes – yes it is.' She turns on her heel and heads back to the door. 'On second thoughts, why don't we go to the kitchen? You must be thirsty after that long drive. I'll make us a drink. Would you like a hot chocolate?'

'Oh, OK,' I say as she hurries past me and out of the room.

I glance back at the photograph. Judith looks so innocent and sweet. It's horrible thinking of her travelling alone across Europe at such a young age trying to escape the Nazis. I wonder why the Gestapo were after her and if she managed to reach the safety of America.

'Would you like me to tell you the next part of the story?' Sofia calls as I make my way to the door.

'Yes, please.' I take a final look at the photograph. I'd assumed that the big reveal of this job would be the mystery surrounding Sofia's supposed death, but something tells me there are deeper, darker secrets to uncover, possibly involving this sweet young girl.

16

LISBON, 1940

Judith's revelation that she was on the run from the Gestapo certainly put a dampener on things, and we left the botanical gardens and made our way back to the station in silence. My mind was going ten to the dozen though as I tried to process what I'd just learned. And I couldn't shake the burning question: what on earth would the Gestapo want with a sixteen-year-old-girl, especially one as sweet and unassuming as Judith? It didn't make sense. But I didn't want to rattle her any more than I already had. If I wanted to help her, I had to first win her trust.

'Would you like to come to my place when we get back?' I asked as we reached the station. 'I could make us some dinner.'

'I don't know,' she replied, glancing anxiously up and down the platform. 'It's probably safer if I go straight back to mine.'

'Are you sure? What if that man spots you again?'

'I meant safer for you,' she said quietly, digging her hands into the pockets of her coat.

'Oh.' I looked at the other people lining the platform, scanning them for potential threat. It was a horrible insight into what life must have been like for Judith, and I was simultaneously frightened and furious that it should be happening – and in Portugal too. 'I'm not scared of that creep,' I said with a lot more gumption than I felt. 'I scared him off before, and I'll do it again.'

'How exactly did you scare him off?' Judith asked, eyes wide.

'I got a *varina* to ambush him,' I replied.

'What's a *varina*?'

'A woman who sells fish. You might have seen them walking around Lisbon.'

'In the brightly coloured clothes with the baskets on their heads?'

'Yes. I used to be one, and when I was following the man following you, I got one of them to block his path – which is how he ended up with fish all over him. He collided with her and sent the basket flying.'

Judith let out a giggle, but her smile soon faded. 'I'm so glad neither of you got hurt. Kurt Fischer is a monster.'

I thought of the knife I'd seen him take from his pocket but decided against telling her. Judith already knew how dangerous he was – there was no point in making her even more scared.

I heard the chug of a train approaching and grabbed her arm. 'Please,' I begged. 'Come back to my place. I can't bear the thought of leaving you all on your own.'

To my relief, she nodded.

I looked at her jagged hair and had a brainwave. 'I've had a genius idea!' I exclaimed. 'Something to make sure that monster never recognises you again.'

When we got back to Rossio station, we slunk out via a back exit and stuck to the side streets and alleyways all the way to my apartment. The fact that we'd been reduced to scurrying around in the shadows infuriated me even more and made me more determined than ever to help Judith evade her pursuer.

Once we reached the apartment, I ushered Judith inside and locked and bolted the door.

'This is lovely,' she said, gazing around at the eclectic mix of furniture and the brightly painted walls. 'It's the kind of place I dream of having one day – although I'd have lots of plants too.'

'I'm afraid I don't have a very good track record with plants,' I said sheepishly, thinking of the potted plants I'd bought when I first moved in. Despite my best efforts to water them regularly, their leaves had all turned brown and dropped off within a few weeks.

'Plants need to feel loved just like humans,' she said with a dreamy expression on her face. 'So, what is this plan you have to make me unrecognisable?'

'Wait here.' I hurried to my bedroom and came back with a blonde wig and an armful of clothes – all perks of my job as a singer. 'With this wig and a different wardrobe, you'll no longer look as if you've just got off the train from Germany – you'll look like a glamourous blonde who stars in movies or sings on stages.'

She gave a nervous laugh. 'Are you sure?'

'Of course,' I answered confidently, although I really wasn't sure at all. Judith looked so mousy and young.

Undeterred, I scraped back her hair and carefully placed the wig on her head. The difference it made was incredible, and I breathed a sigh of relief.

'Take off your glasses and look in the mirror,' I said, ushering her over to the mirror on the living-room wall.

As soon as she saw her reflection, she gasped. 'You're right, I look like a completely different person.'

'Exactly. And once you're out of that old coat and in some other clothes, the transformation will be complete.'

'I'm not getting rid of this coat,' she said defensively.

'Then you may as well wear a sign around your neck saying, "HELLO, I'M A REFUGEE. PLEASE FOLLOW ME, MR GESTAPO!' I replied. It was a little harsh, but I needed to convince her for her own safety.

'But I—'

'I have four coats and you're welcome to take your pick,' I interrupted. 'Not that you'll need one – the weather's getting warmer by the day.'

'I'm not getting rid of this coat,' she said again, looking tearful, and it dawned on me that maybe the coat had some kind of sentimental value, and I kicked myself for being so insensitive.

'I'm not saying get rid of it; just don't wear it. You don't want that man, Fischer, to recognise you.'

'But you don't understand.' She looked down at the tatty old coat.

'What is it?' I asked gently.

'I have to keep it with me at all times.'

'Did it belong to your grandmother or something?' It certainly looked old enough. 'Is that why you don't want to lose it, for sentimental reasons?'

'What? No!' she exclaimed.

'Then why on earth would you be so attached to it? I don't mean to be rude, but it's hardly a priceless mink.'

'Actually, it's worth a lot more than a mink,' she whispered. 'It's worth about half a million dollars.'

I stared at the threadbare fabric and the fraying hem, wondering what on earth I was missing. Two thoughts popped into my mind in quick succession. One: Judith was experiencing some kind of trauma-induced delusion. Or two: she was a compulsive liar. As I stared at her sweet face and trembling bottom lip, I felt certain it had to be the first option.

'How about I make you a nice cup of tea?' I said gently. 'And I'll get you something to eat. You must be so exhausted, not to mention famished.' Perhaps her delusion was due to malnutrition. 'I have some sardines, fresh off the boat this morning, and some bread rolls. Come on – let's go through to the kitchen.'

Judith stared at me, clearly startled. 'Did you hear what I said?'

'Yes, I did, and I think you need to get some nice food inside you.'

'But don't you want to know why it's worth so much?'

Oh Lord. I dreaded to think of what she might come out with next – that the coat was woven from gold by magical elves perhaps. 'Why don't we have something to eat first?' I coaxed, hoping that some food would restore her lucidity. Sardines were considered to be one of the most nutritious fish after all. I hurried through to the kitchen, hoping she'd follow me.

'Tra la la,' I started singing as I busied myself taking the fish from the refrigerator and a pan from the shelf. After a few moments, I heard her come into the room behind me.

'This is why it's worth so much,' she said, and I turned to see her fiddling with the bottom of the coat lining. I braced myself for whatever crazy notion she was about to come out with as she slowly extended her hand towards me.

'What the hell?' I gasped.

There, nestling in her palm, was the biggest jewel I had ever seen – the size of an egg but shaped more like a teardrop, casting beams of gold and white light around the room.

17

LISBON, 1940

'What is it?' I whispered, unable to tear my gaze from the magnificent jewel.

'It's the Vadodara Teardrop,' Judith replied. 'From India originally, and one of the most valuable diamonds in the world.'

'But how—' I broke off, too stunned to speak. All of the gems I'd owned up until that point had been costume jewellery procured from the market stalls of Lisbon and made of coloured glass. Compared to the Vadodara Teardrop they were dull as mud. I'd never seen a jewel so dazzlingly bright. It was as if it were a living, breathing thing, pulsing away in the palm of Judith's hand.

'How do I have it?' she asked.

'Yes.'

'My great-great-great-grandfather bought it from Napoleon's stepson in the early 1800s and it's been in our family ever since. The Nazis knew my father had it, so when they came to take him away, they ransacked our home looking for it.'

'But you managed to escape with it?' I asked.

She nodded. 'My father insisted I take it with me if I had to escape.'

'To stop those thieving Nazis from getting their hands on it?'

'Yes, and to secure my future. The Germans have taken everything from us. It reassured him to think that if I needed to, I'd be able to sell it and start again.'

I felt a pang of sorrow as I looked at the diamond. Its teardrop name suddenly felt all too apt.

'I sewed it into the lining of the coat to stop it from being found – or stolen.' Judith continued. 'I assumed that no one would look twice at this tatty old thing.' She laughed as she surveyed the coat.

'Well, you got that right!' I exclaimed. 'I couldn't understand why you were so attached to it. I thought maybe you were suffering from delusions.'

She burst out laughing. 'Is that why you came rushing in here to make me some food?'

'Yes! I thought maybe hunger was sending you crazy.'

'No, although part of me wishes that it was and the diamond didn't exist.'

'What do you mean?'

She looked at the diamond and sighed. 'Legend has it that the Vadodara Teardrop is cursed. I never used to believe it before, but now I'm not so sure. It's certainly made my life hell since I've had it.'

'The diamond has, or the Gestapo?'

'Good point, but it's been so much pressure trying to keep it safe.'

'I can imagine.' I shuddered as I wondered what lengths the Gestapo would go to get their hands on the diamond. It certainly explained why they were following Judith.

Judith gave a heavy sigh. 'I'll totally understand if you don't want to help me anymore. The last thing I want to do is put you at risk, so if you want me to leave, just say.'

'Don't be ridiculous,' I scolded, suppressing my fear. 'I want to help you.'

'Thank you.' She gave me a relieved smile. 'Hopefully I'll get my passage to America soon, so I won't be here for much longer.'

I nodded, although I knew from my conversations with the refugees who came for lunch at the taberna that getting their precious ticket to freedom could take weeks, if not months. 'I will help you for as long as you need me to,' I said firmly. 'Now, let's have something to eat.'

Judith flung her arms around me and hugged me tight, and I said a quick prayer of thanks to Santo Antonio for this opportunity to help someone so lovely and so in need.

'I can't believe you thought I was suffering from delusions about the coat,' she said, laughing as she tucked the diamond back into its lining.

I squeezed some lemon juice over the sardines and placed them in the frying pan.

'I thought you were about to tell me it was woven from gold by magical elves!'

We both giggled, and I felt a rush of warmth. Despite the crazy and undoubtedly scary circumstances, I gave another prayer of thanks for this unexpected new friend.

After dinner, I insisted that Judith stayed for the night, giving her my bed and making a bed for myself on the sofa. Once she was asleep, I sat in the armchair by the living-room window and began composing my song. Using the jacaranda tree as inspiration, I wrote a classic fado ballad about someone pining for Portugal and wishing they could drift on the breeze like a jacaranda seed and be brought back home. I imagined I was

Judith having to flee my homeland to tap into the emotions of fear and longing. I knew I'd captured the feeling when I started to cry mid-composition.

I was up most of the night, experimenting with the melody and honing the lyrics, and when Judith woke, I made her a breakfast of toast and eggs and sang the song to her while she ate. I felt way more self-conscious singing in front of her than I did singing in a club, but it was because I'd drawn upon her experiences as inspiration – I didn't want her to think me a fraud.

'Well?' I said nervously, after I'd finished and translated the lyrics into English for her. 'What do you think? It's obviously very new and rough around the edges.'

She was silent for a moment, and I thought my worst fears had been confirmed and the song was a dud, but then she wiped a tear from her eye. 'It's beautiful,' she whispered with such sincerity I knew it wasn't empty praise.

'Thank you! And thank you for inspiring it with your talk about jacaranda seeds. I'm so grateful I met you.'

'Me too!' she exclaimed. 'It's *bashert*, I'm sure of it.'

'Yes!' I smiled. It was lovely to think that Judith and I had been destined to meet. It made life feel magical.

After breakfast, Judith returned to her lodgings in her blonde wig and one of her new outfits, with the diamond inside the coat, which was stuffed inside a small case I'd given her for the rest of her new clothes.

As soon as she'd gone, I got ready for my audition, putting on a dress in the same vivid purple of the jacaranda blossom and spritzing myself with a floral scent before setting off for Alexandre's office. It was only when I walked in the door and saw the framed records on the walls that I got nervous. I'd put so much effort into pretending that Alexandre wasn't that big of a deal, I'd almost convinced myself that it was true. Seeing the success of his clients lining the walls made me realise he was a very big deal indeed, and so was the fact that he'd invited me to come and sing for him. I also knew that in this business you didn't get many chances like this so I couldn't blow it.

'I'm here to see Alexandre Fernandes,' I said to the stern-faced secretary click-clacking away on a typewriter behind her desk. She nodded and called him.

Moments later, Alexandre appeared, wearing a crisp white shirt and baggy pants with a sharp crease up the front. 'You came!' he exclaimed, clearly surprised.

I was about to say, 'Of course I did,' then remembered just in time to slip back into the irreverent persona he was expecting. 'Yes well, cleaning my bathroom didn't take as long as expected, so I thought I might as well.'

The sourpuss secretary audibly tutted, but Alexandre let out a bellowing laugh.

'Well, I hope this proves even more rewarding than scrubbing a toilet,' he said, ushering me through a door into a narrow, dimly lit corridor. 'No calls until we've finished, please, Fatima,' he said over his shoulder before taking me into a room that looked half office, half lounge bar.

A dark-haired stocky man with the flattened nose of a boxer was sitting in an armchair by the fireplace. As soon as we came in, he leaped to his feet.

'This is Sofia Castello,' Alexandre said to him before turning back to me. 'Sofia, this is Emilio Almeida, my favourite producer.'

My heart skipped a beat as I shook his hand. Emilio Almeida was a very big cheese in the music business, from Chicago but with Portuguese origins.

'Great to meet you,' he said, smiling warmly. His accent was a weird hybrid of Portuguese with a slight American drawl. 'I've heard very good things about you – and your fado for the fish,' he added with a laugh.

'Yes, well, fish have feelings too,' I said, instantly kicking myself for sounding stupid.

But both men appeared to find it hilarious and laughed heartily.

'I have to admit, I've not felt the same about eating sardines since hearing your song,' Alexandre said. 'I swear I could almost hear them singing up at me from the plate, lamenting the fact that their silvery skin had helped the fisherman catch them.'

We all laughed this time, and I felt myself relax slightly.

'So, did you manage to write anything for us?' Alexandre asked.

'I did.'

'Excellent.' Emilio went over to the piano in the corner. 'You start singing, and I'll pick up the melody.'

'OK.' I took the piece of paper from my bag and instantly remembered Judith tearing it out of her notebook for me. If she had the courage to travel halfway across Europe on her own, on the run from the Nazis, I could sing a damn song to a couple of men in a room. And even better, I'd sing it for her, and everyone like her, so full of saudade, so far away from home.

Alexandre went and sat behind his desk and nodded at me to begin.

I opened my mouth, but nothing came out. The enormity of the moment seemed to have sucked all the air from my lungs. *How can you expect to sing a song for the Exhibition of Portugal?* a sneaky voice inside my head wheedled. *You're just a lowly* varina *who got lucky.*

Closing my eyes, I tried to summon my courage. *You're not a lowly anything*, I heard my mother whisper in my ear, and the skin on my arms erupted in goosebumps. *You're the girl who took care of me when I was dying. You're the girl who came to Lisbon with nothing. You can do anything you set your mind to.*

I opened my mouth and began to sing.

18

LISBON, 1940

All the time I was singing, I lost myself in the emotion of the piece, but as soon as it was over, I became a bundle of nerves. As a freshly composed song, it was undoubtedly rough around the edges, but would they be able to see the potential?

'Well, I see what you mean,' Emilio said to Alexandre, running his fingers along the piano keyboard in a final flourish. Like a true musical maestro, he'd picked up the melody almost straight away, and he'd even begun adding extra harmonies by the last verse and chorus. But what did he mean by 'I see what you mean'? I looked at Alexandre anxiously.

'Well done!' he exclaimed, leaping to his feet. 'That was—' He broke off for a moment as if searching for the right adjective. 'Remarkable!'

'It really was.' Emilio came over to join us. 'The use of the jacaranda seed as a metaphor was wonderful.'

'Thank you!' My words burst out on an exhale of relief. 'I'm so glad you liked it.'

'I didn't just like it; I *loved* it,' Emilio enthused. 'Say, have you thought of adding in a bridge before the final verse. Maybe we could bring it down a key.' He headed back to the piano and started playing around with a few melodies.

'This is a very good sign,' Alexandre said with a grin. 'If you get Emilio this enthused, you know you've got a hit on your hands.'

'Come on over, kid.' Emilio beckoned to me. 'Let's see what we can do.'

The next couple of hours passed by in a blur. At some point, Alexandre sent his secretary, Fatima, to get us some food, and by the time I left, my song had become a clearly defined piece. Emilio had come up with a really catchy hook and I couldn't stop humming the melody, which I took to be another good sign.

'This is definitely the song for the exhibition,' Alexandre said as they walked me over to the door. 'Congratulations, Sofia.'

'Yes, congratulations,' Emilio said, shaking my hand. 'I hope this is the start of a long and very successful working partnership.'

'Are you serious?' I stared from one of them to the other. It had been hard enough believing that I might have a shot at the expo song, I'd never dared to have dreamed of anything else.

'Of course!' Alexandre exclaimed. 'With a talent like yours, you could go all the way.'

'Yup.' Emilio nodded in agreement. 'I can see you going down real well across the pond too.'

'Whoa! What pond are we talking about here?' I said. 'The new Lisbon Marina?'

The men laughed.

'And you've got sass too.' Emilio grinned. 'Americans love a spirited woman.'

It was hard not to get carried away at this point, but the good thing about having taken more than a few knocks by the tender age of twenty was that I was able to temper my excitement with an 'I'll believe it when I see it' attitude.

'All right, all right, hold your horses,' I quipped, determined to maintain a cool exterior. 'So what next?'

'Next we get you into a studio with some musicians to lay down the track,' Alexandre replied.

'I've got some great guys for you to work with,' Emilio added.

'Sounds good to me,' I said as casually as I could muster, although inside I was fizzing like a shaken soda.

The second I stepped outside, I felt completely disoriented. I'd arrived in brilliant sunshine, but now twilight was gathering, casting long shadows along the street. I glanced at my watch and saw to my surprise that it was almost seven. I'd been so immersed in what we were doing, I'd lost all track of time and I was meant to meet Judith in the café at six. I quickened my pace and tried to process my thoughts.

'Can you believe this is happening, Mama?' I whispered, gazing up into the velvet blue sky. The first of the evening stars winked down at me, and I was sure I heard her whisper back: *Of course I believe it – you can do anything you set your mind to.*

I arrived at the café anxious I might have missed Judith, but there she was, tucked away in a corner, with her nose in a leather-bound book. It was so nice to see her, and to be able to share my good news with her, I was hit by a brilliant idea.

'I'm so sorry I'm late,' I gasped, sitting down.

She looked up at me over her glasses, clearly surprised. 'Are you?'

'Yes, it's almost seven.'

She laughed and nodded at her book. 'Once I start reading about plants, I lose all sense of time.'

'That's just like me and singing!' I exclaimed. 'Speaking of which, I have excellent news!'

As I told Judith about my audition, her smile grew bigger and bigger.

'I'm so proud of you!' she exclaimed.

'Yes, well, that's not all the good news,' I said.

'What else?' she asked, eyes shining.

'I want you to move in with me. You'll be safer, and it will be so much fun.'

'Oh no, I couldn't.'

'Why not?'

'I don't want to put you at risk.' She leaned closer. 'If I move in with you, it could make you a target for the Gestapo too,' she whispered.

'I'm not scared of them!' I exclaimed, and I was so buoyed up from my audition success, I actually meant it. Oh, how those words would come back to haunt me!

19

LISBON, 2000

When I wake the next morning, I feel a little like Dorothy in *The Wizard of Oz* when she says to Toto, 'We're not in Kansas anymore.' I look around at the eggshell-blue walls, the polished pine floorboards, and the primrose curtains gently blowing in the breeze and wonder if I'm dreaming. Then I hear the cry of seagulls outside and it all comes flooding back. I've got the job. I'm in Sofia Castello's house. Sofia Castello isn't dead! I'm going to be ghostwriting Sofia Castello's life story – or trying to anyway.

My gaze falls upon my Portuguese dictionary on the nightstand and I remember the words I heard Gabriel say so earnestly to Sofia last night while looking at me – '*a verdade*'. I'd looked it up last night when I went to bed and discovered that it means 'the truth'. The truth about what? I wonder. And why did Sofia shake her head so vehemently? Maybe he meant the truth about her faking her own death. Perhaps he was asking her if she was going to tell me yet. If so, it's disappointing that she said no so vehemently, but it makes me even more determined to win her trust. After last night's revelation about the Gestapo and the diamond, I'm itching to learn more.

I go over to the window, pull the curtain to one side and inhale the salty sea breeze. It's a smell that always makes me think of holidays and instantly makes me happy. Sofia certainly wasn't kidding when she told me I was going to love the view. My room is at the back of the house and looks out onto a small garden, bursting with flowers in a riot of colour. A gate in the white fence at the bottom opens directly onto a small cove. The tide is out, but I can see a head bobbing up and down in the waves. I wonder if it's Sofia. I lean out of the window and look left and right. I'm guessing it must be as there doesn't seem to be another house anywhere nearby. It's been years since I swam, but the water looks so inviting. I wish I'd brought a bathing suit. I could go for a paddle though...

I pull on my new dress and go downstairs. The grass in the back garden is still damp with dew, and it feels wonderfully refreshing beneath my bare feet. I open the latch on the back gate and step onto the sand, which is already pleasantly warm from the early-morning sun. Sofia is now walking out of the water towards me. She's wearing a mismatching turquoise bikini top and bright pink bottoms, and although her tanned skin is wrinkled, it's still incredibly taut for someone of eighty. When she sees me approaching, she waves with delight.

'*Bom dia*, Lily! The water's perfect – come on in!'

'I don't have a bathing suit,' I call back. I wonder if she'd loan me one; she's shorter than me, but other than that we're about the same size.

'That's OK – swim in your underwear.'

'Oh – I – uh – I'm not wearing a bra.' In my haste to get outside, I hadn't bothered putting one on.

'Swim in your knickers then – or your birthday suit even.' She grins at me. 'There's no one around for miles, and there's no better feeling than swimming in the sea naked. It always makes me feel like a mermaid.'

'Oh – well...'

She stares at me, hands on hips, and I get the feeling this might be some kind of test. Am I uninhibited enough to be her ghostwriter? Am I able to throw caution to the wind? Aware that I haven't even started writing her book yet and I'm probably still on some kind of probation, I take a quick glance to make sure there's no one else around, then pull down the straps of my dress and let it slip to the ground.

'Attagirl!' she cries, and then before I can say anything, she whips off her bikini top, twirls it around her head like a lasso and flings it onto the sand. 'Come on!' she cries before plunging back into the water.

Laughing, I run down and meet a wave just as it crashes onto the shore. I shiver as it splashes up my legs. It's cold but exhilarating, and in a bid to preserve what's left of my modesty, I plunge in. The waves roll lazily back and forth, and as I allow my body to drift for a moment, it feels as if I'm being rocked in a cradle.

'Isn't it wonderful?' Sofia calls.

'Absolutely,' I call back. And it is.

I have a sudden flashback to how much I used to love swimming as a kid. Every Saturday I'd go down to the local baths and I'd swim all the stress of the week away. I feel the water having the same effect now, the waves caressing my skin, the salt cleansing me. It feels like such a natural state to be floating in the water like this.

Just like a baby swimming in the amniotic fluid of the womb, I think, and this time a more unpleasant memory intrudes, of the doctor's appointment where I was told I was infertile.

'You have premature ovarian failure,' the doctor said, with a sympathetic smile.

'What could have caused that?' I heard Robin ask above the sudden ringing in my ears.

'We're not entirely sure,' the doctor replied, 'but it's essentially a problem with the follicles inside the ovaries, which house the eggs. It could be that your follicles stopped working earlier than usual, or it may be that they never worked properly, which can be a hereditary condition.'

I felt a double blow at the bitter irony. Not only had my parents abandoned me as a baby, but they could have also denied me the ability to have my own family.

As Robin kept firing questions at the doctor about lifestyle changes and treatment options, I fought the urge to yell at him to shut up. In his desperation to understand the reason for my infertility, it also felt as if he was searching for reasons to blame me. Why couldn't he see that all I needed in that moment was for him to hold me? To help me grieve the children I wouldn't be able to conceive.

As I drift in the sea, I'm overwhelmed by that loss all over again, then I see a little red-haired girl bobbing amongst the waves in front of me, brightly coloured inflatable bands on her chubby arms. Tears begin mingling with the sea spray on my face. I'd thought – hoped – that maybe now I was no longer in London I wouldn't see her again. I should have known it wouldn't be that simple.

I first saw the ghost of my dream daughter about a week after receiving my diagnosis. I'd been lying on my bed crying and crying, and then, when I rubbed my eyes, she suddenly appeared, standing by my wardrobe, sucking her thumb. She had bright red hair in plaits and looked a little like my childhood hero Pippi Longstocking. Before I'd known I was infertile and we were trying to get pregnant, I'd been convinced I was going to have a daughter, and I'd daydreamed for hours about what she would be like. In my dreams, she was just like Pippi, fearless and headstrong and quirky – everything I'd been too scared to be as a kid for fear of upsetting my latest set of foster parents and being shunted off to yet another family. I was so excited at the prospect of being able to provide my child with a stable, loving home. Somewhere she could feel totally free to be herself. But of course, that opportunity has been cruelly denied me.

When my dream daughter began appearing to me after my world fell apart, I didn't feel scared. I found her presence strangely reassuring. But now I'm in Portugal, trying so hard to move on, I find it slightly unsettling. I start swimming away from her, swimming away from the sorrow and pain, my arms scything the waves in a powerful front crawl. My follicles might not work properly, but I still have the rest of my body. I'm still strong.

I'm strong, I tell myself over and over. It's only when my lungs start to burn that I stop and look around.

'Shit!' I gasp when I realise how far I've come. I see Sofia's head bobbing up halfway between me and the shore, and I start swimming towards her, against the tide, and suddenly my body feels heavy as lead.

'I thought for a moment you were swimming back to Britain,' she jokes when I finally reach her.

I laugh. 'I'm so sorry. I'd forgotten how therapeutic swimming can be. I used to go a lot as a kid, to help deal with the stress at home.'

Sofia moves closer, treading water. 'Oh really? What was your home life like, if you don't mind me asking?' she calls above the sound of the waves.

'Not great. I grew up in foster care.'

She instantly looks concerned. 'Please tell me you weren't abused.'

'Oh, no, nothing like that. It was more that it was unsettling. I got shunted around a lot.' I normally feel awkward telling people this – I can't help seeing it as some kind of admission of not being good enough – but it's as if the waves have stripped me down to the core, washing away any need for pretence.

'I'm so sorry.' Sofia looks so genuinely sad for a moment I totally forget who she is, and we're just two women bonding.

'Thank you, but it's fine. It was a long time ago – and now look where I am!' I gesture around at the sea shimmering in the sunshine.

Sofia laughs. 'Race you back to shore!' she cries, and off she darts through the water like a little fish.

I start swimming after her, wondering if it's unfair to beat someone more than twice my age.

Turns out I needn't have worried as she beats me fair and square.

'Well, that was exhilarating,' she says as I walk out of the water towards her. She clearly has no qualms about me seeing her half naked, and her freeness is infectious.

'It certainly was.' I tilt my face up to the sun, close my eyes and take a deep breath. The seaweed draped all over the rocks nearby makes the warm air smell even more salty.

'I'm really sorry about your childhood,' she says, retrieving her bikini top from the sand. 'Do you mind me asking what happened to your real parents?'

'I have no idea,' I reply, slipping my dress on over my head. 'But it really doesn't bother me anymore – it was so long ago and so much has happened since then. And is continuing to happen.' I look at her and smile. 'You offering me this job and bringing me here, it...' I fall silent for a moment, unsure how to articulate how I'm feeling. 'It's more than work to me.' I turn and see that she's staring at me intently. 'It's bringing me back to life again, after my break-up and everything – if that makes sense.'

She nods, her expression deadly serious. 'It makes perfect sense.' She steps closer. 'So, we're bringing each other back to life then.'

I smile. 'Yes!'

She links her arm through mine. 'Come on – let's get some breakfast.'

Back at the cottage, I have a shower in my en-suite bathroom, which is tiled in the beautiful turquoise-and-white mosaic of mermaids. Then I put on my jeans and T-shirt and decide to let my hair dry in its natural wavy state. Given that I hadn't been expecting to start the job right away and only brought a backpack with me, I really need to buy some more clothes as soon as possible. Hopefully there will be some stores within walking distance.

I head downstairs and into the kitchen to find Sofia already there, freshly showered, wearing a scarlet kaftan and smelling of lavender. She takes a jug of orange juice from the fridge and places it on the worn pine table. 'Please, help yourself to a juice; the coffee will be ready soon.' She nods to a silver pot on the stove. 'And while I'm making us some breakfast, I thought you might like to look at these.' She takes a folder from the side and places it on the table in front of me. 'There's some memorabilia from the Portuguese World Expo and a couple of other things that I'd like to tell you about today. Things that really changed the trajectory of my life story,' she adds mysteriously before heading over to the fridge.

I pour myself a juice and take a sip. It's delicious, freshly squeezed, and so tart it makes my taste buds tingle. I open the folder and see an old flyer, yellowed with age, advertising the expo. Beneath it is a printed list of events, and I notice Sofia's name about halfway down, next to 'Jacaranda Sonhos', which I guess must have been the title of her song. The next thing I find is an old vinyl 45 record in a paper sleeve. The label in the centre of the disc also says 'Jacaranda Sonhos', along with Sofia's name.

'Your first ever record!' I exclaim, holding it up.

She looks over her shoulder and nods. 'And a first edition too. It's the only record I took with me when I... when I died.'

I put the record down and pick up the next thing in the pile. It looks like some kind of invitation, with elegant gold handwriting embossed on a cream card with the words 'Exposição do Mundo Português' in the centre.

Next, I take out an old greeting card, also yellowing with age, with the faded picture of some daisies on the front. I open it and see handwriting in faded pencil. It takes me a moment to realise that the words are in English, the writing is such a tiny scrawl.

Dear Sofia,

Thank you for being the best bossy big sister in the world and for all you've done to help me. I can't wait until we can properly celebrate in America!

All my love,

Judith

I feel a wave of relief. 'So, Judith made it to America safely then?'

'What?' Sofia, who had been bringing a plate of cheese over to the table, stops dead.

'This card.' I point to the writing. 'She says she'll see you again in America.'

'Oh.' Sofia sits down at the table and it's as if all the life has drained from her. 'Unfortunately, Judith was being a tad optimistic when she wrote that.'

'No! What happened?' I ask, feeling a sudden chill.

'That monster, Kurt Fischer, happened,' she replies ominously.

20

LISBON, 1940

Over the next few weeks, Judith and I fell into an easy routine. Judith spent her days queuing at Lisbon's main post office in Commercial Square to see if her cousin in Brooklyn had written back.

I went with her once and it broke my heart to see the queue for the poste restante counter. It always snaked out way beyond the door, a long line of anxious refugees all waiting to receive word from a relative or benefactor overseas who would help them escape – or at least that was the hope. The tension was palpable as they watched the clerks painstakingly sorting through the boxes of letters, postcards and telegrams arranged in alphabetical order, wondering if today would be their lucky day, and trudging away despondently at the apologetic shake of the clerk's head.

I spent most of my days rehearsing for the expo in a studio with Emilio and the band he'd put together and pinching myself on a regular basis that by some miraculous twist of fate I was now a recording artist. And the Vadodara Teardrop, which had come to feel like a third person in our friendship such was its importance, remained hidden inside the old coat, which remained hidden under the mattress on my bed. Every night, after checking the diamond was still safely in place, Judith and I would spend hours at the kitchen table, talking, laughing, eating and becoming effortlessly closer.

One night, as we sat down to a dinner of tender garlic-infused pork and fried potatoes, she presented me with a posy of wildflowers, their stems tied together with a pink satin ribbon.

'I wanted to get you something to say thank you for all you've done for me,' she said, smiling sweetly.

'They're beautiful!' I exclaimed. 'I love their vibrant colours.'

'They say that the earth laughs in flowers,' she said. 'Or, at least, that's what Ralph Waldo Emerson once said.'

'I love that!' It really tickled me to think that every time the earth was amused, it chuckled up a primrose or a daisy.

'I know they're not much, but one day, when I've finally made it to America and this stupid war is over, you'll have to come and visit me and I'll get you a real thank-you present. I could take you to see a show on Broadway, or to a restaurant by Central Park.' Her eyes shone with hope.

'You really don't need to thank me at all – you've done way more for me than I have for you.'

She pulled a comical pout. 'Hmm, protecting me and the Vadodara Teardrop from the Nazis is hardly nothing.'

'But you inspired the song that helped me win the competition to sing at the expo, which could change my career forever. And it's not just that.' I fiddled with the ribbon on the cheery flowers. 'Having you stay here, getting to know you...' I looked back at her, my eyes swimming with tears. 'It's the closest thing I've felt to family since my mother died.'

'Oh, Sofia!' She leaped up, came around the table and hugged me tight. 'I feel exactly the same. It's like you're my sister – my jacaranda seed sister.'

I laughed through my tears. 'Yes! I'm so glad we ended up being blown together.'

She sat back down, and I raised my glass.

'To the jacaranda sisters!'

'The jacaranda sisters,' she said, giggling as she chinked her glass to mine.

The next day we arranged to meet for a late lunch at the Santo Antonio tavern on my break from rehearsals. As soon as I walked in the door, Judith came flying over to greet me, a beaming smile on her face.

'I finally heard from my cousin,' she exclaimed, waving a telegram in my face. 'She's helped arrange my entry visa. I can go to America!'

'Yes!' I cried, and we hugged and danced for joy. 'So, what does this mean?' I asked once we'd sufficiently calmed down and taken a table in the corner. 'What will you have to do next?'

'I'll have to register with a shipping line. And I'll need to get my vaccination before sailing. Apparently, there's a six-week wait for tickets to sail, but that's OK – at least I know I can go, and it gives me more time with you.' Her face beamed with joy.

I felt a sharp pang as I realised the full implication of her news. It was one of the most bittersweet moments I've ever experienced. Judith would be safe, but I would be losing my best friend. 'I'm really going to miss you,' I murmured.

'But it won't be goodbye forever,' she said. 'We're jacaranda seed sisters, remember. We'll see each other again as soon as the war is over.'

'You're damn right we will!' I exclaimed. 'And that's an order from your bossy big sister.'

'You're the best bossy big sister ever!' she exclaimed, grabbing my hands and clasping them tightly.

'OK, I'm going to go and boss the chef into giving us a special celebratory dish,' I said, laughing as I got to my feet.

I'd only been in the kitchen a minute when Judith came flying in after me, her face white as a sheet.

'Sofia, he's here!' she gasped, instantly turning my blood to ice. I didn't need to ask who; there was only one man capable of making her look so terrified. My heart sank, heavy as a stone. It had been so long since I'd last seen Fischer I'd allowed myself to get a little complacent, even hoping that he'd forgotten all about Judith and that wretched diamond.

'Don't worry, you've got your wig on – he won't have recognised you,' I consoled, hurrying over to the kitchen door and opening it a crack. Sure enough, I saw Fischer, sitting at a table by the window with another smartly dressed man in a suit. The notion that members of the Gestapo should turn up bold as brass at a lunch for refugees made me overwhelmed with dread. It was like a pair of cats turning up at a lunch for mice.

'Do you think he knows I'm here?' Judith asked, trembling like a leaf in a breeze. It made me so sad to see her so vulnerable and scared again. In the time we'd been living together she'd really come into her own.

'Of course not. You look completely different.' I quickly cast my gaze over her blonde hair, make-up and plum-coloured dress, as much to reassure myself. She didn't look like a refugee at all now, but, given the setting, that would make her stand out in a totally different way. 'You need to leave by the back door and go straight home to the apartment,' I said.

'Aren't you coming with me?' she asked, her eyes wide with fear.

'I'll be back soon; I just need to make sure that he stays here so you can get away safely. If he leaves, I'll come straight after you.'

'OK.' She nodded and gave me a grateful smile. 'Thank you.'

'Of course.' I gave her a quick hug. 'Now get home safely – and that's an order from your bossy big sis!'

She gave a nervous laugh before exiting through the back door.

I hurried back to the door to the restaurant and peered through the crack. Fischer was still at the table, but his companion was nowhere to be seen. He must have just gone to the bathroom, I told myself.

I turned back to see the chef about to throw some fish into the bin.

'Why are you throwing them out?' I asked.

'They're on the turn,' he replied.

'In that case, I want you to make them for the gentlemen sitting at the table by the window,' I said, and he frowned at me like I was crazy. 'They're in the Gestapo,' I whispered.

He raised his eyebrows. 'It would be my pleasure to undercook these fish for them,' he said, reaching for one of the frying pans hanging from hooks in the ceiling.

I laughed and breathed a sigh of relief. It had been a close shave, but Judith had got away and she'd soon be on a boat to America, and that monster Fischer was about to get his just desserts in the form of a rotten mackerel!

As soon as the fish had been served, I hotfooted it out of there and back to the rehearsal studio. Thankfully, Emilio didn't keep us for too long, and I set off for home at just gone five. On the way back to the apartment, I stopped off at a store to get Judith a new leather-bound notebook, as I'd noticed she was nearing the end of her current one, and a set of pens as she would surely need them to keep her occupied on the long voyage to America.

'Your bossy big sister has a gift for you!' I cried as I came through the door.

Everything that happened next seemed to take place in slow

motion. The room looked as if a bomb had hit it. Most of the furniture had been upended, and all the drawers in my cabinet were lying upside down on the floor, their contents scattered about.

'Judith?' I said, my voice coming out like a squeak. 'Are you here?'

I crept through to the bedroom to find her old, battered case open in the middle of the room, with all of her clothes strewn around. In a fit of panic, I tried to reassure myself that maybe she'd been looking for something in a hurry. But then I saw her beloved book on plants had been torn to shreds.

'Judith?' I said weakly, hoping she might be hiding somewhere. I checked the bathroom, where I found my marble pot of talcum powder emptied into the sink. And then I saw something that chilled me to the core. Judith's blonde wig was in the bath. Surely, she wouldn't have gone out without it on.

'Judith!' I called more urgently, running over to the wardrobe and flinging it open. All my clothes had been pulled from their hangers and were lying in a tangle at the bottom. My knees buckled and I sat down on the bed, overcome with fear. 'What's happened to you?' I whispered.

This didn't make sense. Kurt Fischer had stayed in the tavern after she left. He couldn't have seen her, could he? But what about the other man he'd been with? I'd assumed he'd gone to the bathroom, but what if he'd slipped out and seen Judith leaving. What if he'd followed her to the apartment?

'Oh no!' I cried. And then I remembered the diamond. 'Oh no, oh no,' I muttered as I saw the old brown coat on the floor at the end of the bed, the lining torn out. I picked it up and felt it in desperation. But there was no telltale teardrop-shaped lump. I did find something in the pocket though – an envelope with my name on it in Judith's handwriting. I opened it with trembling fingers.

Dear Sofia,

Thank you for being the best bossy big sister in the world and for all you've done to help me. I can't wait until we can properly celebrate in America!

All my love,

Judith

My heart sank. She must have bought me the card after getting the good news about her visa, just as I'd bought her the notebook and pens. I looked at my gifts to her lying on the floor where I'd dropped them in shock and I felt sick to my stomach. Having tried so hard to keep herself and the Vadodara Teardrop safe from the Nazis, they'd found her, just when it seemed like her luck had changed. Just when she'd been given the promise of freedom from their clutches. And even worse, I could have been to blame by telling her to leave the taberna without me and, in doing so, serving her up to the Gestapo like a fish on a platter. The thought was horrifying.

21

PORTUGAL, 2000

'Are you all right?' I ask Sofia as her voice peters out and she wipes away a tear.

'Yes.' She clears her throat and takes a sip of water.

'Judith sounds so lovely,' I say tentatively.

'She is – *was*,' Sofia replies, inadvertently answering my next question. I ask it anyway, just to be sure.

'It must have been horrendous finding your apartment like that. Did you... did you ever find out what happened to her?'

'I'm really sorry, but would it be OK if we take a little break?' she murmurs. 'I hadn't realised quite how painful it would be to relive all of this. And this is only the beginning.' She gives a wry laugh. 'God knows how I'm going to cope when we get to the really tricky part!'

'I'm sorry, I didn't mean to push—'

'I'm actually feeling very tired.' Sofia stands up abruptly. 'I think perhaps I'll take a nap.'

'Of course.' I stop the tape recorder and stand up too, nervous and unsure what to do. While part of me is desperate to find out more, there's no way I want to upset Sofia and make her clam up. I have to tread very carefully if I'm to coax the story out of her. 'I'll make a start on writing some of it up.'

'Please yourself,' she mutters.

I listen to the creak of her footsteps on the stairs as she goes up to her room. I'm not surprised she's upset, reliving what happened. I'd grown fond of Judith just hearing about her, and I loved learning about the special sisterly bond they'd formed. It must have been devastating for Sofia to lose her in such brutal and scary circumstances. I open the folder she gave me and take out the card. As I reread Judith's message inside, it feels even more poignant.

I'm gathering my things to take up to my room when the phone starts to ring. I glance up at the ceiling, wondering if Sofia has an extension in her bedroom. Perhaps I should answer it anyway as she's gone to take a nap.

'Hello?' I say instinctively as I pick up the receiver before realising that whoever's calling would speak Portuguese. 'Sorry, I mean *ola*,' I say, cursing myself for sounding even more stupid.

There's a long silence and then the click of the phone being put down. Whoever called probably thought they'd got the wrong number when they heard my voice. But they don't call back, so I head upstairs and start transcribing the recording onto my laptop.

After an hour or so, I save what I've written to a floppy disc, then plug my laptop cable into the telephone socket in the wall. I need to email Jane to give her an update and let her know all is well.

But as soon as my AOL account tells me that I've got mail, I see a name in my inbox that instantly makes my pulse quicken: Robin. I never hear from him now, and my mind whirs as I try to imagine why he might be emailing me. The subject matter of the email simply says 'hello'. Perhaps it's something to do with our apartment, although we sorted out the financial side of things ages ago. Maybe he wants to meet up for a coffee?

I feel a pinprick of hope that instantly makes me feel embarrassed for being sad enough to feel it, but I allow myself to think the thought anyway – perhaps he's realised that the last ten months have all been a huge mistake and he wants us to get back together? Heart racing, I open the email and start to read.

Dear Lily,

I hope all is well with you. I just wanted to let you know before you hear from anyone else – we're having a baby!!!

I stop reading, momentarily confused. What does he mean, we're having a baby? We're most definitely *not* having a baby. That's why we're no longer together. Then the awful truth dawns and I feel sick to my stomach. I'm no longer the other half of Robin's 'we'. He and his new girlfriend are having a baby. I stare at the screen in disbelief; the row of jaunty exclamation marks feel like they're mocking me.

As my vision blurs and Robin's words start bleeding across the screen, I'm cast back in time to the day he told me he was leaving – three whole days after the doctor told us about my faulty ovaries. It was a Sunday morning and, as usual, we were sitting in bed with a pot of coffee and the papers, a ritual we'd begun when we moved in together after university. A ritual that, I can see now, perfectly reflected the demise of our relationship. Back in the heady early days of our living together, the Sunday papers and their numerous supplements would end up strewn across the floor as we spent most of the morning making love. Then, over the years, the lovemaking became shorter and the paper reading more in-depth. And, once we were actively trying and failing to become pregnant, sex came to feel like another household chore, and the papers a sweet escape, where no supplement went unread.

That particular Sunday – the Sunday of The End – we'd

had a stupid squabble about one of the newspaper headlines, which was claiming that on New Year's Eve planes might start dropping from the sky due to it being a new millennium and the computers not being able to cope with the calendar change. I thought the paper was fearmongering, but Robin thought they might have had a point, and how did I know the clock's change wouldn't cause chaos? Then he dropped the bombshell.

'I think it's time we called it a day,' he said quietly. And his voice was so calm and measured, I assumed that he was talking about our argument.

'Fair enough,' I replied, folding up the paper and preparing to get out of bed.

'You agree?' he said, clearly surprised.

'Yes, there's no point wasting our energy arguing about it. We'll have to just wait for New Year's Eve – and make sure we're not celebrating under the flight path to Heathrow.'

'Oh.' His face fell. 'I wasn't talking about the millennium. I was – uh – talking about us.' His gaze remained fixed on a croissant flake on the duvet in front of him.

'You think it's time we called it a day?' I murmured, feeling sick to my stomach.

'Yes. It just... it doesn't feel the same anymore.'

Panic flooded me. Robin couldn't leave me. He couldn't. Things might have been tough lately, but our relationship, the life and the home we'd built together was my mooring. The prospect of being cut adrift was utterly terrifying. 'But things have only been tough because of the struggle to get pregnant. It always puts a strain on a relationship. But now we know I'm infertile, we won't have the pressure of trying anymore.'

'But you know how much I want a family,' he said to the croissant flake.

'Yes, we both do,' I said crossly. 'But now we can focus on adoption. There are so many kids out there in need of loving parents and loving homes. I know that better than anyone.'

He shrugged in the annoying way he always did to show that he'd given up on something, and I knew in that moment that we were a lost cause. What I wasn't prepared for was what came next.

'I, uh... I've met someone else,' he muttered, still gazing at that bloody pastry flake. I reached out and swept it off the duvet.

'What... what do you mean?' I stammered, unable or unwilling to believe what I was hearing. 'How? Where?'

'At work.' Finally, he looked at me and I saw that his eyes were shiny with tears. 'It happened by accident.'

'What do you mean? What happened?' I asked, my mind racing.

'Falling in love,' he mumbled, and it was as if he'd stuck a knife right in my heart.

Now, I blink hard and look back at the screen. This only happened ten months ago. How can she be pregnant already? Surely they couldn't have planned it so soon, could they? The thought that it might have been an accident, that after all the blood, sweat and tears I endured trying to conceive, they could have become pregnant so effortlessly and carelessly makes me want to rage at the injustice of it all. I swallow my anger and carry on reading.

> I know things ended badly between you and I, but I hope you can find it in your heart to be happy for us.

I stare at his words and shake my head. Still no apology for what he did to me. Still, oh so subtly, implying that the onus should be on me to make things OK because, ultimately, I'm the one at fault.

> All best wishes,

Robin

And signing off as if I'm a business acquaintance, rather than the person he shared his life with for sixteen years. The person who was his shoulder to cry on when he found himself struggling to cope with the pressure of his post-university banking career. The person who encouraged him to change jobs and supported him financially for almost two years while he figured out his true calling. The person who ran herself ragged trying to provide him with a child, who he then callously dumped for someone else when I couldn't deliver. And now he's asking me to 'find it in my heart' to be happy for him.

I hit reply, my vision blurring with anger and tears. But what can I write? What can I say? If I dare to express the rage I have building inside of me, I'll be accused of being bitter and heartless. I picture him showing his new partner – Meredith – my email and both of them shaking their heads.

'It's so sad that she can't find it in her heart to be happy for us,' I imagine him whining to her, in his stupid nasally voice.

'Yeah, what is her problem?' I imagine her replying, but with a sly side-smirk, like the cat who got the cream.

I want to scream. I rip the cable from the wall to stop myself from sending anything and start pacing around the room. I hate him. But more than that, I hate myself, especially when I remember how, for a second, I thought he might be emailing to see if I wanted to get back together. I am so, so stupid.

I march over to the window and look outside. The breeze has picked up and the sea is looking a lot livelier than it was this morning, the frothy white tips of the waves like the manes of horses all racing to the beach. I think of how good my swim felt this morning and I feel the water calling to me again. One thing's for sure – I have to do something with this anger I'm feeling.

I storm downstairs. There's no sign of Sofia, so she must be still napping. I slip out of the back door and into the garden. I'm so angry and upset I'm halfway down the path before I notice someone tending to one of the flower beds.

'*Boa tarde!*' she calls, and I stop and see an elderly woman with snowy white hair peering out at me from beneath a giant straw sunhat.

'Oh, sorry, *boa tarde*,' I mutter.

'I'm the gardener, Rosária,' she says in faltering English.

Ordinarily, I would have complimented her on the excellent job she's done, but I'm so distraught all I can mutter is, 'Oh,' before heading out of the garden and closing the gate behind me.

The sand is almost uncomfortably hot beneath my feet, and all I want is to get in the water. All I want is to feel that same feeling of comfort I felt this morning. Without a second thought, I pull my dress up and over my head and throw it down on the sand. I'm wearing a bra as well as knickers this time, so it's practically the same as wearing a bikini. But just like me, the mood of the ocean seems to have become darker since this morning, and as I wade in, a huge wave hits me full force in the face.

'Go to hell!' I yell as I bob back up and wipe the salt water from my eyes. I picture Robin in front of me and I start thrashing my arms through the water in a vicious front crawl. *Why? Why? Why?* That one word keeps ringing in my head over the crashing of the waves. Why did this have to happen? And why did it have to happen now, just when I was starting to get my life back together? Just when I was starting to believe that maybe I wasn't a totally lost cause?

The words of Robin's email come back to haunt me, spoken out loud in my mind in his patronising tone. 'I hope you can find it in your heart to be happy for us...' *What about you finding it in your heart to be empathetic to me?* I argue back in my head as I swim out further against the tide. *What about you acknowl-*

edging that your news might be a little painful for me to receive? What about softening the blow with some kind of apology for leaving me for someone else?

'Why do you have to be such a selfish arsehole?' I yell just as a wave rolls over me and my mouth fills with water. I start choking and spluttering and tread water for a moment to try to catch my breath. Seagulls circle above me, crying wildly, and then I hear something different, something deeper, like a man's voice. I glance around, but there's no one else in the water. Then I turn and look back to the beach.

A man is standing on the sand frantically waving his arms at me. I've come out so far that I can't be certain, but I have a horrible feeling it might be Gabriel. Shit, shit, shit!

I turn away and pretend I haven't noticed him. Maybe if I just swim in circles for a while, he'll go away. The waves send me rising and falling as if I'm as weightless as a cork, and it feels strangely pleasant to be at the mercy of such a powerful force. I bob about for a few minutes more, enjoying the sensation of the waves battering the disappointment and pain out of me.

I'm just starting to feel vaguely human again when I hear the man's voice once more – but much louder this time, much closer. My heart plummets as I turn to see a dark head and tanned arms powering through the water. I turn away, still pretending that I can't hear him, but moments later I feel a hand grab my shoulder.

'What are you doing?' I cry as I turn to see Gabriel, his wet curls clinging to his scalp.

'Are you OK?' he says, still gripping my shoulders tightly. 'You looked like you were in trouble.'

'I'm fine!' I yell, all my anger bubbling back to the surface.

'You might be now, but there can be a really powerful undertow,' he gasps, out of breath. 'I was worried it might drag you away.'

'Well don't be.' I'm aware I'm acting like a brat, but I'm so angry and embarrassed, I can't help it.

And now I see anger sparking in his eyes too. 'OK, I won't!' he snaps and starts swimming away.

Another wave hits me, and I suddenly feel completely exhausted, so I start slowly swimming back to land. As I draw closer to the beach, I see Gabriel standing next to a small boat in the corner of the cove. Thankfully, it's the opposite corner to where I left my dress, although due to the small size of the cove, that only means a few metres.

Once I reach the point where I'm able to stand with my head above water, I quickly glance at him again and see that he's busy with something in his boat. Good. Hopefully I can slip into my dress and back up to the house without having to speak to him. But as I walk out of the water, my dress is nowhere to be seen. At first, I think Gabriel might have taken it as some kind of childish prank. But then I realise how far the tide has come in. Damn! It must have been swept out on the waves. I scan the water frantically, but there's no sign of it.

I glance back at the boat. Gabriel is looking over now, and I'm acutely aware that I'm dressed only in my underwear.

'Everything OK?' he calls.

'I lost my dress,' I call back as my embarrassment grows.

'Is that so?' Gabriel reaches into his boat and pulls something out, then starts heading over. I look down at my scrawny pale body and shudder. 'Here,' he says when he reaches me, holding out a chequered man's shirt.

I take it and hastily put it on. 'Thank you.' Due to our difference in size, the shirt almost comes down to my knees.

'So, what was that all about?' he asks, looking out to sea. He doesn't seem angry now, more concerned.

'I had some bad news,' I mutter as my fingers fumble with the buttons. 'And it made me angry. I'm sorry for yelling.'

He shakes his head. 'It is OK; I am used to you yelling at me by now.'

I meet his gaze and see that he's grinning, his green eyes sparkling like the sea in the sunlight. My heart softens a little. 'I'm not normally like this.'

'Like what?' He raises his eyebrows.

'So – shouty.'

'Is that so?'

'Yes. You clearly bring out the shouty part in me.' I grin back at him, grateful for a chance to relieve the tension.

His face lights up as if he's had some kind of brainwave. 'Have you ever gutted a fish before?'

'What? No!' His question is so unexpected, I can't help laughing.

'Well then, I think it is time you learned. Come with me.' He takes a bucket from the boat and starts heading up the beach towards the cottage. I stare after him, feeling bewildered. I can't decide if Gabriel is amusing or intensely annoying, but I find myself curious to find out, so I set off up the beach behind him.

22

PORTUGAL, 2000

'OK, first we need to rinse them,' Gabriel says, taking the bucket of fish over to the sink. 'And then we cut them open.' He takes a knife from his belt and hands it to me, staring at me intently, and I realise that this must be some kind of test. He's trying to see if I've got the guts to gut the fish, so to speak, or if I'll get squeamish and bottle out. *Well, you've picked the wrong woman, on the wrong day to mess with*, I think, grabbing the knife from him.

'Let's do it!'

Gabriel harrumphs and turns on the tap.

Once he's rinsed the fish, I stand beside him at the kitchen counter, knife in hand, and he hands me a mackerel and takes one for himself.

'First you lay it on its back, like this,' he says, laying his fish down on the wooden chopping board in front of us. I follow suit. 'Then you open its gill covers.'

He pulls open two flaps either side of the fish's head and he grins at me mischievously, as if he's waiting for me to cry out in horror. There's no way I would give him the satisfaction, so I swallow hard and copy what he's doing, cutting a kind of cord in the fish's mouth and then pulling out something that wouldn't look out of place in the climactic scene of a horror movie, but I maintain my composure and keep my expression neutral.

'We have to remove the gills because they are full of – how do you say? – blood and that would make the fish taste very bitter,' he says, with what looks like a decidedly evil smirk.

Fighting the urge to retch, I throw the bloody gills in the bin.

'That's good,' he says, looking and sounding quite surprised. I smile at him defiantly, my jaw clenched. 'Now put the fish on its side, like this.' I copy him and turn my fish on its side. He places the tip of his knife by a small hole towards the tail. 'Now, we need to cut from – how do you say? The anus?'

Oh God. The only good thing about this horror show is that it's completely taken my mind off my earlier pain and anger. I place the tip of my knife by the tiny hole and copy Gabriel, slicing up the belly of the fish.

'And now we pull out the guts,' Gabriel says gleefully, and at this point I half expect him to throw his head back and cackle. But, still determined not to give him the satisfaction of seeing me cringe, I grit my teeth and plunge my fingers inside the fish and pull out the slippery innards.

'*Muito bom!* Good work,' Gabriel says, nodding approvingly.

Much to my annoyance, I feel a small glow of satisfaction at having won his praise.

I'm about to say something sarcastic when I hear the kitchen door opening. I turn and see Sofia dressed in her robe, her black hair messy and her face flushed from sleep. She frowns at Gabriel, then switches her gaze to me and, more specifically, Gabriel's shirt on me.

'What is going on?' she asks, her voice taut.

'I'm, er, teaching Lily how to gut a mackerel,' Gabriel answers, his face flushing.

Still staring at the shirt, Sofia says something to him in Portuguese. She sounds angry. Gabriel replies in Portuguese, his voice rising and his tone defensive.

'He saved you from drowning?' she says to me in English.

'No!' I exclaim. 'He thought he was saving me, but I was absolutely fine.'

'Is that his shirt?' she asks, like a headmistress interrogating a naughty schoolgirl.

'Yes, my dress got washed out when the tide came in, so he lent it to me.'

Sofia turns back to Gabriel and barks something at him. He heads straight for the sink and washes his hands as Sofia continues to berate him.

Gabriel gestures at me and mutters something, and I'm able to catch the final word, which I repeat in my head to try to remember it so I can look it up. *Segredo*.

He dries his hands and gives a laboured sigh, then stomps out of the back door without a backward glance.

'Is everything OK?' I ask cautiously.

Sofia sits down at the table and gives a heavy sigh. 'Yes, I just don't want him getting overly familiar with you. You're here to work on the book and I don't want him overstepping any boundaries.'

'Oh, don't worry, he didn't,' I say, sitting down across the table from her. 'To be honest, I get the feeling he doesn't really like me all that much. I'm pretty sure he was only teaching me how to gut a fish in an attempt to make me sick – but I wouldn't give him the satisfaction,' I can't help adding. 'I actually find him kind of annoying.'

Finally, she cracks a smile. 'OK, good.' She places her hand on top of mine and gives it a squeeze. 'I'm sorry, you must think I'm a terrible drama queen. It's just that this book is so important to me – and it's kind of terrifying too, revisiting all of these ghosts from my past, and preparing to reveal all to the world, especially given the nature of what I'm going to reveal.'

Please tell me! I feel like begging but manage to refrain. 'I can imagine,' I say instead. *Gently does it*, fast becoming the mantra for this job. 'But you mustn't worry. Your story means so much to me. There's no way I'd let an irritating fisherman and his fish innards distract me from helping you tell it.'

Sofia throws back her head and snorts with laughter, then she looks at the fish on the counter. 'Speaking of fish, shall we make a start on cooking them?'

'That would be great.'

We go over to the counter and she inspects the gutted fish. 'We need to wipe the insides first.'

'Fantastic!' I say sarcastically, and she laughs again.

'Don't worry, as soon as you taste your first mouthful, it will all be worthwhile. There's nothing better than fish fresh from the boat.'

She tears two lots of paper towel from a roll on the side and hands one of them to me before showing me what to do.

'So, what made you go for another swim?' she asks as we clean the mackerel.

As much as I don't want to relive what happened, I know that opening up to Sofia will help build the trust between us and hopefully make her more inclined to open up to me too. 'I... I had some bad news from back home and it... it made me really hurt and angry, and I needed to get it out of my system. I thought maybe going for a swim would help.'

'I'm sorry to hear that.' She looks at me, clearly concerned. 'And did it?'

'Yes, I think so.'

Sofia looks at me expectantly.

I take a breath before continuing. 'I heard from my ex that he and his new partner – the woman he left me for – are having a baby.'

'Oh.' She raises her thin black eyebrows.

'We'd been together forever – well, since university.' I turn my attention back to my fish, hoping that by avoiding eye contact it will be easier to confide in her. 'And we'd been trying to have a baby for ages, but then I found out that I'm infertile, and he immediately traded me in for someone else.'

'And now she's pregnant?' Sofia says softly.

'Yep. And they've only been together for ten months – that I know of anyway. I'm guessing there might have been an overlap.' As I speak my worst suspicions out loud, I feel sick, and the sight and smell of the gutted fish in front of me really isn't helping. I glance at Sofia.

She gives me a sympathetic smile. 'I'm so sorry.'

'It wouldn't have been so bad if he hadn't broken the news the way he did. His email was really pompous and insensitive. He asked me if I could find it in my heart to be happy for them.' My anger starts bubbling back to life. 'Me, happy for them, with no mention of the pain they've caused me. No apology.'

'What a rat!' Sofia exclaims. She looks so outraged on my behalf it makes me want to hug her. 'If you ask me, I think you have dodged a bullet,' she says firmly. 'Who wants to be with someone who can be so insensitive at a time like this? And someone who could so callously leave you when you've just been told you can't have children.' She starts uttering a stream of words in Portuguese, which I'm pretty sure are expletives. She finishes by muttering 'son of a bitch!' with such vehemence it makes me giggle.

'You're right.' I throw my dirty paper towel in the bin. 'It's funny, when we first broke up, all I could think about were the good things I'd lost. All the good things about him – and the good times we had. But I'm starting to realise that they all happened years ago – years before we broke up. If I'm brutally honest, our relationship had come off track long before it actually ended.'

'Attagirl!' Sofia exclaims. 'That's a very important realisation. It means you are finally free.'

I look at her questioningly. 'Free of what?'

'Free of being trapped in a nostalgia-tinted reality – or non-reality.' There's something about the earnestness in her voice that makes me think she's speaking from personal experience, and I risk giving her a gentle nudge.

'Is that something you've done before?'

'Oh yes!' she exclaims with a bitterness to her tone. 'In fact, you could say I've made it my life's work to become mired in nostalgia – or, rather, my death's work.' She laughs wryly.

'How do you mean?' I ask softly, praying I don't scare her into clamming up again.

'I mean being forced to pretend to be dead creates a deep wistfulness for the life you've left behind.'

I'm intrigued by the fact that she said she was 'forced' to pretend to be dead, and instantly my mind fills with the questions: who by and why?

'I constantly have to remind myself that being a famous singer wasn't all sweetness and light,' she continues before turning her attention back to her fish. 'Anyway, now you're able to see the reality of your relationship, you're free to move on to something much better.'

'Yes, and I think I already have.'

She looks back at me. 'What do you mean?'

'This job, coming here, meeting you. You've already made me feel so much better and I've only known you for two days! I'd give you a hug, if my hands weren't covered in fish slime.'

She laughs as she turns on the tap and rinses her hands. 'A little fish slime doesn't bother me. I was a *varina*, remember? I used to handle fish every day.'

'Oh yes!' I feel a rush of gratitude as she comes over and hugs me tight. She's surprisingly strong for one so small. 'Thank you so much, and I'm so sorry for being so unprofessional.'

She stares at me as if I'm deranged. 'What do you mean unprofessional?'

'Look at me!' I gesture at Gabriel's shirt. 'I can honestly say I've never ended up losing my dress and becoming an emotional wreck on a job before!'

Sofia shakes her head. 'You're not an emotional wreck; you're being emotionally honest. There's an important difference.'

I feel a wave of relief as her words sink in. It's OK to feel how I do, and it's OK to express it too. 'Thank you,' I say softly. 'Seriously, you've really helped me.'

'I have?' She looks so shocked at this, it takes me by surprise.

'Of course. And you've helped loads of other people too, through your songs.'

She frowns. 'Hmm, I think that's more to do with the power of dying young. There's nothing like a tragic death to help immortalise a person and their work. Just look at James Dean and Buddy Holly.'

'I'm sure your songs would have stood the test of time even if you hadn't died,' I say firmly. 'And like I said, you've really helped me and I know that you aren't tragically dead.'

She stares at me intently. 'Do you really mean that?'

'Absolutely. I'm loving spending time with you. You're an inspiration.'

I'm not sure if it's a trick of the light, but her eyes are suddenly shiny, as if they've filled with tears.

'*Obrigada*,' she says quietly before clearing her throat. 'And I'm sorry about before. The way I spoke to Gabriel. What's that saying the British have about being grumpy when you wake up? I must have got out of the bed on the wrong side.'

I laugh and nod. 'There's no need to apologise. You got angry at him, not me.'

'I know, but it must have made you feel uncomfortable.' She

sighs. 'Talking about Judith made me more emotional than I'd expected.'

'That's understandable. Did you... did you ever find out what had happened to her?'

She nods, grim-faced. 'But I think I'm going to need a glass of wine before I can tell you the next instalment – a very large glass. Maybe you could do with one too?' She looks at me hopefully.

'Sounds great.' I nod. 'I'll just have a quick shower and get dressed.'

'Of course. And, Lily?'

'Yes?'

'Thank you for what you said.' She looks so genuinely grateful. I could never have imagined a tiny powerhouse like Sofia needing reassurance or validation, but I'm really glad I was able to give it to her. I feel as if it's brought us closer.

I hurry upstairs and into my room. But before going into the bathroom, I fetch my Portuguese phrasebook and turn to the words beginning with S. I scan the page for something resembling *segredo* – the word Gabriel had said to Sofia while looking at me. I shiver as I read the English translation. It means secret.

23

LISBON, 1940

Once I'd recovered from the initial shock of my ransacked apartment, I sat on the sofa clutching Judith's torn coat. 'Please be OK,' I whispered over and over, but I couldn't ease my growing dread. The Gestapo had got the diamond – why did they have to take Judith too? And what were they going to do to her? I buried my face in the fabric and inhaled the musty scent. Would I ever see my beloved friend again?

I didn't sleep a wink that night, trying to figure out what to do and coming up with a big fat zero. I was due back in the studio early the next day to put the finishing touches to the record, which was the very last thing I felt like doing given what had happened. As soon as I trudged in, Emilio gave me a look of surprise.

'Geez, you look rougher than a two-cent steak,' he exclaimed.

Normally, I would have come back with a witty retort, but that morning I could barely think straight, let alone make wisecracks.

'Late night?' he asked, pulling out a chair for me at the mixing desk beside him.

I'd planned to not tell him anything, but I was so desperate to share my concerns, I couldn't help blurting it out.

'I think my friend's been kidnapped – or worse!' I exclaimed, plonking myself down on the chair.

'Say what?' His grin instantly disappeared.

'I know it sounds crazy, but she's Jewish and a refugee. She came here from Germany – well Germany originally, via France and Spain – and she told me that a Gestapo agent had tried to capture her in France but she managed to escape, but then she saw him here in Lisbon recently and I think it's him. I think he's the one who's taken her.' I paused to take a breath.

'OK, let's slow down the tempo,' Emilio said calmly, 'and take it from the top. What happened exactly?'

So I told him the story of how Judith and I came to meet and how she'd helped inspire the song for the expo, and how I'd asked her to move into my apartment and how close we'd become. My voice broke as I reached the part about returning home to find the apartment trashed.

'But why would the Gestapo be interested in a young girl?' he asked.

'She had something they wanted.'

'What, France?' he quipped, and I shot him a frown. 'I'm sorry, but I don't understand why they'd follow her all the way here.'

I hesitated for a moment before deciding that, as the Gestapo now had the Vadodara Teardrop there was little point in keeping it from him. 'She has – or had – a diamond,' I whispered. 'A very valuable diamond. The Nazis knew her father owned it, but he gave it to her to take with her when she left Germany.'

Emilio took a pack of cigarettes from his pocket. 'Wow. So did they get the diamond too when they ransacked your apartment?'

I nodded glumly and took the cigarette he offered me. ''Fraid so.'

'Damn!' He shook his head before lighting our cigarettes. 'OK, we need to move you out of that apartment, just to be on the safe side.'

In all the time I'd been working with Emilio I'd only seen a light-hearted, fun-loving side to him, but now, as he frowned and ran his hand through his thick, silver-flecked hair, a more serious grown-up persona appeared.

'But—'

'No buts, Castello – those guys ain't playing. There's no way I want you going back there, knowing they could come back. And there's no way Alexandre would either. I'll talk to him today, get you moved into a hotel.'

'But—'

'What did I say?' He put his chunky finger to his lips. 'Shh.'

I nodded. As much as I hated having to give up my apartment, it felt good knowing that Emilio had my back. He was such a solid and reassuring presence and good to his word. By that evening, Alexandre had booked me into the exclusive Hotel Aviz, close to his office at the end of the Avenida da Liberdade, and Emilio and the guys from the band helped me move my essentials from my apartment.

Despite his assurances that the hotel was a known haunt for Allied agents, so no Gestapo would dare set foot there, I spent the first night pacing the room, going out of my mind thinking about Judith. In the end, I decided to take refuge in my old failsafe for stressful times and take a bath. Thankfully, I'd got the guys to bring my huge pot of lavender salts. As I sat on the edge of the tub, throwing handfuls under the cascading water, I said a prayer to Santo Antonio. 'Please keep Judith safe.'

I plunged my hand into the salts for one more scoop and my fingers brushed against something hard. My throat tightened as my fingers wrapped around the object – the tear-shaped object. Hardly able to breathe, I took my hand out and held it up to the light. There, sparking and glowing in my hand, was the Vadodara Teardrop.

'Oh, Judith,' I whispered. 'What have you done?'

24

LISBON, 1940

The summer of 1940 was swelteringly hot, even by Portuguese standards, which didn't do anything to help ease my nerves. I spent the days preceding the expo opening ceremony wracked with tension and fear, my thoughts swinging like a pendulum.

I couldn't decide if Judith successfully hiding the diamond from the Gestapo was a good or bad thing. In my more negative moments, I thought it was the worst thing ever – if they thought she didn't have it, then surely she'd have no more purpose for them. And if they still thought she knew its whereabouts, what would they do to her to try to extract the truth? Either way didn't bear thinking about. And, of course, the responsibility for the Vadodara Teardrop and where to hide it had now fallen upon me. Given that I had zero vested interest in the damned thing, other than its importance to Judith, it felt a little like being lumbered with an unwelcome guest. I wasn't sure I believed that a gem could be cursed, but having to hide it from the Gestapo sure as hell felt like one! Every day, I hid the diamond in a different place in my hotel room, paranoid someone might find it.

When I wasn't in the studio rehearsing, I was pounding the

streets searching for Judith. Of course, deep down, I knew that my search was futile, but I felt that if I stopped looking, it would be like admitting defeat and that my beloved jacaranda sister was gone forever.

On the morning of the opening ceremony, I sat in front of my dressing-table mirror staring at the gold embossed invitation trying not to think of who I'd be singing for. But, of course, that was impossible. The Head of the Portuguese State, Marechal Carmona, would be there, and the President of the Council and our soon-to-be dictator, Oliveira Salazar. My mouth was so dry, I could hardly swallow, and even the spirit of my mother seemed too intimidated by the enormity of the event to be able to help me. Instead of offering words of encouragement, I pictured her smiling sympathetically and shrugging. If Judith hadn't disappeared the way she did, I might have felt differently; in fact, I'm sure I would have. I would have got her an invitation to the expo and turned the whole thing into a fun adventure, but now the very concept of celebrating in such an ostentatious way while the rest of Europe was suffering and my beloved friend was missing felt truly grating.

I took a deep breath and began applying make-up to my clammy skin. I couldn't back out now. I couldn't let Alexandre down. I'd become really fond of him and, me being one of his artists, his reputation was on the line as well as my own.

The opening ceremony took place on a stage in the Plaza of the Empire at the centre of the expo which was flanked by two pavilions – one dedicated to Honour and Lisbon and the other to Portuguese in the World. The place was packed, and I'm not sure if I was projecting my own paranoia, but it seemed to me that there was a tension crackling in the air, a bit like the moments before a gathering storm finally breaks. The only people in the crowd who seemed truly carefree were the American sailors from the ships amassed in the harbour as part of the ceremony. 'We're just here for a last hurrah,' their boyish grins seemed to say. 'Soon we'll be on the other side of the Atlantic, safe in the land of Uncle Sam and a world away from your war.'

I was scheduled to sing close to the start of the ceremony, which suited me just fine as it meant less hanging around wishing I could flee – or stow away on a boat bound for Kathmandu. I'd been billed as Alexandre Fernandes' brightest new star; I only hoped that the event didn't make me famous for all the wrong reasons.

I don't remember a thing about being backstage, other than I was made to wait in a stuffy room with bright orange walls, which did little to ease my tension. And then, in a blur, I was bustled into the wings of the stage. I heard an announcer call my name, and I thought for one horrible moment that I might faint. *What if I forget my lines?* I panicked as I walked onto the stage.

The sun was beating down on me, which in some ways was a blessing because it meant that I was too dazzled to see the audience. As I stepped up to the mic, my mind went as blank as a fresh sheet of paper. What were the lyrics? *Jacaranda seeds*, I heard Judith whisper in my ear. And her voice was so crisp and clear, I had to look behind me to check that she wasn't there.

The musicians all gave me encouraging nods, and I turned back to the audience and grabbed the mic, leaning on the stand for support. *Jacaranda seeds*, I heard Judith whisper again, and I couldn't help wondering if it was her ghost that I was hearing, and I had the strongest, saddest knowing that I would never see her again.

I cleared my throat and took a breath, and not trusting myself to make any kind of opening gambit, I nodded to Charlie, the piano player, that I wanted to go straight into the song.

As soon as I started singing, all I could think about was Judith, and I poured all the angst and sorrow and pain I'd felt since her disappearance into the words. Even though the emotion was overwhelming, it was in a strange way a godsend, as it stopped me from thinking about my audience.

I only made one slip-up, when my voice tremored with pain and went slightly off-key, but I kept going and didn't let it put me off. Then, when I reached the final chorus, where the instruments faded away and there was nothing but my voice left, I let my voice fade too. This wasn't something we'd planned in rehearsals, but in the emotion of the moment, as I was saying farewell to Judith, it felt perfectly natural. I came to an end and closed my eyes, still clinging to that mic stand for dear life.

There were a couple of seconds of silence, which seemed to stretch forever, and I was just about to panic and prepare to flee the stage when the whole place erupted in rapturous applause. My knees almost buckled from the relief, and I squinted in the bright light to make sure my ears weren't deceiving me, but no, everyone was clapping and cheering and hooting and hollering. I turned to look back at the band and saw that they were all on their feet clapping me too. I turned back to the mic and said '*obrigada*' over and over again, dazed with disbelief, until the applause finally faded.

Afterwards, Alexandre bustled me around meeting and greeting people and giving journalists impromptu interviews. At one point, I remember shaking hands with a man with dark eyes and greying, slicked-back hair. It was only afterwards that I realised it was Salazar!

'I hope you're ready for your world to turn upside down and inside out,' Alexandre said to me later, over a nightcap in the Aviz bar. 'I think you just made all of Lisbon fall in love with you. And once the record comes out next week, it will be all of Portugal.'

'Oh, I don't know about that,' I replied. I wasn't being cute or deliberately bashful; I still couldn't quite comprehend the enormity of what had just happened, especially with thoughts of what might have happened to Judith plaguing me.

The next day, when I went to the café to study the morning papers as normal, I had the fright of my life. There was a picture of me on the front of the *Avante!* under the headline, *From Humble* Varina *to Voice of Portugal*. And so the fairy tale that was to become my life had begun. Little did I realise that I'd never have control of the narrative again. The day before the opening ceremony, the Germans began their occupation of France and the cataclysmic events this unleashed would come to affect me more than I ever could have imagined.

25

PORTUGAL, 2000

On my second day at Sofia's, I wake with a start. Once she'd told me about the expo, Sofia requested a pause, and after a delicious dinner of fresh fish and potatoes sautéed in paprika and garlic, she'd declared the day over and retired to bed. It had taken me ages to fall asleep, I had so many questions going round and round in my head. In an attempt at emptying my mind, I'd written them down in my notebook. I reach across to the bedside table and pick it up, squinting at the words.

Why was Sofia 'forced' to pretend to be dead?
What happened to Judith?
What happened to the diamond?!
Was the plane crash that supposedly killed her linked to the diamond?
What is 'the secret' and 'the truth' that Gabriel spoke about?

As I reread the page now, another question comes to me, and I scribble it down at the bottom of the list...

Why do they seem to keep arguing about me?

'Lily!' I jump as I hear Sofia calling me and shove my notebook under the pillow. 'Lily! Are you awake?' she calls again, and I realise that her voice is coming from outside, in the garden.

I go over to the window and peer out. Sofia is standing on the footpath with her gardener. A rusty old bike is propped up between them.

'*Bom dia!*' Sofia cries as soon as she sees me. 'I asked Rosária to bring you this, so you can get into town easily to buy some new clothes.'

Rosária tips her straw sunhat back and grins up at me.

'*Obrigada,*' I call back. 'I'll be right down.'

Before going to bed, I'd told Sofia that I needed to buy some new clothes, a need that was even more urgent than before given that my new dress had been swept out to sea. I'm not sure how much easier the bike will make it though, as it looks ancient.

I have a quick shower and get dressed and head down to find Sofia sitting at the kitchen table, sipping a cup of coffee. A jug of juice and a bowl of boiled eggs and a rack of toast have been placed at the centre of the gingham tablecloth.

'Is Rosária not joining us?' I ask as I sit down.

'Oh – no – she had some work to be getting on with.'

'Shame, I wanted to congratulate her on the garden. The flowers are so beautiful.'

'Like the earth laughing,' Sofia murmurs.

'The earth is laughing a *lot* in your garden!' I joke, helping myself to some toast.

As soon as we've finished eating, we go outside to the bike, which is now leaning against the wall of the cottage.

'Are you sure it's safe to ride?' I ask as Sofia blows a cobweb from the handlebars.

'Of course!' She gives the bike a loving gaze. 'Amália was my main mode of transport until last year.'

'Amália?'

'Her name,' she says indignantly, as if naming one's bike is a perfectly reasonable thing for a grown adult to do. 'Named after Amália Rodrigues, the Queen of Fado,' she adds.

'I see. So what made you stop riding her last year?' I ask, eyeing the scuffed saddle.

'A tree got in my way and I ended up in a heap.' Sofia gives a mournful sigh. 'Gabriel banned me from riding after that – he said that if I broke my hip at my age, I might never recover.'

Gabriel needs to mind his own business, I automatically think, but on the other hand, I suppose he did have a point. Sofia is eighty. Her bones are bound to be more fragile by now.

'How long has it been since you rode a bike?' she asks.

'Not since I was a kid.'

She looks at me as if I'm insane. 'Don't people ride bikes in London?'

'They do, but it's a little too daunting for me. The traffic is horrendous,' I add when she looks at me questioningly.

'Ah, well you won't have that problem here.' She grins. 'Apart from the occasional tractor or truck going to and from the vineyards, the road into town is pretty deserted.' She blows the remaining cobweb from the handlebars and starts pushing the bike around the side of the cottage. 'All you have to do is take a left at the end of the track and follow it for about twenty minutes.' She looks me up and down and frowns. 'Maybe closer to thirty, given that you haven't cycled in years. And I did cycle like a maniac – according to Gabriel anyway.'

I nod. 'I'll definitely be taking it slow at first.'

'When you get to the crossroads, take the road to the left, and you should reach the high street about five minutes later.

It's not the biggest town, but there are a couple of clothes stores. My personal favourite is a boutique called Borboleta. I get most of my clothes there.'

'OK, great.' I take the bike from her, hoping she'll disappear into the house before I set off, but to my dismay she stands there, arms folded, clearly wanting to watch me go.

'OK then,' I say nervously as I swing one leg over and prop myself onto the saddle. What if I've forgotten how to do it? I panic. What if I'm about to make a total idiot of myself? I take a breath to try to calm myself. Of course I'll be able to do it. Riding a bike is famous for being impossible to forget after all. 'Bye then.' My voice comes out like a squeak as I put one foot on the pedal and push myself off.

'Good luck,' Sofia says, and I can hear the amusement in her voice. But it's just the motivation I need, and, determined not to look stupid in front of her, I push myself off and, after an initial wobble, start cycling down the bumpy track.

'Stop off at the bakery while you're there,' she calls after me. 'They do the best pastel de nata in all of Portugal. The custard filling is orgasmic.'

'Will do!' I call back gaily, trying not to laugh at her description and narrowly avoiding a pothole.

Once I reach the end of the track and I'm on the road, the smoother surface makes things a lot easier, and it's not long before I'm sailing along, the warm breeze whistling through my hair.

I have a sudden flashback to my third foster family, which I went to when I was eleven. They lived close to an abandoned railway track where you could cycle for miles without having to stop for traffic. I loved taking off on my own along that track, pedalling as fast as I could, dreaming that if I went fast enough, my bike might magically sprout a pair of wings and I'd be able to fly away. Sometimes I'd dream that I'd flown right up to heaven, where my birth parents were. I had no idea if they were dead or not, but it felt strangely comforting to imagine that they were – that they'd been taken from me tragically rather than chosen to abandon me.

Immersed in the memory, I cycle faster and faster along the narrow, winding road. After about ten minutes, I see a sign for a vineyard and suddenly the landscape changes and all I can see are neat rows and rows of waist-high vines, stretching all the way to the horizon. I tilt my head back and drink in the thin wisps of white cloud drifting across the cornflower-blue sky. I feel so light and free it's as if I'm made of cloud too, a wisp of a woman drifting through the air. It occurs to me that I never once felt like this in all the time I was with Robin. When we were together, I felt all too solid and weighted down. Of course, that's what I'd wanted at first. Back when we met, I craved security and to feel grounded.

The words of his email flicker back into my mind, but this time his patronising tone doesn't infuriate me; it's more like an irritating niggle. I pedal faster and harder and feel a huge wave of gratitude for Sofia and how our chat yesterday helped me see things more hopefully and maybe just maybe I'm now free to move on to something better.

It takes me precisely twenty-three minutes to get into town, which I make a mental note of to tell Sofia as a point of pride. I padlock the bike to a lamp post and take a moment to catch my breath. I feel hot and sweaty from the ride but blissfully free from caring. I look up and down the main street and see a higgledy-piggledy row of old buildings in beautiful pastel shades of pink, green and blue, with terracotta-tiled roofs. As I stroll along, I feel nervous about the language barrier – surely in this more rural area people won't be as fluent in English, but then I remind myself that I've managed OK so far.

I spot a sign with a butterfly painted on it, and as I get

closer, I see a beautiful array of clothes in the window and the word BORBOLETA stencilled in gold on the glass. Sofia's favourite store. I push open the door and step inside.

Fifteen minutes later, I leave the store, the proud owner of three new dresses and a bathing suit in shocking pink. Buoyed by my purchases, I make my way to the bakery and order a bag of tarts to take back with me. I'm so happy as I head back to the bike, I catch myself whistling. But then I see a toy store and I fall silent. Maybe it's because it's the most beautiful toyshop I've ever seen, its window crammed with wonderful brightly painted wooden toys, or maybe it's a delayed reaction to Robin's email, but suddenly an apparition of my dream daughter appears right there in the window, laughing as she pushes the wooden train around the track. Damn. Why did she have to appear now, just when I was feeling so happy?

Because I don't want you to let me go, I imagine her calling at me from inside the shop.

I quickly look away, tears burning in my eyes.

No matter how hard I try, on the ride back to Sofia's I can't quite recapture the feeling of euphoria I'd experienced on the way into town. The sun feels too bright and the air too humid.

I arrive at the cottage to find Sofia sitting on the living-room floor, an old brown leather trunk open in front of her.

'Lily, my dear, how did you get on?' she asks, but she looks distracted.

'Very well, thanks,' I say breezily as I perch on the edge of the chaise longue. There's no way I can tell her I'm being haunted by the ghost of my dream daughter. 'What's this?' I ask, pointing to the trunk.

She sighs. '*This* is my Pandora's box.'

'Oh dear.' I give a nervous laugh. 'Hopefully you aren't about to unleash a load of evils upon the world.'

She stares down into the case. 'I'm afraid that I am. Or, rather, we are.'

'We?'

She glances over her shoulder at me. 'By writing this book.'

'I don't understand.'

'No, but you will,' she murmurs.

'How can you telling your story be evil?'

She looks away. 'Trust me, there's going to be plenty of evil in those pages.'

I try to reassure myself that she must be talking about the Gestapo, but why doesn't she just come out and say this? Why do I get the feeling that she's sitting on a shocking plot twist I won't see coming?

I lean closer and peer into the case. I can see a newspaper, yellowed with age, a small tin box, some neatly folded clothes and a gas mask with a snout-like nose that I recognise instantly from school history lessons. 'You have a gas mask?' I gaze at it transfixed. It's so strange to see one for real, rather than in a picture.

'What?' she says, clearly still distracted. 'Oh – uh – yes.'

'Why? Surely you didn't need them in Lisbon. Or did they issue them as a precautionary measure?'

She shakes her head. 'No. I got it in London.'

'You went to London?' I stare at her, wondering why she's never mentioned this before, given that it's my home city and has come up in conversation several times.

'Yes, for my sins.'

I wonder what she means by this, but before I can ask, she slams the lid of the trunk shut and gets to her feet.

'Did you get the pastel de natas?' she asks.

'I did.'

Her expression brightens. 'Excellent! I'll go and get some plates and make some coffee.'

I watch her go, my head once again filling with questions.

Why did she say 'for my sins'? Previously, she seemed so positive about Britain and our quaint sayings. What could have happened to have prompted this change in her mood?

I glance at the trunk feeling certain that the reason must be lurking inside. My gaze drifts around the room, falling on the mantelpiece, and I do a double take. The framed photograph of Judith is nowhere to be seen.

26

LISBON, 1940

The months following my expo performance passed in a blur. Alexandre had been right when he told me that my life would turn upside down and inside out. 'Jacaranda Seeds' was a smash hit in Portugal, and I immediately returned to the studio to record an album with Emilio. He and Alexandre felt strongly that the album should be a mixture of different kinds of songs and that I shouldn't limit myself to fado. This suited me just fine as I approached my songwriting in the same way I approach my food – always eager to try something new. It was an attitude I'd adopted when it came to the opposite sex too, and I thoroughly enjoyed the buffet of men all eager to woo me as my star ascended.

Not that many succeeded in their attempts. My experience with Bing had left me bruised and determined that I should never be made to feel like that again, so I crafted a suit of armour made up of cutting wisecracks and withering stares to protect my heart. Of course, this only seemed to make me more popular, as men do so love the challenge of the hunt. None of them came close to getting past my armour though. I didn't like any of them enough, and besides I was too distracted by other things, such as my beloved Judith and 'That Pesky Diamond', as I'd come to think of it. I'd continued rotating the Vadodara Teardrop between various hiding places in my room, but every time I returned to the hotel I felt a surge of panic as I opened the door, praying I wouldn't find the room ransacked and the gem gone.

The war was now raging across Europe, and the Germans were blitzing Britain with their bombs. Lisbon had become flooded with refugees and even though the lights still shone and the music still played in Portugal, there was a growing sense that they could be switched off at any moment, and I couldn't shake the feeling that we were a little like the band who kept playing on the deck of the sinking *Titanic*. Every time I saw a refugee wandering the streets like a startled rabbit blinking in the dazzling sunshine and overdressed in their winter clothes, I thought of Judith and felt yet another pang of loss. But all my searching for my beloved friend remained in vain.

Then, one morning in October, I was walking to the studio when I saw a young man coming towards me. I knew instantly that he was a refugee. The heavy woollen coat was an immediate giveaway. He had the same haunted expression I'd seen in Judith too. The hollow look of the hunted animal.

As I drew closer, I gave him a beaming smile, to try to let him know that he was welcome in Lisbon and that we Portuguese were no threat to him. But then, from out of nowhere, a car came screeching to a halt beside us and a man leaped out. There was something familiar about his pinched face and thin moustache, and then I realised – it was Kurt Fischer. I saw a look of horror upon the refugee's face as Fischer grabbed his arm.

'Hey!' I exclaimed. Finally, this was my chance to try and find out what had happened to Judith.

'Shut up!' Fischer hissed at me over his shoulder. Then, in a trice, he bundled the young man into the back of the car and slammed the door shut behind them.

'What are you doing?' I cried, pulling at the door handle. But it all happened too fast, and the car went speeding off down the hill, almost taking my hand with it. As I stood staring after it, my blood turned to ice. Had Judith been bundled into a car like this too? I stumbled my way down the hill, my head a jumble of panicked thoughts.

I burst into the studio to find Emilio hunched over the mixing desk.

'Well, someone's keen to get started this morning!' he exclaimed with a grin.

'I've just seen something,' I gasped. 'Something awful. A Gestapo agent, snatching a refugee off the street right in front of me. It was the same guy I'd seen following my friend – the friend who was taken.'

'Whoa, take it easy.' He beckoned me to come and sit beside him. 'OK, what happened?'

I took a breath before telling him what I'd seen. 'I know it was the same man my friend pointed out to me in the restaurant the night she got so spooked. I recognised him immediately. His face is pointy like a weasel's.'

Emilio frowned. 'Does he have blond hair and a thin moustache?'

'Yes! Why, do you know him?'

'I think I might know *of* him.' Emilio went over to his coat hanging on a peg by the door. 'Is this him?' he asked, taking a photograph from the pocket.

I shivered as he showed me the picture. I recognised Fischer instantly, sitting at a café table. Clearly the picture had been taken in stealth as he seemed to be blissfully unaware of the camera. 'Yes, that's him. But why do you have this picture?'

Emilio shifted his chair closer to mine. 'I've started helping the Allies,' he whispered.

'With what?'

'Gathering intelligence on German activity here in Lisbon.'

'Wow. And here I was thinking you were just a mild-mannered music producer,' I quipped.

'What do you mean, "just"?' he retorted. 'In fact, my music career makes the perfect cover.' He paused for a moment before leaning even closer. 'It could be the same for you too – if you wanted to help. Especially if your album sells as well as we're expecting it to.'

'Are you kidding me? Of course I want to help!' I exclaimed, although I wasn't entirely sure what this would entail.

'Shh!' He looked at the door anxiously.

'I'm sorry,' I whispered. 'But yes, I'd do anything to help defeat those monsters. Anything to help my friend.'

'Awesome.' Emilio slipped the photograph into his trouser pocket. 'I'm sure you've already figured this out, but Alexandre has big plans for you. He doesn't just want you to be a star here in Portugal – he's aiming for America and Britain too. And as your profile rises, so will your access to certain social circles.'

'Such as?' I asked, surprised.

'The kind of circles German agents like to infiltrate. You could be a very useful observer for the Allies, or even a courier.'

'A courier of what?' I whispered, my excitement growing.

'Top-secret information.'

I gave a laugh of disbelief. I'd thought that my rise to fame as a singer was a crazy twist of fate, but the thought of becoming some kind of courier for the Allies seemed even more fantastical. 'Count me in!' I exclaimed.

'Excellent!' Emilio clapped his hands together. 'We'd better start making a best-selling record then.'

I sprang to my feet and began doing my vocal warm-ups, racing up and down those scales like a lark. After weeks of feeling helpless in the face of Judith's disappearance, I finally felt a sense of purpose and direction again. I was going to do everything in my power to help my jacaranda seed sister – that's if she was still able to be helped. If it was too late and those monsters had killed her, I was going to do everything I could to get revenge.

27

LISBON, 1941

The second single I released was a jazzy little number called 'This Doll', which Emilio and I came up with when we were fooling around in the studio one night. Emilio felt we should do something fun and light-hearted to give people something to smile about, so in the song I eviscerate a man for trying to play with my heart and underestimating my wit and intelligence. I used Bing for inspiration – which made it all the more infuriating when, after my death, he claimed he'd been the inspiration for 'Ocean Longing'. I mean, as if!

'This Doll' came out at the end of 1940, and Emilio had called it perfectly. People clearly did need something to make them smile, and it was an instant hit in Portugal. By the new year, it was also a hit in Britain. It turned out that the Brits loved my tongue-in-cheek humour, and as soon as the record started being played on the BBC airwaves – courtesy of Alexandre's contacts in London – people began singing it around the pianos in pubs. Some of my original fans were a little offended that the 'Voice of Portugal' should now be singing in English and accused me of selling out in order to become famous, but I didn't care. I knew the real, deeper reason for my ambition – the more famous I became, the more I could be in a position to help the Allies, not to mention Judith and others like her.

In February, I was invited to Estoril, a town in Cascais on the Portuguese Riviera – to sing at the swanky five-star Hotel Palácio. Alexandre had booked me a room for the night. Although I tried really hard to keep my feet on the ground throughout my growing fame, the moment I arrived and was whisked in through the grand revolving door, I have to confess I felt a little light-headed. How had a humble girl from Ovar ended up staying at a hotel that regularly hosted the great and the good, including members of royalty? Only a couple of years previously, I'd been walking around Lisbon barefoot with a basket of fish on my head! Once the porter had shown me to my room, I threw myself onto the sumptuous bed and began laughing my head off.

'Can you believe it, Mama?' I cried, gazing up at the ornate coving on the ceiling.

Of course I can, my darling, I imagined her whispering. *And you deserve it more than most because you will appreciate every second of it.* It was in moments like this that I truly believed I was communing with my mother's spirit, as only she was capable of such wisdom and she stopped me from getting too carried away with myself.

I was just putting the final touches to my make-up, ready for my performance, when there was a rap on the door. The hotel was so fancy it even had one of those new-fangled spyholes, so you could check who was calling before letting them in. I peered through the fish-eyed glass and saw Emilio, glancing anxiously up and down the corridor.

'Everything OK?' I asked as I opened the door.

'I need to talk to you,' he said quietly as he walked in. His expression was deadly serious. 'I have a job for you, for the Allies. Here tonight.'

A shiver ran up my spine. Ever since he'd asked me if I'd

like to help, I'd been on tenterhooks, waiting for my first assignment. 'What is it?'

He took two cigarettes from his pack and handed one to me. 'This place is a hotbed of spies,' he said before lighting them. 'They're mostly allies, but there are some Germans too.'

I took a deep inhale, trying to stay calm.

'And we think there might be one who is working for both sides.' It was strange seeing the normally laidback Emilio look so tense, and it really brought home the gravity of the situation.

'A double agent?' I felt a wave of disgust. To my mind, there was nothing worse.

'Yup. He's from England and meant to be working for the Allies, but we think he might have been turned by the Nazis.' He sighed out a thick plume of smoke. 'Sadly, the Germans have more than a few fans in Britain even in the highest sections of society. Even amongst royalty.'

'Royalty?'

Emilio nodded grimly. 'Why do you think Churchill whisked Edward and his American wife off to the Bahamas? Rumour has it the Nazis were planning on making him their puppet king if they managed to take Britain.'

'Shit.' I'd been under the impression that I was well informed due to my avid reading of the newspapers, but clearly I still had a lot to learn.

'Exactly. The man we'd like you to meet is called James Sinclair. He's six feet tall with blue eyes and auburn hair. He's known to the Germans as Teeblatt, meaning Tealeaf, which I'm guessing is a reference to the British love of tea. He's also a known ladies' man. After you've done your set, we want you to mingle in the hotel bar.' Emilio gave a wry smile. 'He's bound to be in there as he's also known for his fondness for liquor. And you're sure to be the belle of the ball, so I'm certain he'll want to get to know you. Who knows? He might even invite you to have a nightcap with him.'

I frowned. 'Exactly how friendly do you want me to get with this potential traitor to king and country?'

Emilio instantly looked concerned. 'I'm not suggesting you do anything that makes you uncomfortable; we'd just like you to keep an eye on him. See if he talks to anyone suspicious, or if he looks like he could be passing a message to anyone. And, of course, if you did gain access to his room, you might be able to have a snoop around.'

'Right.' I sat down at my dressing table and gazed at my reflection. I looked a whole lot paler than before. I'd been so eager to do my bit to help I hadn't quite realised the enormity of what I'd signed up for.

'If anyone has the balls to pull this off, it's you, Castello,' Emilio said, coming to stand behind me.

I met his gaze in the reflection and glared. 'Save the flattery for someone dumb enough to fall for it.'

He burst out laughing. 'That's the spirit!' His smile faded and he placed his hand on my shoulder. His thick gold wedding band glinted in the lamplight. 'Seriously, though, if you do well tonight and blow his cover, it would be a huge help for the British secret service and it could lead to other opportunities.'

I nodded.

'But only if you want to.' He gave my shoulder a squeeze. 'I meant what I said. I don't want you doing anything you're not comfortable with. If he is Teeblatt, then he could be a very dangerous customer.' He met my gaze in the mirror. 'I don't want you putting yourself at risk, Castello; you're one of my favourite recording artists.'

'Hmm, I bet you say that to all the girls you record with.'

He laughed. 'No, actually, I don't.'

There was a beat of silence and something passed between us. Something extremely awkward given the wedding ring on his finger.

I looked away. Now was not the time to be thinking about

Emilio's marital status. Now I had to focus all my thoughts on Judith and doing everything I could to help her and other poor souls like her. That was the reason why'd I'd volunteered for this in the first place.

'I'm in,' I said through gritted teeth.

28

LISBON, 1941

Agreeing to sing a thirty-minute set *and* try to identify a Nazi double agent certainly added an extra level of frisson to that night's performance. As I stepped into the spotlight and gazed out at the silhouettes of the audience at the small round tables, I wondered if that rat of a traitor was there, looking up at me. Well, if he was, it was my job to make myself as enticing to him as possible. I thought of Judith again and tried to send her a telepathic message. *If you only knew the things I'm doing to try to save you, my jacaranda sister!*

I began my set with a couple of the tracks from my soon-to-be released album then, once I'd got the audience nice and warmed up, I performed 'This Doll', making extra effort to wither and pout my way through it. When the song came to an end, most of the men in the bar hollered and whistled. I wondered if James Sinclair was one of them.

I finished the set with 'Jacaranda Seeds', pouring every ounce of emotion I could into it as I thought again of Judith. The place erupted in applause, and as the house lights came up, I gazed out into the audience, looking for someone with auburn hair, but no one fit the description Emilio had given me. I stepped down from the stage feeling a wave of disappointment. As I made my way towards the bar, people's praise rang in my ears. I glanced left and right, smiling graciously and saying thank you, but there was still no sign of anyone resembling Sinclair. The only thing I could think to do was sit at the bar and hope that if he was present, he'd make his way over to me.

I sat on a stool, crossed my legs, making sure to pull the hem of my dress above my knee, and then I took my cigarettes from my purse. As if by magic, a hand holding a silver lighter appeared over my shoulder. Maintaining my composure, I put a cigarette in my mouth and lit it. Then I turned and felt a mixture of excitement and fear as I saw a man with blue eyes and red hair right behind me.

'So, what do you do for your next trick?' I asked drolly, my heart pounding.

'I make you disappear,' he replied. His words were slightly slurred, and I could smell the liquor on his breath. I felt a little sick. What did he mean by making me disappear? Did he somehow know that I was working for the Allies? 'And reappear in my suite,' he continued with a grin.

I fought the urge to retch. I might not have known if he was guilty of being a double agent yet, but he was definitely guilty of being a sleazeball.

'I think you have me mistaken for someone else,' I said, blowing a thin plume of smoke in his face.

He frowned. 'No, I know who you are. I just watched you singing on—'

'Someone with no class,' I cut in.

His face flushed red. 'Oh no, I didn't mean... I just meant that I'd like you to see my suite. It has a piano and a corner bar. It really is something else.'

'Hmm, well, how about you make a bottle of champagne magically appear and maybe I'll think about it?'

His face broke into a smile of relief. 'Of course!' he replied as he waved to the bartender.

Emilio was right – Sinclair had a weakness for both women and alcohol, and by the time the bottle of champagne was finished, with him having quaffed most of it whilst ogling my breasts and legs, he was eager as a puppy.

'Come on then – let's see this piano of yours.'

'Are you sure?' In his eagerness to vacate the bar stool, he went careering into a waitress. 'Watch where you're going,' he slurred at her crossly, and I had to bite my lip to stop myself from giving him a piece of my mind.

I took a final sip of my drink for Dutch courage. My hope was that he would be too inebriated to make any kind of advance and I'd be able to have a snoop around for anything potentially incriminating. Our conversation so far had been useless – he was too drunk and dull to offer anything more than a series of monologues on his prowess at various different sports. It took all my self-restraint not to suggest that he add World Champion Bore to his list.

Sinclair guided me through the bar and into the lobby, one hand pressed into the small of my back. Feeling his touch made my skin crawl, but my loyalty to Judith and desire to help overrode my fear. As we waited for the lift, he started swaying like a poppy in the breeze.

'You're so beautiful,' he murmured.

And you're so disgusting, I thought, all the while smiling sweetly.

The lift doors opened, and I stepped and he staggered inside.

'And so talented too,' he murmured, lurching at the buttons and stabbing the one for the top floor.

As soon as the doors closed, the smell of alcohol emanating from him became overpowering. I really hoped Emilio and whoever he was working for appreciated the lengths I was going to.

We arrived at the top floor, and he stumbled out ahead of me. 'This way,' he said before letting out a loud belch.

In my admittedly patchy history with men, this was fast becoming the worst experience of them all. *I only have to get inside his suite and have a snoop, then I can make my excuses and leave,* I reminded myself.

After several bungled attempts, Sinclair finally managed to unlock his door, and I followed him into the room.

'Ta-da!' he cried, turning on the light.

His room was pretty much identical to mine, but not wanting to burst his bubble, I feigned delighted surprise. 'How incredible!' I cooed.

'*You're* incredible.' He smirked and staggered towards me. I deftly stepped to the side, and he went teetering past.

'How about we have a nightcap?' I suggested, trying not to roll my eyes. With any luck, one final drink would be enough to tip him over the edge and into oblivion.

'Excellent idea.' He lurched over to the drinks cabinet in the corner, and I glanced around the room, looking for anything incriminating. I made a mental note of a briefcase in the corner, although I wasn't sure if a double agent would be so obvious.

Just like the day I sang at the opening of the Portuguese World Expo, I was struck by how surreal my life had become. It all felt like a dream – or, rather, a nightmare – as Sinclair came staggering towards me holding two crystal tumblers of what looked like whisky. The glasses were so full and he was so incapable of walking straight, the drink sloshed over the sides as if he was aboard a ship on a roiling sea.

'So you were lying then,' he said, thrusting one of the glasses into my hand.

My skin instantly prickled. 'What do you mean?'

'In your song. This doll is for being played with after all.'

He gave a suggestive sneer, a glob of saliva gathering in the corner of his mouth.

'Hmm, that all depends,' I said, trying desperately to think of what to say next.

He opened his mouth to speak and another belch escaped. How he had the arrogance to think I'd want anything to do with him was beyond me.

'Depends on what?' he asked, beginning to hiccup. I made a mental note to kill Emilio if I made it out of there without first killing Sinclair.

'On what we're playing.'

'Oh, I think we both know what we're playing,' he said menacingly, taking a lurching step towards me.

29

LISBON, 1941

I took another quick step to the side and put my glass down. 'Why don't you go and make yourself comfortable over there?' I gestured at the bed. 'And I'll go and freshen up in the bathroom.'

He gave a smirk. 'With pleasure.'

I watched him weave his way over to the bed, nearly upending a coffee table en route. I was hoping he was so drunk, he'd pass out as soon as his head hit the pillow. If he didn't, I'd have to feign a sudden illness and make my escape. As much as I wanted to help the Allies and Judith, there was no way that grotesque hiccupping creep was coming anywhere near me.

I went into the bathroom and locked the door.

'Don't be long,' he called out between hiccups.

'I won't,' I called back, perching on the side of the bath and glancing around. What if he stayed awake and got violent when I rejected his advances? I needed some kind of weapon, just in case.

I looked at the glass bottle of bath salts on the counter by the sink. It was hefty enough to do some serious damage, although I'm not sure Emilio would be impressed if I ended up clouting a

Brit to death with a bottle of bath salts, even if he did die smelling of roses. And it would hardly help my reputation as we looked to build my singing career. No, I needed something else. Something more subtle.

I went over to the bathroom cabinet, hoping there might be some sleeping tablets in there that I could grind up and put in his drink. Just enough to make him have a long, deep nap.

I opened the cabinet to find a tube of toothpaste, a toothbrush and a hairbrush with a few red hairs caught between the bristles. Perhaps I could give him a smack with the hairbrush if he got too handsy. I fought the urge to laugh and went and pressed my ear to the door, hoping to hear drunken snores. To my dismay, I heard more hiccupping and then – I took a step back and shuddered – vomiting.

'Help!' Sinclair cried between retches.

Bracing myself, I hurried out of the bathroom to find him hunched over, vomiting into an ice bucket.

'Oh dear,' I said, although inside I was cheering. There would surely be no drunken advances made now. Although the sour smell now filling the room slightly dampened my euphoria.

He opened his mouth to speak and spewed up again. Thankfully, nursing my mother through the later stages of her cancer meant that I had a hardy constitution when it came to such things.

'Are you all right?' I asked sweetly, trying not to breathe in the smell.

'Yes,' he gasped and promptly vomited again. 'My case,' he rasped, pointing to the wardrobe. 'Can you get my case?'

'Of course.' I made my way past him and opened the wardrobe. A brown leather suitcase sat at the bottom beneath a rail of neatly pressed suits.

'There should be a tin of Andrews liver salts inside it.'

I put the case on the floor and kneeled in front of it, my pulse quickening. This might be a truly hideous situation, but he was giving me permission to look through his things. I was going to be able to snoop right in front of him!

I opened the case and started riffling around. I found the jar of liver salts straight away but ignored them.

'Did you find them?' he called before retching again.

'Not yet.' I reached inside an inner pocket and pulled out a matchbox. I was about to put it back when I felt whatever was inside make a dull thudding sound instead of the rattle of matches.

'I'm sure I packed my liver salts. I take them everywhere with me,' he called.

I stuffed the matchbox into my purse and grabbed the tin of liver salts. 'Found them!'

'Oh, be a doll and put some in a glass of water for me.' He looked up at me imploringly. His pale face was covered in a sheen of sweat and the corners of his chin were covered with flecks of vomit. Another new low point in my encounters with men.

Eager to get out of there as quickly as possible, I did as instructed and passed him the drink. 'I'm going to leave you to recover now,' I said, edging over to the door.

Thankfully, even he wasn't deluded enough to think that I ought to stay, and he nodded and turned away.

I closed the door behind me and raced along the corridor. Not wanting to wait for the lift, I made my way down the stairs. When I reached my room, I locked the door behind me and went over to the desk, turned on the lamp and took out the matchbox. Opening it slowly, I saw a dark object inside. I held it up to the light to examine it more closely and realised that it was a tiny camera. It was so small, I wondered for a moment if it was for a doll. But before I could think any more, I jumped out of my skin at a loud knock on the door.

I tiptoed over to the spyhole, saying a prayer of thanks for the genius who invented it. I was fully expecting to see Sinclair swaying there, hiccupping and with vomit around his mouth, demanding to know why I took his camera, but to my huge relief it was Emilio.

I opened the door and let him inside.

'Are you OK?' he asked, looking concerned. 'I saw you go up to his room with him and I got worried.'

'As well you should have done,' I retorted.

He gripped my arm. 'Did he try anything on with you?'

'Only vomit.'

He gave a confused frown.

'You were right about him not being able to handle his drink. He puked up everywhere.'

'Oh!' Emilio began to grin.

'It wasn't a complete disaster though. He got me to look in his case for some liver salts and I found this.' I went over to the desk and picked up the tiny camera. 'It was hidden inside a matchbox.'

'A spy camera,' he exclaimed.

'Yes,' I muttered, relieved I hadn't told him that I thought it might have been for a doll.

'This is excellent,' he said, his smile growing. 'This might contain proof that he is working for the Germans. Good work, Castello.'

'Thank you, Almeida.'

He threw his arms round me and hugged me tight. 'I'm so glad you're OK. I was worried,' he murmured into my hair.

He kept holding me, but I didn't pull away. After the nerve-wracking events of the previous hour or so, it felt good to be held by someone I trusted. It felt good to be able to let go.

'You're clearly as talented a spy as you are a singer,' he said softly, and just like before, when we caught each other's gaze in the mirror, it was as if something in the atmosphere shifted. I still didn't pull away though, and he held me tighter. 'I think about you all the time,' he whispered.

'I should think so too – you're my producer,' I quipped, thinking of that wedding ring on his finger.

'No, I don't mean...' He leaned back a little so he could look me in the eye. 'I mean I *think* about you.'

'Shouldn't you be thinking about your wife back in Chicago?'

'Yes, but...'

Finally, I broke away. If he had said, 'Yes, but our marriage is over,' or even the old chestnut, 'Yes, but she doesn't understand me,' I think I might have wavered. I liked Emilio, and the creative spark between us could have easily ignited into something else. But the fact that he fell silent seemed to say so much. His marriage wasn't over and his wife did understand him – he was just looking for a one-night thing, a chance to fool around while there was an ocean between them. It was a realisation that suddenly made me feel acutely empty.

'I think you should go. I'm feeling pretty tired – what with having to sing and make my undercover debut all in one night,' I added, wanting to show him that there were no hard feelings. I didn't want any awkwardness affecting our working relationship.

'Yes of course.' He took a step back, looking really embarrassed. 'I'm sorry, Sofia. I hope I didn't overstep the mark.'

'Of course not. It's been an eventful night. We weren't thinking straight.'

He gave a grin of relief. 'Excellent. Sleep well.'

I walked him to the door and locked it behind him, my feeling of emptiness increasing as I looked around the room. I wasn't the kind of woman who needed a man in order to feel whole or any of that kind of nonsense, but still. It would have been nice if for once I could have met a man who was both kind and single – and sober. Downstairs, I heard people laughing and chatting as they made their way to their cars, and my feeling of loneliness grew.

30

LISBON, 1941

Of course, I'm not one to stew in my own juices, so by the time I saw Emilio again – a week later at the Hotel Aviz – I'd given myself a stern talking-to and I was over my malaise. As he strode through the bar towards me, I extended my hand as if greeting a business acquaintance.

'I trust you'll be able to control yourself if we shake hands,' I said drily in greeting.

His face flamed red. 'I was kind of hoping you'd forgotten,' he said sheepishly.

'Forgotten what?' I gave him a brisk handshake and a wink.

He laughed. 'Thanks for being such a sport.'

'Well, at least you didn't vomit on me, and speaking of which...' We made our way to a table in the far corner, partially obscured by a silk screen with the picture of a lotus flower on it. 'Did you have any joy with the camera?'

He nodded and pulled his chair closer to mine. 'There were pictures on the microfilm that shouldn't have been there,' he whispered. 'Pictures of secret files – that would be extremely useful to the Germans.'

'Whoa!' I hadn't dared allow myself to get too excited about my find in case it didn't amount to anything. Hearing this made it all worthwhile.

Emilio grinned. 'Exactly.'

'So, what happened?'

'He's been dealt with,' he said with a knowing look.

'But won't he realise that I was the one who gave you the camera? He knows I was looking in his case. What if he's told the Germans?' My initial excitement gave way to feelings of alarm.

Emilio shook his head. 'He wasn't able to tell anyone anything. He was spirited off to Britain that evening before he'd even had a chance to leave his room.'

'Oh.' I felt a chill come over me.

'We shouldn't talk about it anymore here,' Emilio said, waving at a waiter. 'We don't know who could be listening.'

I glanced around the bar and nodded. It was starting to feel as if even the cutlery might have ears.

My debut album came out March, and Alexandre arranged a whirlwind of interviews to help publicise it. We had some practice interviews beforehand to make sure I had the fake story of my childhood straight, in which my father was a good-for-nothing ne'er-do-well and my mother a ghostly figure hovering in the background, doing nothing. It baulked a bit to portray my mother in such an insipid way, but I cared more about protecting the truth of her. I didn't see why I should serve up my personal details for all and sundry – surely my music should be enough for them? I did bare my soul in my songs after all.

But after the first couple of interviews, I started to enjoy it. It felt as if I was playing a role, and I became quite accomplished at pulling a harrowed expression as I denounced my brute of a father, and any time I felt the interviewer was getting a little too prying for comfort, I would instantly feign sorrow – even making tears spring to my eyes – telling them it was too painful to recount any more. All I had to do to make myself cry was think of my mother's final moments and the sound of the last breath escaping her parched lips, like the gasp of a baby bird. To this day, I can't think of the moment I lost her without welling up.

To promote the album, I did a tour around Portugal, returning to Lisbon to play at the Queen Maria II Theatre at the end of April. After the show, I was meant to be going for drinks with the band, but I couldn't bear the thought of being around people all wanting to know me – it felt fake. Because it was fake. They were only interested in my celebrity. So I made my excuses and slipped out of a fire exit and found myself walking down to the river.

It felt as if I was walking back in time as I thought back to my sixteen-year-old self treading this exact same path as she arrived in Lisbon. If I'd told that feisty kid that in just a few years she'd be a recording artist and singing on the best stages in the city, she would have been so excited I'm sure, but now it was all starting to feel like smoke and mirrors. There was a loneliness to fame and fortune that I hadn't anticipated.

I walked down to the edge of the Tagus and looked at the moon shimmering silver on the water. It wasn't that I wanted to go back to life as a *varina*, but I craved the companionship I felt in those days, the camaraderie, and of course, I missed Judith acutely. I gazed up at the sky and found a star shining brighter than the others and focused my gaze upon it.

'I'm not entirely sure that you exist,' I whispered – the opening line to most of my prayers to God – 'but if you do, I would really appreciate your help.'

I waited for a moment, as if expecting a booming voice from the heavens above to respond. But all I heard was music drifting from a bar somewhere.

I closed my eyes. 'Please bring me someone – someone I can be close to. Thank you!'

I opened my eyes and gave a sigh of relief. I still didn't know if God existed, but I felt better for speaking my desires out loud at least. I set off for the Aviz feeling comforted.

The next day I went for a meeting with Alexandre at his office.

'So, Sofia,' Alexandre said as soon as I sat down, 'how do you fancy singing in Queen's Hall?'

I frowned at him. 'The only Queen's Hall I've heard of is in London.'

Alexandre's smile grew. 'Exactly!'

'But... but...' I had so many questions, I didn't know where to begin.

'Your album is going over a storm in Britain, and the owner of your record label there has asked if there is any chance you'd consider playing a concert or two in London, to raise morale. They've been taking such a pounding by the Germans.'

I'd been reading all about the Blitz in the London papers. 'Are they still having concerts in spite of all the bombing?'

'Oh yes. It's incredible really.'

I nodded. I had to admit I was hugely inspired by their defiant spirit.

'But, of course, everyone would understand if you said no. It would be really dangerous – even flying there has its risks.'

I pursed my lips. 'I hope you're not implying that I'm a lily-livered coward.'

'No, of course not. Never!' he exclaimed with a laugh.

'Good, because I'd be delighted to do it. I always wanted to see London in the spring,' I added breezily and with all the naivete of one yet to experience a bombing raid.

'That's fantastic!' Alexandre leaped to his feet and lit us

both a celebratory cigarette. 'The Brits are going to love you for this; the benefits for your career will be huge, I'm sure.'

I shrugged off his gushing words. I wasn't interested in that. I was just so relieved to have something new to think of and a reason to leave Lisbon and my loneliness for a while. 'How long are you thinking of sending me for?'

'I think three days should be enough. It will give you the chance to do a show, and I'll try to set up an interview with a friend at the BBC. Then we'll need you back here to start recording some fresh material.'

'Sounds good.'

Alexandre picked up his phone. 'Fatima, could you bring us in some fizz – we're celebrating.'

A moment later, his secretary appeared with a bottle of champagne.

'So, what are you celebrating?' she asked, her normally sour face softening slightly.

'Oh, just that Sofia's song has done really well in Britain.'

Fatima gave a distinctly unimpressed nod and left.

'Why didn't you tell her the whole story – that I'm going to London?' I asked Alexandre as soon as she'd left. 'Then she might finally start to like me.'

Alexandre laughed. 'She does like you! She just doesn't like to smile.' His expression grew serious. 'We can't tell anyone – it's too risky. Not until after you've been and you're safely back home. There's way too many Luftwaffe buzzing around up there.' He looked skyward. 'We don't want to make your plane a target. By going to entertain the Brits, you'll be seen as siding with the enemy.'

'I'll be proud to be seen as an enemy of the Nazis!' I exclaimed, although his words caused my stomach to churn. The prospect of going on a plane for the first time was nerve-wracking enough, but the knowledge that the skies would be riddled with enemies was terrifying.

. . .

Two days later, Emilio came to see me in my room at the hotel. As soon as I opened the door to him, I blinked in shock. I'd never seen him look so dishevelled. His chin was covered in a dull shadow of stubble, and his hair looked greasy at the roots and greyer than ever at the temples.

'What the hell happened?' I asked. 'You look rougher than a bucket of fish guts.'

'Gee thanks.' He shook his head and sighed. 'I don't want to talk about it. But I do want to talk about your exciting news.'

I raised my eyebrows.

'You're going to London,' he whispered once I'd shut the door.

So much for Alexandre not telling anyone.

'Yes,' I whispered back. 'The Brits are crazy for me apparently. According to Alexandre's friend at the BBC, they think I'm' – I cleared my throat and put on my best British accent – '"a jolly good sport!"'

'Well, of course you are, old chap,' Emilio replied in his own hammed-up British accent. 'Seriously though, this is awesome news.'

'I know. Alexandre seems to think I could become a best-seller there if I just get a little more airplay.'

'Not only that.' He smiled. 'It's the perfect opportunity to help the Allies again.'

'Please tell me you don't have another drunken Brit lined up for me.' I rolled my eyes. 'I don't think my stomach could take it.'

He laughed. 'No, but you could pass some information on to them.'

'Information for who?'

'The SOE,' he whispered.

'The British secret service?'

'Yes. We have some information from the French Resistance. We can code it into some sheet music, which, of course, you would be taking for your concert so it wouldn't arouse any suspicion.'

'Of course. Who would I be passing it to?'

'One of their agents. His code name is Trafalgar. But don't worry about finding him,' he replied enigmatically. 'He will find you.'

And so, once again, the path of my life took a fateful twist. Although I had no idea at the time quite how much I would come to regret it.

31

PORTUGAL, 2000

'Perhaps now would be a good time to take a break,' Sofia says, leaning back on the sofa and closing her eyes.

'No!' I can't help exclaiming.

She looks at me quizzically.

'You can't leave it on such a cliffhanger,' I joke, although the truth is I'm deadly serious. I feel like she's getting close to the heart of her story now, and I'm scared that if she stops, she might decide against telling me what happened.

'I'm sorry, Lily, but I can't. I just don't have the energy.'

The afternoon sunlight is pouring through the window and falling like a spotlight upon Sofia's face, giving her parchment-like skin a translucent quality. She looks so tiny and vulnerable, like a baby bird, and it feels cruel to push her anymore.

'No problem at all,' I say softly. 'Can I get you anything? Something to eat? A drink?'

She gives me a grateful smile. 'No, thank you. If you don't mind, I think I'll take a little siesta.' She settles back on the cushions and pulls her blanket over her.

'Of course.' I gather my tape recorder, notebook and pen and take them upstairs.

The sea twinkles and shimmers in the sunlight through the window, and I feel a sudden burst of happiness. This is my life now. Whatever happens, I've made the break and I never have to go back to the lethargy and hopelessness of the last ten months. The realisation feels equal parts liberating and scary. But it's a good kind of fear. And learning Sofia's story is empowering. If she could find the courage to work for the Allies to help defeat the Nazis, then I can definitely find the courage to change my life for the better.

I plug my laptop into the internet and wait for the home page to load. I'll check my emails, then go down to the beach. It feels like a good time to start brainstorming ideas for exactly how I want my new life to be.

My home page finally loads and AOL cheerily informs me that I've got mail. Right at the top is a reply from Jane.

Dear Lily,

I can't tell you how happy I am to hear that it's going so well and that you're enjoying Portugal too. Please eat a pastel de nata – or ten! – for me. And please do keep me posted.

In other news, Laurence Bourne's autobiography has gone to the top of the Sunday Times chart again, after the release of his new film. I suggested a celebratory lunch with him once you're back from Portugal and he was only too happy to agree. Congratulations! I'm so happy to see things going so well for you again.

All my love,

Jane

As I read her words, I feel a warm glow of gratitude for this woman who has become so much more than an agent to me. My last set of foster parents were perfectly nice people and they kept me clean and fed, but I always felt a bit of a disconnect with them – a sense that I was one of many kids who'd passed through their home and they didn't really have the time or emotional bandwidth to really get to know and understand me. Over the years, Jane has come to fill that void, and knowing that she's always rooting for me means the world.

I quickly type a reply.

> Don't worry, plenty of custard tarts are being eaten! Thank you again for arranging this job for me. You were right. I think – or at least I hope – that it's going to be truly life-changing. I think it's just the jolt I needed to get me out of the butterfly soup. And that's amazing re: Lawrence's book! Really looking forward to that lunch!
>
> Lots of love,
>
> Lily

I look back at my inbox and see a message from my best friend Nikki. As soon as I read the title, I feel a little lurch in my stomach. 'Robin and Merrie.' Whenever Nikki and I have talked about Robin's new partner, we've always referred to her by her proper name, Meredith.

I open the email, dread growing in the pit of my stomach. *Hello,* it begins, another sign that all is not well. Normally, Nikki and I begin messages to each other with the lighter-sounding 'hey'. It seems like such a small thing, but in the familiarity of a long-term friendship, even one extra syllable can speak volumes.

I read on.

> I have something to tell you and as you're away I can't call you...

You could if you joined the rest of the world and bought a mobile phone, I think, but Nikki has remained resistant to the new mobile phone craze, convinced that it won't last.

> And this is something I'd much rather say to you over the phone – or in person – but I really don't want you to find out from someone else.
>
> Robin and Merrie have asked me and Dave to be godparents to their baby. I'm cringing as I type this as I really don't want to hurt you, but I'm in a bit of an awkward position as Dave really wants to do it – and he is Robin's best friend. I can't stress enough that I don't want to hurt you, and if you really don't want me to do it, just say so and I'll tell Robin. I'm sure they'll be able to find another godmother.
>
> I so wish I could call you, so do let me know if there's a number I can get you on in Portugal.
>
> I love you and I hope you're having a wonderful time.
>
> Nik xxxxxxxxx

I stare at the screen feeling shell-shocked. Although I logically know that it isn't Nikki's fault that Robin asked her to be godmother, the fact that it has happened – that Robin had the insensitivity to ask my best friend to be godmother to his baby, to the baby I wasn't able to have – feels like yet another punch to the gut.

I stand up and pull the internet cable from the wall. I am so, so sick of getting knocked back down every time I try to pick myself up.

Needing to do something with the disappointment and hurt growing inside of me, I march downstairs, out into the back garden and down onto the beach. Why couldn't Nikki have turned the role of godmother down without telling me? I wonder as I stalk across the sand. Does the fact that she did tell me mean that she really wants to be godmother and is hoping to get my blessing? But how can I give my blessing?

I picture Nikki and Dave standing at a church font with Robin and 'Merrie', all of them smiling and laughing at their adorable gurgling baby, and my hurt grows. If Nikki's life becomes inextricably linked to theirs, will I lose my best friend? It will probably be easier for her to be best friends with Meredith – especially as they will all have kids. A montage of happy family scenes starts playing in my mind. The two couples and their growing brood on shared holidays, birthday barbecues, Christmases. All scenes from the life I should have been living. The life I've been kicked out of because of my stupid, incompetent womb.

I reach the end of the cove and start scrambling across the rocks. Why did this have to happen? Why does it keep getting worse? I stand on a rock and look out at the sea.

'Why?' I yell at the top of my voice.

'Why what?' a man's voice calls back, causing me to freeze from a mixture of embarrassment and shock.

I take a moment to try to compose myself before turning around. Gabriel is standing beside the rocks in a pair of swimming shorts grinning up at me.

'Why do you always turn up?' I mutter.

'I live here,' he replies. 'So, actually, I should be asking you why you always turn up. Especially when you always interrupt my peace and quiet.'

Accepting that he does have a point and trying to ignore how tanned and muscular he looks in his trunks, I say, 'Fair enough,' and scramble back onto the sand.

'More bad news?' he asks.

'Yes, actually.'

'Wow.'

'What?'

'You seem to be a very unlucky person.' He shakes his head but is still grinning.

'Very funny.'

'It's true! One day, I have to rescue you from drowning and walking around naked. The next, you're here on the rocks yelling.'

'You didn't have to rescue me and I wasn't naked; I still had my underwear on, and you didn't have to stop me from yelling either. It was actually helping.'

His grin grows. 'Oh, I'm sorry. Please continue.'

'I can't with you watching.'

'Maybe I could join you. My day is not going so great either.' He pushes his wavy hair back from his face.

'Why not?' I ask, instantly curious.

'I got interrupted from my – how do you say? Treasure hunting.' He gestures at a pile of driftwood behind him on the beach. 'So, come on, let's yell together.'

'Really, it's OK. I—'

'Why?' he yells at the top of his voice. 'Why does this woman keep interrupting me?'

It's so theatrical and over the top, especially in his strong Portuguese accent, I can't help laughing.

'OK, OK, I'm sorry. I'll let you get back to your treasure hunting.' I turn to leave.

'Do you want to see what I found?' he asks.

'Oh, well...'

'It might cheer you up.'

'I don't need cheering up,' I snap.

'Is that so?' He tilts his head to one side and frowns.

'All right, if you insist,' I reply, feeling a little guilty for taking my frustration out on him.

As I follow him over to the pile of wood, I notice the tattoo of an ornate, old-style anchor in the small of his back. I pull my gaze away, back to the driftwood. 'What are you going to do with it?'

'I make things with it. Look, here is something I made yesterday.' He reaches into the pocket of his shorts and pulls out a little rooster carved from driftwood and hands it to me.

'Wait – did you make the driftwood lamp in the living room?'

He nods.

'Wow!'

'Why are you so surprised? Did you not expect a humble Portuguese fisherman to be capable of such things?' He raises his eyebrows.

'No! I didn't expect anyone to be capable of such things. They're really beautiful.'

He stares at me for a moment as if trying to decide something, then shakes his head as I attempt to hand the little rooster back to him. 'You keep it. It's a Barcelos Rooster, a traditional Portuguese symbol of good luck.'

'Oh, no, I—'

'I want you to,' he interrupts. 'Anyway, it seems like you need all the luck you can get at the moment.'

I have to admit that he does have a point, and his words bring a smile to my face. 'My life isn't that tragic, honestly. Well, it was until recently, but I'm trying really hard to change things.'

His smile fades. 'Is that so?'

'Yes. Why do you keep saying that?'

'What?'

'Is that so. You say it a lot.'

'Is that so?'

I start to laugh.

'Isn't it an English saying?' he asks.

'I suppose so, but I've never heard any English person say it as much as you do – at least not in this century.'

'Well, this century is only two months old so...' He grins.

'Damn, I keep forgetting!'

'You forget that it's a new millennium?' He stares at me in surprise. 'How could you have missed it?'

'Let's just say I wasn't really in the mood for celebrating.' I suppress a shudder as I think back to my pitiful New Year's Eve, lying in bed trying in vain to sleep while all of London erupted around me in fireworks and cheers. I'm not sure I'd ever felt so disconnected and alone.

'Is that so?' Gabriel says again and we both laugh, and for the first time since we met I feel the tension between us dissolve. I also feel a strange fluttering sensation in the pit of my stomach and it's so unfamiliar it takes me a moment to realise that it's a feeling of attraction.

No, no, no, I tell myself. This is definitely not the time or the place for that part of me to finally resurrect!

'Would you like to join me for a glass of wine?' he says, and the fluttering sensation grows stronger.

'Where?' I ask, trying to ignore my disobedient body. Surely Gabriel isn't suggesting we go into town after the way Sofia berated him for spending time with me. And we can hardly sit down over a bottle at the cottage!

'Right here,' he replies, and I watch as he fetches a rucksack from behind his pile of driftwood and pulls out a bottle of wine. 'I only brought one glass because I wasn't expecting company,' he says with a sheepish grin, 'but maybe we could share. I always have a glass of wine while I whittle,' he adds, gesturing to the wood.

I picture him sitting here in the sun while the sea laps at the shore, his tanned arms whittling away at the driftwood. His tanned, muscular, strong arms... *Oh for God's sake!*

'Yes, I'll have a drink,' I say, a lot more curtly than I'd intended.

We sit down on the sand, and Gabriel pours a glass of red wine and hands it to me.

'*Obrigada!*' I raise the glass before taking a sip, hoping it might help me relax.

'You are welcome,' he replies. 'So, would you like to tell me what's been bothering you? What made you yell at the sea? A problem shared is a problem doubled.'

I burst out laughing.

'Did I get that wrong?'

'Er, yes, I definitely don't want to double my problems, thank you.' I pass him the drink, and he takes a sip. It feels strangely intimate, this sharing a glass with him, and when he passes it back and our fingers briefly touch, I feel a jolt inside. It's so alien to me, I instantly feel awkward and embarrassed. I can't remember the last time I felt an attraction this strong to Robin – or if I ever did.

'What should I have said?' he asks.

'A problem shared is a problem *halved*.'

'Ah.' He nods. 'Well, go on then. Halve your problems with me.'

It's such a funny way to put it, yet it feels quite appealing.

I take another sip of wine for Dutch courage.

'I'm not able to have children,' I blurt out.

But instead of looking shocked or confused, Gabriel simply nods. 'Go on.'

'When I found out, my partner left me – for another woman.' To my surprise, I don't feel vulnerable sharing this, so I carry on, keeping my gaze fixed on the froth-tipped waves building and crashing further down the beach. 'And now the other woman is pregnant. They're going to have a baby together.' Gabriel remains silent, but it's a comforting silence so I keep talking. 'And they've asked my best friend to be the godmother. Her husband is my ex's best friend and they've asked him to be the godfather, so I suppose it makes sense, but still—' I break off, my eyes beginning to smart.

I hear a movement beside me and I realise that Gabriel has stood up. Instantly, my cheeks flush. I've said too much. He feels awkward and wants to leave. But instead he stands in front of me and holds out his hands.

'Come. Stand up,' he says softly.

Instinctively, I reach out and put my hands in his. They feel warm and strong and unlike Robin's hands, which always felt so soft. I can feel callouses on his palms. 'What are we doing?' I ask as he pulls me up.

'Going back to the rocks.'

I stand dead still. 'Why?'

'Because you have a lot more yelling to do.'

'I don't understand.'

'You deserve to be angry. You should be angry. I'm sorry I interrupted you. But now I'm angry too.'

'Why are you angry?' I stare at him, confused.

'Because of your piece-of-shit boyfriend. That was a... a...' He pauses as if searching for the right word. 'A diabolical thing to do.'

His feistiness reminds me of Sofia, and I can't help laughing.

'Why do you laugh?' he exclaims, although I can see the twinkle of a smile in his eyes. 'You need to get your anger out. Come on.' He leads me back to the rocks and gently guides me to where I'd been standing. 'OK, carry on yelling,' he says.

I give an awkward laugh. 'I feel a bit self-conscious.'

He gives a melodramatic sigh and pushes his hair back as the wind blows it into his eyes. 'I guess I will have to lead the way. What is your boyfriend's name?'

'Robin.'

'Ha!' He gives a knowing laugh. 'Like Batman's weedy sidekick.'

I giggle. 'Yes.'

Gabriel raises his arms to the sky and begins to yell. 'Robin, you are a piece of shit!'

I laugh even harder.

'Stop laughing, start yelling!' he calls to me above the crash of the waves.

'Robin, you're a piece of shit!' I yell, and it feels so good, the comedy of the situation instantly defusing my anger. 'And you're a piece of shit too, Meredith!' I cry. 'Meredith is his new woman,' I explain to Gabriel.

'Two pieces of shit, go to hell!' he yells enthusiastically.

'Yes, go to hell!' I scream, inspired by his passion. 'And my stupid follicles can go to hell too!' I cry.

'Your what?' He looks at me blankly.

'It's a medical thing,' I say.

'Oh, OK.' He clears his throat. 'Go to hell, stupid follicles!'

Hearing him yell this is so funny, I bend over double in a fit of giggles.

'Why are you laughing? You're supposed to be angry,' he says, looking genuinely confused, which only makes me laugh harder.

'It was just hearing you telling my follicles to go to hell,' I gasp, clutching my side. 'It was so funny. Thank you. You've made me feel so much better.'

His face lights up with a massive grin, and his obvious pleasure at having made me happy warms my heart. 'Shall we go back down?' he asks, gesturing at the sand.

'Yes, let's.'

He takes my hand and we carefully make our way across the slippery rocks. When we reach the sand, we exchange glances, and I feel another spark of attraction pass between us – or within me at least.

He gives my hand a squeeze before letting it go. 'I'm really sorry you went through all that,' he says quietly.

'Thank you – and for making me laugh.' I can't quite believe how much my mood has shifted.

'Of course. Any time!' he says with a grin.

'I should probably get back to the house,' I say, somewhat reluctantly. 'We probably woke Sofia from her nap with all our yelling, and I don't think she'd be too happy if she finds us together.'

He shrugs. 'Don't worry about her. I can handle her hot temper.'

'Is that so?' I reply drily, and he looks at me for a second before bursting out laughing.

'OK, OK, I shall try not to say it so often.' He picks up the driftwood rooster and hands it to me. 'Don't forget your Barcelos Rooster. I hope it brings you good luck.'

'*Obrigada*,' I reply, and then, as I turn to leave, I can't help adding, 'I think it already has.' I glance over my shoulder and see that he's grinning from ear to ear.

I return to the cottage with a spring in my step, ready for the next instalment in Sofia's untold story.

32

LISBON, 1941

I didn't sleep a wink the night before my flight, I was so nervous and excited. It didn't help that the plane was leaving at the crack of dawn from an airfield in Sintra – a resort town in the foothills of the mountains just outside of Lisbon – so it seemed pointless to even try to get some sleep as Alexandre was sending a driver to collect me at 4 a.m.

As I paced up and down my hotel room, I veered between excitement at flying for the very first time and fear of encountering the Luftwaffe – if not in the air then during one of their many bombing raids once I'd arrived in London. And on top of all that, I also had the issue of what to do with 'That Pesky Diamond' while I was away. I decided that taking it with me would be way too risky, so I hid it in a pot of cold cream, which I hid inside a glove, inside a hatbox, inside my wardrobe.

Thankfully, my driver was a man of few words, which suited me just fine as I was way too nervous to hold any kind of conversation. I sat snug inside my fur jacket on the back seat, gazing out of the window as we wove our way along the narrow hill roads. As the pre-dawn sky lightened from black to darkest blue, I could see the silhouettes of Sintra's grand villas and palaces on the horizon, like something out of a fairy tale. *Oh, Mama, if you could see me now*, I thought with a sigh. *I can, my darling*, I thought I heard her whisper back, although it could have been the breeze coming in the car window.

We arrived at the airfield, and after fetching my case from the trunk of the car, the driver grunted goodbye and a member of airport staff bustled me over to a camouflaged plane waiting by the runway. I tried not to think about the German plane parked just a few yards away. Although it was now operated by BOAC, Alexandre had explained to me that the plane I'd be taking had originally belonged to the Dutch airline KLM and had been flown to Britain before the German occupation of the Netherlands.

As I was shown up the steps and into the cabin, I saw a sign on the inside wall saying 'KLM – Still Flying', which was unexpectedly inspiring. There were about fourteen seats in total and the windows of the plane had all been covered with black cloth. I noticed some men sitting hunched over in the back seats, some of them sporting bandaged limbs or heads. As I took my seat in front, I overheard one of them talking quietly and realised that they were British, and although they were in civilian clothes I realised that, due to their injuries, they had to be soldiers – soldiers who had escaped the Nazis. I hugged myself to suppress a shiver.

Before we took off, the co-pilot, a Dutch man, addressed us all quietly, explaining that in order to avoid enemy aircraft, we would have to take a longer route to Britain, via the Bay of Biscay and, due to it being too dangerous to land anywhere near to London, we'd be going to a place called Whitchurch near a city called Bristol, in the west of England. I thought again of the German plane parked nearby and what Alexandre had said about the Luftwaffe, and I shivered again. The war was starting to feel ever closer and ever more real by the second.

· · ·

When we finally touched down at Whitchurch airfield, I felt a rush of anxiety. Alexandre had assured me that one of his music business contacts would be there to meet me, but what if they didn't show up? What would I do? I instantly scolded myself for being so pathetic. I would find the nearest train station and make my own way to London, that's what.

I stepped out of the plane and into a decidedly gloomy morning. The sky was heavy with grey clouds, pressing down on the surrounding fields. Not to worry, I reassured myself. The world would be a very boring place with relentless sunshine. Variety was the spice of life, and besides, weren't the Brits always moaning about the weather as they twirled their umbrellas? I was lucky to be getting the authentic British experience.

As my head buzzed with forced positive thoughts, I heard someone calling my name and saw a young woman in a tweed suit, with cheeks as rosy and plump as a pair of apples, waving at me.

'Miss Castello!' she called again, hurrying over.

'Hello!'

'Hello!' She looked at a scrap of paper in her hand. 'I'm Mary; I work for your record label here. Welcome to England,' she said in faltering Portuguese.

'Thank you very much, but don't worry, I speak English.'

'Oh you do – oh thank goodness!' She gave me a sheepish grin. 'I'd been practising really hard, but languages are definitely not my strongest suit.'

'It's fine, honestly.'

'OK, let's get to the station. I have a taxi waiting.'

She led me across the tarmac and into a small building, where a balding man was waiting. As soon as he saw me, his eyes seemed to pop out of their head.

'Good – good morning!' he stammered, backing away almost reverentially.

'Good morning,' I replied, shooting Mary a bemused look.

'He's clearly a fan,' she whispered as the man took my trunk and led us outside to a car.

In all the drama of the flight, I'd forgotten that I was coming somewhere I was already well known. It was quite a surreal realisation.

'Please, allow me,' he said, opening the back passenger door for me with a flourish.

'Why, thank you,' I replied, rather enjoying myself. It felt a little like being in a British film, and I had to be careful not to slip into my hammy British accent.

After a relatively short car journey, which I spent face pressed to the window, drinking in my first sights of Britain, we arrived in Bristol and pulled up outside the station. After Mary had paid the driver and he'd bid me a fond farewell, we made our way inside.

'I'm really glad you're here,' I said to her as she fished around in her bag and produced two train tickets. 'I don't think I'd have ever found this place on my own. I haven't seen a single road sign.'

She grinned. 'That's to confuse the Germans.'

I frowned at her. 'Now you've confused me too. What do you mean?'

She laughed. 'In case they invade. We've taken all of the road and station signs down so they won't know where they're going.'

I laughed at the thought of hundreds of German soldiers all scratching their heads as they stumbled around the British countryside. But then the gravity of what she'd said hit me.

'You don't think they will invade, do you?'

'I hope not, but I can't help thinking it's only a matter of time.' She gave me a grateful smile. 'That's why it's so wonderful of you to come now. Your fans here are going to love you even more for it. It's such a brave thing to do.'

'Oh, it'll take more than Hitler to scare me off,' I quipped, but my skin erupted in a clammy sweat. What if the Germans invaded while I was here? What if I wasn't able to return to Portugal? The dark grey clouds seemed to press down even lower, and the air felt too cold and damp to breathe. Thankfully, at that moment there was a piercing whistle and a train came chugging down the track towards us.

'All aboard!' Mary cried gaily as it came creaking and hissing to a stop beside us.

The door closest to us opened and a guard leaped down onto the platform.

'Good morning, Miss,' he said to Mary before turning to me. 'Good morning, M—' He broke off mid-sentence, frowning. 'Don't I know you from somewhere?'

'No, I'm sure you don't!' Mary exclaimed before bustling me onto the carriage. 'Don't worry,' she muttered as we made our way along the narrow corridor. 'I booked us our own compartment, so hopefully you won't be bothered for the rest of the journey.'

'Oh, it's no bother,' I replied. The truth was, I was really touched that the Brits had taken me to their hearts at a time when so much was at stake. It was humbling, and it made me want to do anything I could to repay their kindness.

I thought of the sheet music that Emilio had given me the night before, now tucked inside my case. Whatever had been coded into the music had been extremely well hidden as I'd tried my hardest to find it but hadn't been able to. I just hoped it would help the mysterious Trafalgar person it was bound for.

As the train chugged its way through the British countryside, Mary talked me through my itinerary for the next few days.

'Your show is on Saturday at Queen's Hall, and you're having dinner at the Savoy tonight with Bertrand Montague, the owner of your record label and my boss, and—'

'Wait a second, do you mean *the* Savoy?" I stared at her in surprise.

'Yes, of course – that's where you'll be staying. And hopefully you'll get a chance to do some sightseeing too. Although I'm afraid some of the London sights are looking a little the worse for wear thanks to Jerry and their blasted bombs.' Mary's plummy accent made her sound like a Pathé newsreader.

I nodded gravely. 'Has it been as bad as they say in the papers?'

'Oh yes, they bombed us every night for fifteen nights at the start of the Blitz,' she said wearily.

The thought of Lisbon being bombed for fifteen nights straight was too enormous and horrifying to comprehend. How had the British been able to live through this? 'And now?'

'Most nights – unless there's no moon or it's foggy.'

'Why unless there's no moon?'

'The bombers can't see their targets as well in the total darkness. On a clear night with a full moon, it's terrible. We've come to expect a real drubbing.'

My heart sank as I thought of the moon I'd seen on my way to the airport that morning. It had been pretty fat, but was it waxing or waning?

'But you mustn't worry,' Mary said, as if reading my mind. 'The Savoy has a wonderful bomb shelter. It even has its own dance floor!'

I tried to imagine a bomb shelter with a dance floor but drew a blank. The pictures in the *Daily Mail* all showed Londoners huddled together on the platforms of underground stations, or in weird little corrugated metal shelters, crammed together like sardines in a tin.

I sat back in my seat and wiped some of the condensation from the window so I could look out. As I gazed at the leaden sky and barren fields, I felt as if I'd travelled to another world.

33

LONDON, 1941

We arrived in London several hours later, and the first thing that struck me as we made our way across the concourse was how normal it seemed – or normal in the context of the footage and films I'd seen of London before the war. The place bustled with people on their way home from work. Suited men in bowler hats and the obligatory umbrellas tucked under their arms, and smartly dressed women in tight skirts and heels. Then I saw a soldier and another and another, with kitbags slung over their shoulders. They all looked so young and their expressions so sober. I wondered where they were headed. Or perhaps they were home on leave. Either way, it was a jolt to the system, and the contrast with Portugal was stark. Back home, people often joked that Hitler would be able to conquer Portugal just by making a telephone call, our lack of military was so laughable.

We emerged from the station, and Mary hailed a black taxi-cab, the kind I'd seen many times in films, but to see one in the flesh so to speak was a real thrill.

'The Savoy, please,' Mary instructed the driver as we clambered into the back.

I watched from the window, my heart in my mouth as we

made our way along the London streets. Evidence of the Blitz was all around. There were piles of sandbags by doors and windows, and jagged craters pockmarked the road. I knew from reading the London papers that the large signs with the letter S signalled air raid shelters. We turned up a side street, and I couldn't help gasping as I saw a building with the entire front blown off. It was like looking inside a giant doll's house as I saw a living room on the second floor, all the furniture still in place, and pictures still hanging on the walls.

'What happens to the families who live in the bombed buildings?' I asked Mary.

'They have to go and stay with relatives or friends,' she replied. 'My poor auntie Beryl had to go and live with her mother-in-law in Harrow after her house got bombed, and between you and me, I think she would rather have moved in with Hitler.'

I couldn't help laughing at this. 'Oh dear.'

'Indeed.'

When we arrived at the Savoy, a bellboy in a pristine uniform came running over to carry my case.

'I'll see you to your room, then let you get freshened up before your dinner with Bertrand,' Mary said as we walked up to the grand main entrance.

As we drew closer, I saw that the glass panels in the revolving door had been painted dark blue.

'The glass has been painted for the blackouts,' Mary explained, clearly noting my puzzled gaze.

'Oh, of course.'

One thing refugees always commented on when they arrived in Lisbon was how great it was to see so many lights shining at night, unlike the rest of Europe, blanketed in blackouts night after night.

'Wow!' I gasped as we stepped inside the lobby. I was used to glamorous hotels in Lisbon, but this was beyond anything I'd ever seen. Music and chatter drifted over from a bar at the back.

'That's the American Bar,' Mary said. 'Feel free to go and have a drink before your dinner if you'd like. The new bombproof restaurant is down the stairs over there.' She pointed to a doorway. 'They moved it downstairs once the war started, and it's right by the shelter, which is down in the basement.'

As Mary checked me in, I pictured the swanky guests all huddled together in a darkened basement. It was certainly the most memorable hotel check-in I'd ever experienced.

Once Mary had got my key, she accompanied me up to my room on the third floor. 'In the event of an air raid, you need to go down to the basement as quickly as possible, but make sure you take the stairs, not the lift.'

'Why not the lift?' I asked, thinking that surely it would be quicker.

'You don't want to get trapped in it if a bomb were to hit the building.'

'Oh yes, of course.' I wanted to kick myself for sounding so stupid.

'But it hasn't been hit since November, so hopefully you'll be fine.'

'The hotel was bombed in November?' I tried saying this as calmly as possible, but my voice came out like a squeak.

'Yes, they got the roof,' she says as matter-of-factly as if she was talking about the weather.

As she unlocked the door, I clenched my free hand into a tight fist. The war was becoming more and more real with every second.

'I had some essentials delivered to your room ahead of your arrival,' she said, pointing to the huge four-poster bed. It was the kind of bed with curtains around it that kings and queens sleep in in fairy tales. On the bed there was a folder, an envelope and a strange-shaped shiny leather case with a long strap just like the one she was wearing.

'What is this?' I asked, going over and picking it up.

'Your gas mask – just in case Jerry decide to drop a poisoned bomb on us.'

'Would they do that?' I stared at her, horrified.

'Well, they had no hesitation in using mustard gas in the trenches in the Great War,' she replied. Then, clearly sensing my fear, she added, 'But, having said that, we've had the masks since 1939 and they haven't gassed us yet, which is really annoying because they're so cumbersome to carry around.' She rolled her eyes.

I fought the urge to make a jibe about carrying a container being a hell of a lot worse than a dose of poisoned gas. 'Perhaps we ought to jazz them up a little, add some sequins or something, to make them a fashion accessory,' I joked instead, wanting to show her that I wasn't fazed – although, of course, I was.

'Excellent idea!' she exclaimed before checking her watch. 'I'll leave you to get settled and freshen up. You have an hour and a half before your dinner.'

I fought the urge to beg her to stay. The prospect of being left on my own in a city under almost constant bombardment was unsettling to say the least. How I wished Judith were there. I felt a wistful pang as I realised that if only I'd been able to keep her safe, I could have brought her with me to England. She might be at the mercy of the bombers, but at least the Nazis weren't snatching innocent people off the London streets.

I forced my mouth into a cheery smile. 'OK, great, thank you.'

After she left, I browsed around the room, taking in the velvet drapes and the mahogany furniture and the creamy thick stationery on the desk. But I couldn't fight the jittery feeling, and much to my annoyance, the loneliness I'd been fighting off at home in Portugal, which I'd hoped this trip would alleviate, rushed back with a vengeance. It must have been triggered by thoughts of Judith.

I went through to the bathroom and saw a sight that instantly lifted my spirits – a beautiful kidney-shaped bath on brass legs with clawed feet. I turned on the taps and searched for the complimentary jar of bath salts. It was smaller than I'd imagined a hotel like the Savoy having. A card had been propped against it – the elegant script explaining that they'd had to cut back due to the rations. I felt a guilty pang that while the rest of Europe was suffering so much, Portugal should have more than enough. As if it would make any difference, I refrained from using any bath salts.

I took off my clothes and stepped into the warm water, and as I sank down, the warmth began soothing me and I got my thoughts in order. I didn't need to feel guilty – I'd come to Britain to help, and not just by boosting morale through my singing. I thought of the sheet music in my case and wondered when the member of the British SOE, Trafalgar, would get in touch.

I smiled at the code name. What would I choose for my spy name? I wondered. Pastel de Nata perhaps, or maybe Sardine. But before I could think up any more ludicrous names, the air filled with a piercing wail and my skin erupted in goosebumps. It was something I'd heard in films and newsreels but never in real life before. The unmistakable sound of an air-raid siren.

34

LONDON, 1941

I quickly scrambled from the bath, my wet feet slipping and sliding on the marble floor as I gathered up my discarded clothes. Damn, damn, damn, why did I have a bath? I put my dress back on but didn't bother with my stockings, and slipped my shoes onto my still damp feet. I needed to get downstairs as soon as possible.

I grabbed my suitcase and slung my gas mask over my shoulder and hurried out into the corridor. It was totally deserted, but I assumed most guests were out already or downstairs in the restaurant or bar. I hurried down the stairs – down and down and by the time I got to the bottom I was red-faced and out of breath. I saw some hotel staff ushering guests along a corridor, so I followed them. None of them were carrying luggage or their gas masks, I noted and felt a little embarrassed.

We reached a door with a tower of sandbags either side, and I was ushered inside. I'd been expecting to emerge into a darkened cellar-like space, but it was nothing of the sort. A female member of hotel staff greeted me with a smile, asking for my room number, and then I was whisked off to a cubicle with a bed that might not have been as fancy as the four-poster in my room but was just as comfortable, and made with the same fancy green, blue and pink bed linen.

I sat on my bed watching as other guests started pouring in. Most were British, talking in clipped regal tones, but there were some Americans too, and I began to distract myself from the fear of an imminent bomb strike by imagining backstories for them. The chain-smoking American guy in the baggy suit was a journalist, I decided. The elderly woman in a fur coat and pearls, a member of the British royal family.

As I thought of the royal family, I remembered what Emilio had said about Edward, the man who would have been king. It was chilling to think that while ordinary Brits endured so much in their fight for Europe's freedom, some of those at the very top of their society were betraying them, like that creep Sinclair. I felt a surge of pride that I'd helped catch him.

After an hour or so, the all-clear sounded.

'Must have been a false alarm,' I heard one of the hotel staff say to a guest.

'For now,' the guest replied ominously as I walked past. 'We're bound to get a visit tonight, especially with the moon getting fuller.'

My heart sank. I'd been so excited about my first trip to Britain, but I was fast learning the realities of living in a country at war and embarrassed at my naivety.

After returning to my room to get changed, I hurried downstairs for my dinner date. I wasn't entirely sure if my guest would even be there, given the commotion with the air-raid siren, but when I told the maître d' my name, he gave an instant smile of recognition and led me over to a table in the corner, where a ruddy-faced middle-aged man with slicked-back grey hair was sitting sipping on a cocktail. As soon as he saw me approaching, he leaped to his feet.

'Sofia Castello!' he exclaimed, clapping his hands together. 'I'm Bertrand Montague. Welcome to Britain!'

'Thank you so much,' I replied, shaking his hand. His palm was clammy and his fingers squidgy. 'I'm sorry I'm a little late. I was down in the shelter due to the siren going off and—'

'Oh goodness me, no need to apologise!' he interrupted. 'We're so used to it by now, hardly anything or anyone is on time anymore, which is a godsend for people like me.' He grinned, revealing what looked suspiciously like a set of false teeth. 'I've always been a terrible timekeeper.'

I laughed. "Yes, I suppose you always have the perfect excuse now.'

'Exactly.'

A waiter appeared at our table, like a penguin in his smart black-and-white uniform.

'What would you like?' Bertrand asked but almost immediately held up his hand as if to stop me from replying. 'No, no, I know what you must have – one of their White Lady cocktails. They're renowned for them. The London dry gin is exquisite'

If a man had done this to me back in Portugal, I would have deliberately ordered something different, just to establish that I could make my own choices thank you very much, but feeling slightly vulnerable being all alone in a strange city and one that was regularly being bombed to boot, I put my pride aside for the sake of diplomacy.

'That sounds perfect,' I said, smiling sweetly.

'Excellent! Well, off you go then,' he said dismissively to the waiter, instantly making me bristle again.

'Yes of course,' the waiter, who was barely more than a kid, stammered, his cheeks flushing red. 'I just thought you might like to order some food?'

'Good heavens, give us a chance, boy,' Bertrand boomed. 'We haven't even looked at our menus yet.'

The waiter backed off, muttering his apologies, and I saw that diners at the nearby tables were all staring at us curiously.

'I'm sorry,' Bertrand said to me, shaking his head. 'The Savoy would never have employed someone like that before the war. Trouble is, all our best men are off fighting.'

Is that why you're here then? I felt like responding, I was so annoyed at how he'd treated the waiter. But I forced another smile. 'Maybe it's his first night working here.'

'Maybe,' he sniffed. 'Anyway, we have way more important things to talk about. Firstly, thank you so much for coming to Britain. I can't tell you how much we appreciate it. Did Mary take care of you?'

'Oh yes, she was very—'

'She can be a bit of a wet lettuce leaf,' he interrupted, 'but she is reliable.' He leaned forward conspiratorially. 'That's the one good thing about dull, mousy girls – they're very reliable.' He leaned back and gave a hoot of laughter.

I'd never had to work so hard to control the muscles in my face responsible for withering stares. How on earth was I going to spend an entire meal in the company of this pompous fool? I found myself in the strange position of almost wishing for the air-raid siren's wail, although the thought of being trapped in the Savoy shelter with him was even harder to bear.

'I found Mary to be exceptionally well organised,' I replied, desperately wanting to leap to her defence.

'Exactly!' he cried, so loudly it made me cringe.

I glanced at the table beside ours and saw a young man peering over his menu at me. I could have been mistaken, but his eyes seemed to be twinkling with amusement. I suppressed a sigh and looked back at Bertrand.

'Your fans are so excited for your shows,' he said, 'as are the musicians we've got lined up to play with you. Speaking of which, will you be able to go to a rehearsal with them tomorrow?'

'Of course.' I felt a burst of excitement. It would be so interesting to meet some British musicians. Hopefully they wouldn't be as insufferable as Bertrand. But even if they were, it would be great to get back to my music and the comfort it always brought me.

The waiter returned with our cocktails on a tray. His hands were shaking so much, I could hear the rattle of the glass on the silver.

'Thank you very much,' I said, taking my drink and treating him to the biggest, most heartfelt smile I could muster.

His face flushed and he smiled back.

'Are – are you ready to order any food yet?' he asked nervously.

I cringed, preparing for Bertrand's inevitable tirade as we still hadn't looked at the menu.

'Yes, we'll have the steak,' Bertrand replied.

Well, this was an arrogant assumption too far as far as I was concerned. '*He'll* have the steak,' I said through gritted teeth, 'but I'd like something different. Tell me' – I smiled sweetly at the waiter – 'do you have any fish dishes?'

'Oh, yes, we do,' he said gratefully and picked up a menu.

I glanced at Bertrand while the waiter was showing me the fish dishes and saw, to my satisfaction, that his cheeks had gone a purplish shade of red. I ordered salmon, and as the waiter left the table, I noticed the young man on the table adjacent to ours raise his glass to me as if to say, 'Well played.' Now he no longer had a menu hiding his face, I saw that he really was quite attractive with his thick shock of dark hair and large blue eyes. I stifled a smirk and looked back at Bertrand.

'Once a fish woman, always a fish woman, eh?' he said with a smile, but there was a meanness in his eyes now which made it clear he meant it as an insult. But what dimwits like him fail to realise is that when a person is truly happy with who they are and where they've come from, such pathetic insults fall on deaf and disinterested ears.

'Absolutely!' I exclaimed, raising my glass and shooting a glance at the adjacent table. The young man grinned at me again.

I somehow made it through the entirety of the main course as Bertrand waxed lyrical about his various talents as a fox hunter, record label owner and, of course, entertainments producer, through mouthfuls of steak and potatoes. As far as I was concerned, his only talent was being an insufferable bore, and the only thing that kept the evening entertaining was exchanging knowing looks with the man at the next table. When he paid his bill and got up to leave, I could barely contain my disappointment.

As soon as I'd finished my dinner, I picked up my bag and stood up. 'Please excuse me, but I need to use the bathroom.'

'Of course,' Bertrand replied, taking a cigar from his jacket pocket.

The thought of him spouting clouds of foul-smelling cigar smoke at me was even more unbearable, and as I got out into the corridor, I fought the urge to march up the stairs and out onto the London streets. If it hadn't been for the threat of an air raid at any minute, I might have done just that. Instead, spirits flagging, I went into the ladies' room and locked myself in a cubicle.

'My God, what an insufferable idiot,' I began ranting in Portuguese, taking advantage of the fact that the room was empty. '"Once a fish woman always a fish woman,"' I mimicked, slamming my hand on the wall in frustration. 'What a pompous idiot.'

'Oh, how I wish I knew what you were saying,' a man said from the cubicle next to mine, causing me to almost jump out of my skin.

I'd been so sure that the bathroom was empty. Then a terrible thought occurred to me – had I been so blinded by my annoyance with Bertrand that I'd come into the men's room by accident? There were a few moments of silence and I dared to hope I might have imagined the voice.

'I bet there were a fair few choice swear words in there,' the man continued. He had an English accent, but it wasn't prim and proper like Bertrand's or Mary's. It was much softer round the edges. Unfortunately, it only served to increase my embarrassment.

I cleared my throat and attempted to compose myself. 'I'm very sorry,' I said. 'I appear to have come into the wrong bathroom.' I took a breath and opened the door. The door of the cubicle next to mine was now closed, but I could have sworn it was open when I'd come in. 'Sorry for disturbing you. Please continue with your business.'

As soon as the words left my mouth, I stared at my reflection in the mirror above the sink in horror. *Please continue with your business?* But before I could flee in shame, I saw the door behind me slowly start to open in the mirror.

'Oh, you didn't disturb me at all,' the voice said. 'And you didn't come into the wrong bathroom either.'

I gaped at the mirror as the man from the table next to mine stepped out of the cubicle, staring at my reflection intently. I instinctively gripped the edge of the sink. He might have seemed all friendly and fun in the restaurant, but following me into the dimly lit bathroom put a way more sinister spin on things, and now his twinkling eyes seemed to have taken on a menacing glint.

35

LONDON, 1941

'*Al credo!*' I muttered under my breath as the man came and stood beside me. He was now wearing a fedora hat and an overcoat, his hands thrust into the pockets. Torn between whether to attack or flee, I remained rooted to the spot.

'What does that mean?' he asked, meeting my gaze in the mirror.

'Oh God,' I muttered, finally coming to my senses. 'I need to get back to my dinner guest,' I said in my most efficient and businesslike tone, as if there wasn't anything remotely peculiar about this turn of events at all.

'But do you *want* to?' he asked.

'What do you mean?' I turned to look him in the face. *Show no fear,* I imagined my mother whispering – the advice she always gave me when I was little and frightened of the stray dogs that roamed our neighbourhood. *Make them think that you're the leader of the pack.* I pulled my shoulders back and stood a little taller.

'From what I could tell, your dinner guest is what we Londoners would call a right old bottle and glass.'

I stared at him blankly. 'I take it that isn't a good thing.'

'No. It's a very bad thing, trust me. So, I have a suggestion.' He smiled, causing the skin at the corners of his eyes to crinkle and a dimple to appear in his right cheek. It was hard to be afraid of someone who looked so boyish and happy, so I allowed myself to relax a little.

'Go on.'

'Why don't you escape with me?'

'Hmm, are you proposing that I leave the safety of this hotel with a man I know nothing about who has just followed me into the ladies' bathroom?' I said sternly, although he was so affable his proposition seemed a lot less menacing than it might have done coming from someone else.

'Yes, exactly!' he exclaimed, clearly missing my point – or choosing to miss it. 'But I ought to state for the record that I didn't actually follow you.'

'What, this is all just some bizarre coincidence?' I smirked. 'Do you make a habit of using the ladies' bathroom then?'

He remained annoyingly unfazed. 'No, I guessed you'd come in here. I knew you'd need a reason to get away from that bottle and glass, and excusing yourself to go to the bathroom was the most obvious one.'

'Can you please tell me what a bottle and glass means? Obviously I know what a bottle and glass are, but why is it an insult?'

'It's cockney rhyming slang, innit. Bottle and glass – arse.' He grinned and pointed to his backside, and I had to bite my lip to stop myself from smiling.

'I see. Well, for your information, I was contemplating walking straight out of the hotel, he was so insufferable.'

'There you go then!' he said with a cheeky grin.

'There I go where?'

'Escape with me. It makes total sense, seeing as you were going to leave anyway.'

'But I'm a guest here. And the bottle and the glass, as you

call him, is a work colleague of mine. And... and there could be an air raid.'

'So? So? So?' He grinned, causing that annoyingly cute dimple to appear again.

'What do you mean?'

'Who cares about any of that?'

'I do.'

'Do you though?' He sighed. 'I had you down as being way more fearless.'

'I am! But...'

'You're scared?'

'No!' I stared at him defiantly. And I really wasn't by this point. I was too annoyed at his impudence.

'Perhaps I could take you to *Trafalgar* Square,' he said.

'I have no need for a tour guide, thank you very—' I broke off. 'Wait a minute, where did you say?'

'*Trafalgar* Square.' His grin returned. 'It's very nice this time of year. I hear they might even have some *music* there.'

'You're—' I broke off again.

'Yes,' he said, lowering his voice. 'I am your contact and it's a pleasure to meet you!' He tipped his hat at me. 'They didn't tell me who I'd be meeting, just that it would be a musician. I thought it was going to be some crusty old tuba player, so when I saw you come into the restaurant, I couldn't believe my luck.'

'And what on earth makes you think your luck is in?' I said sharply.

He at least had the grace to blush. 'Oh no, I didn't mean my luck was in. I meant, you look like excellent company – unlike your dinner guest.'

'Hmm.' I gave him one of my most withering stares, but I had to admit, I was starting to feel like my luck was in too. Now I knew who the man was, and why he was in the bathroom, I could fully relax.

'So, how about it?' he said. 'I don't mean to rush you, but I don't have much time left.'

'How very dramatic. Why, are you about to expire?' I arched an eyebrow.

'No!' he exclaimed. 'I mean before I get caught loitering in a woman's bathroom. I don't think they look too kindly on that kind of thing here at the Savoy.'

I nodded. 'Ah yes, you could have a point.'

'So, what do you say? Do you fancy a night out on the town with me?'

'But aren't I supposed to give you—'

'Yes, I know,' he interrupted. 'But I can collect the music from you later. Let's go and have some fun before there's another bloody air raid.'

I instantly relaxed some more. He was clearly who he said he was, and the prospect of throwing caution to the wind and seizing the moment certainly appealed to my sense of adventure. 'OK. Let's go.'

We hurried into the corridor and upstairs to the lobby.

'You go ahead; I'll meet you outside,' I said to Trafalgar before asking one of the receptionists to tell Bertrand that I'd been taken ill and had retired to my room. Something told me that I wouldn't be caught out as he wasn't nearly empathetic enough to think of checking I was OK.

Once the receptionist had left for the restaurant, I hurried outside and onto the street. It was so dark, it took a moment to spot Trafalgar, who was leaning against an unlit street light smoking a cigarette.

'You came,' he said with a grin as I hurried towards him. 'I thought you might have chickened out.'

'You thought what?'

He laughed. 'Chickened out. I'm guessing you don't have that saying in Portugal. It means to be too scared to do something.'

'I'm not too scared to do anything,' I retorted. I'd wanted to appear cool, but as soon as I said it, I felt idiotic. For some reason, the twinkly-eyed Trafalgar was denting my impenetrable armour.

'Oh really?' He looked at me, clearly amused.

'Yes. So where are you taking me then – on this grand tour of London?'

'I'm going to take you somewhere real,' he replied.

'And this wasn't real?' I gestured at the grand silhouette of the Savoy.

'Not really, no. Not for most Londoners, any 'ow.'

I was becoming intrigued by his accent. 'Where are you from?' I asked as we started walking along the street. It was bustling with people all doing an awkward dance of trying not to bump into each other in the dark.

'London!' he replied indignantly, as if offended that I didn't know.

'I'm sorry, I didn't mean to... It's just that your voice is so different to the other people I've met.'

He stopped walking. 'Clearly you haven't met any proper Londoners then,' he said. 'But don't worry, we're gonna fix that.'

'OK then,' I replied, feeling more intrigued by the minute.

'Quick,' he called, 'there's the bus.'

I ran after him to the corner of the street, where one of the iconic red double-decker London buses had come to a halt. Trafalgar leaped onto the opening at the back and held his hand out to me. I ignored it and jumped on just as the bus pulled away.

'We timed that well,' he called, ushering me up the curving stairs to the top deck. 'It's a shame it's not light,' he said as we sat in the seat at the very front. 'This is one of the best ways to see London.'

'That's OK, I can still see some things,' I replied, peering out. An almost full moon hung in the sky in front of us, casting the buildings of London in an ethereal glow. It was all quite magical, until I remembered what I'd overheard in the shelter earlier. The moonlight made it easier for the German bombers to see too. I shivered and sat back in the seat.

'You cold?' he asked, about to take off his jacket.

'No, I'm OK, thanks,' I replied, but I appreciated the gesture and the fact that he'd noticed. 'So where is this real part of London you're taking me to then?' I asked.

'We're going to start at Billingsgate,' he said.

'What is that?'

'A fish market. I thought you might like it.'

I instantly bristled. Was he mocking me the way Bertrand had? 'If that's meant to be a joke, you're wasting your time,' I said curtly. 'I'm proud to have been a *varina*, and I will be until my dying day.'

To my surprise, he looked genuinely shocked. 'Of course it isn't a joke. I know all about your background. It's why I like you as a singer. I really admire people who've worked hard to get where they are.'

Now it was my turn to be shocked. I hadn't been sure if he even knew who I was other than being a musician.

'I thought you might be interested. I read an article about you in the *Evening Standard* when your song "This Doll" came out,' he continued. 'I loved the fact that you went from selling fish to singing smash-hit records. That was what interested me the most about you.'

'Why?' I asked, trying to work out if he was just feeding me a line.

'Because it gave you substance,' he replied matter-of-factly. 'And it made me look up *varinas* in the Encyclopaedia Britannica.'

'Really?' If he was feeding me a line, he was going to extraordinarily detailed lengths.

'Yes, which made you even more intriguing.' He looked out

of the window. 'We don't have to go to Billingsgate if you don't want, but I thought it might be fun. And it's a beautiful building.'

'OK, I'm sold – let's do it.' I glanced sideways at him and saw that he was grinning from ear to ear.

The bus continued trundling its way along the street, collecting more passengers as it went. To my surprise, everyone appeared to be in good cheer. It must have been the infamous Blitz spirit I'd read about in the British newspapers. I had to admit it was very impressive. How people managed to get on with their lives in the face of such relentless bombing was beyond me.

We turned a corner, and I saw a huge crater between two of the buildings and couldn't help gasping.

'There used to be a row of shops there,' Trafalgar said. 'Got hit by a parachute mine – destroyed the whole lot.'

As I stared out at the crater, I thought of the Great Lisbon earthquake of 1755 which destroyed most of the city. The bombed-out buildings in London reminded me a little of the Carmo Convent, one of the few buildings to survive the earthquake, although the stone roof of the church was completely destroyed and never rebuilt. But of course, the empty shell of the church hadn't been caused by other human beings. Knowing that the devastation in London had chilled me to the core.

We reached another turning, and I saw water shimmering in the dark.

'And there on our right we have the River Thames,' Trafalgar said, adopting the official tone of a tour guide.

At that moment, a conductor appeared and issued us with tickets, which Trafalgar paid for. As the conductor gave me mine, he stared at me curiously.

'Is that? Is she...?'

'My cousin Mildred from Wolverhampton?' Trafalgar said

quickly. 'Yes, indeed she is.'

'Oh.' The conductor set off along the swaying upper deck, looking disappointed.

'I hope you don't mind me saying that,' Trafalgar said apologetically. 'I just assumed that you didn't want to be recognised.'

'I don't, so thank you.'

'There's London Bridge.' He leaped up and pressed a button that rang a bell.

We went downstairs and leaped off the back of the bus as it came to a stop. This time, he didn't offer me his hand, which I felt strangely disappointed by, even though I would have obviously batted it away.

'I've decided to make a slight alteration to my tour,' he said, sweeping his hand out and gesturing across the water. 'First stop, the Tower of London.'

I peered across the river to a building with thin slits of light shining from its walls. 'I thought there was a blackout,' I said, puzzled. 'I can see the lights inside.'

'Yes, they had a few problems blacking out the old gun slits in the tower walls, so now, at the first sign of an air raid, an electrician cuts the power to the tower instead.'

'Ah, I see.' I looked back at the thin slits of light feeling slightly comforted. As long as they were shining, there was no attack imminent.

'Do you know about the history of the tower?' Trafalgar asked as we began walking across the bridge towards it.

'I know about the child princes who were murdered in their sleep. My mother told me the story of them when I was a kid. She loved history.'

'Your mother?' He looked at me, confused.

'Yes, why should that be such a surprise?'

'I thought she...' He fell silent, and I realised what must have happened.

'Ah, I guess the article you read about me talked about my tragic backstory of alcohol, neglect and abuse.'

'Yes, I'm sorry, I'm not prying at all. I'm sure you don't want to talk about it.'

Normally, this would be my cue to feign distress and change the subject, but for some strange reason, it felt important that Trafalgar should know the truth about me and, more importantly, my mother. He was a member of the SOE after all – surely he could be trusted with a secret.

'My backstory is – how should I put this...' I paused for a moment. 'A complete work of fiction.'

He looked at me and laughed. 'Really?'

'Yes, but you can't tell anyone. It was my manager's idea. He thought it would help capture the public's imagination and sympathy. And, to be honest with you, I didn't mind at all. I prefer keeping the truth about my mother and my childhood private.'

'What about your father?'

'I never knew him. So, I suppose you could say he was neglectful. But there was no alcoholism or abuse. Sorry.'

'Don't apologise!' he exclaimed. 'I'm glad. And it makes you even more intriguing.'

'It does?'

'Yup.'

Hearing that Trafalgar found me intriguing made me fizz with excitement, and once again I was shocked at how he'd somehow managed to break through the barrier I'd erected around my heart after Bing. It was slightly unnerving but also invigorating – like waking up after a long, deep sleep. But before I could give it any more thought, the glowing slits of the tower were suddenly plunged into darkness and, seconds later, the air-raid siren began to wail.

36

LONDON, 1941

'Do you know where the nearest shelter is?' I asked, trying to keep the panic from my voice as people began running across the bridge.

'Do you believe in fate?' Trafalgar called over the siren's screech.

'What?' I stared at him, bewildered. Maybe I'd misheard. 'I said, do you know where the shelter is?' I yelled.

'And I said, do you believe in fate?' he yelled back.

What on earth? I glared at him. 'Do you really think this is the best time for a philosophical discussion?'

'Of course!' he replied. 'What better time to philosophise than when you're facing death?'

'Are you crazy?'

'Maybe.' He looked at me, his eyes wide.

A man wearing a uniform and a helmet with ARP painted on it ran past blowing a whistle. 'Get in the shelter – the Germans are coming,' he screamed.

'Could we please have this scintillating discussion about fate in an air-raid shelter?' I asked, looking at the sky nervously.

'Mary told me you only get about ten minutes' warning once the siren starts.'

'Who's Mary?'

'That doesn't matter.'

'Do you believe in fate?' he asked yet again.

'I don't know, but I can tell you that you're fated to be punched on the nose unless you take me to a shelter this instant!'

He began to laugh. 'OK. Fair enough. Come on.'

We started running after the other people and off the bridge, where I thankfully spied a sign for the London Underground. We raced down the steps into the station. The ticket barriers had been opened to allow us to swarm onto the platforms to shelter. It was so crowded when we got there, people were down on the tracks too. The air was musty and humid and smelled of urine and alcohol.

'It's not too late to change your mind, you know,' Trafalgar muttered in my ear.

'And go where? Back outside to get bombed to smithereens?'

'I know somewhere. Somewhere safe-ish where we can be alone and watch.'

'Watch what?' I stared at him, confused.

'The sky. It really is quite something once the searchlights and anti-aircraft fire get going.'

I was about to call him crazy again when a red-faced man grabbed my arm.

'Hang on a moment, ain't you that singer?' he asked, breathing beery fumes into my face.

My heart sank. The last thing I needed was to be recognised in such a crowded and confined space. I glanced at Trafalgar.

'Come on,' he said, grabbing my arm, and, unsure what to do for the best, I found myself following him back up the stairs, against the current of people still streaming down.

'Where do you think you're going?' A warden standing on duty at the entrance demanded just as the air filled with a low ominous hum.

'Here they come,' Trafalgar exclaimed. 'Quick!' He grabbed my hand, and we started running back towards the river.

'Where are we going?' I cried as the hum of the planes grew louder. Then I heard a rattling sound and looked up to see trails of silver lights streaking across the night sky like fireworks. The beam of a searchlight swept across in an arc, and I glimpsed the outlines of planes flying in a V formation, like an arrowhead aiming straight for the heart of the city.

'Quick!' Trafalgar yelled, pulling me towards a set of stone steps next to the bridge. We raced down and onto the muddy bank of the river. 'Under here,' he called, ushering me beneath the arch of the bridge.

While I was relieved to have something to shelter beneath, I wasn't sure how much good it would be if the Germans were to bomb the bridge, I felt my fear begin to rise again.

'What are you thinking?' he asked as the planes roared by overhead.

I could barely breathe, let alone think as I prayed with all my might we weren't about to be blown sky-high. One by one, the planes roared over and then they were gone. But any relief I felt was short-lived as I heard the boom of an explosion, followed by another and another, causing the ground beneath us to tremble.

'I think you're completely insane,' I said, biting on my lower lip to stop it from quivering. There was no way I was going to let this crazy person see me cry. I'd just have to wait it out under the bridge with him and then demand we go back to the Savoy, give him the sheet music and never, ever see him again. And to think that I'd given up somewhere with a cosy shelter complete with beds and a dance floor for this. Even sitting through another ten courses with Bertrand would have been preferable at this point.

'I get the feeling you're angry with me,' he said as I crouched on the ground.

'Really?' I replied sarcastically. 'Whatever gave you that idea?'

'I'm sorry, I just...' He sat down beside me and gazed glumly at the water lapping at the riverbank.

'What? Have a death wish?'

'No. I'm just sick of...' Again, he fell silent.

'Sick of what?'

'Being made to feel scared,' he said quietly, sounding really subdued.

I stared at him, completely baffled. 'So, in order to feel less scared, you come outside during an air raid?'

'Yes.' He took a pack of cigarettes from his pocket and offered them to me. I practically tore one in half in my haste to grab it. He lit our smokes and took a long drag on his before continuing. 'It's my way of saying up yours to the Jerrys.'

'Up your what?'

'Up your arse.'

'Don't you mean, bottle and glass?' I said, softening just a little.

He laughed. 'Yes! We'll make a cockney of you yet.'

'But the Germans can't see what you're doing, so what difference does it make?'

He looked at me. 'That may be so, but *I* know what I'm doing and, let me tell you, it makes me feel a whole lot better than cowering in a shelter.'

I nodded. I still thought he was crazy, but I could see a certain logic to his hare-brained thinking. As someone who has always hated being made to feel a victim, I quite liked the notion of saying 'up your arse' or the equivalent to the Germans – even if it did make you more likely to be killed.

'And I believe in fate,' he added.

'So you keep saying.' I took a drag on my cigarette. 'Well, go on then, explain.'

'I believe that certain things are meant to happen. Important things – like when you're born...' He paused. 'And when you're going to die.'

'You believe that we all have a predestined date of death as well as a date of birth?'

'Yes. So, if my number's up, it's up, but in the meantime I'm not going to let those bastards ruin my fun.' There was a bitterness to his tone which felt like a stark contrast to the sunny disposition I'd seen from him so far, but I guessed that nine months of relentless bombing could do that to even the cheeriest person. I felt myself soften towards him again.

'I think I understand,' I said. 'I'm just not sure if I believe that the way we're going to die is predestined. Or rather, I don't know if I want to.'

'Why not?'

'Because then it would mean that my mother was fated to die of cancer when I was just sixteen,' I muttered.

'Oh shit, I'm sorry.' He moved a little closer so that our arms were almost but not quite touching. 'So that's the true story?'

'Yes.'

'I can see why you'd want to keep that private; it must have been very painful.'

I nodded.

'I didn't mean to be insensitive.'

'I know. You weren't to know what had happened to her.'

'But still. You only just got here and I dragged you out into an air raid.'

'My first ever air raid,' I added.

'I'm sorry. I just thought that...'

'What?'

The air seemed to thicken around us, and the explosions faded into the distance.

'You seemed like such a good sport.'

'I am!' I replied indignantly. 'I just don't want to die.' I paused for a moment. 'Especially when I'm having so much fun.'

'Being here in London?' he asked.

'Yes, and being in London with you,' I said so quietly my voice could barely be heard over the rattle of the anti-aircraft fire. I couldn't believe how forward I'd been, and it left me instantly feeling vulnerable.

Trafalgar leaped to his feet and punched the air. 'Yes!'

'What was that for?' I couldn't help grinning. He was such a live wire and so unpredictable, but I found it strangely intoxicating. Once again, I had the sensation of being jolted wide awake after a very long, deep sleep.

'You said you like me,' he replied.

'Er, no I did not.'

'You said you were having fun with me.'

I nodded.

'And have you ever had fun with someone you don't like?'

I thought for a while before nodding again. 'Yes, if I'm torturing them with my quick wit and biting sarcasm.'

'Damn!' he sighed.

'But that's not what's happening here,' I found myself blurting out.

'It's not?' He started to grin again. 'So, you do like me?'

'Potentially,' I replied, although I already knew that I did. If I'm really honest, I knew it the second I caught sight of his twinkling eyes peering over that Savoy menu at me.

Oh, if only I'd known what fate – or rather misfortune – had in store for me.

'She potentially likes me!' Trafalgar cried, and, as if on cue, a silver stream of anti-aircraft fire blazed a trail in the sky above his head.

37

LONDON 1941

For the next couple of hours, we sat under the bridge on the bank of the Thames talking and talking. To my surprise and delight, Trafalgar turned out to be that rare breed of person who is genuinely interested in another and good at listening. And I mean truly listening, not just nodding along while thinking of what he was going to say next, which so many are so talented at. He asked me all about Portugal and my childhood and my mother and what it was like going to Lisbon at sixteen to sell fish for a living.

'My manager likes me to tell people that it was the most gruelling existence,' I said with a laugh. 'Pounding the streets in bare feet with a basket of fish on my head.'

'You didn't wear shoes?' he exclaimed.

'It was too much hassle, having to wade into the water to get the fish from the boat,' I replied with a shrug. 'It was easier to keep shoes out of the equation.'

He laughed, but in a warm, not mocking way. 'You really are a fascinating woman, Sofia. No wonder you aren't fazed by being outside during an air raid.'

'Hmm, if you remember correctly, I wasn't exactly happy to be dragged outside.'

'But now?' He looked at me hopefully.

'Now I might have changed my mind.'

But then the hum of aircraft filled the air and my body instantly tensed.

'It's OK,' he said. 'They're heading back to base.' He moved closer so that our sides were touching, and I appreciated the subtle yet comforting gesture. 'You're shivering,' he exclaimed, and in a second he'd wriggled out of his coat and was putting it round my shoulders.

'Thank you.' I didn't have the heart to tell him that I was shivering from fear rather than cold.

But thankfully the planes flew over without dropping any bombs, and a loud volley of anti-aircraft fire rang out as if bidding them farewell.

As we scrambled up the riverbank, the long singular tone of the all-clear signal rang out across the city, and relief washed over me.

'What a night!' I exclaimed as we reached the road.

'Yes, I suppose I should get you back to your hotel and collect the sheet music. Billingsgate market will have to wait,' he added, somewhat glumly.

Up on street level, the air was strangely musty and hard to breathe.

'What's that smell?' I asked.

'Bricks,' Trafalgar replied. 'Or, rather, the dust from the bricks of the buildings that have exploded.'

'Oh.' I shivered at the thought that we were inhaling the remains of people's homes and shops and workplaces. Then I thought of the poor souls I'd seen down in the Underground station. What must it be like to emerge from the shelter not knowing if you still had a home or workplace to go to?

We walked on alongside the river in silence, and I saw the

outlines of iconic London buildings begin to emerge in the first light of dawn. The fat round dome of St Paul's Cathedral and, in the distance. the elegant turrets of the Houses of Parliament.

'It looks like a fairy-tale palace,' I murmured.

'Hmm,' Trafalgar replied as if he wasn't so impressed.

'What?'

'Let's just say that not everyone in the palace is a fairy-tale hero.'

'What do you mean?'

'Never mind. Come on.' He grabbed my hand and quickened his pace.

As we hurried along, I pondered why he might have said what he did. Then I remembered what Emilio had said about influential Britons being sympathisers of Hitler. Could that include Members of Parliament as well as royalty? Being in the SOE, Trafalgar would probably know. I decided not to press the point as he clearly didn't want to talk about it.

The walk back to the hotel soon dampened our spirits. Evidence of the German bombing raid was all around, with fresh craters in the roads and buildings still smouldering.

'How can people do this to one another?' I murmured.

'They've always done this to one another,' Trafalgar replied. 'It's just that they've invented ways to be even more deadly.'

'But that's just so...' I paused to try to find the right word in English. 'Obscene – it's obscene.'

He stopped and gently put his finger to my lips, causing a charge to rush through my body. 'Let's not think about that. Let's focus on the good – like the fact that we've met.'

I nodded, feeling another rush of warmth at his words. It did indeed feel like a good thing that we'd met, even in such stressful circumstances.

We arrived at the hotel, and the doorman greeted us with a weary smile.

'The Bosch have been busy again,' he said with a sigh.

'Yes, more's the pity,' Trafalgar replied.

'I hope you two were able to find proper shelter.'

'Oh yes, we were grand.' Trafalgar looked at me and winked.

When we arrived at my room, I found a note pushed under the door. It was from Bertrand. '*Sorry you were taken ill. I hope you'll be OK for your rehearsals tomorrow! B*' I scrunched it up and threw it in the bin.

Trafalgar looked at me questioningly.

'It was from my dinner date – panicking that my supposed illness might affect the show I'm doing for him.'

'Ah.' He laughed. 'When is your show?'

'The day after tomorrow – or, rather, today!' I looked at the clock on the mantel. It was almost seven in the morning. I hurried over to my case and took out the folder holding the sheet music. 'This is for you,' I said, handing it to him.

'Thank you.' He put the folder down on the armchair beside him. 'So...'

'So,' I echoed. The tension between us felt almost unbearable – for me at least.

'I know that our business is done, but I'd really like to see you again.'

'I'd really like that too!' I exclaimed, once again marvelling at how he'd managed to break down my defences so effortlessly.

He looked so relieved, it warmed my heart. 'Are you free tonight?'

I nodded.

'Excellent. I shall come and call for you.' He stood looking awkward for a moment. 'Well, goodnight. Or good morning.'

I laughed. 'Good morning.'

'Thank you for a great time.'

'Thank you.' I felt so uncharacteristically tongue-tied and shy, it was very disconcerting.

He took his hat off and held it to his chest. 'I'm going to

remember yesterday's date forever. Wait a minute, what *was* the date yesterday?'

'Thursday the eighth of May, 1941.'

'Thursday the eighth of May, 1941,' he echoed softly. 'The date fate brought us together.' Then he kissed me lightly on the cheek, put his hat back on and left.

I stood rooted to the spot, gazing after him, feeling dazed. Maybe it was all of Trafalgar's talk about fate, but I had the certain knowing that the eighth of May 1941 was the date my life had changed forever. And, of course, I was right, but for reasons I never, ever could have anticipated.

38

PORTUGAL, 2000

I stop typing and wipe my eyes. When Sofia was telling me how she and Trafalgar met, I was in full ghostwriter mode, gently prompting and probing to coax more out of her. But now it's almost midnight and I'm alone in my bedroom transcribing the recordings onto the page, they're having a much deeper impact.

I gaze out of the open window into the dark. The sea is gently lapping down below like sighs against the sand. I swallow down the lump in my throat and wonder why Sofia's words have affected me so deeply. Even though she's been heavily hinting that things do not end well with her and Trafalgar, her description of the chemistry between them has left me with a bone-deep longing. I think back to earlier when I was with Gabriel on the beach and how I'd felt when our fingers had touched and when he'd held my hand. It had been so exciting to feel myself spark into life like that, but now I can't help feeling wistful that I've never experienced anything like it before.

I stand up from my desk and go and sit on the wide windowsill where I'd placed the little driftwood rooster Gabriel had given me. I pick it up and hold it tight. A warm breeze perfumed with the fragrance of the garden flowers drifts past me into the room. My wistfulness grows as I realise that, at thirty-five, I've never, ever experienced the kind of powerful attraction Sofia had with Trafalgar.

As I gaze out into the darkness, a memory comes back to me, a memory that immediately makes me cringe.

About five years ago, I ghostwrote a self-help book for a relationship therapist who has a regular slot on a morning TV show. The book was called *Rekindle* and it was for couples looking to reignite the romance in their relationships. One of the chapters was all about rekindling sexual desire and it was full of exercises designed to bring the spark back to your love life. In my desperation, I decided to give one of them a try. It was called 'Hide and Peak' and it involved hiding in your home fully naked, as a 'sexy surprise' for your partner when they got home from work. According to the therapist, this would be guaranteed to whip them into a frenzy.

Sadly, she hadn't factored Robin getting stuck on a broken-down train into the equation. Or me falling asleep hiding in our walk-in closet while I waited. When he finally returned home in a foul mood an hour late and found me, his reaction was one of shock and ridicule, which in turn made me feel desperate and ridiculous, none of which was conducive to whipping anyone into a frenzy.

Thinking back on that evening now, I'm able to see that a kinder, more good-natured man would have been able to laugh at what had happened and appreciate my efforts. The thing that had drawn me to Robin in the first place – his sensible, strait-laced nature – had ended up feeling more like a straitjacket.

I look at the driftwood rooster and stroke its intricate feathers. I hope Gabriel was right and that it will bring me good fortune.

I return to my laptop and gingerly log on to AOL.

'You've got mail!' the cheery automated alert announces, sending a shudder right through me. Ever since Robin's and

Nikki's emails, the notification has taken on a way more menacing tone. I cautiously look at the screen, but thankfully there are no new emails from them. There is one from Jane though, intriguingly titled: *The crack in the chrysalis*. I open it and begin to read.

Dear Lily,

I'm thrilled to hear that you feel that your Portuguese adventure will jolt you out of your butterfly soup and, without wishing to overdo the metaphor, I thought it might be useful to share another butterfly fact with you – or perhaps a butterfly misconception might be more accurate. I think most people assume that when the butterfly is ready, it just bursts out of the cocoon like a rabbit from a magician's hat. But, actually, the act of bursting out of the cocoon is a very delicate and dangerous process. The butterfly has to squeeze itself through a tiny crack in the chrysalis – and it's the tightness of the squeeze that forces fluid into its brand-new wings and gives them strength. If it happens too early or if the butterfly is helped in any way, it won't be strong enough to fly away.

I wanted to share this with you as I'm aware that you've been through so much this past year – and, who knows, there might be some more trying times to come. But trust me, Lily, it's the tough times that will be the making of you, and I can't wait to watch as you step into the strength and wisdom that these experiences have given you.

All my love,

Jane

'Wow,' I whisper as I finish reading her email. It is so

perfectly timed and so beautifully put. What if all the pain I've felt over the past ten months has been helping me grow stronger? What if, instead of feeling wistful that I haven't experienced what Sofia did with Trafalgar, I can feel hopeful that now I'm no longer with Robin, I've at least created the potential for it to happen?

I click on reply.

Dear Jane,

Thank you so much yet again for your words of wisdom. I can't tell you how helpful and timely they were. Today has been a bit trying, but now I can comfort myself with the thought that it's all making me stronger. And I really believe that it is.

Thank you for being so much more than an agent to me. I'm so grateful.

Lots of love,

Lily

I press send and turn off my laptop and, as it powers down, I recall there being something strange Sofia said at the end of our session together today. What was it?

I pick up my voice recorder and rewind the tape a little before pressing play.

'"The date fate brought us together." Then he kissed me lightly on the cheek, put his hat back on and left. I stood rooted to the spot, gazing after him, feeling dazed. Maybe it was all of Trafalgar's talk about fate, but I had the certain knowing that the eighth of May 1941 was the date my life had changed forever. And, of course, I was right, but for reasons I never, ever could have anticipated.' Then there's a clatter as Sofia stood up and

knocked her empty wine glass over on the coffee table. *'Shit!'* she exclaimed. *'OK, that's enough exorcising demons for one night. I need to go to bed.'*

'Are you all right?' I hear myself ask, and then the recording clicks off.

I stop the tape. Why did she get so rattled all of a sudden? And who or what were the demons she was referring to? Presumably she meant Trafalgar, but why? Normally when I ghostwrite an autobiography, the client is only too happy to talk about their lives and themselves – in fact, in many cases, I find myself having to rein them in, visions of their book's word count spiralling out of control. But in Sofia's case the reverse is true. The real challenge in this job is getting her to open up fully.

I return to the windowsill and gaze up at the inky black sky, trying to imagine what it would feel like to know that bombers could appear at any moment. To be afraid of a full moon because it made it easier for the enemy to hit their targets. There's something so perverse about this notion, it makes me shudder. I look up at the thin crescent moon glowing silver in the sky and feel overwhelming gratitude that I haven't had to go through that.

I'm about to get ready for bed when a light goes on downstairs and I hear the back door creaking open. I quickly turn off the lamp so I won't be seen and peer out. Sofia is standing motionless with her back to me in her dressing gown, illuminated by the shaft of light spilling through the back door. What is she doing up at this time? I notice a trowel in her hand. Surely she can't be about to do some gardening.

I watch, mesmerised, as she sets off along the path, coming to a halt by a rose bush about halfway down. She mutters something under her breath, then gets down on her knees and starts digging a hole, tearing at the earth with the trowel like a woman possessed. I wonder what her gardener, Rosária, would have to say if she could see her. Something tells me she wouldn't approve.

Sofia's still muttering, but I can't hear or understand what she's saying, although it's clear from her tone that she isn't happy. She stops digging and fumbles in her dressing-gown pocket, taking out a small box. I watch, hardly daring to breathe, as she shoves it into the ground and hastily covers it with soil. What on earth is she doing?

She stands up and I quickly step back behind the curtain. As I hear her come closer, I risk peeping out. She's only visible for a split second before she goes back inside, but it's long enough to see that she's been crying. Her face is streaked with black from her eyeliner. I contemplate going down to see if she's all right, but that would mean revealing that I saw what she was doing, and something tells me she would not be happy to know that I witnessed her late-night digging spree.

I move away from the window and start getting ready for bed, unable to shake a growing sense of unease. What was in the box Sofia has hidden and why would she go to the lengths of burying it in her garden? The only person she can be hiding it from is me.

39

PORTUGAL, 2000

The next morning after a fitful sleep, I take a quick shower and hurry downstairs. I hear Sofia before I see her, violently whisking some eggs in a bowl.

'Good morning. Everything OK?' I ask cheerily, although inside I'm plagued by questions about what I saw last night. Is Sofia hiding things from me because she doesn't trust me?

'Yes. Why wouldn't it be?' she replies sharply. She's still in her dressing gown and her face is completely bare of make-up, with dark shadows beneath her eyes.

'No reason, it's just that you seem to be beating those eggs to within an inch of their lives. Are you all right?' I ask, gently placing my hand on the back of her shoulder. I need to make her feel safe, and that she doesn't need to hide things from me.

'Oh!' She stops beating and gives an embarrassed laugh. 'I'm afraid I didn't sleep very well, so I guess I'm taking my frustration out on them.'

'Well, rather them than me,' I joke before going over to the table and pouring us both a glass of orange juice. 'I've typed up all of yesterday's recording, so I'm ready to carry on whenever you are,' I say breezily, so I don't seem like I'm pressuring her, even though I'm desperate to hear the next instalment.

'Oh,' she replies flatly before pouring the eggs into a pan on the stove. 'I'm not sure if I'm in the right mood for it today, to be honest.'

Disappointment courses through me, coupled with panic. My instinct must be right. For some reason, she no longer trusts me. What if she decides to quit the project altogether? What if I never find out what happened? And then, even worse, what if I have to go back home? Perhaps I ought to let her know how much her story is affecting me? She might find it encouraging.

'That's a real shame. I enjoyed hearing about Trafalgar. Although it did make me a little wistful.'

'Wistful for what?' she says as she stirs the eggs, giving me a disbelievingly look over her shoulder.

'For that kind of love.'

She slams her spoon on the counter. 'That wasn't love!'

'Oh, I'm sorry, I thought...' Once again, I'm on the back foot, trying to think of something to say to make things better. 'It sounded like you had such a powerful connection.'

She opens her mouth to speak, then closes it again, and I notice her hands clenching into fists by her sides. 'Appearances can be deceptive,' she finally mutters before removing the eggs from the heat.

I watch as she opens a cupboard door and gazes inside. Then she goes over to the fridge and does the same, without taking anything out of either.

'Are you OK?' I ask softly.

'I just feel a little unsettled.' She gives me a weak smile. 'All of this dredging up the past.'

I contemplate telling her that I saw her in the garden last night but quickly decide against it. She seems way too volatile, and I don't want to push her. 'We don't have to do any more today. I could spend the day going over what I've written so far

– and then if you like, I can show it to you.' I wouldn't normally show a client my rough first draft of their chapters, but maybe it would help her to see how powerful her story is, and that it needs telling.

She nods. 'That might be for the best.'

'Would it be OK for me to take another look at the suitcase of memorabilia? So that I can describe things like the gas mask in more detail.'

'Oh, yes, of course.' She starts dishing up the eggs. 'It's in the living room where we left it.'

After we finish breakfast, Sofia goes for a walk on the beach and I take the suitcase up to my bedroom. Part of me is hoping that I'll find some sort of clue as to why Trafalgar turned out to be such an unhappy memory for her. I root through the old newspapers and the card from Judith and the gasmask and clothes, and then I realise that the tin box is missing. Before I can give that any more thought, I hear the front door open.

'*Ola*, Sofia?' I hear Gabriel call, and I relax. But then I see Sofia making her way back up the beach. If she comes home and finds Gabriel and I together again, she might freak out, especially given the mood she's in, so I decide to stay silent and pretend I'm not here.

I listen to Gabriel moving about in the kitchen and then, thankfully, I hear the front door open and close again and all goes quiet. I creep downstairs into the hallway just to make sure and see that the kitchen is empty, but I notice a folded piece of paper propped against the jug of juice on the table. My curiosity getting the better of me, I go over and unfold the paper. There's only one sentence, but of course it's in Portuguese, so I can't understand it. Then I see a word I know only too well – Lily. The note is about me.

I think back to the furtive conversations I've overheard

between Sofia and Gabriel, and I get the strongest urge to translate it. Perhaps it will give me a clearer idea of what's going on. I peer out of the kitchen window. Sofia hasn't reached the garden yet. Hopefully I'll have time to translate enough of it to work out what it means. I take the note and race upstairs to get my Portuguese dictionary. I manage to translate the key words, writing them down in English in my notebook. *Sofia, We need to talk about Lily – urgently!* G

I'm so stunned I forget to check to see if Sofia's coming and I jump at the sound of the back door closing downstairs.

'Lily!' she calls from the kitchen. 'Where are you? I've had a change of heart – I think we should continue with the book today.'

Shit! I look at Gabriel's note. How on earth am I going to explain taking it upstairs? I can hardly say that he gave it to me.

'OK great!' I call back. 'I'll be down in a second.'

I start pacing the room, praying for inspiration. One thing's for sure: I have to get the note back in the kitchen because it's only a matter of time before Sofia sees Gabriel and he'll ask her if she's read it. I shove it in my pocket and gather up my tape recorder, notebook and pen.

I find Sofia in the kitchen, looking a lot better than she did before. The fresh sea air has clearly invigorated her, and her eyes are sparkling and her cheeks are rosy.

'I'm sorry about earlier,' she says as soon as I come into the room. 'I told my problems to the sea, and it told me not to be so self-pitying.' She gives a sad smile. 'One thing no one really tells you about becoming older is how damn infuriating it can be.'

'Infuriating?' I ask, sitting down at the table, wondering if there's any way I could slip the note back against the jug without her seeing.

She nods and comes and sits opposite me and pours herself a glass of juice, instantly putting paid to my plan. 'Yes, when you realise that there's nothing you can do with all of your regrets – there's no time left to try to rectify them.'

I wonder what she means by this, and if it's connected to Trafalgar. Before I can ask, I hear a cough from outside and, to my horror, I see Gabriel striding up the garden path.

'It's Gabriel!' I squeak, hoping she doesn't detect the panic in my voice.

'Oh yes.'

I watch, heart racing, as she gets up and goes over to the door.

'Did you get my note?' Gabriel asks Sofia as soon as he sets foot in the kitchen. When he sees me, he smiles, but unlike yesterday on the beach, his smile looks slightly strained.

'What note?' Sofia asks.

Fingers trembling, I reach in my pocket for the note under the table and throw it onto the floor.

'The note I left on the table.' Gabriel looks at the table and frowns. He looks back at me and his frown deepens. 'I put it by the jug.'

'How strange.' Sofia comes back to the table and looks at the jug. 'I just had a drink and there was no sign of any note.'

Now they both stare at me. I shrug, hoping I don't start to blush.

Sofia looks under the table. 'Oh, hang on.' She bends down and retrieves the note. 'Is this it? It must have blown under in the breeze.'

I relax a little and watch as she unfolds it and starts to read. This should be interesting.

'Oh.' She shoots a glance at me, then looks at Gabriel. 'Yes, some fish would be lovely,' she replies in a fake-sounding voice.

Gabriel looks confused for a moment, then the penny obviously drops and he nods enthusiastically, as he obviously realises she's making something up because I'm there.

'OK, I'll bring some later.' He gives a sheepish smile, and I feel stupidly disappointed and embarrassed that I should have read so much into what happened between us on the beach. My embarrassment grows as it dawns on me that this might be the 'urgent' thing he wants to talk to her about. Is he going to tell her that he's concerned I have a crush on him?

To make matters even worse, he mutters something to Sofia in Portuguese and she gives a brisk nod. What the hell is going on?

I stare at Sofia, and when she catches my gaze, she instantly looks away as if embarrassed.

'Well, we'd better get back to our book writing,' she says in a tone so falsely jolly it sounds really jarring. 'Good luck with your fishing, Gabriel.'

'OK. Thank you,' he replies awkwardly before looking at me. 'Good luck with your book.'

'Thanks,' I mutter but with zero enthusiasm.

Desperate to vent my frustration, I decide to email Jane.

'I just have to catch up with some correspondence,' I say to Sofia as Gabriel leaves. 'I'll be back in a minute.'

I go upstairs and connect to the internet. There's a response from Jane waiting for me in my inbox.

Dear Lily,

I'm so glad to hear that my email helped and just wanted to check in with you that everything is OK after you said you'd had a trying day. Anything I can help with? Just let me know if you need me to go to bat for you...

All my love,

Jane

As soon as I read her words, I feel a surge of relief. Jane is so warm and kind-hearted, I sometimes forget that she's also a formidable powerhouse of an agent, and on the rare occasion she's had to 'go to bat' for me, due to a celebrity client messing me around or a publisher reneging on a clause in my contract, she's a force to be reckoned with. As much as she was excited about this job, I feel certain she wouldn't even be intimidated by Sofia Castello. As I click on reply, I can't help smiling at the prospect.

> Good morning, Jane!
>
> Thanks so much for your email. No need to go to bat for me – yet at least – but things have got a little strange here. I really like Sofia, but I feel like she's keeping something from me. I've no idea what it could be, but she's been acting weirdly and hiding things from me. There's a guy who lives locally, who's kind of like her Man Friday, and I've caught them talking about me in Portuguese a couple of times about some kind of secret. I know I must sound really paranoid, but it's all a little unsettling, especially as I'm so far from home. I hope you don't mind me venting to you, but obviously I can't say anything to her as I don't want to jeopardise the job and you're the only person I can talk to about this. No need to reply as I know there's nothing you can do, but thank you for reading and for always being there!
>
> Lots of love,
>
> Lily

I press send, then reread the email Jane sent me about the butterfly breaking out of the chrysalis, and I feel a sense of determination growing inside of me. I'm not going to allow Gabriel and Sofia's weird behaviour to intimidate me. I am strong and I am wise and I'm really experienced at my job. And I absolutely can be trusted. So I'm going to go downstairs and I'm going to coax Sofia's story out of her even if it kills me.

40

LONDON, 1941

I was so wired from what happened that first night in London with Trafalgar that I barely got a wink of sleep. Thankfully, I was so excited by what had happened, I didn't really need any, and I turned up promptly at the rehearsal studio in a part of London called Maida Vale.

For all his obvious flaws, I'll give Bertrand credit that he provided me with some fine musicians to work with. The guitarist and drummer were both from America, and the keyboard player and saxophonist were Brits but considerably older. It didn't occur to me until afterwards that this would have been due to all the younger British men being conscripted into the army and, of course, America was yet to join the war. I was relieved and flattered to discover that the guys had done their homework and knew all my songs and were ready and raring to go. All the way through our rehearsal, thoughts of Trafalgar hummed away like a bassline in my mind, and I kept coming back to two questions. Would he still want to see me that evening, and if so, where would he take me?

We finished up at the studio at around four in the afternoon, and after a quick bite to eat, I took a cab back to the

Savoy. I checked at the reception desk to see if there were any messages for me, and my heart lifted as the woman fetched me an envelope. I tore it open right there and then, but my heart sank as I saw it was from Bertrand, giving me some final details about my show the following day.

I went up to my room and sank down onto the bed, feeling suddenly exhausted and trying to fight the creeping feeling that I'd been stupid and I'd never see Trafalgar again. This feeling grew as the afternoon turned to night and there was no sign or word from him. I eventually fell asleep, fully dressed on top of my bed.

The next morning, I woke feeling greatly refreshed and much more my normal self. So what if Trafalgar had turned out to be a disappointment? I'd successfully accomplished my mission for Emilio and the Allies, and I was in London for my first ever show there. I still had plenty to be grateful for.

A car came to fetch me at three and took me to Queen's Hall. Even though I knew it was London's premier music venue, I was completely unprepared for the splendour of the building. Situated on Langham Place, with a grand, rounded front and a domed roof adorned with glass panels, it was nothing short of majestic, and I could see instantly why Londoners had nicknamed it the People's Palace.

As I made my way to the entrance, I noticed brass busts of Wagner and Handel in the wall. They were both German of course, and it gave me a pang of sorrow. If only we could return to the days when people made music to uplift each other rather than bombs to kill one another. But that was exactly what I was there to do, I reminded myself, and I vowed to give the hardy Londoners in attendance that evening a show they'd never forget.

When I stepped onto the stage that night, beneath the

largest set of organ pipes I'd ever laid eyes on, I felt like a woman possessed. Possessed by the desperate desire to bring hope to a people who'd endured so much. The show passed by in a blur and was a wonderful success, ending in the longest standing ovation I've ever received. After giving three encores, I hurried into my dressing room, ears still ringing from the applause. I'd done it! I'd performed my first show in England.

'Oh, Mama, I wish you could have seen it,' I gushed as I sat down at my dressing table. 'I even had those formal Brits up dancing in the aisles! It was absolutely bloody brilliant,' I added in a jokey posh English accent.

'It certainly bloody was,' a voice replied.

I gasped in shock and spun around, but the room was empty.

'What did you say?' I asked, my voice quivering.

'I said it certainly bloody was bloody brilliant,' the voice said, and I realised it was coming from the wardrobe. And although he was also putting on a posh accent, I felt certain it was Trafalgar.

I bit on my lip to stop myself from grinning like a fool. After he'd had the audacity to not show up last night, there was no way I was going to let him get back into my good graces without an apology and a bloody good explanation, as the Brits might say.

'So, are talking wardrobes a British thing?'

'I'm afraid not,' Trafalgar replied in his normal voice. 'Getting dressed would be a lot more fun if they were.'

There was a pause and I continued staring at the wardrobe door, wondering how he'd managed to get backstage and how long he'd been in there. I guessed that being a member of the SOE, sneaking around was part of the job description.

'So, is it safe to come out?'

'Why would it not be?'

'You might want to kill me for standing you up last night.'

'No, I do not want to kill you.'

'Phew!' The wardrobe door opened and Trafalgar stepped out. He was wearing a smart, charcoal-grey suit and a flat cap and looked infuriatingly handsome.

'I am obscenely disappointed in you though,' I quickly added, not wanting to let him off lightly.

'Obscenely?' He raised his eyebrows, and I had the feeling he was trying not to laugh. 'Yep, I can understand that, but I can explain. Well, I can sort of explain.'

I rolled my eyes. 'I really think I deserve more than a sort of explanation.'

'Yes, but—' He broke off, and I realised that he looked genuinely distressed. 'I'm not actually able to tell you.'

'I see.' I turned back to the mirror, annoyed at how hurt I felt by this. For some unknown reason, Trafalgar really seemed able to hit my weak spot – a weak spot I didn't even know I had. 'I think I can guess. You don't want me to know that you were with another woman?'

'What?'

'Or, even worse, your wife.' I began angrily wiping off my stage make-up.

'What wife? I'm not married.' He met my gaze in the mirror and seemed to be genuinely upset. 'I'm not. And why the hell would I want to be with another woman when you're here in London?'

I felt elated at this but made sure not to let it show on my face. He'd shaken my trust and made me realise that I'd been far too open when we first met – now I had to keep my guard up. 'So why aren't you able to tell me what you were doing?'

'Because I was—' He broke off and looked around the room. 'I was working,' he said, lowering his voice. 'And it's not the kind of work that comes with a predictable schedule.'

I felt a pang of guilt. Of course his work would involve

unpredictable hours. I should have known. I cursed Bing for making me so distrusting of men.

Trafalgar came and stood behind me, meeting my gaze in the mirror. 'I'm so sorry. I feel awful about letting you down, and I'd really, really like to make it up to you – if you'd let me?'

'And how do you plan to do that – take me dicing with death again?'

He looked genuinely crestfallen. 'I thought you'd enjoyed it.'

'I-I did.' I felt my resolve begin to weaken. 'I really enjoyed it.'

A smile lit up his face. 'I'm so happy to hear that because I did too and I haven't stopped thinking about you. Even when I was asleep, I dreamed about you – although in the dream you were really yelling at me because I hadn't been able to come and see you.' He shook his head and gave an exaggerated sigh. 'Blimey, you were raging!'

I laughed. 'Well, I'm glad that the dream version of me didn't stand for any nonsense.'

'Something tells me that the real you wouldn't either.' His grin grew. 'So, what do you say? Will you allow me to try to make it up to you? Can I take you for a late dinner? You must be starving after the show – I'm guessing you didn't eat at all before.'

'How do you know?'

'I studied drama at school. I remember what I was like when we put on a play. Anyway, I know this great little place in Soho, a proper authentic Italian café.'

'You want to take me for an Italian meal in England.' I frowned. 'What about British cuisine?'

'I could take you for some jellied eels if you'd prefer?'

I shuddered at the thought. 'Italian will be fine.'

'Great. Oh, and one more question?'

'Go on?'

'Do you have anything against motorcycles?'

'No, why should I?'

'I mean riding on them and, more specifically, on the back of one.'

'Are you talking about now?'

'Yes.' He went back over to the wardrobe and reached inside, producing two helmets with a flourish. 'I brought one for you just in case.'

'In case I really am crazy,' I muttered as I wiped the rest of my make-up from my face. 'OK then.'

'Yes!' He punched the air with delight, and again I had to bite my lip to stop myself from smiling. For the truth was, as much as I hated to admit it, I was as happy as he clearly was at this turn of events.

I instructed Trafalgar to wait in the corridor outside while I quickly got changed. I'd performed in a tight satin number that would have been hugely impractical for riding around town on a bike. Thankfully, I'd worn a pair of trousers and a silk shirt to the venue. Before I left the dressing room, I looked in the mirror. The only make-up I was wearing was a thin coat of rose-pink lipstick. But I felt no need to slap on a mask. Trafalgar was bringing out a wild and natural part in me – and I loved it.

'Obviously, the roads are more perilous these days because of the blackouts,' he said once we'd reached his motorcycle, which he'd parked down a side street.

'Not to mention the bombs,' I muttered.

'Well, quite.' He handed me my helmet. 'So I'm afraid this really is compulsory. They have at least painted the edge of the kerbs white now to try to stop all the pedestrians from being killed, but still...'

'Of course!' I snatched the helmet from him and put it on.

'Oh.' He looked at me, surprised.

'What?'

'I thought you might have been worried about your hairdo. Most ladies get a little anxious that it might get flattened.'

'Well, firstly I'm not most ladies,' I retorted, trying not to think about the other ladies who'd ridden with him before, 'and secondly, I'd far rather my hair was flattened than my skull.'

He burst out laughing. 'You really are quite something.'

'I really am quite starving, so if you don't mind, how about we go to this Italian restaurant of yours.'

'Yes, of course, m'lady.'

I grinned. It felt great to be bantering with him again and back in the rhythm of our first night together.

As we set off along the street, a huge full moon came into view, and I gripped Trafalgar's waist a little tighter. Hopefully the German bombers wouldn't have anything too horrible in store for us.

41

LONDON, 1941

About ten minutes later, we pulled up on an unassuming side street. I only know it was ten minutes because I checked my watch, otherwise I would have sworn it was ten hours. For some reason, Trafalgar spent most of the journey weaving from side to side, often quite violently. I wasn't sure whether he was deliberately trying to unnerve me, but if so, it had worked a charm.

'What the hell is wrong with you?' I yelled, getting off the bike and pulling off my helmet.

'What is it? What's the matter?' he replied, taking off his own helmet and looking baffled.

'Are you so desperate to feel a woman's arms around you that you have to terrify her into doing it?' I yelled.

A couple walking by, arm in arm, slowed down and I heard the woman giggle.

'What are you talking about?' Trafalgar asked, still looking bewildered.

'The way you were driving!' I began waving my arms left and right to demonstrate.

'I was trying to avoid all of the holes in the road from the bombs and the shrapnel,' he replied.

'Oh.' I was thankful for the dark for hiding my embarrassed blushes.

'And it's hard to see them with no headlights. I only see them at the last minute, so I have to swerve. I'm sorry.'

'No, I'm sorry. I shouldn't have shouted. I should have thought. I just got shaken up.'

He looked at me for a moment, then flung his arms around me and hugged me tight. 'I'm so sorry,' he said in my ear, and my knees seemed to turn to jelly. 'And I'm not apologising because I want an excuse to throw my arms around you,' he added, quickly letting go and stepping aside.

'I know.'

'I would never, ever want to hurt you,' he said softly.

'Thank you.'

'In fact, right now all I want to do is...' He paused and my pulse quickened. Was he going to kiss me? 'Feed you!' he exclaimed, taking hold of my hand, and as much as I was hungry, I couldn't help feeling a pang of disappointment. 'Come on – let's get our picnic.'

'Picnic? But I thought we were going to an Italian place.'

'We are, but we're not eating there. I have somewhere far more fun to take you.'

I couldn't help laughing as I ran to keep up with his long-legged stride. He was so boyish and bubbling with energy it was infectious.

'Please don't tell me we're having a picnic under a bridge.'

'No – the opposite in fact.'

'On top of a bridge?' I exclaimed.

'Shh! All will be revealed.'

We turned a corner and a tiny café came into view. Once again, I felt a burst of gratitude for having met Trafalgar. Ever since the start of my singing career, I'd been taken to fancy restaurants and bars – places I never felt able to be my true self in – but this place – Bruno's, as the hand-painted sign informed me – was much more my cup of tea, as the Brits like to say. We stepped inside, straight into a steamy fug scented with the rich aroma of tomatoes, onion and garlic, which instantly triggered a ravenous hunger in me. Trafalgar had been right about nerves killing my appetite, but once the performance was over, it always came rushing back with a vengeance.

A large, olive-skinned man with curly black hair was standing behind the counter yelling instructions to people behind him in the kitchen. As soon as he saw Trafalgar, his face lit up.

'Mister Smith!' he cried, and I felt a fizz of excitement. Was this Trafalgar's real name?

'Good evening, Bruno. I have a very special guest visiting and I wanted to treat her to one of your famous meatball sandwiches.' He turned to me and smiled. 'Is that OK? They're honestly the best thing you'll eat here in London – thanks to Bruno's top-secret tomato sauce.'

'Ah yes, the secret sauce,' Bruno said, tapping the side of his nose knowingly.

'Well, now I'm intrigued,' I replied with a grin.

Bruno wiped his chunky hands on his apron and offered me one to shake. 'Welcome, *signora!*'

'*Grazie*,' I replied, using the one Italian word I knew.

Bruno seemed to really appreciate this, grinning even more before hollering our order to the kitchen.

We sat at a table by the window to wait, and Bruno immediately plonked a couple of complimentary glasses of wine down in front of us. I wiped a clear patch in the steamy glass and marvelled at all of the people hurrying by – the men in their neatly pressed suits and hats, the women in dresses and heels, all clearly dressed up for a night out.

'Do you think the Germans will bomb tonight?' I asked, feeling anxious on their behalf.

Trafalgar nodded. 'I'd say so. They always like to when the moon is full.'

'So I heard. I love that people are going out and about anyway – that they haven't given up on living their lives. It was so inspiring seeing so many people at Queen's Hall this evening.'

'We can't give up living. Then the Germans really will have won.' He lit us both cigarettes. 'I know you probably think I'm crazy after the other night, but it's honestly the only way I'm able to cope – by refusing to let them wear me down. War is just as much about beating your enemy mentally as it is physically, you know.'

I nodded and felt a pang as I thought of Judith and how jittery she'd been at the mere thought of the Gestapo. 'I totally understand.'

'You do?'

I nodded. 'I was friends with a German girl – a Jewish refugee who came to Lisbon. I saw how frightened she was of the Gestapo. She was like a hunted animal. Literally.'

'What do you mean, literally?' Trafalgar put his elbows on the table and leaned closer.

'Those bastards hunted her down and they took her away.' I took a sip of my wine to try to stop the lump forming in the back of my throat.

'I'm so sorry,' he said softly.

'Yes, well, that's why I'm here.' I stared at him defiantly. 'To help defeat those monsters.'

'That's the spirit!' He leaned closer and cupped my hands in his. 'I'm so glad we met,' he said earnestly. 'I don't know if I'm just trying really hard to find reasons to be hopeful in a terrible situation, but I feel as if we were supposed to meet.' He let go of my hands and looked out of the window, as if embarrassed, which only endeared him to me more. It was nice to see a more vulnerable side to him – it made me feel less self-conscious about my own.

'I feel that too,' I replied, and I felt a strange sensation in my heart, a sense that it was expanding bigger and bigger, and glowing brighter and brighter. 'Maybe it's *bashert*,' I added.

He looked back at me with a beautiful, hopeful smile on his face. 'What's *bashert*?'

I laughed. 'Oh, you'll like it with all your talk of fate. It's a Yiddish term for people who are destined to meet. My Jewish friend told me about it.' I refrained from telling him the part about soulmates. He might have made me lower my guard, but I hadn't abandoned all my defences.

Trafalgar's smile grew. '*Bashert*,' he echoed softly. 'I love it.'

By the time Bruno appeared with our food, wrapped in foil inside a brown paper bag, I felt a new closeness between Trafalgar and I – a sense that we'd seen beneath each other's masks, and not only that but we liked what we saw. Or I did at least.

Thankfully, we didn't have to get back on the bike, and he led me through a rabbit warren of cobbled streets and narrow passageways, made even more atmospheric by the moonlight, finally coming to a standstill in front of a large building. A huge, jagged hole gaped like an open mouth halfway up the wall.

'Welcome to our picnic venue,' Trafalgar announced.

'This is it?' I'd been picturing an enchanting walled garden or some kind of courtyard, or London's famous Hyde Park. 'What is it?'

'It's a library,' he said proudly. 'Or at least it was. It was bombed by the Germans back in December and had to be vacated.'

'So, we-we're having a picnic in a bombsite,' I stammered.

'No,' he replied, and I felt a surge of relief.

'We're having a *moonlit* picnic in a bombsite,' he said proudly.

42

LONDON, 1941

'Oh, I'm sorry. How romantic,' I remarked drily, once I'd overcome my initial shock.

'I thought so too!' he exclaimed, completely missing my sarcasm.

He looked so excited, I couldn't help smiling. His exuberance was infectious.

'Come on,' he said, taking my hand and leading me round the side of the building.

'Are we allowed to do this?' I asked as we picked our way over the rubble.

'We're in the middle of a war – normal rules don't apply,' he replied. 'Once you understand that, life becomes a lot more fun.'

I had to admit that since meeting him, my life had become a lot more fun, so who was I to disagree?

When we got to the back of the building, Trafalgar magically produced a crowbar from a pile of rubble by the door and jimmied it open just enough for us to slip through. As he shut the door behind us, we were plunged into total darkness.

'Don't worry,' he said cheerily, 'I have a lamp.'

'You have a lamp?' I echoed in disbelief. I heard a match being struck and Trafalgar's face appeared in the soft golden glow. 'You seem very well prepared. Do you come here often?'

He laughed. 'Not that old chestnut.'

'What old chestnut?' I looked around, confused. All I could see was a darkened corridor.

'In England, asking a person if they come here often is what's known as a chat-up line.'

'Well, in Portugal it most definitely isn't,' I retorted, and he instantly looked crestfallen.

'I do come here quite often, as it happens. It helps me to think, and it looks incredible. Can I show you?'

'Of course.'

'It might be safer if you hold my hand, due to the bomb damage – but I'm not just saying that because I'm desperate to get a woman to hold hands with me,' he added hastily.

'OK, I'll take your word for it,' I said drily, but as he took my hand, I felt my heart begin to glow again.

We cautiously made our way along the corridor and through a set of double doors that were hanging from their hinges like a pair of giant loose teeth.

'*Et voilà!* As they say in France,' Trafalgar announced, waving the lamp in an arc.

'Wow!' I exclaimed as I looked around. The explosion had formed a huge crater slap bang in the middle of the library, with only the shelves lining the walls still standing. Most of them were still full of books. There was an eerie beauty to it that was hard to describe.

'Do you like it?' he asked eagerly.

'I love it. It's very atmospheric. Eerie and yet romantic.'

He laughed. 'That is exactly the kind of atmosphere I wanted for our date.'

'Hmm, I'm not sure if eerie is something to aspire to on a

date,' I quipped, but the fact that he had called it a date caused the warmth in my heart to grow.

'Come.' He gripped my hand tighter and led me deeper inside the library, or what was left of it anyway. As I looked down, I saw that the floor was covered with fragments of pages and covers. We were walking on a carpet of books.

'Here we are,' he announced, leading me into an alcove that had remained untouched by the bomb damage apart from a framed painting of Shakespeare that was now hanging slightly skew-whiff on the wall. As Trafalgar shone the lamp around, I saw that a picnic blanket had been set up in the centre of the alcove, along with some cushions, a bottle of wine and two glasses and plates.

'You set this all up for us?' I asked, staring at him in disbelief.

He nodded. 'Of course, I didn't know if you'd accept or not. I had a horrible feeling that after last night you might tell me to get stuffed, but I have always been an eternal optimist.'

'Get stuffed?' I raised my eyebrows. 'What do you mean, like a chicken?'

He chuckled. 'It's a British saying. It means go away – and not in a polite way.'

'Ah, OK. Well, I don't want to stuff you like a chicken or to go away.'

'Phew! And even if you do hate me, at least you'll be able to say that you've been on an eerie yet romantic date with a difference.'

I nodded. 'That's true. And just for the record, I don't hate you either.'

'Thank you!' he said, grinning from ear to ear. 'And I don't hate you.'

'I should think not!' I exclaimed.

He clapped his hand to his mouth, clearly aghast. 'I'm sorry. I can't believe I said that. I'm just so nervous.'

'You are?'

'Yes.'

'I didn't think a cool customer like you felt any fear,' I said drolly, trying to hide my excitement at why he might have been nervous.

'Yes, well, that's the effect you have on me.' He laughed. 'I can face down the German bombers, but a fascinating Portuguese woman makes me a quivering wreck. Please, sit down.' He gestured at one of the cushions.

We sat down, and he poured us wine and unwrapped the meatball sandwiches and put them on the plates, the air filling with the most delicious aroma of meat and tomatoes. All the while, my mind buzzed with excited chatter. I made him nervous. He thought I was fascinating. We both felt the same. Could this be *bashert*?

As I took the first bite of my sandwich, I can honestly say that I'd never felt such joy. The combination of the delicious food, the atmospheric setting and Trafalgar's company was a feast for all the senses. I wanted so badly to freeze the moment so I could revel in that feeling for as long as possible.

'This sauce is divine!' I exclaimed, licking my lips.

'What did I tell you? Bruno guards his recipe like it's a state secret.'

We carried on eating in a warm, companionable silence, broken only by the sound of us munching and the occasional murmur of appreciation.

'I can't believe all of the books are still here,' I said, once we'd finished, looking up at the shelves.

'I know. It makes this place even more special.' He smiled shyly. 'Sometimes when I come here, I play a game with them.'

'What kind of game?'

'If I have a question or a decision I need to make, I ask the books for their advice.'

'How do you mean?' I stared at him, intrigued. He was such

an interesting mix – one minute wild and exuberant, the next thoughtful and introspective.

He looked away, clearly embarrassed.

'It's all right, I already think you're crazy, so you've got nothing to lose by telling me,' I joked.

He laughed and stood up. 'OK, let's say for example that I'd met a woman I couldn't stop thinking about and really wanted to see again, but I didn't know what to do.' He gave me a pointed look, as if trying to make it clear that he was talking about me. 'I'd ask the books for their advice and then I'd close my eyes and let my intuition guide me to pick one of them.' He closed his eyes and reached up into the darkened shelves and took down a book. 'Then I'd pick a random number and turn to that page and read the first line.'

'And that will be the answer to your question?' I said.

'Yes, exactly.' He brought the book over and sat down.

'Go on then – do it,' I urged, amused and intrigued. 'Pick a number.'

'Twenty-seven!' he declared before leafing through the pages.

'And?' I asked as his eyes scanned the page.

He laughed. 'It says, "Never underestimate the importance of planting potatoes in the sun."'

I burst out laughing. 'How profound!'

'Yes, well, sometimes it works better than others.' He grinned and shook his head. 'Just my luck to find a book on gardening in the fiction section!'

It sounded like the kind of book Judith loved to read. 'Maybe it was meant to be there,' I murmured, thinking of my beloved friend. Maybe the library had wanted to remind me of her. On this extraordinary and magical night, anything felt possible.

'Why, were you in need of some advice on potato planting?' Trafalgar asked with a bemused grin.

'One can never know too much about the humble potato,' I joked.

'This is true.' He gestured at the bookshelves. 'Why don't you have a go?'

'OK, let me think of a question,' I replied, although there was only one question on my mind – what was going to happen between us?

I stood up and made my way over to the shelves.

'Make sure you close your eyes,' he called.

'I will.' I closed my eyes and picked a book.

'And what page number will you choose?'

'I choose page seventy-nine,' I said, feeling a burst of anticipation. But just as I returned to the picnic blanket, the air-raid siren began to wail.

43

LONDON, 1941

'What do we do?' I asked, terror gripping me. 'Where should we go?' Surely a building like this would have some kind of cellar or basement.

'Up on the roof,' Trafalgar said, springing to his feet and passing me a couple of cushions.

'Are you—'

'Crazy? Yes.' He grabbed the lamp and my free hand. 'But in this case it makes sense – the building is already weakened and we don't want to end up trapped beneath it.' He must have noticed the horror on my face because he gave me a reassuring smile. 'I'm sure it won't come to that. The Germans have already bombed this place – the chances of them striking it again are minimal.'

'Oh really,' I muttered as we hurried back to the stairwell. 'And is this based on some kind of scientific law or study?'

He laughed. 'Well, they do say that lightning never strikes twice. Here's hoping the same applies to the Luftwaffe. And, anyway, we don't have the time to get anywhere else. They'll be here within minutes.'

This didn't exactly do anything to calm my nerves, but he seemed so self-assured it gave me a strange sense of comfort.

We reached the top of the stairs and he led me through a door onto the flat roof of the building, where we sat down on our cushions beside a large chimney stack. The huge full moon hung in the sky to the right like a giant silver bauble. It would have been a beautiful sight before the war – or before I'd come to London – but now all I could see was a beacon for the German bombers, causing fear to pool in the pit of my stomach. Searchlights began arching across the sky and my fear grew.

'Remember what I said,' Trafalgar called above the siren's wail. 'This is our way of fighting back and not letting those monsters beat us in here.' He tapped the side of his head.

I nodded and drew upon the well of courage inside of me – the same courage I drew upon after my mother's diagnosis, and when I headed to Lisbon on my own at sixteen.

That's my brave girl, I imagined my mother whispering to me.

A distant hum filled the air, growing louder by the second.

Trafalgar grabbed my hand and squeezed it tight. 'It's OK, Sofia – we've got each other.'

I looked at him and nodded, and my eyes filled with tears.

'It's OK,' he repeated, moving closer, and he wrapped his arm around me and pulled me into him, and once again, in spite of everything, I felt comforted by his presence.

The hum grew even louder and the planes appeared in the distance. The air filled with the rattle of anti-aircraft fire, but it seemed to make little difference. I heard distant boom after boom after boom, and the horizon ignited with white flashes, followed by an orange glow.

'They're dropping incendiaries over to the east,' Trafalgar muttered. 'They must be hitting the docks.'

'What are incendiaries?' I asked.

'They're smaller bombs designed to start fires,' he replied.

'But isn't that better? Doesn't it mean that less people will be killed?'

He shook his head, grim-faced. 'They do it to illuminate the target for the next wave of bombers.'

'The next wave?' I echoed with a growing feeling of terror.

'Yes – the ones with the real bombs.'

I watched in horror as the orange blaze on the horizon grew bigger and brighter. It might have appeared beautiful, but just like the silvery moon, all it signified was imminent destruction and death.

44

LONDON, 1941

'What do you want to do?' Trafalgar asked as the last of the planes disappeared, leaving the London skyline in the distance ablaze. 'We could make a break for it before the next lot come and try to get down to a shelter.'

I thought of the Underground station we'd gone to previously and the smell and the noise and the bodies all crammed in together, and I wondered what would happen if there was a direct strike on the station. Would we all be buried alive in there? At least up on the roof, we could see what was going on and there was less of a feeling of claustrophobia.

'Could we stay here?' I asked, my voice wavering.

'Of course. We're probably safer here anyway.'

I looked at him hopefully. 'How so?'

'The first planes didn't drop any incendiaries here.' He pointed to the burning horizon. 'All of the fires are focused over to the east – so that's where the next lot will be attacking.'

Any relief I felt at this was very short-lived. As I gazed at the fires blazing on the horizon, I thought of the people there – all the mothers, fathers, brothers, sisters, friends, lovers – and my eyes filled with tears. Hopefully they'd all made it to the relative safety of the shelters, but the thought of them coming back to find their homes, workplaces and shops destroyed was heartbreaking.

'I'm so sorry,' Trafalgar said, for once sounding defeated. 'I'd wanted this to be a really special night, especially as you're leaving tomorrow.'

'It still is a special night – I'm not going to forget it in a while, that's for sure.' I looked at him anxiously. 'So how long do you think we've got until the next lot arrive?'

'Not long, I'd imagine.' He glanced down at the book I'd picked from the shelf, now on the roof beside me. In the mad rush to get up there I hadn't even realised I'd still been clutching it. 'Why don't we see what your book's answer was, to take our minds off things?'

'Good idea.' I examined the book's cover. It was called *The Lord and the Scullery Maid*. 'I can't remember the page.'

'Seventy-nine,' he replied instantly.

'Thank you.' I turned to the page, and he held up the lamp so I could read.

'Oh my!'

'What does it say?'

'It says, "You are nothing but a cad and a liar, Lord Douglas, and there's no way on God's green earth that I'm going to kiss you."'

Trafalgar frowned. 'Did you make that up?'

'No, look!' I handed him the book.

'Why?' he cried theatrically to the book.

'What's wrong?'

'Now you'll never let me kiss you.'

'What makes you think that was my question?' I asked, trying not to laugh. As silly as our conversation was, I was very grateful for the distraction.

'Because this is the answer!' he exclaimed, pointing at the page. 'And now you'll think that I'm a liar and a cad like this fool – this fool...' He looked back at the book. 'Lord Douglas!' He threw the book down in disgust, and I burst out laughing.

'You could argue that the book is telling me not to kiss a lord,' I said. 'So that lets you off the hook, doesn't it?'

He grinned. 'Oh – yes – so it does.'

There was a moment's silence, and he put the lamp down and moved closer, causing my heart to race. But then the hum of a plane filled the air.

'Oh no,' I exclaimed.

Trafalgar extinguished the lamp and leaped to his feet. 'They're back,' he said grimly, looking up at the sky. 'Shit!'

'What?'

'There's so many of them.'

I stood beside him and watched, terrified, as the orange sky on the horizon filled with a cloud of planes. From this distance, they looked like a swarm of hornets. Silver streams of anti-aircraft fire shot up to meet them, but there were too many, and the white flashes of more explosions began. It was like watching some kind of macabre firework display.

'Oh no!' Trafalgar exclaimed as the noise grew louder.

'What is it?'

'Some of them are coming our way.'

'But I thought... There aren't any fires here.'

'They're obviously planning something big tonight. I've never seen so many of them.' He stood gazing up at the sky.

'Should we take cover?' I asked, somehow keeping my growing fear under control.

'It's too late,' he replied. 'It's safer to stay here. Come.' He ushered me behind the huge chimney breast. We crouched down, and he grabbed my hand and held it tightly. 'It's going to be OK,' he said. 'We're going to be OK.'

I wasn't sure if he was trying to reassure me or himself.

The roar of the planes grew louder and louder, as did the rattle of the anti-aircraft artillery. I looked up and saw the dark silhouette of a plane directly overhead. It was so close, I could see the markings on its side. I couldn't breathe. I couldn't move. I felt a rushing sensation in my head; a sense that I was hurtling towards my death, and my body began shaking violently. I saw something drop from the plane and I knew that was it. It looked as if it was going to be a direct hit. I closed my eyes tight, but then I heard a strange rustling sound, and I saw some kind of fabric floating down towards the building.

'Oh no,' Trafalgar exclaimed. 'It's a parachute bomb.'

'What?'

'They have timers,' he yelled over the din of the planes. 'They time the detonator to go off in line with the rooftops.' And with that he pushed me flat and flung himself on top of me.

There was a swishing sound and I peeped over his shoulder. The bomb had landed on the roof, the silky fabric of the parachute cascading down all around it. I closed my eyes tight. Waiting. Waiting. For the end.

45

LONDON, 1941

But nothing happened. I could still hear the hum of the planes and the boom of explosions and people crying out and the wail of the sirens, but there on the roof, I was still breathing. We were still breathing. I could feel Trafalgar's chest going up and down on top of mine.

I dared to open my eyes and saw the folds of parachute silk all over the roof beside us, and the cylindrical shape of the bomb beneath. It was only a few yards away. Why hadn't it exploded?

Trafalgar was clearly thinking the same. He wriggled off me and grabbed my hand.

'Quick,' he said, and he led me over to the door and we raced down the stairs.

'What happened? Why didn't it go off?' I gasped.

'It must have a faulty detonator. It happens sometimes.'

We burst out onto the street and started to run. A deafening boom reverberated through the ground, seeming to shake the buildings from their very foundations, and there was the sound of glass shattering as windows exploded. Trafalgar wrapped himself around me, and it took me a moment to realise that he was trying to shelter me from getting hit by the shrapnel and shards of glass raining down. Screams rang out from nearby. We turned the corner to see an apartment building with part of its front blown off. The air was filled with a choking cloud of dust.

'Use your scarf like a mask,' Trafalgar instructed before doing the same with a handkerchief.

We hurried over to the rubble in front of the building and started helping the wardens, digging people out.

I'm not sure how long we were there – time became this strange thing I was no longer conscious of as the bombing went on and on.

'Do you think it will ever end?' one of the wardens asked at some point.

One of the other helpers shrugged. 'That bastard Goering has really lost his temper tonight. I don't think he's going to stop until he's destroyed all of London.'

Finally, the all-clear sounded. As the last of the ambulances left, Trafalgar looked at me and gave a heavy sigh. His dark hair was grey with dust, his shirt was torn and his face streaked with dirt. We walked back to the Savoy in stunned silence. At one point, I saw a severed hand lying in the middle of the road. It was like being in a surreal nightmare that just wouldn't end.

Thankfully, the Savoy was still standing and had escaped any damage. The lobby was abuzz – it was the worst attack of the war yet. Apparently even the Houses of Parliament had been struck, and most shockingly of all, Queen's Hall had suffered a direct hit from an incendiary bomb and been left in ruins. Hearing this utterly devastated me, and the last thing I wanted was to be around other people. I didn't want to be on my own though either. We reached the lifts and I turned to Trafalgar.

'I don't want to leave you,' he whispered, echoing my thoughts.

'I don't want you to,' I whispered back.

We went up to my room in stunned silence. I caught sight of myself in the mirror and gasped. I was so covered in dust, I looked like a ghost. My ears were still ringing from the noise, and my body was still numb with shock.

'I should have a bath,' I murmured. 'Wash this off.' But I wasn't able to move.

Trafalgar nodded and went into the bathroom, and I heard the sound of water running. Some time later, he reappeared and took my hand and led me into the room. The bath was full, and the steamy air smelled of the rose salts.

'Can I?' he asked softly, reaching for the top button of my blouse.

I nodded, and he began to undress me. But it didn't feel sexual. It didn't feel like anything, I was still so numb. Even when I was standing in front of him in my underwear, I didn't feel self-conscious.

'Would you like me to leave?' he asked, and I shook my head.

I slipped out of my underwear and stepped into the water. It was the perfect temperature. Almost too hot but not quite, and it quickly warmed me to the bone. I slid down further and further until my head was completely submerged. When I came back up, Trafalgar had taken his clothes off and was stepping into the tub. I still didn't feel a thing. But I was glad of his closeness. I couldn't bear the thought of being left alone. I kept thinking of Queen's Hall and how, just a few hours previously, it had been full of music and life and defiance. And yet, in an instant, it had been reduced to rubble.

I brought my knees up to my chest to make room for him. He kept his gaze on me, and I couldn't look away either. That connection was all that was keeping me grounded. It was all that was keeping me from drowning in fear and despair. Then he reached under the water for one of my feet and gently pulled it towards him, bringing it to rest on his chest, where he gently caressed it. It was such a simple thing and yet it was the most intimate and reassuring experience of my entire life. I closed my eyes and leaned back in the water, my body slowly starting to relax as Trafalgar stroked the life back into it.

46

PORTUGAL, 2000

Sofia gestures at the tape recorder, and I press stop.

'Wow,' is all I'm able to say. Her account of London during the Blitz was so raw and so real, I felt as if I was there in the middle of the dust and the debris and the devastation. And her description of her interactions with Trafalgar were so tender and heartfelt. He can't have been one of the demons she spoke about exorcising before. She must have been talking about the Germans.

'Wow indeed,' she says crisply, and at first I think she's being sarcastic, but then I look closer and I see that her face is ashen and her eyes shiny with tears.

'I'm so sorry you experienced that.'

She waves her hand dismissively, as if batting away a fly. 'It was nothing compared to what those poor Londoners endured for years.'

'I can't believe Queen's Hall was destroyed.'

She nods sadly. 'At least it was empty when they bombed it, so no one was killed there.'

'But still, it must have been really traumatic.'

She sighs. 'The concept of trauma wasn't a thing back then. We just had to pick ourselves back up and get on with it.'

'Even so, it's a lot to keep stored inside you for so long.'

'Trust me, I'm the queen of storing things up. I'm like a... a giant bank vault, I've got so much stored up inside of me!'

She reaches for the bottle of wine on the coffee table and tops up her glass. Mine is still full as I was too gripped to even think about drinking while she was speaking.

Sofia raises her glass before taking a sip. 'I have to say it felt a hell of a lot easier keeping it in than letting it out.'

'Hopefully in the end it will feel cathartic,' I reply, reaching for my drink and praying that she doesn't want to finish for the day. I have to know what happened with Trafalgar.

'I very much doubt it,' she says glumly. 'But my sense of justice is currently outweighing my common sense. Although only marginally.'

'What do you mean?' I ask cautiously, aware that any wrong move on my part could cause her to clam up again.

'I have to put right the wrongs,' she says ominously. 'I need to set the record straight.'

But this only confuses me more. What 'record' could she be talking about? In all my research on Sofia prior to coming to Portugal, I didn't find a single negative thing written about her. Surely she can't be talking about idiots like Bing claiming to have been her first love, or the made-up story about her childhood. She helped perpetuate that myth after all, and it hardly seems serious enough to warrant such ominous insinuations.

'How about we take a break from talking about me and you tell me some more about yourself?' she says before lighting a cigarette.

I laugh. 'Are you sure? I've had a very dull life compared to you.'

'I already know enough about you to know that that isn't the case.' She takes a long drag on her cigarette and looks at me intently. 'Why don't you tell me some more about your childhood and what it was like being fostered?'

I feel a little unsettled by this sudden change of tack combined with the directness of her question, but if it helps to get her settled again, then so be it. 'Well, if I had to sum it up in a word, I suppose I would say that it was disappointing.'

'How so?' She looks genuinely fascinated, although I really don't understand why someone with a life as dramatic and interesting as hers would be. I'm guessing she's feigning interest to shift the attention from her.

'It was difficult, seeing the other kids in school with their proper parents and normal families. I used to fantasise about having a proper family of my own – when I wasn't daydreaming about being with my real parents in heaven,' I add with a wry laugh.

Sofia's eyes widen. 'What do you mean?' She leans closer. 'Are your real parents dead?'

'I have no idea. A social worker once told me that my mum was a drug addict, and I don't have a clue about my dad or who he was as he wasn't named on my birth certificate.'

'And you've never felt the desire to try to find out about him?'

I shake my head. Just the idea makes me uncomfortable and always has. 'I honestly don't want to. Why bother looking for someone who clearly doesn't want to be found.'

'But what if he doesn't know you exist? Your mother might have never told him she was pregnant.'

'I suppose I'm scared of what I might find. I don't think I could take any more disappointment in the parental department,' I attempt to joke, but it falls flat, and Sofia keeps staring at me, her expression deadly serious.

'But he might be really nice.'

My discomfort grows. I get that she wants a break from talking about herself, but why the fascination with my birth father? Thankfully, at that moment the phone starts to ring from its side table in the corner.

'Hold that thought,' Sofia says cheerily before going over to answer it. '*Ola!*' she cries cheerily into the receiver.

Almost immediately, her face clouds over.

'*Não, não, não,*' she says firmly, looking at me.

I wonder who she's saying no to and why. Maybe it's Gabriel, reiterating what he said in his note about urgently needing to talk about me. My skin starts to prickle as Sofia starts talking rapidly in Portuguese. There's an almost panicked tone to her voice, a sense that she's pleading with the caller. Then she falls silent and listens.

'*Adeus,*' she says curtly before replacing the receiver on the rest with a heavy clunk.

'Everything OK?' I ask casually as she returns to the sofa.

'Yes, it was just my gardener, Rosária, telling me that she – uh – she wants to plant some more flowers.'

This is such a blatant lie, it would be laughable if I weren't the one being lied to. There's no way Sofia would react so vehemently against having more flowers in her garden, and the way she keeps blinking and biting her bottom lip is a textbook giveaway, which I know from a book I ghostwrote for a body language expert. One of the unexpected perks of being a ghostwriter is that you become an unlikely expert in the most random things.

'Anyway, I'm sorry about before,' she quickly continues. 'I didn't mean to pry about your father and I'm sorry if it made you feel uncomfortable. Why don't you tell me some more about your work instead? I guess you must have met some very interesting people.'

I nod, grateful that she's finally changed the subject but also aware that suddenly changing the subject is another textbook tactic of a liar. 'I have – although they've been a little less interesting recently – until you of course.'

She laughs. 'Glad to hear it! But why so?'

'The last couple of clients couldn't have been less interested in their books, which made it slightly challenging.'

She frowns. 'Why would a person not be interested in their own book?'

'When their manager has negotiated a book deal on their behalf, purely in order to make them more money,' I reply, although I realise that I no longer feel bitter about my previous two jobs. Working with Sofia, as challenging as it might be at times, has changed everything. As has coming to Portugal. I already know that whatever happens, I'm never going to return to the life I found myself in last year. Just like a butterfly trying to squeeze itself back into a cocoon, it would be physically impossible.

'I see.' Sofia takes a sip of wine. 'So, who would you say was the most interesting person you've worked with – until me?' She grins.

'Hmm, well, Joyce Daniel, the Olympic runner, was very inspiring, but I guess the most interesting and well known is the actor Sir Lawrence Bourne – have you heard of him?'

She nods. 'Yes, of course – who hasn't?' She stubs out her cigarette and clears her throat. 'So, shall we crack on with the book then?'

'Oh, yes, absolutely!' I exclaim. 'I need to know what happens with Trafalgar.'

Her face instantly clouds over, and she tops up her glass to the brim. Then she looks at me. 'Before we continue, can I just say that I think you're a wonderful woman, and you mustn't let what happened with your real parents affect your confidence. And you're absolutely right: if you did get to meet your real father, you could discover that you were way better off without him.'

'Yes, exactly.' I smile, but as I get my recorder and notepad ready, I can't help feeling uneasy. I'm not sure if all of Sofia's weird secretiveness is making me paranoid, but I can't shake the feeling that she knows something I don't. Something about me. But how can she?

47

LONDON, 1941

Trafalgar and I didn't speak a word to each other during our bath, and then, when the water had turned lukewarm, we silently dried ourselves and made our way to the bed, where we lay, wrapped up in each other, until sleep finally found us. Or found me at least. I woke about an hour later to find him looking through the desk drawer.

'What are you doing?' I mumbled.

'I'm sorry, I didn't mean to wake you.' He came and sat on the edge of the bed beside me. 'I was looking for a pen to write you a note.'

'What kind of note?' My brain felt sluggish with exhaustion.

'To say goodbye. I didn't want to wake you. You'd only just fallen asleep.'

'What time is it?'

'Just after seven. I'm so sorry. I need to get to work. I'll be needed after last night...'

I nodded. 'I understand, and I have to leave soon too. A driver is coming to take me to my plane at half past eight.' I looked up at him, feeling suddenly hollow with loss. 'So this is goodbye then?' After what we'd been through together, the thought of parting so soon and having an ocean between us felt devastating.

'That depends,' he said, smiling down at me.

'On what?' I shifted into a seated position.

'On whether you want to see me again.'

'Of course I do!' I blurted out.

'Yes!' he exclaimed. 'I was hoping you'd say that.'

'But how will we see each other? I'm about to go back to Portugal.'

'I'll work something out, don't worry.' He reached out and stroked my hair. 'It's so funny.'

'What?'

'I feel so close to you. Closer than...'

'Closer than what?' I sat up a bit more, keeping the sheet up to my chin, suddenly acutely aware that I was naked.

'Than to any other woman I've had a relationship with,' he muttered.

I couldn't help wondering at the implication of his words. Did he now see us as being in a relationship? 'Well, I suppose surviving the worst night of bombing in London together will do that,' I said drily.

He shook his head. 'It's more than that. A lot more. It's that word you taught me.'

'*Bashert*?'

'Yes.' He looked at me as if he wanted to say something else, then sighed and glanced at his watch. 'I have to go. I'm so sorry. But we will see each other again,' he said firmly, and then he leaned in and kissed me. And, once again, I lost all sense of time, but this time for the very best of reasons.

It took me a moment to catch my breath after he'd left. The events of the night before and the suddenness of his leaving when I was still half asleep was a lot to process. With every second that ticked by, it felt more and more like a dream. But then I went through to the bathroom and I saw our damp towels draped over the side of the bath. It hadn't been a dream. It had all been beautifully, painfully real.

I'd thought that my car to the airport might have been cancelled due to London being decimated the night before. But it turned out that Londoners were made of sterner stuff, and when my driver arrived to take me to the airport, the streets were bustling with people picking their way over the rubble on their way to work. Many of them looked grim-faced and pale, but they were still in their suits and getting on with their lives.

As we came to a halt at a traffic crossing, I saw a bookshop with half of its front blown off. A handwritten sign had been stuck outside saying 'MORE OPEN THAN USUAL' and people were inside browsing the shelves. It reminded me of my date with Trafalgar in the library and that wonderful moment of joy I'd experienced there. I might not have been able to freeze time, but I'd always have that memory to treasure forever.

I felt something inside of me spark back into life. If these people could pick themselves up and carry on after almost a year of relentless bombing, then I most certainly could and should after a couple of days. And besides, I had so much to look forward to. After the pain of losing Judith, I'd been gifted with another special soul in the form of Trafalgar. The heartfelt prayer I'd made on the bank of the Tagus prior to coming to London had miraculously been answered – and in the most magical of ways.

'You seem different since London,' Emilio said to me, a couple of days later over dinner in my hotel room.

I felt my cheeks grow warm. 'Yes, well, I guess a brush with death would do that to a girl.'

He frowned. 'You seem so happy though, and you haven't been sarcastic to me once since you got back. It's very out of character.'

I laughed. 'I suppose it's made me more compassionate for the less fortunate.'

'Very funny.'

I studied his face. He looked different too, but not in a good way. His eyes were ringed with dark circles and his jaw was grey with stubble. 'Talking about out of character, what's with the unkempt look?'

He shifted uncomfortably in his seat. 'Oh – I, uh, haven't been sleeping all that well. I have some personal issues going on back home in Chicago.'

'Oh, I see. I'm sorry.'

'It's fine. Nothing compared to what some people are going through.' He took a sip of his whisky before continuing. 'So, Alexandre is keen for us to start coming up with some new material. I assume you've been too busy dodging German bombs to have been thinking about songwriting.'

'Actually, I found my trip to London really inspiring.' I rooted around in my bag for my notebook. Inspiration had struck as soon as the plane for Lisbon had taken off and I'd spent most of the flight scribbling down ideas. 'I have an idea for a song inspired by the spirit of the Londoners – something that captures their air of defiance.' Of course, this idea had been inspired by one particular Londoner, yelling at the German planes on the banks of the Thames. 'Something rousing that people could sing along to, to help inspire them to resist.'

'That sounds awesome!' Emilio exclaimed. 'I've been tinkering around with a couple of upbeat melodies – perhaps we could see if your lyrics fit.'

'Excellent!' I grinned at him. 'I love how you and I are always in synch. It's the perfect partnership.'

He grinned back, and I suddenly remembered the awkward moment in the hotel when he'd almost kissed me. It felt like another lifetime ago.

'The perfect *creative* partnership,' I added.

'Yes.' He nodded, and I felt a moment of unspoken understanding pass between us. That he, too, knew that anything other than a creative partnership would have been a huge mistake.

'And I have an idea,' I continued, 'for a love song.'

'Oh!' He looked surprised.

'It's a ballad about longing, in true fado tradition.'

'Alexandre will be pleased. He was asking me if you had anything like that in the pipeline. He thinks it's time for another "Jacaranda Seeds".'

'Wonderful!' I was barely able to hide my relief. The truth was, my new composition meant just as much to me as 'Jacaranda Seeds'.

There was a beat of silence.

'So, can I ask what, or who, inspired it?' Emilio looked at me expectantly.

I hadn't been planning on telling Emilio the backstory to the song, but I saw an opportunity to make it clear that I didn't harbour any romantic feelings for him and get rid of any residual awkwardness between us for once and for all. 'Someone I met in London.'

'Oh.' He looked surprised. 'But you were only there for three days.'

'They were a very intense three days.' I grinned across the table at him. 'Everything felt magnified because of the bombing.' Of course, I knew it was way deeper than that.

'I see. So who's the lucky guy then?'

I started to regret telling him. I didn't want what happened with Trafalgar to be picked over by someone else, I wanted to keep our precious time together hidden away, just like Judith's pesky diamond, concealed in the wardrobe, for only me to see.

'Oh, just a guy I met in the restaurant at the Savoy.' I couldn't help smiling at the memory of the twinkly-eyed Trafalgar peering over his menu at me.

'Wow, you have got it bad.'

I stared at Emilio. He was smiling, but there was a slight edge to his voice that made me think he wasn't just teasing.

'Yes, well, I'll probably never see him again, but hey, if we get a good song out of it...' I quipped, trying to downplay it.

'Absolutely.' He nodded. 'It's all good material. OK, let's hear what you've got.'

'What do you want to start with?'

'Let's hear the ballad.'

I turned to the page in my notebook where I'd scribbled the first notes for what would become 'Ocean Longing'. It's so strange to think that I had no idea when I sat hunched over in that plane, daydreaming of Trafalgar and consumed with a bone-deep longing, that these scrawled words would go on to work their way inside the hearts and minds of millions of people all over the world – and continue to do so! Back then, I was just trying to express what I was feeling in its rawest, truest form. But maybe that is the secret to good art – it's the rawness that resonates the most with people.

Feeling a little self-conscious, I started to sing, pretending I needed to look at my notes when, in truth, the lyrics had instantly committed themselves to my memory. I turned away slightly and closed my eyes and thought of how I'd felt that morning I'd said goodbye to Trafalgar, and my voice wavered slightly, but I got through it. When I reached the end, I took a moment before turning back to look at Emilio. His expression was unreadable, and instantly the doubts began flooding my mind. The song had been too personal; it had meant too much to me and clouded my judgement. It was soppy nonsense.

'That was... that was...' Now his voice was wavering.

I held my breath and waited for him to continue.

'That was your next smash hit,' he said quietly.

I was elated at his response, little realising that the song for which I am still so well known would come to haunt me like a curse.

48

PORTUGAL, 2000

'But why?' I blurt out as Sofia stops talking and closes her eyes.

She opens her eyes and frowns at me. 'Why what?'

'Why is it a curse?' I know by now that I shouldn't push her, but I can't help it. 'It's meant so much to so many people,' I continue, wanting to lift her spirits whilst simultaneously trying to work out what she might have meant. I suppose if things didn't end well with Trafalgar, it might make the song somewhat painful to her, but still, a curse?

'Yes well, it hasn't to me,' she snaps, and it's as if a cloud has passed across the sun, her dramatic change in mood bringing a sudden chill to the room.

'It did to me,' I say defiantly.

She gives a derisory snort. 'When you were crying over a man who wasn't worthy of your time in the first place?'

There's a sharpness to her tone that reminds me a little of how Robin used to get when he was determined to win an argument, and it sets me on edge. 'You don't have the monopoly on pain, you know,' I snap.

She stares at me, then goes to pour herself another glass of wine, but she's finished the bottle. 'I might not have the monopoly on pain,' she says, placing the empty bottle down, 'but I feel certain that what I've been through in my life is worse than you being dumped by that idiot. You said yourself that your relationship was over a long time ago. So by leaving you he actually did you a favour, which you'll realise one day, whereas...' She falls silent and downs the last of her wine.

A former version of me – the version who put up with Robin's patronising put-downs – feels close to tears. But then another part of me kicks in and what feels like a lifetime's unexpressed rage comes roaring to the surface.

'Actually, when I listened to "Ocean Longing" I wasn't longing for my ex; I was longing for the child I wasn't able to have – that I'll *never* be able to have.'

I see a flash of red out of the corner of my eye, and the ghost of my dream daughter comes running into the room and scrambles up onto the sofa beside me, sucking her thumb and gazing up at me. Tears begin forming in my eyes, but I'm determined not to let Sofia see them.

'You might think that I'm pathetic for letting that get to me, but I'm not. I'm human. And I know you're keeping something from me too,' I add for good measure. 'So, if you want to continue with me as your ghostwriter, I need you to be honest with me. Totally honest.'

I stand up, knocking my notebook onto the floor, but I don't bother picking it up. 'I'm going to go for a walk to give you a chance to think about it, but if you're not prepared to be straight with me, then I'm going to leave.' I've played my trump card and it may well backfire, but I'm so angry and upset I don't actually care.

I march into the kitchen and fling open the back door. Gabriel is standing there holding a bucket of fish, his hand mid-air as if he was about to knock.

'Oh great!' I mutter.

He instantly looks concerned. 'Lily? What's wrong?'

'Ask Sofia. Maybe you could write another note about me while you do it.'

I know I sound childish, but I get some satisfaction from seeing the look of shock and embarrassment on his face. I march down through the garden and onto the beach.

49

PORTUGAL, 2000

After stomping around on the beach for a while, I still don't feel any calmer, so I march back into the living room, fired up and ready for a potential confrontation, but there's no one there.

'Hello?' I call out cautiously, but there's no response.

I jump at the sound of a click from the sofa, and I see my tape recorder sitting on the arm. The click was the sound of the tape coming to an end. I must have left it recording.

I left it recording!

I grab it and race up to my bedroom, closing the door behind me and sitting down on the bed. I rewind the tape a few minutes and press play. It's silent. I rewind it some more and this time when I press play, I wince as I hear my own voice.

'... for the child I wasn't able to have – that I'll *never* be able to have. You might think that I'm pathetic for letting that get to me, but I'm not. I'm human. And I know you're keeping something from me. So, if you want to continue with me as your ghostwriter, I want you to be honest with me. Totally honest. I'm going to go for a walk to give you a chance to think about it, but if you're not prepared to be straight with me, then I'm going to leave.'

I sit dead still and listen to the sound of me leaving the room.

'My God!' I hear Sofia mutter.

I hold my breath, then hear the creak of the door opening and Gabriel's deep voice booms out of the recorder. He's speaking in Portuguese, but whatever he's saying sounds urgent and I hear my name. I stop the tape and replay it, pausing after every couple of words to translate them using my Portuguese dictionary, writing them on a piece of paper.

What... is... wrong... with... Lily?

Then Sofia starts speaking, and again I slowly translate, writing the words in English.

I... upset... her.

I go through the rest of the recording like this, translating the key words, then figuring out the sentences and writing them down...

'How?' Gabriel asks. 'Has she found out?'

My skin erupts in goosebumps. Have I found out what?

'No,' Sofia replies. 'Although she knows I'm keeping something from her.'

'Shit,' Gabriel says. 'I think she read my note to you too.'

I stare at the tape recorder. So whatever the big secret is, Gabriel is clearly in on it. I glance at the driftwood rooster on the windowsill. After he gave it to me, I thought I could trust him. I thought we were friends. Have I been an idiot? Was I reading things into the situation that just weren't there?

I press play, and Sofia speaks. I flick through the dictionary like a woman possessed, to translate what she's saying.

'What should I do?'

'Tell her the truth.'

There's that word again – *verdade*. Truth. But the truth about what? Or, I reflect, who? I shiver as I think back to Sofia's questions about my real dad. Is this somehow connected to him? Does she know who he is? Is that the secret they've been keeping from me? Of course it isn't, I tell myself – that would be ridiculous.

I press play again and translate Sofia's next sentence.

'But if I tell her the truth, she'll hate me.'

My stomach churns. What on earth are they keeping from me?

'You will have to tell her in the end,' Gabriel responds.

'But we haven't finished the book yet. We're not even close. Oh God!' Sofia's voice rises in panic.

I hear the sound of movement. 'We need to go and get...' Gabriel says, his voice fading, and I realise that they were leaving the room. Sure enough, I hear the door creaking closed.

What do they need to go and get? Where have they gone? And what should I do?

I go over to the window and look down at the garden. As my gaze falls on the rose bush, I remember Sofia burying the box beneath it. Could that hold the key to all the secrecy?

I race downstairs and into the garden, buzzing from a mixture of anger and adrenaline. Was this whole project started under some kind of false pretence? Was I specifically picked to ghostwrite the book for some kind of nefarious motive? I'm aware that my thinking is becoming increasingly far-fetched, but how else can I explain all the strange goings-on?

I crouch by the rose bush and start digging at the earth with my bare hands. I should have thought to use a spoon at least, but I need to get the box before Sofia returns. Mud clumps beneath my nails and covers my skin, but I keep digging, and finally I feel something solid. I tug at the box and pull it free, sprinkling earth everywhere. I open it a crack and see that it's full of newspaper clippings. But before I can properly look at them, the back door of the cottage bursts open, flooding the garden with light.

'Lily!' I hear Sofia cry. 'What are you doing?'

50

PORTUGAL, 2000

'How about you tell me what *you're* doing?' I march over to Sofia and stare at her defiantly, deciding that attack is the best form of defence – my *only* form of defence. 'Why did you bury this box in the garden?' I ask, stepping inside. As I hold the box out to her in the bright light of the kitchen, it suddenly seems a lot more innocuous and rather anticlimactic, but then I notice Sofia's stunned expression.

'How did you know?' she gasps.

'I saw you last night.'

Gabriel bounds into the kitchen, holding a bag of groceries. 'Lily!' he cries cheerily, putting the bag on the table and coming over. 'How are you? Oh...' His smile fades as he looks at the box in my muddy hands. 'What is that?'

'She knows,' Sofia says glumly, looking away.

'No, actually, I don't know!' I exclaim. I go over to the table and place the box in the centre. 'I saw Sofia burying it in the garden,' I say to Gabriel, although I'm sure he already knows she did this. I glare at him. 'I take it you know what's inside it?'

Gabriel looks at Sofia and throws up his hands helplessly.

'I don't understand,' I say. 'Can one of you please explain

what is going on? And before you lie to me again, I heard you talking on the tape before you went out.'

'What tape?' Gabriel asks, clearly horrified.

'I accidentally left my voice recorder on when I walked out earlier.'

Sofia and Gabriel look at each other, and then she lets out a laugh. 'I think this is what's known as being caught red-handed.'

'But being caught doing what?' I cry. 'Why did you feel the need to hide a box full of clippings from me?'

'You did see them?' Sofia's eyes widen.

'No, you turned up before I was able to read them.'

'You have to tell her,' Gabriel says, and, to my relief, Sofia nods.

'But first I need a strong coffee.' She gives me an apologetic smile.

'I'll put some on.' Gabriel goes over to the stove.

'Come.' Sofia picks up the box and beckons at me to follow her into the living room. She sits down on the sofa and pats the space beside her for me to join her. 'First of all, I'm so sorry.' She clasps my hand tightly as I sit down. 'I've handled this so badly.'

I feel myself soften a little. 'Please just tell me what's happening. And tell me the truth,' I add firmly.

'Of course. But before I do...' She clears her throat. She looks so nervous. 'I want you to know that it seemed like a good plan at the time.'

'What did?'

'Hiring you to write the book. But I didn't contemplate how it would feel once I'd got to know you – and grown to care for you – care for you a lot.' She looks down into her lap, like she might be about to start crying. 'I guess I was driven mad by anger and the need for justice.'

'Can you please just tell me!' None of this is making any sense and I can feel myself starting to panic.

She nods. 'But to explain fully I'm going to have to go back to where we left off, when I returned to Lisbon.'

'Oh... OK,' I say, although I'm not exactly sure how going back to 1941 is going to explain the secret she's been keeping from me. I really hope she isn't fobbing me off.

She lets go of my hand, and we both settle back on the sofa.

'All right, here goes nothing,' she says, and I realise that her voice is trembling.

51

LISBON, 1941

When Alexandre heard 'Ocean Longing', he decided to release it as soon as possible, for which I was very grateful. I wanted the record to be played in Britain. I wanted Trafalgar to hear it and to realise that it was about him. By the time the record came out in September 1941, it had been four months since we'd seen each other and in that time I hadn't heard a thing from him. I'd been so shell-shocked when he left me at the Savoy, I'd completely forgotten to tell him I was living at the Hotel Aviz and, of course, I had no way of contacting him. I didn't even know his real name.

The more time that passed, the more our experiences during the Blitz took on a dreamlike quality. The emotions contained within the lyrics felt a little like capturing smoke in a bottle, reminding and reassuring me that I hadn't dreamed it, and the feelings I'd experienced were real. But why, oh why, hadn't Trafalgar found a way to contact me since?

On my more optimistic days, I told myself that he'd been sent on some top-secret undercover mission, rescuing Allied pilots who'd been downed over France perhaps, and that as soon as his mission or the war was over, he'd be on the first plane to Lisbon. On my more pessimistic days, I tortured myself with thoughts of him perishing at the hands of the Germans, although since that terrible night in May, they'd stopped bombing London so frequently. The reason for this became apparent a month later when the Germans invaded Russia and the Luftwaffe became otherwise engaged.

Alexandre arranged a string of gigs for me in Lisbon when the single came out, the first of which was in Estoril at the Hotel Palácio.

'I still can't come to this place without thinking of vomit,' I said to Emilio with a shudder as we arrived in the lobby.

He laughed. 'Well, you'll be glad to hear I don't have any jobs for you tonight – other than to knock 'em all dead with the new song.'

'I'll try my best.' I felt suddenly afraid. 'Ocean Longing' was so personal to me, just as much as 'Jacaranda Seeds'. If people didn't like it, it would sting. 'Do you fancy a drink?'

To my surprise, he shook his head. 'I think I'll go to the casino. See if I can get those cards to pay me back, it's about time they fell in my favour.'

'Ah, has Lady Luck been unkind to you then?'

'You could say that,' he said with a sigh. 'I'll see you later.'

'OK.' I frowned as I watched him go. He used to stride into a room, but now his broad shoulders were slumped and there was no sign of his old swagger. I'd asked Alexandre what was going on with Emilio, but he'd just shrugged and muttered something about his wife not being well. Now I wondered if it was more to do with a gambling debt.

I went through to the bar and ordered a martini. As I sat there sipping it, it struck me how much I'd changed since I'd last been at the Palácio, sitting on that very same bar stool, hitching up my dress, hoping to lure Sinclair into my trap. It had been less than a year, but I felt as if I'd aged by ten. Not in a bad way though. My trip to London and coming face to face with death seemed to have stretched me as a person, and I felt strengthened by the experience. If I encountered Sinclair now, I wouldn't feel the slightest bit ruffled. I'd stood on the bank of the Thames and yelled obscenities at the Luftwaffe, for God's sake. I'd survived a parachute bomb. After that, anything else seemed small fry.

I took a sip of my drink, feeling pretty pleased with myself, but then I saw a sight that sent a chill right through me. A mean-faced man with blond hair and a thin moustache had entered the bar and was looking around. I knew right away that it was Kurt Fischer. I hadn't seen him since he'd abducted the refugee from the street right in front of me. But now there he was again, the proverbial bad penny.

I turned away and pretended to study the bar menu, my heart pounding. I needed to let Emilio know Fischer was there. Perhaps we could apprehend him and try to find out what had happened to Judith. But then I remembered that I still had the pesky diamond. If I let Fischer know I was connected to Judith, it would make me a target of the Gestapo for sure. And now I was so well known, there'd be no hiding place from them – for me or the Vadodara Teardrop.

I glanced over my shoulder and saw Fischer leaving the bar. Despite my concerns, I couldn't let him go; he was my one remaining link to Judith. I didn't know what I could do, but I knew I had to follow him. I slid off my stool and hurried into the lobby just in time to see him disappearing through the main door.

I followed Fischer down the winding path from the hotel towards the casino, my mind racing. Perhaps if I saw who he was here to meet, it might help me find out about Judith. I knew I was clutching at straws, but I had to do something.

When we reached the casino, Fischer marched along the central aisle, clearly looking for someone. But who? I gulped as I thought of the wealthier refugees who'd made Estoril their home since fleeing the Nazis. Was he going to snatch one of them to send to the German prison camps? I had to find Emilio. I had to try to stop Fischer.

I glanced at my watch. I had less than an hour before my performance. Keeping one eye on Fischer, I scanned the clusters of people gathered around the roulette wheels and poker tables. Where the hell was Emilio? As my tension grew, everything else seemed to become heightened too – the voices and the laughter, the music and the spinning of the wheels. Even the huge chandeliers glimmering from above seemed garish and gaudy.

I watched as Fischer hovered by a roulette table, scrutinising the people sitting there. Was he closing in on his prey? I was so busy watching I didn't look where I was going, and I crashed right into someone.

'Watch it!' I snapped, even though I'd been the one to blame.

'Sofia?'

I turned to see Emilio. His collar was undone and his tie skew-whiff, and there was a look of panic on his face.

'What are you doing here?'

'I was looking for you,' I hissed. 'And following a member of the Gestapo.'

'Who?' His look of panic grew.

'The one I saw kidnapping the refugee. The one who was following my friend. He's here in the casino.' I looked back at the roulette table. Fischer had disappeared. 'Damn!'

'What?'

'He's gone.'

Emilio grabbed my arm. 'You need to get out of here too. It's almost time for your performance. Alexandre will kill me if you're not there on time.'

'But—'

'But nothing! Come on – we need to go.' Emilio began steering me back towards the entrance.

'But I wanted you to see him,' I cried. 'I thought maybe we could try to find out what happened to my friend.'

'It's too dangerous,' he muttered.

I stared at him. He looked really rattled.

'I don't understand.'

'Wait till we're outside.'

We hurried out and along the footpath. Then Emilio stopped and glanced all around to check the coast was clear.

'There's an operation going on here tonight,' he whispered.

'What kind of operation?'

'We have intelligence that the Gestapo are here to meet with a member of the British aristocracy – someone with close ties to their government who will be giving them some top-secret information – information that could jeopardise the lives of thousands of Allied troops.'

'Shit!'

'Exactly!' He linked my arm again, and we carried on walking. 'So you mustn't do anything to put it at risk.'

'Of course.' I felt crushed. I completely understood what he was saying, but my heart broke thinking of Judith.

'There are people planted in the casino – undercover agents – trying to find out who the traitor is.'

'Oh, I see.' Everything began falling into place. No wonder Emilio looked so stressed. 'And that's why you're here?' I whispered.

'Exactly.' He nodded. 'And I need to get back as soon as I've got you to the hotel safely.'

'Go!' I exclaimed. 'I can get back by myself.'

He shook his head. 'No way. I need to make sure you're safe.'

I frowned at him. 'Why would I not be safe?'

'You're a high-profile singer. Everyone knows you went to London to perform. The Nazis will have seen that as you siding with the Allies.' He gave my arm a reassuring squeeze. 'I'm sure it's all right, but it's better to be safe than sorry.'

I nodded but still felt bitterly disappointed. I didn't care about being safe. All I cared about was Judith. It just about killed me that the man who undoubtedly knew what had happened to her was in such close proximity and yet I couldn't do a thing.

We returned to the hotel in silence. When we reached the lobby, I gave Emilio a hug. 'Please stay safe,' I whispered in his ear, and as I felt him grip me tighter, I could tell that he was scared too.

'Good luck, Castello – knock 'em dead,' he said but with none of his normal zest. Then he turned and hurried off.

After a much-needed glass of wine and cigarette in my room, I got changed into a midnight-blue satin dress with matching heels and made my way downstairs to the bar. It was now buzzing with people, and my fear grew. My conversation with Emilio had unsettled me, and as I waited in the wings to go on, I had a moment of panic as my mind went blank and I couldn't recall any of my lyrics.

The hotel compère welcomed me to the stage, and the house lights dimmed. I walked into the spotlight, encouraged by the warm smiles of the musicians. I gripped the microphone, leaning into the stand for support. The band began playing the opening bars of 'This Doll' and the jaunty beat kicked me back into focus, and once again the magic of music took over and the words all came back to me.

The rest of the set passed by in a blur, and before I knew it, it was time for the final song. I'd kept 'Ocean Longing' till last as it had become such a huge hit, and, sure enough, as soon as I sang the first line, the place erupted in cheers. I closed my eyes and thought of Trafalgar, the lyrics conjuring up memories of the events that had inspired them. I poured every ounce of my longing into the song, my voice cracking with emotion as I reached the final chorus. What if I never saw him again? *Please, God, let me see him again*, I thought as I sang the last line.

What happened next seemed to happen in slow motion. I opened my eyes. The place erupted in applause. The lights came back up. And I saw Trafalgar standing in front of the stage, staring up at me, open-mouthed in shock.

52

LISBON, 1941

I stumbled down from the stage, certain I had to be hallucinating. But no, Trafalgar was still standing there, dressed in a smart black suit, crisp white shirt and tie. He looked as stunned as I felt. I was about to ask him what he was doing there when it dawned on me – he must have been one of the agents sent to identify the British aristocrat who'd been selling secrets to the Germans. And for all I knew, Gestapo agents could be watching us right now. I needed to be discreet, so I wiped any trace of recognition from my face.

'Good evening,' I said politely.

'Good evening,' he replied, holding out his hand in greeting.

I shook it and stepped closer.

'I feel like I must be dreaming,' he whispered in my ear.

'Me too. But you're not. Room 402,' I whispered back before releasing his hand and stepping back.

He gave me the briefest nod and strode away, and I was swept up into a sea of people wishing to congratulate me on my performance.

I was finally able to return to my room about half an hour later. As I let myself in, I was hoping Trafalgar might be there already. I even checked the wardrobe! But there was no sign of him, and I felt a growing disappointment. He was there on a work mission; he probably wouldn't be able to come at all. So close and yet so far.

I went over to the window. A half-moon hung in the sky, partially obscured by cloud. Down below, the palm trees swayed in the breeze like a row of hula dancers, and beyond them I could just make out the dark line of the sea. On the surface, this place seemed so much safer and more beautiful than bombed-out London, but when you knew that it was crawling with Nazis and traitors, all you could see was the ugliness of humanity. I thought of Judith and how sweet and kind she was, and it made my heart break. It seemed so unfair that the good people of the world should suffer so much while evil triumphed.

I was startled from my contemplation by a soft knock on the door. I let out a soft gasp of delight. He'd come! I ran over to the door and flung it open.

'Oh, it's you!' I was unable to hide my disappointment when I saw Emilio standing there.

'Gee, thanks!' he exclaimed. 'Don't sound too happy to see me.'

He walked in, and my heart sank. Now, if Trafalgar did arrive, it would be all kinds of awkward.

'Were you expecting someone else?' Emilio looked at me almost accusingly.

'Possibly.' I felt my hackles begin to rise. He had no right getting uppity about me having a visitor. He had a wife back home in Chicago for Christ's sake. 'How did it go? Did you catch your guy?'

'Not yet. I just came to see how the show went and to make sure you're OK,' he replied huffily.

'I'm sorry, it's just that...'

'What?'

I decided to go for broke. 'The guy I wrote "Ocean Longing" about is here,' I whispered.

Emilio instantly looked at the bathroom door. 'Here?' he whispered back.

'In the hotel. He's coming up to see me, and I haven't seen him since London and—' I broke off, hoping that this would be enough to send Emilio on his way, but he remained rooted to the spot.

'Who is this person?'

'I told you, someone I met in the Savoy when I was staying there.' I started ushering him back over to the door.

Emilio's expression was impossible to read. 'And he was just another guest at the hotel?'

'Yes! I told you all this.'

'OK,' he said but very reluctantly.

I opened the door, praying Trafalgar wouldn't be standing there about to knock. Thankfully, the corridor was empty.

'Please be careful,' Emilio said quietly as he stepped outside. 'You're famous now – you don't want people taking advantage of you.'

I let out a snort of laughter at the nerve of him saying this. 'He's not taking advantage of me – and he isn't married either,' I added for good measure.

Emilio took a step back, looking stung. 'I – uh...' He gave a sigh. 'OK, Castello. I guess I'll see you in the morning then.'

'Maybe.' I shut the door and sighed. I was sick of him acting as if he was my boss.

I marched over to the crystal decanters on a side table and poured myself a brandy. I'd only taken a couple of sips when there was a knock on the door. My heart skipped a beat, but I told myself not to get too excited as it could very well be Emilio returning to give me another lecture.

I opened the door and my spirits soared as I saw Trafalgar

standing there. He walked in, and I closed the door, my body fizzing with excitement.

'Now do you believe in fate?' he asked, his eyes gleaming. 'I had no idea you would be here today. Then I walk into the bar and there you are, singing.' He grabbed my hands. 'Don't you think it's incredible?'

'Yes, but...' As much as it was incredible to see him, I also felt a little disappointed. Had he come to Portugal with no plan to see me?

'I'm here for work,' he said quietly, as if reading my mind. 'One night only.' He sighed. 'It was torturing me, knowing that I was in the same country as you and yet not able to see you. But fate had other plans!' He went over to the open window and flung his arms open wide to the sky. 'Thank you!' he cried.

I started to laugh. 'You're crazy!'

He laughed. 'Yes. Crazy about you.'

'That has to be the worst line I've ever heard – and, trust me, I've heard a few.'

'Ow!' He clasped his hands to his heart. 'OK, how about this for a line? Since Thursday the eighth of May 1941, I haven't stopped thinking about you. I could have written that song you were singing tonight about how I've longed for you.'

'I actually wrote it about you,' I murmured, looking away, suddenly embarrassed. 'I thought you might have heard it. It sold very well in Britain.'

'I've been away,' he replied. 'And I mean really away,' he added enigmatically. 'You know, work.'

I nodded, my heart racing as I wondered what kind of derring-do he might been involved in. It made me all the more relieved to see him standing in front of me, safe and sound.

Trafalgar started to laugh.

'What's so funny?'

'I'd been so worried you'd forgotten all about me.'

'Why would I forget about you?' I stared at him, baffled.

'You're a famous singer. You must get men throwing themselves at you all the time. Men who take you to fancy places like this. I took you to a bombed-out library.'

'And don't forget our night beneath a bridge,' I added with a grin, touched to see this vulnerable side to him. Yet more reassurance that he was genuine and could be trusted.

He laughed. 'Exactly! I almost got you killed. Twice.'

'And that's why I'll never forget you,' I said softly. 'And why you're so much more interesting than all the rest.'

He looked at me for a moment before turning back to the window. 'Thank you!' he cried to the sky again before coming towards me. 'Thank you,' he whispered, taking hold of my hands. 'So, we have a choice.'

'Go on,' I said, my excitement building.

'I only have two hours before I have to leave for my flight back to England.'

My heart sank.

'So we could spend those two hours talking about the weather.'

I looked at him, confused. 'Since when have we ever talked about the weather?'

'I'm British, we always talk about the weather.'

'Fair enough.'

'Or we could do what we are supposed to do. What we are fated to do.'

'Which is?'

'*Você me permite te beijar.*' He looked at me, concerned. 'Did I say that right? I learned it specially for this moment.'

I felt a burst of excitement. 'But you said you didn't know you were going to see me tonight.'

'No, but I knew I would one day. How many times do I have to tell you, Sofia? I believe in fate!' he exclaimed. 'And fate brought us together for a reason on Thursday the eighth of May

1941,' he said grandly before adding, 'So, did I get the Portuguese right?'

'Yes, you got the Portuguese right, and yes...'

'What?' He looked at me hopefully.

'Yes, I will allow you to kiss me.'

He clapped his hands gleefully, and I prepared myself for the kiss, but before I knew it, he was back over at the window exclaiming 'Thank you!' again.

'*Meu deus!*' I rolled my eyes. 'Are you going to spend your two hours shouting at the sky or kissing me?'

'Kissing you!' he cried, bounding back over.

And then finally, all my longing was over. And fate began hammering another nail in my coffin.

53

LISBON, 1941

I'd never understood why sex was called 'making love' until that night with Trafalgar. Prior to that, I'd always thought that it would be more accurate to call it 'making believe' or 'making awkward shapes with my body', or, in the case of that terrible night with Bing, 'making a damn fool of myself'! But that night, as Trafalgar and I gave ourselves to each other, I could feel the love being made between us. Everything that had happened in London was the prelude – the conversations, the laughter, the fear as we faced death together, and the bath where he caressed the life back into me; now, finally, we had the chance to pull all those moments into their natural crescendo. And as we came to rest, we looked at each other and, in perfect synchronicity, both said, 'I love you.'

'And now I have to leave you!' he said, looking at the clock and instantly ruining the moment.

'No!' I cried, clinging to his arm.

'But I'll be back.' He took my hand and held it tight. 'I promise. As soon as I can, and for longer. And if you ever come back to London to do another show...'

I nodded eagerly. In that moment, I didn't care one bit

about the bombs or the danger. All I could think was that I couldn't spend another four months longing for him until it hurt.

He got out of bed and picked his clothes up off the floor. 'I hate this,' he sighed, sitting on the edge of the bed and pulling on his trousers. 'I hate leaving you.'

Then don't, I wanted to say, but obviously I couldn't. It would have been different if he had an ordinary job, but there was no way I would expect the SOE to say it was fine for him to abandon his work for the Allies to stay with his lover.

'Did you achieve what you came here for?' I asked, remembering what Emilio had told me.

He looked a little startled. 'Here?' he said, pointing to the bed.

I laughed. 'No, here in Lisbon.' I leaned closer. 'I know about it,' I whispered.

He looked even more confused.

'One of my contacts here told me – about the member of the British aristocracy.'

He continued staring at me bewildered, and I wondered if he was pretending not to know because he'd been sworn to secrecy. But surely he knew he could trust me, given how we first met.

'Well, I hope you caught him,' I said.

'Oh, right, yes,' he said quickly, and I realised that I shouldn't have said anything. I didn't want him scared that I'd blab about it to anyone else.

'I'm really going to miss you – especially now,' I said, eager to change the subject.

'Me too.' He leaned down and kissed me. 'Is there any way I can call you, once I'm back in London?'

'Of course! I'm living at the Hotel Aviz.'

'The Hotel Aviz,' he echoed as if committing it to memory.

His expression became grave. 'God, I hate this war,' he muttered before standing up and putting on his shirt.

'Me too.'

He came and sat beside me. 'When this is all over, I hope fate brings us together for longer. I hope it brings us together for...'

I looked at him questioningly. 'For what?'

'Forever?' he said, but as if asking my permission.

'I hope that too,' I whispered, and we kissed again.

After he'd gone, I lay there for about an hour, trying to relive every moment of our all too brief time together.

When I heard the birds beginning their dawn chorus outside, I had a bath and got dressed, whistling along with them. I don't think I'd ever felt so full of joy.

By the time Emilio arrived, I was ready to go. But as soon as I opened the door to him, I did a double take. He looked even more dishevelled than before, with his shirt untucked and half unbuttoned and no sign of his tie.

'Are you all right?' I asked as he strode into my room.

'It's been a very long night,' he said, making his way straight over to the drinks table.

'And clearly it isn't over yet,' I remarked as he poured himself a large Scotch.

He turned back to me. 'So, did your mystery suitor turn up?'

'He did. How about you? Did the aristocrat turn up? Did they meet with the Gestapo?'

'Yes, but then he managed to give us the slip.' Emilio sighed. 'I've spent all night searching high and low, but it's as if he vanished into thin air.' He plonked down in one of the armchairs by the fireplace.

'I'm sorry,' I said, perching on the arm of the chair opposite him, trying to rein in my joyous spirit in sympathy.

'It's OK. At least we know who he is now, so we can keep tabs on him. Hopefully next time he meets with the Gestapo, the SOE will catch him red-handed.'

'Who is it? Am I allowed to know?'

'The Earl of Beaumont.'

I pictured a ruddy-faced earl puffing on a cigar and drinking a glass of port.

'You've actually met him.' Emilio looked at me over his glass.

'I have?' I stared at him, confused. 'When?'

'When you were in London.'

I immediately thought of the ruddy-faced cigar-puffing Bertrand. 'Does this Earl of Beaumont own a record label by any chance?'

'No. He's a member of the SOE.'

'He's in the SOE and I've met him?' I said faintly. The room seemed to tilt on its axis.

Emilio nodded, grim-faced. 'He's the contact you gave the sheet music to. The one code-named Trafalgar.'

54

PORTUGAL, 2000

Sofia stops talking as Gabriel enters the room carrying a pot of coffee and two cups.

'So – uh – everything is OK?' he asks as he places them on the low table in front of us.

Sofia nods.

Gabriel looks at me anxiously, and I nod too. I'm still too busy reeling from the Trafalgar bombshell to think about anything else. He pours us both cups of coffee then backs off. 'OK, I'd better go and, you know...' He looks at Sofia, and she nods.

I wait until he's left the room and I hear the front door close behind him.

'I think I might know why you've been keeping this from me,' I say as Sofia takes a sip of her coffee.

'You do?' she splutters, causing the coffee to spill onto her chin.

'Yes,' I reply, eager for the chance to prove I'm not quite as naive as she might think. 'Is this something to do with my real father?' I take a breath before continuing, my heart pounding. 'Am I related to Trafalgar?'

'What?' Sofia exclaims, putting her cup back on the table.

'Did you hire me to write your book because you found out that I was related to Trafalgar? I'm guessing he must have been my grandfather though.' I study the expression on Sofia's face. 'Were you hoping to track him down through me? Is that why you asked me if I'd ever tried to find my real dad? Do you know who he is?'

Sofia stares at me, but rather than look guilty as I'd expected, she looks stunned. 'Oh my goodness!'

Does this mean I'm right? Maybe she's stunned at my ingenuity at working it all out? I wonder, and I feel a flicker of excitement laced with dread. Am I finally going to find out who my real father is – or was? But does this mean that my grandfather was a traitor? And then the craziest thought of all occurs to me. What if Sofia became pregnant after sleeping with Trafalgar? I stare at her wide-eyed.

'Oh my God, are you my grandma?'

'Oh, Lily.' She grabs hold of my hand, and I begin to well up. 'How I wish I was, but no, I'm not your grandmother and Trafalgar isn't your grandfather. I was only asking those questions about your parents because I found it fascinating that we both have that in common – that we never got to know our real dads.'

'Oh.' I feel a rush of disappointment before realising that she said 'isn't' rather than 'wasn't' when it came to Trafalgar. 'Wait a minute, you said "isn't" – does that mean... Is Trafalgar still alive?'

'Yes, and...' She glances nervously at the muddy box on the table.

'And?' My breath catches in my throat. Why is she looking so anxious? What could be on those newspaper clippings that she doesn't want me seeing?

'And this is who he is.' Sofia opens the box and hands it to me.

I take out the top clipping and stare at the headline.

'But... but...' I stammer as I'm overwhelmed by a choking sense of horror. 'How is this possible?'

55

LISBON, 1941

Emilio stared at me. 'Why do you look like you just found out Santa doesn't exist?'

Utterly shell-shocked by his revelation, I somehow managed to gather myself enough to respond. 'I – uh – I can't believe he's a traitor. Are you sure? The man I met was so young. And he seemed like an ordinary Londoner from the way he spoke. He didn't seem like an earl at all.' I thought of the way Trafalgar had yelled up at the German planes. His anger had seemed so real. Could it all have been just for show? Was the reason he was brave enough to stand on the riverbank because he knew they weren't going to bomb there? Had I just been hoodwinked by the biggest cad ever to have lived?

I looked at Emilio, the last vestiges of hope draining from me as he nodded gravely.

I went to fetch my cigarettes, as much to hide my face so he couldn't see the growing horror written all over it. The reason Emilio couldn't find the British traitor was because I'd been unwittingly harbouring him in my room. I'd been unwittingly harbouring a traitor who had come here to meet with a member of the Gestapo – the same member of the Gestapo I saw capturing a refugee from the street; the same man I was certain was behind Judith's disappearance. Was Trafalgar really capable of such a terrible thing? I felt sick to my stomach as I had a flashback to waking up and seeing him looking in the desk drawer in my room at the Savoy. Was he really looking for something to write a note on, or was he snooping through my things, the same way I'd done to Sinclair? Had he been spying on me for the Germans? Oh God!

I lit a cigarette and took a long, slow drag before returning to the armchair, unable to look Emilio in the eye I felt so disgusting and ashamed, not to mention heartbroken.

'Excuse me?' Emilio said indignantly, instantly making me jump. Did he know? Had he worked it out?

'What?' I said nervously.

'Aren't you forgetting something?'

'What?'

'To offer me a smoke!'

'Oh! I'm sorry. Of course.' I leaned forward and held the pack out to him, hoping he wouldn't notice my trembling fingers.

'Are you all right?' he asked, looking at me intently before taking a cigarette.

'Yes. I'm just a little unnerved. I can't believe I met with a traitor. Do you think he passed the information I gave him in the sheet music to the Germans?' The more I thought about it, the more horrific it became.

'More than likely,' Emilio said grimly.

I glanced over at the bed, at the rumpled bedsheets and the pillow that still bore the imprint of that traitor's head, and I realised that I had to come clean. If I didn't, I'd be betraying the Allies too. 'There's something I need to tell you,' I muttered.

'What is it?'

'Trafalgar, the man I met with in London – he's who I met up with last night.'

'What?' Now it was Emilio's turn to look horrified. He set his drink down on the side table with a loud clink. 'He was here, in this room?'

I nodded, staring down into my lap. 'I'm so sorry. I had no idea. I didn't even know he was going to be here in Estoril. He just appeared in the bar at the end of my performance. I spent quite a bit of time with him when I was in London. He's the one I—' I broke off, unable to say the words out loud, I felt so aghast.

'The one you fell in love with,' Emilio said flatly. 'The one you wrote "Ocean Longing" about.'

I nodded again, unable to speak.

Emilio stood up. 'When did he leave?'

'Ages ago. He only stayed a couple of hours. He said he had to catch his plane back to England.' I clamped my hand to my mouth in horror. 'Oh no, I let him know that the Allies were on to him.'

Emilio's look of horror grew. 'What do you mean?'

'I asked him if he was here to catch the British aristocrat.'

'What did he say?'

'Nothing. I thought he looked confused by my question, but it must have been that he was alarmed. And then he seemed to brush it off, so I thought he wasn't allowed to talk about it. No wonder he left so quickly.' But not quickly enough, I thought, feeling sick to my stomach that he'd stayed just long enough to have sex with me.

Emilio gave a long, low sigh. 'Damn.'

I looked at him imploringly. 'If I'd known, I never would have invited him up here. I never would have said a thing.'

Emilio glanced at the bed, and my shame deepened. 'What a lost opportunity!' he eventually said with a sigh.

'I'm sorry.' I stood up, feeling the sudden urge to cry, which I couldn't bear to do in front of him. I felt pathetic enough as it was. 'I feel terrible.' My voice wavered.

'Are you OK, Castello?' Emilio's voice was softer now,

thankfully, but this only made me feel worse. To think I'd fallen for the traitor's lies. To think I'd let him into my bed. And after vowing I'd never be made a fool of again after Bing.

'I just – I...' I put my cigarette in the ashtray and began to sob.

Emilio put his arms around me and hugged me tight. His cologne was tinged with the odour of stale sweat, but it was familiar. *He* was familiar, and in that moment it felt so comforting.

'I feel like such a fool,' I sobbed into his shoulder. 'He was so convincing. He was a member of the SOE – I thought I could trust him completely.'

'You mustn't blame yourself,' Emilio said. 'You're not the only one he's fooled. Apparently, he's a very talented actor – he'd just graduated from RADA when the war began. The Brits thought his acting skills would make him the perfect spy, but sadly they made him an even better traitor.'

'He's an actor?' I stared at him through teary eyes. A vague memory came back to me, of Trafalgar saying something to me in the dressing room after my performance, something that implied he too had experience of performing. Whatever it was, I knew he'd downplayed it.

'It's OK, Castello,' Emilio said, stroking my hair. 'We're on to him now, and you never know: maybe the Allies can use your friendship with him to their advantage.'

'Of course.' I nodded eagerly, feeling the tiniest glimmer of hope. In that moment, I would have agreed to do anything to make amends for my crass stupidity and get revenge on Trafalgar for deceiving me so thoroughly.

56

PORTUGAL, 2000

Sofia falls silent, and I look back at the old newspaper clipping in my hand. 'A STAR IS BOURNE!' the headline reads, above a picture of the actor Lawrence Bourne.

'Sir Lawrence Bourne is Trafalgar?' I say, my voice barely audible.

Sofia nods.

'But he's one of the most popular actors in Britain – in the world! He's considered a national treasure. I-I ghostwrote his autobiography.'

'I know.'

I stare at her for a moment while the jigsaw pieces slowly begin to fall into place. 'Is that why you hired me? Because you knew I'd written his book? Is that why you were keeping this a secret?' I nod at the muddy box of clippings.

'Yes,' She looks down at her lap as if deeply ashamed.

'But why?' As the implications of this revelation dawn on me, I feel a creeping disappointment. I hadn't been hired on my merits for this job at all. I'd just been used as an unwitting pawn, but why exactly? 'What were you hoping would happen?'

'I was hoping you might be able to give me some information,' she says, still looking guilty. 'About him and his life now and' – her eyes dart around the room as she looks anywhere but at me – 'possibly facilitate a meeting with him.'

'You want to meet with him? But – but...' My mind races. In all my dealings with Lawrence Bourne, he was nothing but kind and fun and full of enthusiasm. It dawns on me that Lawrence's natural exuberance fits perfectly with Sofia's descriptions of Trafalgar – apart from the cockney accent. The Lawrence I met spoke like a member of royalty. But surely he couldn't have been a traitor to the Allies. He had a knighthood for God's sake. 'Are you absolutely certain that he betrayed the Allies to the Germans?'

Finally, Sofia makes eye contact with me. 'Oh yes, absolutely.'

'But how did he never get caught? Why did it never come out after the war?'

'Why did it never come out about Edward and Mrs Simpson?' she says flatly. 'Or any of the other members of the British establishment who were in cahoots with the Germans? Once the war was over and the Allies were victorious, they all slunk back into the fold and it was all swept under the blanket, or whatever that saying is.'

'Under the rug,' I mutter.

'Yes, exactly.'

We're silent for a moment, and I look at more of the clippings. Most of the others are from Portuguese newspapers over the years, charting Lawrence's stratospheric rise to fame as an actor. Then I spot a clipping about his first wedding back in the 1950s. And another from his second wedding in the 1970s. And then his third and final wedding in the 1990s. I think back to the day I'd interviewed him about his marriages, and I remember something he said when I asked why he thought he'd been married so many times.

'All of the women I've married have been wonderful human beings, but they were never able to compete,' he replied.

When I'd asked him if he was referring to his career, he shook his head. 'With my first love,' he'd said softly before telling me that that was strictly off the record, and I was not to put it in the book. And when I'd asked him what had happened with his first love, he'd instantly clammed up.

'Whoa,' I whisper, wondering if he'd been talking about Sofia.

'What is it?' Sofia asks.

'Nothing.' I can't disclose what Lawrence said due to the NDA I signed when I was hired to write his book, but he might not have been referring to Sofia anyway – although the accounts she's given about their time together were so full of passion and what seemed like love. What if his feelings for her had been genuine even if he was a traitor to his country?

'I'm so sorry,' Sofia says. 'I hope you don't think I've been using you.'

'But you have!' I exclaim.

'That's what Gabriel was worried about,' Sofia remarks. 'Right from the start, he felt it was unfair not to tell you.'

'Oh.' I'm momentarily stunned. So that's what his note to Sofia had been about. He'd been trying to look out for me!

'But I felt absolutely certain that you wouldn't carry on if I told you,' Sofia continues. 'I thought you would fly into a rage and spit in my face and leave.'

I can't help smiling at the melodrama.

'And the deeper we got into the project, the more I began to panic,' she says. 'Especially when Gabriel started threatening to tell you. That's why I hid the clippings. I was terrified you'd find them.'

'But I was bound to find out eventually,' I say.

But Sofia shakes her head. 'No because I'd changed my

mind. I decided to change the story I was going to tell you. To omit Trafalgar's true identity.'

'Why?'

'Because I hadn't counted on becoming so damned fond of you!' she exclaims, and all the suspicion and hurt and disappointment I'd been feeling begins to fade. 'When you started confiding in me about all you'd been through, with that dreadful bore of an ex-partner of yours and then about your fertility issues, well...' She gives me a weak smile. 'I'm not made of stone, you know. I do have a heart, despite any appearances to the contrary.'

'How were you going to change your story?' I ask. 'Were you going to edit Trafalgar – or, rather, Lawrence – out entirely?'

She shakes her head. 'No, it would be impossible for me to not include him, but I was going to hide his real identity and not mention him becoming a famous actor.'

There's something about the seriousness of her tone that instantly makes me curious. 'Why would it be impossible not to include him in the book?'

She visibly shudders. 'Because he was responsible for my death.'

It feels as if the temperature in the room has suddenly dropped. 'He's the reason you pretended you'd died and went into hiding, you mean?'

'No, I mean he was actually responsible for my death.' She looks at me grimly. 'As in, he made it happen. Sir Lawrence Bourne was the reason the plane I was supposed to be flying on was shot down.'

57

LISBON, 1941

The next month passed by in a numb haze. It should have been one of the happiest, most exciting times of my life. 'Ocean Longing' became a smash hit on both sides of the Atlantic, climbing to the top of the British hit parade and staying there for weeks. But I couldn't think about chart positions, or America, or the life-changing amounts of money being deposited into my bank account. All I could think about was the way Trafalgar had betrayed me, as well as his country. All I could think about was his connection to the member of the Gestapo responsible for the disappearance of my beloved jacaranda sister, Judith. It made me want to retch when I thought of how I'd confided in him about her, and how he'd pretended to be so concerned. I felt so stupid and naive. But I couldn't allow the shock and the hurt to break me. I was a famous singer now; the show had to go on – literally.

Wanting to build on my sky-rocketing success, Alexandre arranged for me to do some gigs in Portugal, which only increased my pain. Having to perform a song that had been inspired by that dirty rat Trafalgar felt like having all of my teeth pulled in the hot glare of the spotlight night after night – and without anaesthetic. It was torturous.

And then, one evening, about six weeks after I'd last seen him, the phone in my hotel room began to ring.

'Good evening, Miss Castello,' the switchboard operator chirped. 'I have a long-distance call for you from London, a Mister Trafalgar.'

My stomach dropped like a stone, and I quickly sat down in the chair beside the phone. Emilio and I had gone over what I should do in the event of Trafalgar calling, but practising it with him was one thing – having to talk to the rat himself was quite another. In truth, part of me had suspected that I'd never hear from him again after he'd got what he wanted from me that night in Estoril.

I cleared my throat and took a breath. 'Thank you. Please put him through.'

There was a click, and the line hummed and buzzed with static.

'Good evening, Miss Castello,' Trafalgar's voice crackled in my ear. 'I'm calling to see if you believe in fate yet?'

Only that I'm fated to be cursed by dirty rats, I felt tempted to reply, but somehow I refrained. 'Possibly,' I replied instead.

'Yes!' he exclaimed, and I pictured him punching the air in that exuberant way of his. It made me sick to think that I'd once found it so attractive. No doubt it was all just a part of his act. 'I'm so sorry it's taken me so long to call. I've been very busy.'

Yes, busy being a traitor to king and country, I thought. 'That's OK – I understand,' I trilled.

'I knew you would, and I see you've been busy too,' he said, instantly causing my skin to prickle.

'What do you mean?'

'Your new song. It's top of the charts here in Blighty.'

'Oh – oh yes.' I felt a wave of nausea rolling in. But then I remembered what Emilio had coached me to say in this situation. 'As a matter of fact, I was thinking of coming back to London to do another show – to show my gratitude for all of the support.'

'Are you being serious?'

'Of course.'

I heard a clunk, like the receiver had been put down on the side, and then a faint, 'Yes! Yes! Yes!' There was another clunk as he picked it back up, and his voice became clearer. 'Sorry, I was unable to contain my excitement. I thought what happened last time you came here would have scared you off for good – and quite understandably,' he added hastily.

'It takes more than a few bombs to scare me,' I said firmly, but my nausea continued to grow at the thought of having to see him again.

'Attagirl! Oh, Sofia, I'd been feeling a little down since we last met and missing you terribly, but now you've made me so happy.'

'Me too,' I said through gritted teeth.

'And I promise I will spend every available second that I have with you. I'll begin planning things to do and places to go right this minute – or as soon as I get off the phone anyway.'

'Wonderful.' I winced at how strained and false my voice sounded, but thanks to the crackles on the line he didn't appear to notice.

'Shall I call you again in a few days, to see if you have your date and time of arrival?'

'That would be wonderful.'

'OK, I'd better go. I can't wait to see you!'

'Me too,' I said again, like a stuck record.

I put the receiver down feeling sick to my stomach, so sick in fact that I had to run to the bathroom, where I vomited into the sink.

. . .

The following night, I arranged to meet Emilio for dinner at the Britannia Hotel. He arrived looking like his dapper old self, dressed in a sharply pressed suit, with fresh clipped hair and smelling of a new cologne.

'I heard from Trafalgar,' I whispered as soon as the waiter had taken our order and left us alone.

Emilio's eyes widened. 'When? How?'

'He called me at my hotel last night.' I leaned closer. 'I told him I wanted to come back to London, just as you suggested.'

Emilio nodded. 'And?'

'And he was very enthusiastic.'

'This is great.' He beamed at me across the table.

I felt a rush of relief at receiving his approval, but I knew the only way I was going to make full amends for my faux pas was by going to London and getting some dirt on Trafalgar. As soon as I thought of this, my stomach lurched, and I took a quick sip of my iced water.

'OK, you need to speak to Alexandre,' Emilio said. 'Tell him that you're dying to get back to London to thank your fans for their support. Ask him if he can send you for a little longer this time. The bombing isn't as bad there now that Germany are preoccupied with Russia, so hopefully he'll agree.'

'But do you really think I'll be able to catch Trafalgar out?' The more I thought about it, the more unlikely it seemed. 'I let him know that the SOE were on to him – surely he'll be playing it really safe now.'

Emilio took his cigarettes from his pocket and offered me one. I shook my head. Due to my unsettled stomach, just the smell of cigarettes had been making me queasy. 'Yes, but if he's fallen in love with you, that makes him vulnerable to being indiscreet. Perhaps if you were to express a certain dissatisfaction with the Allies yourself, you might be able to entice his pro-German sympathies out of him. And if there was some way of recording him...' He trailed off, looking thoughtful.

'I'm sure he hasn't fallen in love with me. He was probably just using me,' I said casually, although the thought still cut me like a knife.

Emilio looked confused. 'Well, then he's even more of a damn fool.'

'Why, thank you, Almeida,' I said, raising my glass of water. 'But if anyone's a damn fool, it's me for falling for his schemes.'

'You mustn't blame yourself.' He reached across the table and took hold of my hand. 'How were you supposed to know?'

'I honestly thought I was a better judge of character,' I said with a sigh.

He squeezed my hand tightly. 'If it's any consolation, I think you're swell.'

'Thank you.' I smiled across the table at him, overwhelmed with gratitude for my loyal songwriting partner and friend.

Emilio cleared his throat. 'There's something I need to tell you.'

'Uh-oh. Please don't tell me Alexandre is working for the Gestapo; I don't think I could take it – although I could believe it of that sourpuss of a secretary of his...'

He laughed. 'No, it's nothing like that...' He looked down at the table. 'My wife and I are no longer together. We're getting a divorce.

'Oh no; I'm so sorry.'

'It's OK, honestly.' He smiled. 'I've been worried about our marriage for months, but now it's finally over, I actually feel a bit better.'

I nodded, thinking about the strange relief I'd felt when my mother had passed and was finally free from pain. 'I understand.'

'And now that I'm free...' He looked at me hopefully.

'Yes?'

A waiter arrived at our table and put our plates down in front of us. I caught a waft of sardines and suddenly felt sick. I'd been on edge ever since Estoril and it was really affecting my stomach.

'I was thinking that maybe...' Emilio said as the waiter left.

'For goodness' sake, speak in full sentences,' I said, fanning myself with my napkin to try to stop my growing nausea.

'You and I could maybe become an item.' Emilio started fiddling with his silver napkin holder.

'I'm sorry, I—' I stood up from the table so suddenly my chair tipped over backward. 'I have to go to the bathroom,' I gasped, retching into my napkin.

I somehow made it to the bathroom and into a stall before vomiting. Once I was done, I closed the lid on the toilet and sat with my head in my hands. I didn't know whether to be flattered or embarrassed by Emilio's proposition, but one thing was for sure – after what had happened with Trafalgar, I didn't want any kind of romantic involvement with anyone.

I went and freshened up at the sink and returned to the table. Emilio had obviously ordered himself a large Scotch since I'd left, and his dinner was untouched.

'I'm so sorry,' I said, sitting back down.

He looked at me and raised his eyebrows. 'I've certainly had more favourable responses from women.'

I gave him a sheepish smile.

'Are you OK?'

'Yes, I've had a bit of an upset stomach the past couple of days. I thought I was over it, but clearly not.'

'OK, so I don't need to take it personally?' His expression turned to one of hope.

'Of course not. But...'

'Uh-oh.' He took a swig of his Scotch.

'I'm just not looking for any kind of fling at the moment.'

'But it wouldn't be a fling!' he exclaimed. 'We're Almeida and Castello, the dream music team. I mean it, Castello, I'm crazy about you.' He placed his hand on top of mine on the table. 'Please don't rush off to be sick again or you'll give me a real complex.'

I laughed and took a sip of my water. 'But the fact that we work so well together is exactly why we shouldn't get romantically involved. I don't want anything to ruin our creative partnership.' The look of hurt on his face was like a punch to the gut. I hated doing it to him, but I had to be true to myself and what I wanted – or, in this case, didn't want.

'But I thought—' He broke off and took another swig of his drink. Then he cleared his throat as if somehow resetting himself and forced a smile onto his face. 'Of course. You're right. I'm sorry.'

'No need to apologise! To Almeida and Castello – songwriting dream team.' I raised my glass.

He nodded and smiled but didn't clink his to mine, and we returned to our meals with an awkward silence heavy as a storm cloud hanging over the table.

58

LISBON, 1941

The following day, I went to see Alexandre, who, after initially expressing fears for my safety, came round to my request to return to London. While I was relieved at the chance to try to redeem myself, I couldn't help feeling jittery, and on the way back to my hotel, I couldn't shake the feeling I was being followed. But when I turned around, all I saw was a scrawny newspaper boy in a scruffy old coat loitering behind me.

My strange sickness and upset stomach continued, and after about a week, a terrible thought began nagging at me. I kept pushing it away and telling myself that it couldn't possibly be – and that surely I wasn't that unlucky – but after two weeks there was no escaping my growing fear as I'd definitely missed a period. Could my sickness have nothing to do with my feeling on edge? Could it be due instead to me being pregnant?

My rising fame meant that I didn't dare go in person for a pregnancy test, so I ended up confiding in Alexandre, and he despatched his secretary, Fatima, with a phial of my urine to the doctor's. If I hadn't been so terrified at the potential result, I would have found the prospect of old sourpuss being made to carry my urine anywhere highly amusing, ditto the test itself.

Believe it or not, back in the 1940s, a pregnancy test was carried out by injecting the woman's urine into the back of a frog, which sounds crazy now but was surprisingly effective. If the woman was pregnant, the hormones in her urine would cause the frog to produce eggs within twelve hours, which would be visible in a sac on its body. But, of course, none of that interested me then. All I could think was that I might have been impregnated by someone who was prepared to betray his country for the Nazis, and I was filled with stone-cold dread.

The day after I'd given my urine sample, I returned to Alexandre's for a meeting about my upcoming London trip where, to my surprise, Fatima greeted me with a smile for the very first time, and a sympathetic one at that. I stepped inside Alexandre's office, heart pounding, and he leaped to his feet and rushed over to greet me.

'Sofia! Please, sit down.' He gently guided me to one of the armchairs. 'I have very big news,' he said, going over to his desk and taking a file from the drawer. 'You are with child,' he stated, with all the gravity of a prime minister declaring his country was now at war.

'Oh,' was all I was able to say in response.

'Who is... How is your relationship with the father?' Alexandre asked gingerly. Of course, he didn't have a clue who the father was. When I'd told him I needed to take the test, I'd vaguely mentioned that I'd been seeing someone.

I shook my head, too stunned to speak.

'It would be better if – uh – you and he were to get married before – uh...' He trailed off, looking embarrassed.

The thought of me marrying Trafalgar was so preposterous, I let out a slightly hysterical burst of laughter.

'It's just that, your reputation...' Again he trailed off, clearly embarrassed.

'I know,' I said, standing up. 'My reputation will be in tatters.' I felt so angry suddenly, yet unexpectedly defensive of the tiny foetus growing inside of me. 'I need to go and do some serious thinking.'

He gave me a sympathetic smile. 'Of course. And, Sofia?'

'Yes?'

'If you don't want to, you know, have it, that can be taken care of.' He looked so awkward by this point, I was surprised he didn't just slide from his chair into a puddle of embarrassment.

'Oh.' I stared at him for a moment in disbelief. 'OK.'

I returned to my hotel feeling shell-shocked, my head spinning from all that had happened. But one thing I knew for sure now that the fact I was actually pregnant had registered with me was that there was no way on this earth I could have an abortion. And it wasn't because back then abortions were horrendous backstreet affairs – although God knows that would have been enough of a reason. It was because I was experiencing yet another completely unexpected twist in the unfolding tale that was my life. Ever since my mother had died, I'd felt so lonely with no other family, but now I had the seed of my child and my mother's grandchild growing inside me – and that notion was surprisingly comforting.

I lay on my bed and placed my hands over my womb – or where I thought my womb was anyway – and I imagined being the mother to my mother's grandchild, and despite everything, that made me smile. This baby would reconnect me to my mother. This baby would be my family. And although I hadn't given much thought to becoming a mother before, I felt sure I'd be a good parent because I'd grown up with the very best of examples. And I'd also grown up without a father so I knew all about how that felt.

I was drifting into a nap when there was a knock on the door. I opened it to find Emilio standing there, his hair shiny with Brilliantine and smelling of his old pine cologne. It was a smell I'd always liked, but now, thanks to my hormonal upheaval, it made me feel slightly sick.

'Where have you been, Castello?' he said, coming into the room. 'I've been trying to get a hold of you.'

'I was at Alexandre's, why?' There was no way I wanted Emilio knowing about the baby yet, and I'd sworn Alexandre to secrecy. I needed more time to come to terms with it myself.

'I have some excellent news.'

'Oh yes?' I replied, wondering what it could be.

'When you're invited back to London again to do another show, the SOE are going to set up a meeting between you and Trafalgar.' He smiled at me, his eyes gleaming with excitement. 'I'll give you another coded message to pass to him – although this time it won't be genuine of course – and when you've got him alone, you can try to find out more. Perhaps you can use the closeness you've formed with him to your advantage.' There was a slightly knowing tone to his voice that set me on edge, and the thought of being intimate with Trafalgar now was nauseating.

I felt a burst of panic as I thought of the child now growing inside of me. *Our* child, but there was no way I wanted Trafalgar having anything to do with it. Not ever. No way. But what if he realised I was pregnant? And what if he'd told the Germans I was working for the Allies? What if by going to London I'd be walking into some kind of trap?

My nausea grew, and I leaped to my feet and raced to the bathroom.

'You OK?' Emilio called after me.

I turned the tap on full so he wouldn't hear me retching, then hastily cleaned my teeth and splashed some cold water on my face.

'Sorry about that,' I said, returning to the room. 'I'm still having a few stomach issues.'

'Shouldn't you go see a doctor?' Emilio stared at me. I'm sure it was a look of concern, but in my paranoid state, I feared he might have worked out the truth.

'I'm fine, and yes of course regarding London,' I said breezily to try to avert any suspicion. I took a deep breath and forced my mouth into a smile. 'I'll do whatever it takes to catch that traitorous rat.'

Emilio's face broke into a broad smile, and I breathed a sigh of relief – suspicion averted.

'That's fantastic.' He stood up and patted me on the back. 'Good work, Castello!'

After he left, I stood there with my hands on my stomach, staring helplessly at the door. 'What am I going to do?' I whispered to the tiny seed of a child growing inside me. 'How am I going to protect you?'

The night before I was due to fly to London, I didn't sleep a wink. But unlike the previous occasion, when I'd been too excited, this time it was because I was consumed with dread. Try as I might, I couldn't see how my trip could possibly be a success. Despite Emilio's coaxing, I just couldn't imagine Trafalgar being stupid enough to out himself to me. And I couldn't see him believing any sudden change of heart on my part either. Emilio had told me to say that I'd had a meeting with the Portuguese leader, Salazar, and he'd convinced me to support the Germans, which I guessed was vaguely plausible, given Salazar's neutrality, but still.

My pregnancy had knocked me for six, physically and emotionally, and I didn't feel my normal formidable self. Even my old fail-safes, praying to my beloved mother or Santo Antonio, no longer seemed to be working. My panicked thoughts were too loud, and it was as if they were jamming our lines of communication.

At around two in the morning, there was a knock on my hotel-room door. I looked at the clock and frowned. My car to the airport wasn't due for another couple of hours. I padded over to the door and called out, 'Hello?'

'It's hotel reception,' a woman's voice replied. 'We have a message for you.'

I opened the door expecting to see one of the receptionists, but to my surprise what looked like a street urchin was standing there in a tatty coat, with a peaked cap pulled down over their face.

'What the hell?' I exclaimed as they barged past me into the room. I grabbed the closest thing to me to use as a weapon, which sadly happened to be an umbrella – and a broken one at that. 'You'd better get out of here quick smart before I make you sorry,' I said as menacingly as I could muster for one who had been rudely interrupted at two in the morning.

There was a moment's silence as my intruder and I stared at each other, or I stared at their cap at least. And then, to my shock, they began to giggle, causing me to prickle with indignation.

'I might not look scary to you, armed with this mere umbrella, but I can assure you that in the right hands, the humble umbrella can be a lethal weapon and... and this is no laughing matter.'

But my waving the umbrella about as if it were a sword only caused the urchin to laugh even more, and to add insult to injury, they even doubled over, clutching their side from the hilarity.

'What is wrong with you?' I cried, feeling intense irritation.

'Oh, Sofia,' they gasped, and the cap was whipped off to reveal a dirt-streaked face. 'I've really missed you!'

I stared at the scrawny figure in front of me in absolute shock, and I think it took me a full ten seconds to regain the power of speech.

'Judith?' I gasped, my mouth suddenly dry. 'Is it... is it you?'

59

LISBON, 1941

The street urchin in front of me smiled and nodded and, as if by magic, Judith began to emerge from beneath the grime and the matted hair. A much thinner, scruffier Judith, but there was no denying it was my beloved friend.

I dropped the umbrella to the floor and flung my arms around her. 'My God, I thought I'd never see you again!' I grabbed her thin shoulders and stared into her eyes. The same dark almond-shaped eyes that had looked at me so earnestly when we'd first met. 'Not that I ever gave up on you,' I added hastily. 'I tried so hard to find out what had happened to you. I even wrote a song about you.' I was aware that I was gabbling ten to the dozen, but I just couldn't stop. 'Was it him? Was if Kurt Fischer? Was he behind your abduction? I tried to poison him with old fish, but it didn't work.'

'What?' Judith laughed. 'Slow down.'

'Of course. I'm sorry. Please, sit down.' I led her over to one of the armchairs and knelt on the floor at her feet. I was scared of us being too far apart in case she disappeared into thin air again. 'What happened to you?'

'One of Fischer's henchmen caught me. He must have

followed me back to your apartment. I'm so sorry he made such a mess of it. It must have been horrible for you to come back to.'

'Don't worry about me!' I exclaimed. 'Are you all right? What did they do to you?'

'They took me to an internment camp in Spain.' Her voice turned sombre, and fear gripped me.

'Did they... Did they torture you?'

'No. I told them I didn't have the diamond and when they couldn't find it, I guess they decided to believe me and they left me to rot in the camp.' She glanced around the room. 'I don't suppose you found anything surprising in your bath salts, did you?'

'Funny you should mention that.' I went over to my wardrobe and took out the hatbox. I brought it back over to her and took the pot of cold cream from its hiding place inside. 'And I can confirm that it is indeed cursed. Or at least it felt like it was, having to keep it hidden all this time.'

'Oh, Sofia! This is the best news ever – although I'm really sorry you've had the worry of having to keep it safe.'

'It's fine. The Germans clearly never discovered I was connected to you in any way.'

'Thank goodness!' Judith exclaimed. I watched as she unscrewed the lid on the pot of cream and felt inside. Her eyes lit up. 'You are truly the best and bravest big sister ever!' she exclaimed joyfully, and hearing her say that caused my heart to glow.

'And I'm also the luckiest,' I replied. 'I can't believe you're here! How did you get back?'

Judith screwed the lid back on the pot and rubbed the cream on her fingers into her hands, which I noticed were bruised and scuffed. 'I escaped from the camp – a lovely Spanish doctor helped smuggle me out. He and his wife hid me in their attic for about a month, so I could get my strength back.' She gave a dry little laugh. 'Let's just say that the menu at the camp was extremely limited – unless of course you're a fan of cabbage soup.'

I winced as I thought of her having to live in such conditions.

'Then, once I felt strong enough to leave, the doctor and his wife gave me a hand-drawn map, with directions on how to get to the border. It turns out that orienteering isn't my strongest suit, and within a couple of days I was completely lost and ended up having to hide in a forest.'

'No!' I gasped.

'But then the most magical thing happened.' She smiled at me, her eyes gleaming. 'After walking for miles, I finally reached a town, and as I was standing outside a café wondering what I should do and if I should just give up, I heard your song about the jacaranda seeds on the radio!'

'You're kidding?' I exclaimed.

She giggled. 'I honestly thought I was imagining it at first. But then the show's presenter said your name and it felt like a sign, and it gave me hope again. I knew I had to try to find my way back to Lisbon – back to you.'

'Wow!' I stared up at her, shaking my head. 'Every time I sang that song, I thought of you and prayed you'd come back to me. The prayers worked!' I placed my hands on her knees, trying not to grimace at how brittle and bony they felt. 'I'm so sorry you had to go through all of that though.'

'It's fine. I'm fine.' Judith placed her hands on top of mine. 'But how are you?'

'Oh, OK I suppose.'

'You suppose?' She cocked her head to one side like a tiny songbird and looked at me curiously.

'Well, if you must know, I'm not OK at all.' I sighed. 'Without your calm, wise friendship to guide me, I've somehow got myself into a complete and utter mess. But I'm hoping to sort it out. Oh no!' In the shock of Judith's return, I'd forgotten I was about to leave the country. It was the worst timing ever.

'What's wrong?' Judith asked, instantly looking panicked.

'I'm going to London in a couple of hours to give a show. Wait a minute...' An idea began to form in my mind. I wasn't sure if it was a good one, but it would mean we could stay together. 'Why don't you come with me? We can pretend you're my personal assistant.'

Judith looked down at her grimy clothes and laughed. 'I'm not sure I'd look very convincing as the personal assistant to a star.'

'I can transform you.' I grabbed her hands. 'I mean it. You can have a bath. I can lend you some clothes. And once we're in London, I can find you somewhere to live, somewhere safe from the Germans. I can introduce you to my colleague, Mary, and see if she can find some work for you. At least in England you'd be safe from the Gestapo finding you.' I shivered as I thought of Trafalgar.

'Are you sure?' Judith asked, looking slightly apprehensive.

'Of course. Now come on – the car's going to be here soon; we don't have a moment to lose!'

I ran Judith a deep bubble bath and then, while she was bathing, I rooted through my wardrobe for some clothes for her. I stuffed a couple of extra dresses and some underwear into my suitcase and laid another set out on the bed. Judith emerged from the bathroom in a cloud of steam and wrapped in a towel. Her shoulder blades jutted above the towel, causing me to wince. She looked as if she hadn't eaten in weeks.

'When was the last time you had a proper meal?' I asked, feeling a stab of concern.

She shrugged.

I went and fetched some nuts and crackers from the drinks cabinet. 'I'm sorry it's not much, but they might feed us on the plane. And I could get the driver to stop off at an all-night café on the way to the airport.'

'I'm all right, honestly. I'm just so happy to have found you.'

'How *did* you find me?' I asked, in awe of my young friend and how she'd endured so much yet could still find it in herself to be happy and grateful.

'I hung around outside your manager's office, hoping you'd eventually turn up, and you did. And then I followed you back here.'

'It was you!' I exclaimed. 'I thought I saw someone lurking in the shadows the other day, but I thought you were a newspaper boy.'

She gave me a sheepish grin. 'It was so hard to not run up to you and give you a hug, but I didn't want anyone to see me, just in case.'

I shivered, thinking of our encounters with Fischer. 'I understand, trust me.'

Judith took the clothes and went to get dressed in the bathroom. She emerged a couple of minutes later looking downhearted. The dress hung from her tiny frame like a sack.

'Do I look ridiculous?'

'No, of course not.' I fetched a belt from my chest of drawers. 'Let's just put this around your waist, to give it more shape.' I did up the belt and couldn't resist giving her another hug. 'Oh, Judith. I can't believe this has happened. I feel as if I'm dreaming!'

I dried Judith's hair and made up her face, concealing the dark shadows under her eyes and applying a rosy blush to her cheeks. By the time I'd finished, she looked transformed.

'OK, we need to give you another name, for when I introduce you to people, and get you onto the plane. What would you like to be called?' I asked, standing back to admire my handiwork.

'How about Rose?' she replied. 'After my favourite flower.'

'Perfect!'

We both jumped as the phone began to ring, but it was just the hotel reception, letting me know my car had arrived.

'What should we do with the pesky diamond?' I asked, looking at the tub of cold cream.

'I'll take it with me,' she said. 'Relieve you of the curse.'

I laughed, but part of me felt anxious, knowing that the damned thing would put us more at risk – en route to the airport at least.

'OK, let's go,' I said nervously as Judith stuffed the cold cream into the bag I'd given her.

Once we were in the car, I started firming up my plan for Judith when we arrived in London. If Mary wasn't able to help, I would pay for Judith to see the rest of the war out in a hotel. And I would make sure she was safe before I got on with the business of seeing to Trafalgar.

The car swerved around a pothole, and a sudden wave of nausea came over me.

'Oh no,' I muttered as my skin erupted in a cold sweat.

'Are you OK?' Judith asked.

'I think I might be sick.' I leaned forward and tapped the driver on the shoulder. 'I'm so sorry – could you stop please?'

He screeched to a halt, and I flung the door open and vomited onto the road. Thankfully, I'd been too nervous to eat dinner the night before so there wasn't much to come up.

'I'm so sorry,' I said, wiping my mouth with a handkerchief.

The driver grunted, and we continued on our way.

'Are you ill?' Judith asked, clearly concerned.

'No, no, I'm not ill. I – uh – I think the fish I ate last night was bad.' I couldn't risk the driver overhearing, so I'd tell her the truth when we got to London. At the thought of being in London and seeing Trafalgar, my stomach lurched again, but we made it through the winding roads of Sintra and arrived at the airfield without me being ill again.

'Oh no,' Judith muttered as we drove up to the small airport building. There on the tarmac, just a few yards from the BOAC airliner we would be taking, were two German passenger planes.

'It's all right,' I whispered, although I felt anything but. 'All we have to do is check in with the ground crew and then we'll be shown on board. Last time, it was very quick.' I really hoped my star power would be enough to get them to allow Judith to come with me. But I realised in that moment that if they didn't, I would refuse to board. I wasn't going to lose my friend again for anything or anyone.

Judith nodded, but I could tell she was scared.

The driver parked up, and we got out of the car. The sour taste of vomit in my mouth made me feel sick all over again, and I wondered if there was any way I could get a drink of water before take-off. A couple of men in suits were climbing the stairs to the plane, so I guessed we'd have to board straight away. I gritted my teeth and made my way over to a female member of the airline crew who was holding a clipboard.

'Hello, Miss Castello!' the woman exclaimed with a beaming smile.

This was good – she appeared to be a fan. Hopefully it would work to my advantage.

'Hello. This is my assistant, Rose,' I said confidently. 'She'll be making the trip with me.' I decided that telling rather than asking was the best course of action and hopefully the least likely to be met with refusal.

The woman looked at her clipboard and frowned, so I decided to enact a little role play for authenticity.

I turned to Judith. 'Rose, could you please go inside and fetch me a bottle of water?'

'Yes, of course, Miss Castello,' Judith replied.

'There's no sign of your assistant's name on the passenger log,' the woman said.

'My manager assured me that he'd asked his secretary to book her ticket.' I frowned. 'Honestly that woman is so forgetful.' I took my purse from my bag. 'I'm happy to pay for her ticket now. I can sort it out with my manager later.'

The plane's engine rumbled into life, and a member of the crew appeared at the top of the steps. 'We need to board the remaining passengers,' he called down.

The woman looked at me and smiled. 'OK, go ahead. I'll tell your assistant to join you when she comes back with the water.'

When I got to the top of the steps, I saw Judith coming out of the building and beckoned at her to follow me, then I entered the cabin and was shown to my seat. Judith arrived moments later, looking incredibly anxious.

'It's all right – you're allowed to fly with me,' I whispered as she came over to join me.

'You have to get off the plane,' she hissed.

'What?'

'Right now!'

'But—'

'Please!' she begged, tugging my hand, and I could see a real urgency in her expression and that her eyes were shiny with tears.

I undid my seat belt and stood up. 'I'm so sorry,' I said to a crew member. 'There's been an emergency. I have to leave.'

We slipped out just before the plane door was closed and raced down the steps. But instead of heading back to the building, Judith grabbed my arm and pulled me over to a nearby hut used to store mail sacks.

'What's going on?' I called as the plane engine grew louder.

'I overheard two Germans talking in the airport,' she gasped.

'So why on earth did you make us get off the plane?' I glanced nervously at the building. 'If we'd stayed on board, we'd have been heading to safety.'

'They were talking about you,' Judith replied, and my stomach lurched.

'What were they saying?'

'One of them was telling the other that he'd just seen you get on board. They mentioned something about a contact in London. Then they started joking about how you wouldn't be singing for much longer.' She gripped my hands tightly. 'I think they're plotting to kill you in London.'

The roar of the plane grew fainter, and my palms began to sweat as I watched it take off, only to be swallowed up by the dark night sky.

60

PORTUGAL, 2000

I stare at Sofia open-mouthed as she goes over to the bureau by the window and fetches an envelope from one of the compartments inside.

'And that was the plane that got shot down,' I say softly.

'Yes.' She takes a newspaper cutting from the envelope, and I recognise it as one I found on the internet when I was researching her.

PORTUGUESE SINGING SENSATION PERISHES IN PLANE CRASH!

Beloved singer Sofia Castello was killed yesterday when the passenger plane she was travelling on was shot down by the Luftwaffe over the Atlantic. All seventeen souls aboard BOAC flight 777 from Lisbon to Britain, including the four crew members, tragically perished.

Portuguese songbird Castello became her nation's sweetheart when her debut single, 'Jacaranda Seeds', was released in 1940, and since then she has found fame across the globe, being described by The New York Times *as 'the haunting voice of the war generation'.*

Earlier this year, her ballad 'Ocean Longing' became a smash hit on both sides of the Atlantic, perfectly capturing the mood of the times, with so many loved ones currently separated due to the war.

It is a tragic end to a life that began in hardship. After a childhood scarred by the drunken violence of her father, Castello ran away to Lisbon at the age of sixteen to begin her working life as a humble fish-seller on the streets of the city. A couple of years later, her incredible voice won her the attention of music industry movers and shakers, and she was whisked from the streets to the stage. Her fans are bound to be heartbroken that there will be no happily ever after for this rags to riches tale.

'Everyone thought I was on the plane,' Sofia says once I've finished reading. 'The airport log showed that I'd boarded. If it hadn't been for Judith...' Sofia pauses. 'She saved my life. In more than one way.'

I wonder what she means by this, but I have so many other questions clamouring to be answered first.

'How did you escape from the airfield, and with no one seeing you?'

'We hitched a ride on the back of a mail truck.' Sofia smiles. 'Or, rather, we snuck onto the back of the truck when no one was looking.'

'But where did you go? How did you hear about the plane crash? How did you go into hiding?'

'OK, slow down, one question at a time.' Sofia takes a torturously slow drink of her coffee.

'How can you drink coffee at a time like this?' I exclaim, and she lets out a snort of laughter.

I freeze as I remember my first meeting with Lawrence

Bourne and how he'd said that people who snorted with laughter were free spirits who were uninhibited in their joy. A shiver runs up my spine as I think of this now. Had he been thinking of Sofia when he'd said it?

'Are you all right?' Sofia asks, clearly noticing a change in my expression.

'Yes, yes, I'm fine, just trying to process it all. So, what happened next?'

'As soon as the mail truck got back to Lisbon, we managed to slip out,' Sofia replies. 'I'd taken a scarf from my suitcase, which I wore on my head along with a pair of dark glasses to try to disguise myself. Of course, at that point it was more to avoid being spotted by a German agent rather than anyone else, and we hotfooted it to Alexandre's place.' Sofia takes another sip of her coffee. 'And that is where everything changed forever.'

61

LISBON, 1941

Being in the music business, Alexandre was of course a night owl and had only been asleep for about an hour when we arrived, pounding on his front door. After what felt like forever, the door opened and a tousle-headed Alexandre stared out at us.

'We need your help,' I said, barging past him and dragging Judith with me.

'Sofia! But... but why aren't you on the plane to London?' he stammered.

We went into the living room, and Alexandre stared at Judith, who, it had to be said, was a strange sight in her oversized dress and overly made-up face.

'And who is this?'

'My friend Rose.' I sat down on the sofa and hugged myself to try to stop from trembling as the reality of what had happened started to sink in. When we'd been at the airport in the pitch-dark, it had all felt like a surreal dream, but now I was back in Lisbon and daylight was pouring in through the large sash window, reality hit me with the force of a freight train. The Germans were plotting to kill me in London, which meant that

Trafalgar had to be involved and was luring me into a trap. Or, rather, he'd tried to. I gave Judith a grateful smile and gestured at her to sit beside me.

Alexandre made a pot of coffee, and I told him what had happened, omitting the part about my helping the SOE and telling him instead that the Germans must be trying to kill me because of my obvious support for the Allies. The less he knew, the less danger he'd be in.

'I need to get away,' I said, once I'd finished the tale. 'When the Gestapo find out I wasn't on the plane, they're going to come looking for me. And it's not just my life at stake now.' I gave him a pointed look and placed my hand protectively on my stomach.

Alexandre nodded gravely. 'Of course.'

'I need somewhere to hide out until the war is over. Somewhere I can have the baby and not be discovered.'

'The baby?' Judith cried.

'I'll explain later,' I said, feeling sick yet again as I thought of Trafalgar. In his plan to kill me, he would have killed his own child. 'At least my going into hiding will deal with the problem of people finding out about my pregnancy,' I quipped weakly, but Alexandre didn't smile.

'This is terrible,' he said, looking shell-shocked. 'They must have seen your performances in London as an act of support for the Allies, but even so...' He began pacing the room. 'OK, I need to think of somewhere for you to go. And I need to come up with a story to explain your disappearance. Maybe I'll say that you're suffering from exhaustion. You have been working flat out for the last couple of years. You could go to my place up in the mountains at first. It's very secluded and would buy us some time to find you something better.'

'OK.' I felt a slight relief at the thought of being away from Lisbon.

'But we need to wait until tonight,' Alexandre said. 'Better to drive up there under the cover of darkness.'

I nodded. 'That makes sense.'

'Well, there's no way I'll be going back to sleep now.' He smiled. 'Let's have some breakfast.'

We went into the kitchen, and while Alexandre made us some more coffee and toast and eggs, I told him a cock-and-bull story about 'Rose' and how we'd become friends. It was far too dangerous to tell him the truth – for him and for Judith.

We'd just finished breakfast when the phone began to ring. Alexandre hurried into the living room to take it.

'Good morning, Fatima,' I heard him say. 'No, I'm afraid I'm not going to be in today; I'm not feeling too good. I— What?' My ears pricked up at his sudden change of tone. 'What do you mean?' he exclaimed. 'Oh my God! Yes, yes, I'll be there in an hour.'

Alexandre returned to the kitchen, ashen-faced.

'You look as if you've seen a ghost,' I joked.

'I have,' he replied. 'In fact, I'm looking at one right now.'

I felt a sudden chill. 'What do you mean?'

'You.' His voice wavered, and he sat down. 'The plane you were meant to be on has gone missing. And there are reports that the Germans shot it down.'

62

PORTUGAL, 2000

Sofia breaks off at the sound of a car approaching outside. 'That must be Gabriel,' she says, jumping to her feet and instantly looking nervous.

'Hang on a moment,' I say. 'You gave Judith the name Rose?'

'Yes,' she replies, looking even more ill at ease.

'What's the Portuguese name for Rose?'

I hear the front door opening, and Sofia begins pacing around the room.

'Is it Rosária?' I ask.

'What? Oh yes, I...' she stammers, looking anxiously at the door.

'*Boa noite*,' I hear Gabriel call from the hall, and the front door closes.

'Come through,' Sofia calls, wringing her hands.

I hear a woman cough, and I stare at Sofia. 'Who's with him?' I whisper, although I'm pretty sure I can guess, and my mind is blown by this latest development.

'I – uh – invited someone to join us for dinner,' Sofia replies as the door slowly opens.

Gabriel walks in looking just as nervous as Sofia. A woman walks in behind him. A woman with white bobbed hair, wearing a wraparound paisley dress. Her appearance is so unexpected and out of context, it's only when I smell her signature rose perfume that I realise who it is and I cry out in shock.

'Jane!'

'Lily!' she cries and hurries over and gives me a hug. 'Are you OK?'

My mind races as I try to work out why and how she's here. My emails about Sofia must have caused her so much concern, she has come to bat for me. But I can't believe she's come all this way to do so – she could have just sent an email. 'You didn't have to come,' I murmur in her ear. 'I didn't mean to worry you.'

'It's all good,' she replies, holding the sides of my arms and looking into my eyes. 'I wanted to come. I needed to be here.' She glances at Sofia.

Sofia sighs and sits down, looking slightly defeated.

'It's OK – you can trust her,' I say. 'She's been my agent for thirteen years.'

Sofia laughs. 'And she's been my best friend for sixty.'

'What?' I stare from Sofia to Jane and back again.

Gabriel, who's now standing by the fireplace, gives an awkward cough.

'What does she mean?' I say to Jane. 'How have you been friends for sixty years?'

'We met in Lisbon during the war,' Jane says softly.

'She's my fellow jacaranda seed,' Sofia says.

I let out a gasp as the enormity of the revelation hits me. 'Not Rosária? Not the gardener?' I stammer.

'I'm Judith,' Jane says with a smile.

63

PORTUGAL, 2000

'But how... why?' I stammer, staring at Jane. Of all the revelations over the last twenty-four hours, this is by far the most shocking. All the other people in Sofia's story are just that – people in *her* story. But Jane has featured in my life for over a decade. She's one of my closest confidantes. Or so I thought.

Suddenly, Gabriel is at my side, taking hold of my arm and steering me back to the sofa. 'Why don't you sit down?' he says softly. I remember what Sofia told me about him wanting me to know the truth from the start and smile at him weakly as I sit down.

'I'll be in the kitchen,' he adds, as if to reassure me.

I nod numbly, and he leaves the room.

Jane sits down beside me.

'Why didn't you tell me?' I ask, feeling utterly bewildered.

'Sofia wanted to make sure that she could trust you first,' Jane replies.

There's something about her use of the word 'trust' that makes me feel slightly annoyed. 'What about who *I* can trust?' I mutter. I think back to the photograph of Judith I'd seen on the mantelpiece before it mysteriously disappeared. The bobbed hair might be more immaculately cut and white rather than brown, and her face might be lined now, but there was a definite similarity in the heart-like shape of her face, I realise now. 'Is that why you hid the photo of Judith on the mantelpiece?' I exclaim, looking at Sofia. 'Were you afraid I'd see the similarity with Jane?'

'I didn't realise you'd noticed it had gone.' Sofia gives a sheepish laugh. 'But yes.'

I look back at Jane. 'I can't believe you didn't tell me.'

'I'm sorry. I wanted to tell you before you left, but we felt it was too risky.' Jane puts her hand on top of mine, the huge diamond in her ring glinting yellow.

'Wait – if you're Judith, is that the diamond – the Vadodara Teardrop?' I point at the ring.

Jane nods. 'It is. Or part of it at least.'

'I have another part here,' Sofia says, pointing to the jewel in her crescent moon ring.

'We had it cut after the war,' Jane explains. 'To break the curse!'

'Right.' I frown as more jigsaw pieces start falling into place. 'But you knew I wrote Sir Lawrence's book. You got me that job. Was that deliberate? Has this whole thing been a set-up from way back then?'

'No!' Jane exclaims. 'It was after you wrote his book. After we saw what was in it.'

'Or what wasn't,' Sofia adds.

'What do you mean?'

'The way he painted himself as such a hero in the chapter on the war years,' Jane says.

I wrack my brains, trying to remember what Lawrence had said about the war. Most of the book had focused on his acting career. I remember him talking about helping people during an air raid and then another piece of the jigsaw falls into place. 'He talked about the night you almost died in the Blitz!' I exclaim, looking at Sofia.

'Yes, but without giving me a mention,' Sofia replies bitterly.

'Of course he wouldn't mention you,' Jane says drily. 'He was responsible for your death. The last thing he'd want to do is draw attention to any connection between you.'

Sofia nods, and my anger at her fades. She looks so tired and drawn.

'I'm really sorry, Lily,' she says softly. 'I didn't like deceiving you, but reading his book made me so mad. Especially when it did so well and won him even more affection and acclaim. It all felt so unfair. Knowing that he'd effectively killed me and my career and gone on to become this hero of the acting world and – how do you call it in England? A national – national...' She furrows her brow.

'A national treasure,' Jane says drily, in her cut-glass accent.

I turn to look at her. 'How do you have an English accent? Did you end up going to London when the war ended?'

She nods. 'Yes, a few years after. And once I started working in the book world, I decided to get rid of my German accent to try to fit in.'

I hear the sizzle of oil coming from the kitchen and realise that Gabriel must be cooking.

'So what happened after you discovered that the Germans shot the plane down, when you were at Alexandre's?' I ask, remembering where Sofia had left the story.

Jane looks at me solemnly. 'I will never, ever forget that moment.'

'The moment we realised we were supposed to be dead,' Sofia says quietly.

'I can't imagine how it must have felt.' The room is warm, but I can't help shivering. It's such an eerie thought – and it must have been even worse for Sofia, knowing that her lover had played a key role in making it happen. I feel another jolt of disbelief as I think of Sir Lawrence Bourne and the hours we spent together working on his book and how much I'd liked him. It's chilling to think of what he'd done and what he'd been capable of. 'I'm so sorry.'

Sofia shakes her head. 'You mustn't be sorry. Do you remember when I said to you that sometimes things that seem like the end of the world are actually just the prologue for something truly delightful?'

I nod.

'Well, believe it or not, my death ended up becoming the prologue to the most delightful story of all.'

'Mine too,' Jane agrees enthusiastically.

'How?' I stare at them both in disbelief.

'My death allowed me to finally live my life on my own terms.' Sofia snorts with laughter. 'Now that's ironic.'

I look at her, confused. 'But how? You were forced to go into hiding.'

'No, no, no – I *chose* to go into hiding,' Sofia corrects me. 'To protect myself and Judith – and, of course, my daughter.'

'You have a daughter?' I glance around the room. After the Judith revelation, I'm half expecting her to leap out from behind the curtains, crying, 'Surprise!'

'Yes,' Sofia says softly, looking down into her lap. 'Or, rather, I had.'

A heavy silence falls on the room. I so badly want to ask what happened to Sofia's daughter, but I'm aware that it would be straying into deeply personal territory. I see a flash of red and picture my dream daughter running into the room and clambering onto my lap. I blink hard to make her go away.

'Are you all right?' Jane asks Sofia, and she nods. Then a terrible thought occurs to me. Did the Germans somehow get to her – did they kill her daughter?

'It was actually Alexandre's idea,' Sofia says. 'When the news reports started coming out about the plane crash and we realised that no one knew I wasn't on board, he spotted the opportunity. At first it was just to buy us some time to escape to his place in the mountains to figure out what we wanted to do next. But the more time that passed, the more appealing it became to me to never return. Especially when it was confirmed that the Luftwaffe had shot the plane down.' She grimaces. 'Quite frankly, I was terrified. And not just for me, but for my baby, and of course Judith.' She smiles at Jane. 'While I was pregnant, I thought I might one day reveal the truth to the world – that I was alive after all. Once the war was over and if the Allies won.'

'Why didn't you?' I ask.

Sofia picks up the muddy box and tips the newspaper clippings onto the sofa between us. 'After the war, it was as if none of it happened. All of the members of British society who'd come to Lisbon and cosied up to the Germans were instantly forgiven and welcomed back into the fold. Look...'

She fishes through the clippings and shows me an article about Lawrence's starring role in a film made the year after the war ended – the film that propelled him to stardom.

'They were all protected. How could I, a humble former *varina* from Portugal, possibly challenge a British earl? Who would have believed me? Back then, members of royalty and the aristocracy were still seen as being next to godly. And, of course, I hadn't been prepared for the huge outpouring of grief after my death. I was scared that if I suddenly reappeared, people would be furious at me for deceiving them. But more than anything, I didn't want that monster having anything to do with my daughter. I was terrified he'd work out the dates and realise that she was his and try to take her from me.'

'Wow!' I say under my breath. 'So where did you go after you left Alexandre's place in the mountains?'

The women look at each other and laugh.

Jane grins. 'Where we would be least expected.'

'Germany,' Sofia says.

'What?' I splutter.

'Not immediately of course,' she continues. 'We moved there about a year after the war ended.'

'My grandma had a cottage in the forest in Bavaria,' Jane says.

'And of course I'd never become famous in Germany,' Sofia adds. 'I wasn't known there at all, thanks to the banning of my records.'

'That's hilarious,' I say.

Sofia grins. 'I thought so too. And it turned out to be a wonderful place to raise my daughter.'

'So they never found you – or her?' I ask hopefully.

'No. Everyone thought I'd perished in the ocean – they never recovered half of the bodies from the plane – so the fact that they never found my corpse didn't arouse any suspicion. And Alexandre didn't tell a soul, not even Emilio – so we didn't have to worry about it ever coming out.'

'That's incredible,' I murmur. 'When did you come back to Portugal?'

'In 1960. Alexandre sorted out a new identity and a fake passport for me courtesy of a dubious connection he had in Porto.'

'And that's when I went to London,' Jane says.

I lean back on the sofa and shake my head. 'Can I ask what happened to your daughter?'

'She died of cancer two years ago,' Sofia replies quietly, and any last trace of anger I have towards her instantly goes. I can't imagine what it must have been like to lose her daughter the same way she lost her mum.

'Oh, I'm so sorry.'

'It's all right. She's free from pain now, and I like to believe that she's with my mother, so that brings me great comfort.' But her eyes glimmer with tears.

Gabriel comes back holding a bottle of wine, a tea towel draped over his tanned arm. 'Is everything OK?' he asks cautiously.

'Yes, it's all good,' I reply.

He grins. 'Very good. Would anyone like a glass of wine?'

'Yes!' we all chorus with such enthusiasm it makes us laugh, and any remaining tension disappears.

As Gabriel fetches some wine glasses from the drinks cabinet in the corner, Sofia gives me a sad smile. 'Losing my daughter was another factor in me deciding to tell my story. I never told her who her real father was – or who I really was, for that matter – as I wanted to protect her from him to the very end. And then I turned eighty and I realised that I have very little left to lose. If it all backfires on me, who cares? I'll soon be dead.'

'Shh!' Jane says crossly.

'You're going to live to a hundred at least,' Gabriel says, laughing. 'You're too stubborn to die on us – you love nagging me too much.'

Sofia lets out one of her loud guffaws. Then her smile fades and she looks back at me. 'But, most importantly, when it comes to telling my story, I have the blessing of my grandson.'

'Your grandson?' I ask, looking at her surprised.

Gabriel clears his throat.

64

PORTUGAL, 2000

Once the shock of discovering Gabriel's true identity has faded, we take our glasses of wine through to the kitchen. Gabriel has set the table, and two red candles flicker away in the centre, next to a basket of bread rolls and a dish of butter.

'I've made us some salted cod,' he says, going over to the stove, where a couple of frying pans are sizzling away, filling the room with the most delicious smell.

'I love your salted cod,' Jane exclaims, and once again my mind is sent spinning as my perception of reality has to rapidly recalibrate. Gabriel is Sofia's grandson and Jane is Judith, Sofia's best friend, so of course she would know him well enough to have tasted his cooking.

'My – mind – is – blown,' I say slowly for dramatic effect.

'I'm so sorry.' Jane smiles as I sit down beside her. 'It must be an awful lot to process.'

'Yes, but a lot of things are starting to make sense too.'

'Such as?' Sofia asks.

'Such as how Gabriel is so involved in your life,' I reply. 'I couldn't understand why if he was supposedly just the son of a friend.'

'It was very annoying,' Gabriel says. 'Especially when she asked me to follow you in Lisbon.' He points his silver fish slice at Sofia accusingly. 'I thought you were going to get me arrested.'

I laugh. 'Oh yes!' So much has happened since then, I'd completely forgotten about the fiasco with the alarm.

'All I can say is it's a good job you weren't alive during the war,' Sofia remarks drily. 'Imagine if you'd had to tail a Nazi.'

'Then I would have done a much better job!' Gabriel exclaims. 'I just didn't want to stalk an innocent woman!' He gives me a warm smile, and I feel that same spark of connection I felt with him on the beach, and I relax some more. But as Gabriel turns back to the stove, I'm hit by another lightning-bolt realisation.

'So that means Gabriel – he's Lawrence Bourne's grandson?'

Jane nods grimly.

'Only biologically,' Sofia snaps.

'Of course,' I say quickly to placate her before glancing at Gabriel. He has his back to us so it's impossible to read how he feels, but I notice that he's standing dead still. Then I remember something else, and I turn to Jane. 'That email you sent me about having lunch with Lawrence?'

She nods and shoots Sofia a sideways glance.

'Is that part of your plan too?'

'Er, yes, yes it is,' Jane stammers.

Gabriel mutters something in Portuguese.

'It isn't crazy,' Sofia snaps at him. 'It's going to provide me with – how do the therapists say? Closure. And it's going to provide Lily with a wonderful final chapter for our book. The thrilling denouement.'

'How's that?' I ask nervously. I really hope she's not expecting me to confront Lawrence with the truth.

'It will be the scene where our intrepid heroine – that's me by the way,' Sofia adds.

'Naturally,' Gabriel says drily.

'Yes, well, it's the scene where the intrepid heroine finally confronts the villain and gets her revenge.' Sofia takes a hearty swig of her wine.

'You're not thinking of killing him, are you?' I ask, only half joking.

'Only with my razor-sharp tongue,' she replies. 'And, of course, with the revelation that I'm going to be setting the story straight and telling the whole damn world that he's a murderous traitor.'

65

LONDON, 8 MAY 2000

I follow Judith into the Savoy restaurant, my mouth dry and my heart pounding. Even though we've spent the past few months rehearsing the showdown between Sir Lawrence Bourne and Sofia, and preparing for every possible outcome, including Bourne keeling over from shock and whether or not we would try to resuscitate him, I can't shake a feeling of dread. I completely support Sofia's right to set the record straight, especially now I've written the first draft of her book and I know the full story in intricate detail, but I just can't see how this can end well. Sir Lawrence might now be in his eighties, but he was once capable of murder – and Sofia's murder at that. A shiver runs up my spine as I wonder how he'll react to discovering his victim has risen from the dead and at the very place they first met – and on the anniversary of that meeting too, which had been Sofia's idea.

'Hello,' Jane-Judith, as I've come to think of her, greets the maître d' cheerily. 'I have a table for five booked in the name of Jane Hill.'

I feel a pang of sorrow as I think back to Jane telling me how she'd felt the need to anglicise her name from Judith Hilderstein when she'd first moved to London. 'I never wanted to be hunted like an animal again simply because of my Jewishness,' she'd said, and while I understood, I also found it heartbreaking.

'Yes of course, madam – right this way.' The maître d' gives us a beaming smile, blissfully unaware of the carnage that might be about to be unleashed in his restaurant.

We weave our way through the tables, all laid with starched snowy-white tablecloths and ornate gold cutlery. The diners perfectly match the decor, immaculately dressed in expensive clothes. I feel a jolt of panic. This is surely the worst place to have a major showdown. Thankfully, our table is in a far corner, partially hidden behind a wall of large potted ferns.

'Did you book this table deliberately?' I whisper to Jane as we sit down.

She nods grimly.

The waiter leaves us with some menus and a jug of water. As I pour us both a glass, I realise that my hand is trembling. The plan is that Jane and I will begin our lunch with Lawrence, then, shortly after, Sofia and Gabriel will arrive, and Sofia will make her big reveal.

'Don't worry,' Jane says, placing her hand over mine. I look at her ring and think of the journey that diamond has been on – the journey Jane has been on, since being a teenage refugee on the run from the Gestapo. Then I think of how she wouldn't be here at all if Lawrence had had his way, and my resolve strengthens. I can't imagine what my life would have been like if I'd never met Jane. It doesn't bear thinking about. And now I know that she's also the sweet, kind teenager from Sofia's story, I love her even more.

'I'm trying not to,' I reply. 'I know we've rehearsed it about a million times, but can you please remind me one more time?'

'Of course.' Jane places her hands neatly on the table in front of her as if she's about to give some kind of formal address. 'When he first gets here, we'll talk about his book and drink a toast to how well it's doing. Then, when Sofia and Gabriel arrive, I'll tell him that I have someone I'd like him to meet and Sofia will introduce herself, and then we just play it by ear.'

'But what if he gets up and walks out?' I ask, unfolding my linen napkin. 'Surely once he finds out who she is and that she's still alive he's going to panic and leave?'

'That's where Gabriel comes in,' Jane replies, slightly ominously. She gives me a reassuring smile. 'You don't have to do or say anything, other than record it all for the final chapter of the book.'

I reach into my bag for my mini voice recorder and place it under my napkin on the table. 'I hope the waiter doesn't try to move it. Can you imagine if...' I see Jane staring at something over my shoulder and fall silent.

'He's coming,' she whispers, and now even she looks nervous.

I turn and peer through the ferns and see the maître d' escorting Sir Lawrence through the restaurant towards us. As always, his presence creates quite the ripple effect, with the diners either side stopping talking and eating to gaze up in awe. He might be in his eighties, but he's still a commanding presence – tall and wiry with a spring in his step and a thick shock of white hair.

'Jane, my dear, and darling Lily!' Lawrence booms in the voice of a trained theatre actor as he arrives at the table. Normally, he wears flamboyant suits and ties in vibrant colours, but today, to my surprise, he's all in black, with a smart leather satchel slung over his shoulder. 'It's so good to see you.'

We both stand to greet him, and he gives me a hug. I always used to like how affectionate he was. He always seemed so warm and genuine, but now I freeze in his embrace. All I can think is that this is the man who tried to get Sofia – and Jane by default – killed. This is the man who betrayed his country and his lover to the Nazis.

He steps back and takes a look at me and gives me one of his boyish grins. 'You look positively radiant.'

'Oh – uh – thank you. I've – uh – been away.' I sit down and take a gulp of iced water, desperately trying to compose myself.

As Lawrence and Jane embrace, I slip my hand under my napkin and turn the voice recorder on.

Jane orders some wine for the table, and the waiter hurries off.

'Are we expecting some other guests?' Lawrence asks, looking at the two empty seats.

'Yes, I've invited a couple of people from your publishing house,' Jane replies, cool as a cucumber. 'I thought it only right that they join the celebration.'

'Grand idea.' He turns to me and smiles. 'It's so nice to see you again, Lily, especially today. I really miss our chats.'

'Me too.' I force myself to smile at him. 'What do you mean, especially today?' I ask, worried he might have realised that there's more to this meeting than meets the eye.

Lawrence sighs and pours himself a glass of water. 'The eighth of May is always a very sad day for me.'

I shoot a glance across the table at Jane. Her expression is unreadable.

'Oh, I'm sorry,' I reply, my stomach churning. Could he be referring to his meeting with Sofia? 'Do you mind me asking why?'

'It's the anniversary of the best day of my life,' he says quietly, gazing down at the tablecloth.

I shoot Jane another look, and she raises her eyebrows.

'So why is it sad?' I ask softly.

'Oh, that's a whole other story.' He looks up at me and smiles, but his eyes are filled with sorrow. 'And one that never made it into the book.'

I feign a breezy laugh, all the while my pulse quickening. 'I thought you told me everything.'

'Not quite.' He looks around and clears his throat. 'The funniest thing is that this is where it happened, here at the Savoy.'

I gulp hard. He *is* talking about Sofia. He has to be.

'Oh really?' I reply, my voice wavering.

'Yes. And I've spent years avoiding this place like the plague.' He looks across the table at Jane. 'But when you sent me the invitation and I saw the date and the venue, I thought it had to be some kind of sign – fate, you might say – and that maybe it was an opportunity to lay some ghosts to rest.'

He says this just as I take a mouthful of water, and it takes everything I've got not to spit it all over the table.

'How interesting,' Jane says coolly, but my mind is racing. Something about this doesn't feel right. Lawrence seems so genuinely sad.

But he is an Oscar-winning actor, I remind myself. *And he was once a spy. He's well practised in the art of deception.*

I shoot a sideways glance at Lawrence, sitting head bowed in his black suit and tie. But he doesn't know that we're on to him. So, as far as he's concerned, there's no need for him to fake anything.

'Why didn't you include it in the book?' I ask gently.

'Because some things are way too special for public consumption,' he replies. 'Some things are too sacred – they need to be kept private.'

Jane clears her throat, and I see that she's staring over my shoulder again, and my heart skips a beat.

'Our other guests are here,' she says, her voice strained and slightly high-pitched.

I clench my hands beneath the table and pray that this doesn't end in complete and utter disaster. This isn't going how I'd expected at all.

'Hello!' Lawrence says cheerily, getting to his feet.

Gabriel and the maître d' are now right by the table, with the tiny Sofia hovering behind them.

'Someone will be over to take your order shortly,' the maître d' says, gesturing at the empty seats. And then he's gone. And it's just us.

'Nice to meet you,' Lawrence says, offering Gabriel his hand.

'And you,' Gabriel says gruffly, giving it a brisk shake. I know from our conversations that he's been dreading this meeting and that it will take all of his restraint not to 'gut that rat like a mackerel' – a mixture of metaphors that had required all of my restraint not to giggle at.

Gabriel sits down opposite me and beside Jane, so now it's just Lawrence and Sofia standing. I'm so tense, I'm barely able to breathe.

'And very nice to meet you too,' Lawrence says, offering his hand to Sofia, although his tone is a little less self-assured. I'm guessing he must be surprised by her age, given that she's supposed to be from his publishing house.

Sofia stares at him, her mouth agape. She's wearing a vivid green dress and matching shoes, and her short hair has been freshly dyed black.

Say 'nice to meet you too', I silently implore, thinking back to all the times we rehearsed this moment.

'Nice to meet you too,' she mutters, quickly shaking his hand and sitting down at the head of the table.

Lawrence remains standing, still as a statue.

I shoot a panicked glance across the table, but Jane and Gabriel are staring at Lawrence, and Sofia is looking down into her lap.

'I-I...' Lawrence stammers, and I erupt in a cold sweat.

'Are you OK?' I ask, standing up beside him. His gaze remains fixed upon Sofia.

'Is it you?' he whispers.

Sofia gives a little gasp of shock. None of us had expected him to recognise her, and we haven't prepared for this.

'Sofia?' he gasps, placing his hands on the table for support.

Sofia appears to gather herself and clears her throat. She looks up at Lawrence, her expression deathly cold, and she nods.

Lawrence lets out an anguished cry. 'But... but – you're dead.'

Sofia keeps her gaze fixed on his, but I notice that her hands are now balled into tiny fists. 'Surprise!' she replies icily, reverting to her prepared script.

'Oh my God. I must be dreaming. Am I dreaming?' Lawrence looks down at me, his eyes wide with shock. Before I can respond, he turns back to Sofia.

'In a way,' Sofia replies. 'I suppose I must be your worst nightmare.'

'What are you talking about?' Lawrence exclaims. 'You're alive!'

'Yes,' Sofia says. 'And your plan failed.'

66

LONDON, 8 MAY 2000

Lawrence grips the edge of the table, and I see that his hands are shaking.

'Why don't you sit down?' I ask nervously. As much as I'm on Sofia's side in all of this, I don't want him collapsing on us.

Lawrence looks down at me, his face drained of colour. 'You knew?' he whispers.

I nod, annoyed at myself for feeling guilty. But it was one thing thinking of the young Trafalgar from Sofia's story being in cahoots with the Nazis. The much older Lawrence standing before me suddenly looks so vulnerable and weak. And I still can't shake the sense that something isn't quite right. The things he was saying right before Sofia arrived don't make sense. I gesture at his chair. 'Please, sit down.'

Sofia shoots me an annoyed glance, no doubt thinking me disloyal. But she wasn't here when he talked about today being a sad anniversary. She doesn't know that there might be more to all of this.

Thankfully, Lawrence sits down, and before anyone can say anything, the waiter returns with our bottle of wine. We all sit in extremely awkward silence as he fills our glasses.

'Are you ready to order yet?' he asks innocently.

'No!' Jane and I yelp in unison, and he beats a hasty retreat.

As soon as he's left, I feel the urge to speak. I need to try to get to the bottom of this anniversary business, and catch Sofia and Gabriel up on what was said before they got here.

'Were you talking about Sofia before when you said this was a very sad date for you?' I ask.

Lawrence nods, still gazing at her in disbelief. 'Yes, this was the date we first met. Thursday the eighth of May 1941. And this was where we met – or downstairs at least, in the wartime restaurant.' He leans across the table. 'Is it really you?'

Sofia remains stony-faced, so Lawrence looks back at me.

'Is it really her?' he asks imploringly.

I nod.

'But how?' Lawrence returns his gaze to Sofia. 'You died in a plane crash.'

'Ha!' Sofia replies. 'You thought I did.'

'Why are you being like this? Why aren't you happy to see me?' Lawrence's normally powerful voice cracks with emotion. 'Why have you made me believe you were dead all these years? And what did you mean, my plan failed?'

'Your plan to murder me!' she hisses, causing Lawrence to flinch.

'What on earth are you talking about?'

I stare at him, transfixed. He looks genuinely shell-shocked but not at all scared or panicked as I'd been expecting. There's no sign of a guilty conscience. He's either giving the performance of a lifetime or there's something badly wrong with Sofia's account of things.

'There's no point lying,' Sofia says, her eyes sparking with anger. 'I know what you did. I know that you were a traitor to your country and how you helped the Germans kill me – or at least you thought you did.'

'What are you talking about?' Lawrence's voice is growing

stronger now, and he sounds almost indignant. 'I would never have betrayed my country to help those bastards. And why would I ever help anyone kill you?' He bangs his hand on the table, causing his cutlery to jangle. 'You were the love of my life!'

Sofia gulps, and for the first time since her arrival, I see a flicker of doubt in her eyes. 'Liar!' she exclaims. 'I was told by a very reliable source that you were a double agent.'

Lawrence frowns and shakes his head. 'I'd like to meet that reliable source of yours because they're talking utter horse shit!'

'Don't raise your voice to her,' Gabriel pipes up protectively, but Lawrence completely ignores him.

'You were the only person who knew I was on that plane,' Sofia continues. 'The only person who could have told the Germans.'

'That's not strictly true,' I say quietly.

Sofia glowers at me. 'There's no way Alexandre would have betrayed me. He was the one who took care of me after this asshole tried to kill me.'

'I know, but...' I start mentally scanning the chapters of Sofia's book leading up to the plane crash, trying to work out who else might have known.

'But nothing,' Sofia retorts, glaring at Lawrence. 'This son of a bitch killed me, and now everyone's going to know about it!'

Before anyone can respond, the waiter reappears through the wall of ferns. 'Are you ready to order now?' he asks cheerily.

'No!' we all chorus this time, and again he beats a hasty retreat.

'What are you talking about?' Lawrence says to Sofia, and to my surprise he now seems just as angry as her. 'How could you possibly think I'd want you dead? I've spent the last fifty-nine years of my life pining for you. I've wrecked three marriages because I was still in love with you! And do you want to know what I do every year on this day?'

Sofia seems to have lost the power of speech.

'Yes please,' I murmur.

'I go to London Bridge with a letter for you. Look – *look*,' he booms, grabbing his leather satchel from the floor.

'Stop raising your voice to her,' Gabriel says again.

Again, Lawrence ignores him and tears the satchel open. 'Look!' he practically yells, taking out an envelope and shoving it across the table to Sofia. 'Read this!'

'Do not tell me what to do!' she barks back at him, and I have to fight the nervous urge to laugh. It's like watching a battle between two aging but still fearless boxers. And I realise that it's reminding me a little of the scenes I've already written featuring them – that same spark still burning strong.

'I will absolutely tell you what to do if I think you're being a stubborn old fool!' he retorts.

'Don't call her a fool,' Gabriel says, and finally Lawrence looks at him.

'Who *are* you?' he asks, and I feel a jolt of alarm.

'Never you mind,' Gabriel replies, much to my relief. The last thing we need right now is anyone being gutted like a mackerel.

I return my gaze to Sofia, who is staring suspiciously at the envelope.

'Oh, for God's sake!' Lawrence snatches the envelope back and tears it open. 'I shall read it to you then.' He takes the letter out and clears his throat. 'My dear Sofia...' As soon as he begins, his tone softens. 'So here we are, another year gone and still I feel your loss so acutely. I know they say that time is a great healer, and in other things I've certainly found that to be true. But not with you. With you, it feels as if every year the loss becomes more acute and the secret I've borne in my heart all this time grows larger and aches even more.'

'Aha!' Sofia cries triumphantly.

Lawrence glares at her. 'The secret of our *love*,' he

continues pointedly. 'The secret I'll take to my grave. When I've seen the way others have cashed in on your memory over the years, it's infuriated me. Especially the monster who deserves to burn in hell for the way he betrayed you. If he hadn't drunk himself into an early grave, I swear I would have happily killed him for you.'

'What are you talking about?' Sofia interrupts. '*Who* are you talking about?'

'The bastard who betrayed you.'

'The clipper pilot?' I say. 'Bing?'

Lawrence looks at me blankly, then shakes his head.

'Who?' Sofia asks again.

'Your music partner. Emilio Almeida. He sold you out to the Germans to pay off a gambling debt.'

67

LONDON, 8 MAY 2000

'Wh-What?' I stammer.

'What?' Jane echoes.

'What the hell are you talking about?' Sofia snaps.

'Emilio Almeida,' Lawrence replies. 'The fellow you wrote your songs with.'

'What do you mean, he sold me out to pay off a gambling debt?' Sofia looks ashen-faced.

'Exactly that.' Lawrence sits back in his seat and sighs. 'I found out last year when I had dinner with an old SOE colleague. Emilio was the one who told the Nazis you were on that plane.'

'No!' Sofia gasps. She looks at Jane, panic-stricken. 'He can't have been. He was one of my closest friends.'

Once again, I trawl my memories of her book and the scenes I wrote featuring Sofia and Emilio, and I start feeling sick.

'But you did spurn his advances,' I say cautiously. 'And what about the night at Estoril? The night you followed the Gestapo agent Kurt Fischer into the casino and you bumped into Emilio there. Is there any way Emilio could have been meeting Fischer instead of Lawrence? You did say he looked really panicked when he saw you.'

'Yes because he was there to try to catch Lawrence,' Sofia replies, but her tone is a lot less harsh now.

'Me?' Lawrence replies.

'Is anyone else really confused?' Gabriel mutters, and I shoot him a sympathetic smile.

'Are you talking about the night we spent together in Estoril?' Lawrence asks Sofia.

She nods.

'I was there with the SOE,' he says indignantly. 'We were trying to find out who was passing secrets to the Germans, but whoever it was gave us the slip.'

'No,' Sofia mutters. 'No, no, no.'

'Are you lovely people ready to order yet?' the waiter asks, reappearing yet again through the ferns.

'No!' Sofia practically screams.

'I'm sorry,' the waiter mutters, backing away. 'Perhaps it would be easier to come and find me when you are ready.'

'We will, thank you,' Jane replies apologetically.

'Are you all right?' Lawrence asks Sofia, clearly concerned.

'Of course not,' she snaps back. 'Almeida can't have betrayed me. He was my songwriting partner.'

'But if he was in love with you, and then found out you were in love with Trafalgar...' I say.

'You *were* in love with me?' Lawrence says hopefully.

'Shh!' Sofia says crossly.

'And he knew you wrote "Ocean Longing" about Trafalgar,' I say more animatedly as events from her book start connecting in my head. 'And I think he knew you were pregnant too!' I blurt out without thinking.

'You were pregnant?' Lawrence exclaims.

'Lily!' Sofia cries. When we'd rehearsed this lunch, everyone had been under strict instructions to never disclose the pregnancy or Gabriel's true identity to Lawrence. But things are different now. Now I'm convinced that Lawrence is innocent.

'You kept being sick around Emilio,' I continue. 'And he knew you'd slept with Trafalgar in Estoril. He must have worked it out, and it probably drove him mad with jealousy.'

'Oh God,' Jane mutters. 'I think she might be right.'

'Of course she's right!' Lawrence exclaims.

'But...' Sofia looks at me, horrified. 'Do you really think I could have been wrong all these years?'

I nod. 'I'm going to say something now, and I hope you don't mind because it will be breaking the terms of our NDA,' I say to Lawrence.

He shrugs. 'Go ahead.'

I turn back to Sofia. 'When I was working with Lawrence on his book, I asked him why he felt his three marriages had failed, and he told me that his wives were never able to compete. I'd assumed he meant with his career as an actor, but he told me, strictly off the record, that it was because he'd never got over his first love.'

'That's right!' Lawrence exclaims. 'I remember that conversation, and I was really worried you'd try to slip it in the book without me noticing.' He looks at Sofia. 'I was talking about you. My first love. My only true love.' He smiles. 'I'd totally forgotten how bloody feisty you can be though.'

Gabriel stifles a laugh.

'I'd assumed you didn't mention me in your book because you didn't want people knowing we were connected – because you'd killed me,' Sofia says hesitantly.

'Poppycock!' Lawrence splutters. 'I was protecting your memory. Our memories. Like I said in my letter.'

'What exactly were you going to do with that letter?' I ask.

'The same as all the rest,' he replies. 'I was going to take it to London Bridge and drop it in the Thames. Every year, I've written one to you, on the eighth of May. Every year since your death.' He reaches across the table to Sofia. 'Please, my darling, you have to believe me. I would never, ever have done anything to hurt you.'

We all stare at Sofia, awaiting her response.

'Apart from nearly getting me blown up twice in the Blitz,' she finally mutters, but I'm sure I can see a twinkle in her eye.

'Well, yes, but I was young and foolish then.'

'You also had a totally different voice,' Sofia remarks.

'Cor blimey, so I did,' Lawrence says, slipping into a cockney accent. 'I was working as a spy and I didn't want anyone knowing my true identity,' he says, reverting to his normal voice. 'But I promise you, that was the only thing I hid from you. And it was only because of the war.'

Sofia nods. 'Do you have any proof that Almeida betrayed me? Anything concrete?'

To my relief, Lawrence nods. 'Of course. My old colleague in the SOE showed me the file they had on him. I can arrange another meeting with him so he can show you. Hell, I can call him right now if you want?'

'But why didn't it come out that he'd helped the Germans?' Jane asks.

'My guess is that the Americans covered it up,' Lawrence replies. 'Just like the Brits covered up so many of their own dirty secrets after the war ended. It might have been different if Almeida had lived longer, but he drank himself to death in 1947.'

'Maybe due to his guilty conscience?' I suggest.

Lawrence nods. 'Could well have been.'

'And there was me thinking it was because he was heartbroken over my death,' Sofia mutters before taking a large gulp from her glass of wine. 'I remember seeing him on the television on the day of my memorial in Lisbon looking like death, and I'd assumed it was because he was so heartbroken I'd died. I'd actually felt sorry for him and bad that he didn't know that I was still alive.' She looks at Jane, horrified. 'That son of a bitch was eaten up with guilt, not sorrow!'

'How *are* you still alive?' Lawrence asks. 'How did you manage to fool the whole world?' He turns to me. 'Have you known about this all along? All the time we worked together.'

'No!' I exclaim. 'I only found out a few months ago.'

'Right. And you?' He looks at Jane.

'I've known from the start,' she says, looking a little sheepish. 'I've known Sofia since the war.'

'And you?' Lawrence looks at Gabriel. 'How are you involved in all of this?'

An awkward silence falls upon the table, and we all turn to look at Sofia.

'He's my grandson,' Sofia replies after what feels like forever.

I reach for Gabriel's hand beneath the table, and he squeezes mine tightly.

'He's *our* grandson,' Sofia adds softly.

EPILOGUE
PORTUGAL, AUGUST 2000

The tide is out, and the sky is streaked copper and pink from the setting sun. I stroll over to the rock pools and plonk myself down on the sand. I smile as I look down at the driftwood bangle on my tanned wrist and the words Gabriel carved into it: '*Is that so?*' book-ended by two hearts. A sudden breeze ruffles my hair, and I turn to see my dream daughter skipping across the beach towards me. I feel a pang of sorrow at what I know I must do.

'I'm so sorry I wasn't able to be your mum,' I whisper as I picture her coming and sitting cross-legged on the rock beside me. 'And thank you so much for coming to see me, but now I need to carry on, on my own.' I start to well up and close my eyes.

When I open them again, she's gone, but I see a flicker of colour on the rock where she'd been sitting. I wipe my tears away and realise that it's a butterfly. Its wings are the same shade of red as my dream daughter's hair, and I smile through my tears as it takes off into the air. Watching it go, I feel a burst of joy.

The past few months have undoubtedly been challenging,

but they've been the equivalent of me squeezing through a tiny crack in the chrysalis. They've given me the strength to finally fly free from the past and into my future – a future beyond my wildest dreams.

Tomorrow, Jane will send out a press release, announcing the imminent publication of Sofia's book. It's being published by the same house that published Sir Lawrence's autobiography and they've somehow managed to keep the whole thing under wraps throughout the editorial process, with only a handful of staff working on it at breakneck speed and in top secret. Tomorrow, the whole world will discover that Sofia Castello is alive after all, and they'll finally get to learn her untold story and the story of her and Sir Lawrence Bourne. Their love story.

I smile as I think of all that's happened since our infamous lunch at the Savoy. That same afternoon, Sir Lawrence took us to meet his friend from his SOE days, who confirmed that Emilio had indeed been responsible for letting the Germans know Sofia would be on the plane. Sofia and Lawrence then went on to London Bridge to commemorate the anniversary of their first meeting together. Gabriel had been a little wary about letting Sofia go off on her own, but after she'd told him in no uncertain terms that she'd still be able to 'fillet a man like a fish' if need be, he acquiesced. The talent for menacing fish metaphors runs deep in that family.

Gabriel and I spent the evening creating some special London memories of our own and now 8 May is an anniversary for us too, marking the day that we officially became a couple.

The next morning, when we came down for breakfast in the hotel hand in hand, we found Sofia and Sir Lawrence draped all over each other at a table in the corner, and they've remained inseparable ever since. As Sir Lawrence movingly put it, 'We have so much lost time to make up for and not a lot of time left to do it.' I only hope that with all the furore the book is bound to cause they're able to do so in peace. Sofia has recorded an interview with Jane to be released alongside the book, and as soon as the announcement is made tomorrow, she and Lawrence will be escaping to his private bolthole in the Bahamas.

Of course, they're not the only ones whose lives will be changed tomorrow. Sofia and Jane have insisted that my name be on the cover of the book as the co-author. Jane reckons that this will have publishers clamouring to sign me, and I'll be able to write my own books again. Part of me is excited at the prospect, another part slightly jaded at the fickle nature of the business. Whatever, I'm going to take my time and wait and see if the muse strikes me.

As well as being credited as co-author, Jane and Sofia have ensured that I get a fifty per cent share of the advance and the royalties, meaning I can afford to take my time before deciding what to do next – or, rather, what to do after my trip to Brazil with Gabriel. Spending time in Portugal has sparked a real wanderlust in me, and I'm craving my next adventure. And the thought of adventuring with someone who makes me feel so seen and loved and makes me laugh so much has been the equivalent of taking a power hose to my relationship with Robin and blasting away all the painful memories. As Sofia once told me, sometimes the things that seem like the end of the world are actually the prologue for something truly delightful, so it makes zero sense to feel bitter. If anything, all I feel now is thankful that, to quote Gabriel, Robin is 'slithery as a bucket of fish bait'.

Taking one last look at the sea, I stand up and begin walking back to the cottage, where Gabriel, Sofia, Lawrence and Jane are all waiting for me.

My new family.

A LETTER FROM SIOBHAN

Dear reader,

Thank you so much for choosing to read *The Lost Story of Sofia Castello*. I hope you found it an interesting and entertaining read! If you want to be kept up to date with all my latest releases, just sign up at the following link. Your email address will never be shared, and you can unsubscribe at any time.

www.bookouture.com/siobhan-curham

Back in 2023, I gave up my home in the UK to join the growing number of people living, working and travelling as digital nomads, and I've been writing my way around the world ever since. As a result, my travels have heavily influenced and inspired this book.

In January 2024, I was invited by the Portuguese publisher of my novel *The Storyteller of Auschwitz* to celebrate the launch of the book in Lisbon, and I instantly fell in love with the Portuguese people and country. I returned a couple of months later to go on a walking tour of Lisbon with a local historian who specialises in World War Two. As soon as I began learning about Lisbon during the war and what a hotbed of refugees, spies and intrigue it became, I knew I had to write a novel set there.

One of the things that most fascinated me was when our tour guide told us about the *varinas* who used to sell fish on the

Lisbon streets. As she showed me an old black-and-white photo of the women in their eye-catching costumes, I felt a spark inside. Maybe it was a spark of recognition in my DNA, from my family members who'd worked in the Scottish fishing industry back in the day, but I knew I had my novel's starting point. And then I discovered fado, and so the story of the fictional star, Sofia Castello, was born.

Once upon a time, I worked as a celebrity ghostwriter, and I've always thought it would be fun to write a novel about that secretive world, and so the character of Lily Christie came to be (incidentally named after my great-great-grandfather's second wife, who was an Aberdeen fish-woman). As well as exploring the ghostwriting world through Lily, I also wanted to show the transformative power of travel, which has so magically transformed my own life these past couple of years. And, of course, create a love letter to Portugal in book form!

I began work on this novel when I was staying in Aberdeen for a month, then I spent five weeks in Ukraine. At that point, I had yet to write the scenes set in London during the Blitz, and I'd been planning to draw upon the stories my grandma had told me about her own experiences, but then, sadly, I got to experience air attacks for myself while I was in Lviv. The setting and the time period might have been different, but the emotions Sofia experiences during the bombing raids were drawn directly from my own personal experiences – and the experiences of all Ukrainians over the past three years.

After I was in Ukraine, I went to Stockholm, where all kinds of emotions started bubbling up inside of me – shock, fear, sorrow and, more surprisingly, rage. The scene where Trafalgar yells at the German bombers from the banks of the Thames was inspired by a dream I had while in Stockholm, of standing on a roof in Lviv yelling at the bombs and drones and channelling my fury that world leaders could terrorise innocent civilians in this way. It breaks my heart that people are still being bombed in Europe today, but I hope that my writing can in some way help to raise awareness and support for the victims of war – and if you'd like to read more about my experiences in Ukraine, you can find them on my Substack letter, Wonderstruck, at siobhan-curham.substack.com.

Finally, when I was writing my World War Two spy novel, *The Secret Keeper*, I came across a true story while I was doing my research that shocked me to the core. The story was about the actor Leslie Howard, who starred in *Gone With the Wind*, and how a passenger plane he'd been travelling on from Portugal to England had been shot down by the Luftwaffe. There are several different theories about why his plane was targeted, but the most popular is that it was because he was working for Winston Churchill, using his fame as a cover to travel to Spain and Portugal to try and influence the 'neutral' leaders there to support the Allies. I found the idea of a successful artist using their fame for good, despite the obvious dangers, really inspiring. I hope that, now you know the real-life inspiration behind Sofia's story, you do too.

Siobhan

www.siobhancurham.com

siobhancurham.substack.com

x.com/SiobhanCurham

instagram.com/siobhancurhamauthor

ACKNOWLEDGEMENTS

MASSIVE thanks as always to Kelsie 'up the mystery' Marsden, my wonderful editor, for pushing me to make the plot of this novel more dramatic and mysterious with every draft, and for always being so supportive of my ideas. Ditto the entire team at Bookouture. I'm so grateful to be with such a supportive and dynamic publisher. Special thanks to Richard King, Saidah Graham, Sarah Hardy, Kim Nash, Noelle Holten, Jenny Geras, Ruth Tross, Alex Crow, Melanie Price, Alba Proko, Ria Clare and Sinead O'Connor, to name but a few. And extra thanks to copy-editor extraordinaire Jade Craddock for always being so positive, helpful and insightful.

This novel wouldn't have come into being if it hadn't been for my wonderful experiences in Portugal last year and all the amazing, warm-hearted people I met there. Most especially Andrea Alves Silva for giving me my first Portuguese book deal and inviting me to come to Lisbon, and Dora Santos Marques, booktuber extraordinaire, for being so supportive of my work. And to the very talented Portuguese artist Alexandre Gaudêncio, and author Rosária Casquinha da Silva, for being such fun new friends and giving me such great guided tours. I hope you enjoy the characters I named in your honour!

HUGE thanks also to all the lovely people who take the time to review my novels on their social media, blogs, Goodreads, NetGalley and Amazon. There are so many, it's impossible to mention you all here, but please know that I read and deeply appreciate every review. I also really appreciate all the messages I receive from readers; it's so encouraging to receive your feedback about my books.

Last but never least, much, much love and gratitude to my family: My wonderful son Jack and my equally wonderful new daughter-in-law Zirka Curham, Michael Curham, Anne Cumming, and 'The Curham Mafia', aka Alice Curham, Bea Curham, Luke Curham, aka the best siblings in the world! To my Number One Niece Katie Bird and Number One Nephew John Arthur, and Danno Arthur, Lacey Jennen, Gina Ervin, David Ervin, Sam Delaney, Carolyn Miller, Amy Fawcett, Rachel Kelley, Charles Delaney. And huge love to my new Ukrainian family – Igor and Natalia and the beautiful Plakhtyna sisters – thank you so much for making me feel so welcome in your family and your beautiful country. And massive thanks to my friends who feel like family: Tina McKenzie, Sara Starbuck, Pearl Bates, Caz McDonagh, Steve O'Toole and Sammie Venn.

Huge gratitude also to the friends who have been so supportive of my books and writing over the years: Charlotte Baldwin, Stuart Berry, Anthony Berry, Sass Pankhurst, Sandra McDonagh, Stephanie Lam, Abe Gibson, Linda Newman, Lesley Strick, Lara Kingsman, Diane Sack Pulsone, Thea Bennett, Jan Silverman, Marie Hermet, Mara Bergman, Jan Silverman, Patricia Jacobs, Mavis Pachter, Suzanne Burgess, Liz Brooks, Fil Carson, Jackie Stanbridge, Gillian Holland, Doug Cushman, Gill Thackray, Page Perrior the Instagram Jewellery Queen, Alina Chyzh, Gill Vernau and to Simon Vernau, Fabio Chiapatti and Barry Stewart – the most fun, floral and delicious book club I've ever attended!

Ever since I started living as a nomad, I've experienced some wonderful Airbnb hosts who have helped make the writing of this book such an enjoyable experience. Special thanks to Sue, for providing me with such a lovely cosy base in Aberdeen, where I wrote the opening chapters. And to Natalia in Lviv where I wrote some of the middle, and for going above and beyond during the air attacks on the city. And to Megan in Hove for providing such a lovely leafy retreat while I wrote the end. And to Eleanor in Margate where I put the very final touches to this novel – your wonderful artwork on the walls was a huge inspiration.

And big shout-out to the fantastic American writer friends I've made on my travels: Linda Joy Myers, Ruth Mitchell, Wendy Taylor Carlisle, Janie Bynum, Jeremy Owens, Allison Landa, Sunshine Knight, Heather Kolf, Robin Carsten, Nina Mukerje, Aileen Basis, KT Sparks, Mayumi Shimose Poe. It's been so much fun getting to know you!

Lastly, thank you to everyone who subscribes to my weekly Substack letter, Wonderstruck, to follow my writing and travel adventures. I'm so grateful for the lovely community we've created over there, and I love writing to you every Sunday. (If you don't subscribe to Wonderstruck, I'd love it if you joined us! You can subscribe for free at siobhancurham.substack.com).

PUBLISHING TEAM

Turning a manuscript into a book requires the efforts of many people. The publishing team at Bookouture would like to acknowledge everyone who contributed to this publication.

Audio
Alba Proko
Sinead O'Connor
Melissa Tran

Commercial
Lauren Morrissette
Hannah Richmond
Imogen Allport

Cover design
Eileen Carey

Data and analysis
Mark Alder
Mohamed Bussuri

Editorial
Kelsie Marsden
Nadia Michael

Copyeditor
Jade Craddock

Proofreader
Laura Kincaid

Marketing
Alex Crow
Melanie Price
Occy Carr
Ciara Rosney
Martyna Młynarska

Operations and distribution
Marina Valles
Stephanie Straub
Joe Morris

Production
Hannah Snetsinger
Mandy Kullar
Ria Clare
Nadia Michael

Publicity
Kim Nash
Noelle Holten
Jess Readett
Sarah Hardy

Rights and contracts
Peta Nightingale
Richard King
Saidah Graham

Made in United States
North Haven, CT
18 July 2025